LITTLE
PIECES
of
ME

Also by Alison Hammer

You and Me and Us

LITTLE PIECES
of
ME

A Novel

ALISON HAMMER

wm

WILLIAM MORROW

An Imprint of HarperCollinsPublishers

P.S.™ is a trademark of HarperCollins Publishers.

HarperCollins books may be purchased for educational, business, or sales promotional use. For information, please email the Special Markets Department at SPsales@harpercollins.com.

FIRST EDITION

Designed by Diahann Sturge

Library of Congress Cataloging-in-Publication Data has been applied for.

ISBN 978-0-06-293487-1 (paperback)
ISBN 978-0-06-305942-9 (hardcover library edition)

21 22 23 24 25 LSC 10 9 8 7 6 5 4 3 2 1

To my parents, Kathy and Randy,
for giving me (mostly) their best pieces

I am made and remade continually.

—Virginia Woolf

Chapter One

FORTY-THREE YEARS AGO TODAY, MY DAD GOT WHAT HE CLAIMED was the best birthday present of his life: a screaming redhead with bright blue eyes who would grow up to share his love for puns. It doesn't seem right to celebrate a birthday without him.

If I had my way, I'd sleep through this whole day and skip ahead to tomorrow. But one of my closest friends, who I love dearly most of the time, thinks he knows what's best for me. And what was acceptable last year won't fly now that Dad has been gone almost two years. Which is why I'm sitting at Dublin's, my neighborhood bar, in the middle of a Wednesday afternoon.

"You're supposed to be happy," Maks says from the barstool next to mine. "There's a reason people say *happy* birthday—not sad and lonely and depressed birthday."

"And you're supposed to be at work," I say, sidestepping the issue of my day of birth.

"Pfft," he says, dismissing the thought, as if a regular paycheck and insurance weren't a big deal. Since I was laid off three weeks ago, I've gotten a new appreciation for things I used to take for granted. "Work is for the horses," Maks says. "There are more important things."

I don't feel like getting into a debate over linguistics, so I don't tell him the saying is actually "for the birds." Instead, I give him an *if you say so* smile and take a sip of the drink I've been nursing for the last half hour.

"I'm serious," Maks says. He pouts, and I smile. It's easy to picture him as a kid, wearing the same distressed jeans and a black band T-shirt, his Ukrainian accent the only thing keeping him from fitting right in.

He takes a sip of his whiskey ginger and turns to me, ready with another attempt to cheer me up. "Did you know the birthday song was written by a kindergarten teacher back in the eighteen hundreds?"

"You told me that last year on my birthday," I remind him. "And the year before that."

He makes a show of rolling his eyes and turns back to the TV, where the commercial break is over, and Maury Povich is about to reveal the paternity of a young boy.

Maks instantly perks up. "Scarlett!" he calls to our favorite bartender, frantically pointing toward the TV.

The bar is relatively empty between the lunch and after-work crowds, so Scarlett obliges and turns up the volume. Maks takes my hand in his, gripping it as if he has stakes in the results.

"In the case of four-year-old Jason," Maury Povich says as he opens the telltale envelope. "Victor"—dramatic pause—"you are *not* the father."

"I knew it," Maks says, pumping our fists in victory. My smile breaks free and I have to laugh at his enthusiasm. Reality TV—even the most unreal kind—has always been Maks's guilty pleasure.

Scarlett mutes the TV again as a phone number comes on-screen, inviting viewers to call if they want to determine the paternal status of someone in their family. I wonder if people know they can get the same results at home with a little spit, a test tube, and a postage stamp. Although they'd miss out on the circus sideshow and whatever compensation they get for airing their dirty laundry on national TV.

"Would you ever go on a show like that?" Scarlett asks, glancing behind her at the TV. Light from the window reflects off her nose ring, casting tiny rainbows on the bar.

"I unfortunately know who my father is," Maks says. His eyes dart toward mine, as if hearing the word "father" will undo me. But I'm stronger than he gives me credit for.

"I took one of those DNA tests a few years back," I tell Scarlett. Maks looks pleasantly surprised that I've joined in the conversation.

"Find anything interesting?" she asks.

"Only that there's a genetic reason I think cilantro tastes like soap. Other than that, I'm a full-bred Jew. Ninety-nine-point-five percent Ashkenazi, and point-five percent Eastern European."

"No Irish?" She gestures toward my curly red hair, which has always been my most defining feature.

"Only on St. Patrick's Day," I say, twirling a strand around my finger.

Maks's ears perk up at the opportunity to rattle off more useless trivia, like the charming human Wikipedia he is.

"It's actually a common misconception that the Irish have a monopoly on red hair," he says. "In twentieth-century Europe, red hair was synonymous with Jews. Most of Shakespeare's Jewish characters had red hair—and Judas is almost always a redhead in Italian art."

Scarlett nods in mock interest. After the great tomato debate last summer, she learned that sometimes it's best not to engage.

The bells on the front door chime as Margaux, the other half of my best-friend duo, walks in. Her arrival plays right into Maks's hands.

"Now this one got the DNA surprise of a lifetime," he says, pointing toward Margaux.

"It's rude to point," she says before wrapping me in a hug, then taking the barstool to my left.

"Hey, facts are facts," Maks says. He turns back to Scarlett and explains. "Turns out our little Francophile is zero percent French, which makes the 'aux' ending of her name ironic, don't you think?"

"So ironic," Margaux says, brushing her smooth black hair behind her ears.

I laugh, remembering the day she found out that only half of her family history was accurate. While Margaux had always known she had a mixture of European and African ancestry, she'd been told the European part was French. But it turned out the white man her great-grandmother had scandalously fallen in love with in the French Quarter of New Orleans had roots in Belfast, not Bordeaux.

We drank so much wine that night—French, of course—as we had a deep discussion about the significance of identity, who and what defines us. Margaux had always been proud of her French ancestry and had attributed her impeccable style and love of wine and cheese to that heritage.

The way I saw it, she was the same person she always had been, no matter what cultures collided to create her. The specifics of her DNA didn't change who she was. If anything, it gave her a more interesting story to tell.

"Where's Jeff?" Margaux asks, looking around the bar.

"He's meeting us later at the restaurant," I say, hoping he's able to get out of work on time. I twirl my engagement ring, missing him. He's been working so hard lately, putting everything into his presentation for a potential client. If it goes well, he'll be the lead candidate to take over when his boss retires next year.

Scarlett sets a glass of white wine in front of Margaux. "Looks like you could use this," she says.

I glance at my best friend, who does look like she's had a day. Her lawyer uniform—a pencil skirt and blouse—is as crisp as ever, but the brightness is gone from her deep brown eyes. She looks defeated.

"How was work?" I ask.

"Ugh," she says. "I don't want to talk about it. How's your birthday been so far?"

"Ugh," I tell her. "I don't want to talk about it."

We laugh and clink our glasses.

TWO AND A half drinks later, I hear the *Jaws* theme song coming from my phone. Maks raises an eyebrow, daring me to answer. I send the call to voicemail, not wanting to put a damper on the day now that I've actually started to enjoy myself.

"Was that Mommy Dearest?" he asks, a mischievous grin on his face. He knows exactly who it is—he's the one who programmed the ringtone for her.

I nod and put my phone back down on the bar. "I don't feel like talking."

"Hey, it's your birthday," Maks says.

"And she's the one who gave birth to you," Margaux counters.

"Not by choice," I remind her.

I may have been my dad's greatest gift, but I was my mom's nightmare come to life. They were in college when she got pregnant, and thanks to my impending arrival, she had to drop out of school and her sorority. They got married, then had me. My twin sisters weren't born until thirteen years later, when my parents actually wanted a family.

The phone rings again, and before I can get to it, Maks picks it up.

"Elizabeth!" he says into the phone. The cheer in his voice is genuine—for some reason the two of them adore each other. "She's right here."

I reach for the phone, but Maks isn't ready to give it up. He nods as if she can see him, then laughs a little too loudly before saying, "Oh, girl, you don't have to tell me."

"Give it," I say, wrestling the phone from his grasp. "Hi, Mom."

"Paigey," she says, using my dad's nickname for me. "Happy birthday, darling."

"Thank you," I tell her, trying to sound sincere.

There's a beat of silence, and I'm reminded how hard it is for us to communicate without having Dad in the middle. I wonder if she's thinking about him, too.

"Did you get my gift?" she asks.

"Not yet," I tell her. "But I got an email about a delivery—I'll pick it up when I get home."

"Okay, then." She sounds disappointed, but not as disappointed as she'd be if I told her the truth.

"Hey, Mom—thanks for calling, but I've got to run," I tell her. "I don't want to be late—we're meeting Jeff for dinner across the street. But I'll see you next weekend."

"Right," she says. "Next weekend. Happy birthday, sweetheart."

I hang up, wishing I'd put my phone in my purse and out of Maks's reach.

"You opened the present before we left your apartment," Maks says, confused.

Margaux frowns. "You didn't like it?"

"No," I tell her. "But you will. More of your anti-aging cream."

Maks groans. "Why don't you just tell her you don't like the stuff?"

"It's too late for that," I tell him.

Three years ago, the first time my mom bought me a jar of the ridiculously expensive anti-aging cream, I accidentally told her I liked it. Now, she buys it for me every chance she gets. At least it doesn't go to waste, thanks to Margaux.

"Your mom is more understanding than you give her credit for," Maks says.

Instead of answering, I drain the last of my drink. Maks makes it sound easy—but he's never been a daughter. And he's never had Elizabeth Meyer as his mother.

Chapter Two

Now

THE PATIO AT CARMINE'S IS CROWDED. IT SEEMS HALF OF CHI-cago had the same idea to dine al fresco and take advantage of the break in the July heat wave.

Jeff is already seated when I walk in, flanked by Maks and Margaux. I can't help but smile at the sight of him. I'd always imagined myself marrying someone Jewish, with brown hair and brown eyes like my dad, but Jeff is as un-Jewish as a man can get, with his angular features, blond hair, and blue-gray eyes.

"There's the birthday girl!"

Half the restaurant turns toward the source of the loud, obnoxious voice at the same time I do. Ross, Jeff's college roommate, current coworker, and dinner-party crasher.

My cheeks flush with embarrassment. I make a beeline for Jeff, keeping my head down to avoid making eye contact with all the strangers I feel staring.

"I'm sorry," he whispers, as he stands to give me a hug. "He asked what I was doing tonight."

"You didn't have to invite him," I whisper back.

Jeff gives me a kiss to keep up appearances, even though Ross is socially clueless and Margaux and Maks know exactly what I'm thinking.

"He invited himself." Jeff's breath tickles my ear, and I smile, even though I'm less than happy about our change in plans.

It's not unusual for Jeff to bring along a stray—it's a side effect of his being a genuinely good guy who puts others' feelings first. Although I would think that he'd put my feelings first on my birthday.

He knew I didn't want to celebrate at all this year. I caved only when he said it could be a small group, just my closest friends. And that does not include Ross, whose only redeeming quality is the fact that he's the one who dragged Jeff out to the bar on the night we met almost two years ago.

I hadn't wanted to go out that night, either. It had barely been a month since my dad's accident, and I was still in a fog of grief. But my two best friends showed up uninvited and went full intervention on me. Margaux turned on the shower while Maks dug through my closet for an outfit he deemed acceptable.

An hour later, we were at Four Farthings, one of our go-to bars for karaoke night. Maks had just finished butchering a Shania Twain song when a preppy man with blond hair and an electric smile took the small stage. He started singing "Friends in Low Places," and I couldn't look away. His voice wasn't anything special, but there was something about his easy confidence that made me smile—which I hadn't done in the past thirty-three days.

The bar was packed, but he found my face in the crowd and couldn't seem to look away, either. By the end of the song, it felt like it was just the two of us standing there. Everyone else disappeared as he stepped off the stage and walked right up to me.

He offered to buy me a drink, and I said yes. Two hours and three drinks later, he asked if I wanted to go somewhere quieter, and I said yes. Six months after that, he asked if I wanted to do the whole forever thing, and again, I said yes.

I'm not usually the type to move so quickly, but like they say, when it's right, it's right. And it felt right with Jeff from the first moment we spoke.

"What do you think, Paige?" Margaux asks, jolting me out of my memories.

"Sorry?"

"Do you want the calamari grilled or fried?"

"Let's get one of each," I say. The grilled is my favorite, but I know Maks likes it fried.

"What she said," Margaux tells our waiter, who smiles before walking away to put in our appetizers.

Ross picks up his glass to make a toast, and I wonder if I've been too hard on the guy.

"Cheers," he says. "To the future Mrs. Parker."

My face falls as I look at Jeff, who lifts his hands in defense. "Don't look at me," he says. "You know I'm okay with you keeping your last name."

"He doesn't really mean that," Ross says.

"Oh, but he does," Jeff says. His voice sounds firm and almost convincing.

"I'm just saying, it's traditional for the woman to take the man's last name," Ross says. He adjusts the Windsor knot in his tie, and I wonder if it's a power move or a sign of insecurity.

"It *was* traditional," Margaux says, getting her lawyer on. "But women are allowed to vote now, too."

Ross laughs, dismissing Margaux, which only fuels her fire. "Paige doesn't have to change her name if she doesn't want to," she says.

"And she's not going to," Maks says, jumping in. "Would you want your initials to be PP?"

I can't help but laugh, grateful for my best friends and my understanding fiancé.

When I found out Jeff's last name the morning after our first "date," I told him I wouldn't be able to take his name if we ever got married. At the time, I was joking. Never in a million years had I thought I'd end up marrying what I thought was just a one-night stand. Being single was as much a part of my identity as my name, and I couldn't imagine changing either.

It had been more than a decade since my last serious relationship, and I'd honestly stopped looking for anything meaningful. I wasn't sad about my single status. Quite the opposite, really. We had big plans to be like the Golden Girls—Maks was our Sophia, and Margaux and I fought over who got to be Blanche.

If Jeff was a Golden Girl, he'd be Dorothy. The responsible one with a good head on his shoulders.

"Enough," Jeff says. "We didn't invite you guys here to fight over whether or not Paige changes her last name—which she's not going to, by the way. We invited you to celebrate her birthday."

After Jeff's declaration, the rest of dinner is blissfully uneventful. My favorite four-alarm chicken calabrese is as spicy and delicious as ever, and Ross is too busy eating to stir up any more debates. Even if he tried, I'm sure Margaux would have squashed it. She seems on edge and ready to rumble. I'm not sure what's going on at work that has her so out of sorts, but I feel bad for whoever is up against her.

Once the waiter clears our plates, Jeff reaches under the table and comes back up holding a giant blue gift bag with yellow tissue paper artfully coming out of the top.

"It's beautiful," I tell him, giving him a quick kiss.

"Don't thank him till you open it," Maks says.

"I'm sure I'll love whatever it is," I say. It's not just a line. Jeff is an excellent gift-giver, which I credit to his growing up with three sisters.

I carefully lift the tissue paper out of the bag. There's more of it than I expected. I keep going, wondering for a minute if anything else is actually in the bag. Finally, my hand knocks against something hard.

My face lights up as I wrap my fingers around what feels like a small jewelry box.

"What did you do?" I ask.

Jeff shrugs, but he looks proud of himself.

I'm less careful with the box's wrapping paper, tearing off the edges to see what's inside. It's a box from my favorite jewelry store. I slowly open the lid and gasp at the sight of a gorgeous diamond tennis bracelet.

"Jeff," I say through a shocked laugh. "This isn't a big birthday."

He takes the bracelet out of the box and clasps it around my wrist. "Every birthday is a big birthday—and it's a chance to celebrate you."

I hold out my arm to admire the bracelet and lean in to give him a kiss. "Thank you."

"We should have gone first," Maks tells Margaux, before handing over an envelope.

"You guys didn't have to do anything," I tell them. "Your friendship is enough of a gift."

"Okay," Maks says, reaching to take back the envelope.

I snap it back from him, quickly opening it up before he changes his mind. I pull out three gift cards—one for Starbucks; one for Hollywood Nails, my favorite nail salon in Lincoln Park; and one for my favorite local bookstore.

"It's like you got me the perfect day," I tell them. "Thank you!"

Maks blushes but shrugs. "It's no diamond . . ."

"I've got a diamond for you," Ross says. I brace myself, hoping he's not going to take another shot at Jeff. I know guys do friendship differently, but I'm over it. "The boss gave me his Cubs tickets for next Friday," he says. "It's a one o'clock game—Jeff can take you."

"That's so sweet," I tell Ross. "But I'm a Cardinals fan."

He laughs a little too loudly and slaps Jeff on the back. "It's not too late to back out of the wedding, bro."

"Never," Jeff says, bringing my hand to his lips.

I force a smile and narrow my eyes at Ross. From the stories Jeff has told me about their office antics, I've gathered that Ross is angling for the promotion Jeff has all but earned. I've worked with enough smarmy men to see right through Ross's plan with the tickets. Get Jeff out of the office and then sweet-talk the boss, trying to convince him that Ross is the one who's been putting in all the late-night and weekend work.

Jeff might be too nice to play hardball, but I'm not. And I'm more convinced than ever that he needs to stay in Chicago next weekend. As much as I'd love to have his steadying presence by my side, he needs to be focused on work. Not driving five hours to sit through an hour-long service at Temple and dinner with my family.

Mom doesn't understand why I'm making the trip, either. There's no religious or societal reason for me to go back home to mark the second anniversary of my dad's passing. There won't be anything official like last year's unveiling of his headstone. But his name will be read out loud during Friday night services, and someone should be there to hear it. If I wasn't going, I doubt Mom or the twins would, either.

Dad would want us to be there for each other. He'd want me to be there. So I'm going. And I'm going to try my best to smile through it.

Chapter Three

Now

"EXCUSE ME. SORRY, PARDON ME," I MUTTER AS I SQUEEZE PAST the bent knees of congregants at Temple Israel, making my way down the row where I hope someone saved me a seat.

Nothing has gone as planned today. I spent three hours waiting for a recruiter to call me back about a job I'm overqualified for, and then I was late to my nail appointment. I could have skipped it—but I couldn't show up at Temple with chipped nails. It was a lose-lose situation. And now I'm the one thing my mother has no patience for: late.

Mom is sitting upright with her usual perfect posture. She doesn't so much as turn her head toward the commotion I'm inadvertently causing.

I want to tell her it wasn't entirely my fault, that there was a line at the rental car counter and huge stretches of 55 were down to a single lane—but it wouldn't matter. Elizabeth Meyer believes excuses are for people who don't want something bad enough.

"Sorry," I whisper to Aunt Sissy as I take the empty seat beside her. "Construction."

She takes my hand in hers and gives it a squeeze. I lean back in the pew, already soothed by her presence. It's no wonder I grew up wishing I'd been her daughter, instead.

My mother's best friend is the yin to her yang—not only does Aunt Sissy know how to let loose and have fun, but she's openly affectionate, always supportive, and genuinely interested in my thoughts and feelings. All the things I craved but never got from my mother.

It's pathetic how hard I used to try, constantly putting myself out there for her to reject me. My hair was too red, I was too "artsy," and, my worst crime, I'd been born a few years too early.

I smooth out the dress I slipped on in the parking lot. The same parking lot where my dad taught me how to drive and also where I let Rich Plum get to second base in the back of his mom's Volvo during Michelle Dash's bat mitzvah.

Mom catches my eye and gives me a thin-lipped smile. I return the gesture, hoping it means my transgression of tardiness has been forgiven.

I lean forward and glance down the row to where my twin sisters, Annabelle and Frannie, sit beside her. They both have their heads bent, looking down at the Gates of Prayer even though the rabbi is speaking words from her heart, not the page. They aren't the first ones to try the cell-phone-in-the-book trick, although in my day it was a Baby-Sitter's Club or Sweet Valley High novel I was sneaking a look at.

Mom looks at me again, and I glance down to make sure I didn't accidentally put my dress on backward. As far as I can tell, nothing is off about my outfit—a simple black dress I used to wear for client presentations—although Margaux would have told me to pair it with some scarf or accessory to give it more personality and style.

When I look back up, Mom is still staring. I watch as she tucks a lock of chestnut brown hair behind her ear and gives me a look that borders on coquettish. I turn and quickly realize I was not her intended target. A few rows back on the left side, an older man is staring back at my mother. It's Joel Levy. He quickly averts his eyes back to the pulpit when he notices me noticing him.

I remember hearing something about Mrs. Levy passing away last year; maybe Joel and my mom are moving on with each other. In theory, it's fine with me—I know sixty-two is too young for my mom to spend the rest of her life alone—but does she have to openly flirt with a man at the service we're attending in memory of her late husband? My late father.

The thought of my dad with his easy smile and gentle voice fills me with a mixture of sadness and gratitude. When it came to parents, I won the dad lottery.

He wasn't quite as lucky, but I tried to be the kind of daughter he'd be proud of. Unfortunately, I didn't inherit any of his mathematical or business skills—politics and religion were of no interest to me, and I'd rather spend my time drawing and daydreaming than watching sports. But he let me be me.

My dad didn't just accept the fact that I was different; he loved me because of it. I remember coming home from college, babbling about my color theory class and how powerful color could be. He didn't change the subject or tell me I should switch my major to something more practical—instead, when I told him that the color orange has the power to make people hungry, he helped me think of all the fast-food places that used orange or a combination of yellow and red in their logos, which was pretty much all of them.

I can't believe it's been two years since I last saw his round, smiling face, with the beard that was always a little too scruffy and the black-rimmed glasses he was constantly cleaning with the soft fabric of the button-down shirts he wore every day, even on the weekends.

We talked the morning he died. Just ten days after our birthday. It was an ordinary conversation, and now I regret wasting those precious minutes telling him about a difficult project at work. When he offered to help me, I laughed and told him that he would be about as helpful with the design of an ad as I would be picking stocks and bonds or whatever else it was financial advisors did.

If I had known that was going to be the last time I'd hear his voice, I would have done less talking and more listening. If I had known, I would have asked one of the questions I assumed I'd have a lifetime to ask. Silly things that I didn't think mattered until he wasn't here anymore to tell me the answer: what he dreamed of growing up to be when he was a kid, how he managed to make pancakes so fluffy, if he still would have married Mom if I hadn't come along.

The last words he said to me were "I love-love you." That was our thing, ever since the day he and my mom brought the twins home. He told me even though there were two of them and one of me, he loved me doubly, since I would always be his first.

I miss him the way I imagine people miss lost limbs—sometimes it feels like it's still there, until you look down and have to go through the hurt all over again.

We don't even know for sure what it was that took him from us. The heart attack and the car accident happened within seconds of each other, so the doctors couldn't tell us which one happened first. Like the chicken and the egg. Dad would have gotten a kick out of that. He loved his puns and riddles.

The rustling of the congregation rising to their feet brings my attention back to the moment. The service is almost over.

"*Aleinu l'shabeiach l'adon hakol.*" I stand and recite the opening line of the Aleinu prayer while trying to find the page so I can read along with the transliteration. The synchronized voices and movement speak to me, even though I'd be a hypocrite to call myself religious.

As the prayer ends, my stomach does a little flip with the realization that it's time for the Mourner's Kaddish. The reason we're here.

"Elaine and Joseph Berger," the rabbi says, reading down the list of names of people the service is honoring, former members of the congregation, going who knows how far back, all who passed away during this week. "Ely Goldstein, Annette Greenberg." I don't realize I'm tapping my finger against my leg until Aunt Sissy reaches for my hand. I shake my head and pull it away. I appreciate the gesture, but I need to feel this pain.

"Joyce Lewin." The rabbi is getting closer to the *M*'s. I hold my breath, releasing it at the sound of his name. "Mark Meyer."

Three short syllables in the rabbi's soft-spoken voice. I wish she would scream it loud enough that even the people sitting in the last row could feel the importance of his name. The name that's spoken only in past tense now, even though the memories of him are anything but.

"*Yitgadal, v'yitkadash,*" the congregation recites. I open my mouth to say the words, but no sound comes out. I wipe a tear from my eye and listen to the prayer, feeling the words settle inside my heart where they don't begin to fill the hole he left behind.

EVERYONE IS SEATED by the time I walk into the private room Mom reserved at Cardwell's. She thinks it was Dad's favorite restaurant, but he only picked it for special occasions because he knew *she* loved it. His real favorite was Sportsman's Park.

The two of us would saddle up to the bar, order a dozen wings each, a plate of their famous toasted ravioli to share, and two beers—Budweiser for him and Bud Light for me. If we were celebrating something, like the Cardinals making it into the World Series or my getting accepted to portfolio school, he'd get an old-fashioned.

The only seat left at the table is next to Mom and across from Frannie. I sit down and apologize for keeping them waiting.

I hadn't meant to be late again, and I was technically there on time—just in the parking lot. After the service, I felt too vulnerable to be around my family. Without Dad there to help balance me, it's like I revert back to my awkward and moody teenage-self.

Plus, Jeff called, and I couldn't bring myself to hang up. He was nervous about his big presentation on Monday, and I talked him through the opening lines. It might have helped him, but it definitely helped me.

As Annabelle drones on about some trivial drama with her friends, I look back and forth between my sisters—three minutes apart and identical, except that Annabelle's face is a little harder, and she's always a few inches taller since she "wouldn't be caught dead" in flats. With the warm brown eyes and olive skin they got from Dad, and Mom's chestnut hair, they're the perfect blend of our parents. No one would ever question their place in our family.

"What did you think, Paige?" Mom asks.

"I'm sorry—what?"

A flicker of disappointment crosses Mom's face, and I can feel the criticism without her saying a word.

"The services at Temple," Aunt Sissy says. "They were really nice."

"I like what they do for Shabbat," Mom says, turning to her best friend. "I've started going a few times a month, if you ever want to join me."

"Now, let's not get carried away," Sissy says, holding up both of her hands to slow my mother down.

Annabelle laughs, and Frannie follows suit, as she tends to do. I look at them and wonder if I'm the only one who realizes there's something strange about Mom suddenly being religious.

Dad was the one who always made me go to Hebrew school and insisted I have a bat mitzvah. Mom, like me, was more interested in the party that took place after the service. Once, she even let me play hooky from class and took me for manicures at Ladue Nails instead. She made me promise not to tell Dad. Of course, that was before the twins were born.

The door to our little alcove opens, and Annabelle perks up as our waiter, a good-looking Italian guy, walks in. He's a little short for my taste, but the older of my little sisters is far from picky these days.

"Good evening," the waiter says. "My name is Tony, and I'll be taking care of you."

"You can take care of me anytime," Annabelle says in a hushed, suggestive voice. Ever since her now ex-boyfriend took the wrong end of an ultimatum, she's been on a mission to find a husband. God forbid she end up being a bride past forty, as she said the last time I was in town.

"Are you here for a special occasion?" the waiter asks.

"The anniversary of our father's death," I tell him.

"Paige," Mom says, a *please shut up, dear* tone to her voice.

"What?" I say. "It's the truth."

Aunt Sissy speaks up, attempting to save Mom and me from each other like she always does. "I'll have a glass of Prosecco."

The waiter looks both flustered and relieved as he fumbles for his pad to write down our drink orders. The twins love the idea of Prosecco, so they decide to get a bottle for the table. But tonight, I want an old-fashioned.

An awkward silence settles around the table after Tony walks away. If Dad were here, he would make a bad joke to ease the tension. I know he'd want me to try to keep things positive.

"So, Frannie and Annabelle," I say, using Annabelle's full name. She started going by Belle in middle school, since it sounded prettier, but old habits die hard. "How's the party planning going?"

Annabelle instantly perks up. Their thirtieth-birthday bash has been her favorite topic of conversation since the day after they turned twenty-nine last September.

"We booked the sickest DJ," she says. "Right, Frannie?"

"Right," Frannie agrees. "The sickest."

My phone buzzes with a perfectly timed text from Jeff, a cute GIF of a teddy bear blowing heart-shaped kisses along with a message: Thanks for your help. Feeling better about the presentation already. Hope dinner isn't too dreadful. Love you!

I'm looking for a GIF to send back when Aunt Sissy says my name.

"Have you decided if you want a DJ or live band at the wedding?" she asks. I love her for trying to involve me in the conversation, although I'm happier in the shadows than I am in the spotlight.

"Not yet," I tell her. "The only detail I've figured out is the groom."

Frannie laughs and Mom smiles, but Annabelle just rolls her eyes.

My phone vibrates again, and I look down, hoping to see another message from Jeff, but it's just an email from FamilyTree, telling me I have a "new leaf." I dismiss the message and put my phone back in my purse.

The next forty minutes are filled with more details of the twins' thirtieth birthday. Somewhere between the idea of passed appetizers and matching little black dresses, I notice Mom staring at my drink. I bet it makes her think of Dad, too.

"Want a sip?" I offer.

She cringes as if I asked her to join me and Jeff in a threesome. "I can't stand whiskey," she says. "The taste, or the smell of it."

I shrug and take a defiant sip, adding whiskey to the long list of things we don't have in common.

"You used to make Mark brush his teeth before he kissed you if he'd been drinking whiskey," Aunt Sissy says, a look of love and lost memories on her face.

Mom blushes and takes another sip of Prosecco. "The girls don't want to hear about that."

"Actually, I'd love to hear a story about Dad," I say. "That's why we're here, isn't it?"

"I've got a few good ones," Aunt Sissy says. She stops when Mom shakes her head. The gesture was faster than a blink, Mom's earrings the only thing still moving, swinging against her frozen face.

Then, because there's nothing Elizabeth Meyer hates more than making a scene, she turns her pursed lips into a smile and lays her napkin next to her barely touched salad. "It's been a long day," she says.

"Yes, it has," I agree, looking down at my own plate, still full enough that it could be served to another guest. My drink, however, is almost empty, and I finish it in one sip.

I can almost hear Dad's voice repeating the words that are burned into my memory. "You're not as different from your mom as you think," he'd say when things got particularly tough. "Be easy on her, sweetheart."

I sigh, wishing it wasn't so hard. But nothing in this family is easy without him.

Chapter Four

Now

THREE DAYS LATER, I'M LYING IN BED WITH MY EYES CLOSED, listening to the familiar sounds of Jeff's morning routine. He's always up earlier than I am, but today he's up before the sun to catch a flight to San Francisco for work.

I hear the soft click of his suitcase handle and open an eye, smiling at the sight of him. "Have a safe flight."

"I was trying not to wake you," he whispers, as if it's not too late.

"And leave without a good-luck kiss?"

"Never."

The expensive mattress Jeff insisted we splurge on for the new apartment doesn't budge as he sits down beside me. Even in the dark, he looks handsome. I reach up my hand and caress his smooth, freshly shaven cheek. His blue-gray eyes sparkle as my hand drifts behind his neck, bringing him down for a kiss.

"Don't forget about me," I say between kisses.

"I'll only be gone a few days." He tries to get up, but I hold on tighter. "I'll miss my flight."

"Fine," I say with a sigh, and release my grip.

"Go back to sleep," he whispers, rolling his suitcase out the bedroom door. "I love you."

"Love you more," I say through a yawn. I used to hate cheesy couples before I became half of one. My thirties and the first year of my forties were a string of casual flings—and one on-again-off-again guy I couldn't quite shake. I thought I wasn't good at relationships, but it turns out those just weren't the right relationships. They weren't with Jeff.

I flip my pillow to the cool side and snuggle back under the covers, grateful there isn't anywhere I have to be today. Both a benefit and a curse of unemployment.

THE SOUND OF an ambulance screaming down State Street twenty-six floors below wakes me again. I reach for my phone to check the time. Ten minutes after ten. If Jeff hasn't landed in San Francisco yet, he will soon.

I curl back under the covers with my phone to get caught up on what's happened with the rest of the world since I've been sleeping. I quit out of the apps and open my email in case the recruiter who ghosted me last week wrote back to apologize.

There are thirty-five new messages: six from various job search sites I signed up for, eight trying to sell me clothes I shouldn't be spending money on, three daily deals, twelve emails on a thread with Maks and Margaux about happy hour plans, five from various food delivery services, and one email from FamilyTree.com.

The FamilyTree email is promotional, trying to get me to upgrade my account to the paid version. I open it out of curiosity but quickly delete it. They really should have hired my old advertising agency when we pitched the business a few years ago.

We would have done a better job designing the email to get more engagement—their version doesn't even have a call-to-action above the fold. At least I got a free DNA kit out of the project in the name of research.

I scroll back in my inbox, remembering the email about a new leaf. I find it and skim the information, dismissing it when I see it's a parent-child connection. I delete the email and get out of bed.

It must be a mistake on their end—I would know if I'd ever had a child. I shake off the thought as I slip out of Jeff's T-shirt and turn on the shower, the water almost as hot as it will go. I stand there for a minute, enjoying the rhythmic pressure on my scalp before reaching for the conditioner.

While the curl-conditioning treatment sits, I squeeze more than the recommended quarter-size amount of body wash onto my loofah. I scrub my stomach, which is soft and flabby despite never having carried a baby. I can't imagine how FamilyTree could make such a big mistake—that I could have a baby in the first place, much less one who was born in 1955. That would make him sixty-three, the same age as my parents.

I stiffen as the thought settles in my mind. *My parents.*

I drop the loofah and step out of the shower, conditioner still in my hair and soapy suds on my skin. I wrap a towel around myself and open my laptop. With shaking fingers, I pull up the "new leaf" email from the virtual trash can, where the words are written in black and white. They aren't saying I had a child.

They're saying I *am* the child.

Chapter Five

Now

JEFF'S CELL PHONE RINGS TWICE, THEN GOES STRAIGHT TO voicemail. I exhale a panicked breath—I need to talk to him. But he has no way of knowing I'm actually calling him for something important this time.

I consider calling again. He knows I wouldn't call twice in a row if it wasn't serious. My finger is poised to tap his number again when a text pops up.

JEFF: About to walk in the meet and greet. Wish me luck. And text if it's good news about a job! xx

I wish that's what I needed to talk to him about—a job. He believes in me more than I believe in myself, and I've started feeling like a failure every time I have to tell him there's still no news on the job front. But right now, that's the last thing on my mind.

Since I can't distract Jeff with this right now, I send him a kiss emoji and text out an SOS to Maks and Margaux. They'll help me get to the bottom of this.

I stare at the words on the computer screen until they become a jumble of letters that don't make sense. I close my eyes and look again, but the message hasn't changed. We've added a new leaf to your family tree, a parent-child match.

TWENTY MINUTES LATER, I'm still wrapped in a towel, sitting in front of my computer, when I hear a knock at the door.

"What's the word?" Maks says, walking past me and heading straight for the kitchen. "Do you have any food?"

"Help yourself," I say automatically, knowing he will anyway.

Maks opens the refrigerator, then glances back at me. He furrows his brow, as if just realizing something's not right. "You okay?"

I shrug, still dazed. "I'm not sure."

He closes the refrigerator. "Talk," he commands.

I take a deep breath and try to formulate the words. I don't know how to start. "I just got some bad news."

"Breast cancer?" he gasps.

"No," I say, and pull my towel tighter around me. I'm shaking, and not only from the cold. "Just the worst news I could possibly get from a DNA test."

"You're related to our illustrious president?" he asks, picking an apple from the fruit bowl on the counter.

"Worse," I tell him, as my stomach sinks further.

"Hmm," he says, shining the apple with the hem of his T-shirt.

Before he starts listing off Hitler, Mussolini, or other historical figures he knows I'd hate being biologically connected to, I spit it out. "FamilyTree sent me an email saying my dad just joined the site."

"Is someone trolling you?" Maks asks between bites. "There are sick people who get off on impersonating dead people. It's like phishing, but worse."

If I don't stop him, I know he'll launch into a diagnosis of my nonexistent troll's psyche. "I got an email saying another man is my father," I tell him. "Andrew Abrams." Saying his name out loud leaves a sour aftertaste in my mouth.

"What the shit?" Maks says, disbelief in his voice. "Show me."

He follows me into my room and sits down in front of my computer. We both read the email.

Dear Paige Meyer,

Congratulations! We've added a new leaf to your family tree, a parent-child match. You and Andrew Abrams (b. 1955) are now connected. To message with him on the site, sign up for our full membership for just $12.99 a month.

Sincerely,
Your friends at FamilyTree, where we're all family

"I bet it's just a marketing scam to get people to sign up," Maks says. "It's pretty smart, actually."

"You think?" I ask, desperate to believe him, even though I know a stunt like that would never make it through legal.

"Maybe?" He doesn't sound convinced. "Or it could be human error."

"That was my first thought," I agree. Logically, it makes sense.

Someone could have entered a wrong letter or number in the DNA sequence and messed up the whole thing. Happens to me all the time with long Internet passwords and account numbers.

"What do you think I should do?" I ask.

Maks spins the chair around, looking me up and down. "Finish showering," he says, giving me a push toward the bathroom.

THE SECOND TIME I get out of the shower, I actually manage to get dressed in yoga pants and a T-shirt from the one and only 5K Margaux talked me into running with her. I hear murmuring on the other side of the bathroom door. She must have gotten here.

"Paige?" Margaux says my name like it's a question, as if she's not sure who I am anymore. *But we don't know yet,* I want to tell her. It might not be true.

I walk back into the bedroom and she pulls me in for a hug. "We can sue the website, or this guy," she says. "We can sue somebody."

I shrug out of her embrace and sit back down at my desk. I need answers, so I go to the one place that can give them to me.

The FamilyTree website has barely loaded before a chat window opens in the bottom corner of the screen.

LISA F: Let me know if I can be of any help!

"Someone's messaging me!" I shout.

Margaux and Maks are instantly beside me, leaning close so they can see the message. I smell garlic on Maks's breath—he must have found the leftovers from Topo.

"Ask if the results are based on probabilities, or if they literally compared your DNA to his," he says. "If it's a cheap test where they don't provide much detail of the genome— Well, it matters how they compare, if they—"

"Shut up, Maks," Margaux and I say in unison.

"I'm just trying to help," he says.

"You can help," I tell him. "Just more quietly so I can type."

USER: I just got an alert that says I share a parent/child relationship with a man who isn't my father.

LISA F: Hello, I would be happy to look into this situation and give you some information. May I have your Family-Tree username?

USER: PaigeMeyer711

LISA F: Can you confirm your date of birth?

USER: 7/11/75

LISA F: Thanks, Paige. Give me a few minutes and I'll look up your account.

My two best friends and I stare at the monitor, waiting for Lisa F to write back. For her to tell me there's been a mistake. She'll apologize for the mix-up and say they sent the email in error. She'll say this strange man is in fact a stranger, not my father.

The sound of bells tolling makes us all jump, and Maks fumbles in his pocket for his phone. "Sorry," he says, then looks down at the screen. "Shitfuck, I'm late for a meeting."

"It's okay, thanks for coming."

"Thanks for lunch." He kisses my cheek, then leaves with a flourish, calling out behind him, "Keep me on the loop!"

The ding of a new message calls Margaux's and my attention back to the computer.

LISA F: Thanks for your patience. Based on the results of your DNA test, it appears the match in question is your biological father.

I hear Margaux inhale a quick breath behind me. But I'm not ready to believe it. Not yet. My hands tremble over the keys as I type a response.

USER: No, he's not. My dad is Mark Meyer. He died two years ago.

LISA F: I understand how this may not make sense or even seem valid, however we do stand by the accuracy of our testing and are confident in the results we've provided. Please let me know if you have any other questions.

They're confident in the results. Confident that this man I've never seen or heard of in my entire life is my father? He can't be. I already have a father.

My eyes are drawn to the picture of my dad that I keep beside my computer. It's not the last picture we took together, but it's one of my favorites.

A year before he died, he had a work conference in Chicago, and he came into town a day early so we could spend time together, just the two of us. I took the day off work, and we played tourists—taking selfies in front of the Bean, riding the Ferris wheel at Navy Pier, and ending the day with a sunset architecture tour on the river. That's where we snapped this picture, the water below us and the sun sparkling off the reflection of a mirrored building behind us.

I pick up the picture and study his face, searching for a piece of myself. His eyes are crinkled behind his black-rimmed glasses, but I've stared at them enough to know they're brown, not blue, like mine. His untamed eyebrows are bushy and wild, which mine would be if I didn't get them regularly waxed. His nose is prominent where mine is small—but we're both right-handed, and we both hate broccoli but love cauliflower. And he always told me I had his mother's sense of humor. He wouldn't lie to me about that.

Relieved, I sit back and find his smile in the picture. It's straight where mine is crooked, his white teeth standing out against the beard that's so dark brown it's almost black. I run a finger over his face, lingering at the bottom. I don't remember what his chin looked like—it was almost always covered by his beard.

I push back my chair, startling Margaux.

"Paige?" she asks.

"I need to find something," I tell her. "A picture."

I drag the desk chair into the closet, and Margaux follows me. She tries to stop me from climbing up, but I need to do this, and she knows me well enough to let me. Still, I'm grateful she's there to hold the chair so it doesn't roll out from under me.

My heart is beating so loud it echoes in my ears as I put one hand on the wall for support and use the other to reach for the hatbox filled with old family photos that I've been meaning to digitize since before Dad died. My fingers graze the bottom of the box, and I start sliding it toward me until it's hanging half off the ledge.

Feeling confident, I let go of the wall and bring up my other hand. I'm holding the box in both hands when my feet start to teeter.

"Careful," Margaux says, but it's too late.

I manage to steady myself, but the box tips out of my hands, spilling hundreds of photographs. I take a moment to catch my breath, then let Margaux help me down from the chair.

I slide down to the floor, sitting in a puddle of family photos.

"What are we looking for?" Margaux asks, sitting down beside me.

"A family portrait," I tell her. "A professional studio one—the twins were two or three."

I can almost see the picture in my mind. The twins were at the stage where they were as adorable as they were annoying, getting into everything, everywhere. As an awkward teenager with braces and pimply skin, I resented them for being everything I wasn't.

Mom refused to let me sit out of the picture; she didn't even give me a choice about the outfit I wore. I remember sweating under the studio lights, the wool dress scratching my thighs. Dad didn't have much of a choice, either. Not after Mom told him the only thing she wanted for Chanukah that year was to have him shave his beard for a family photo.

I remember almost everything about the picture—the cloudy blue-gray background; Dad holding one twin, Mom holding the other; and me, in the middle, wearing a hideous dress, the curls in my hair flatironed away so I was barely recognizable, the pained expression on my face revealing my true feelings.

Mom, on the other hand, looked happier than if she'd just stumbled onto the set of *Knots Landing* and bumped into Gary Ewing himself. I remember Dad's dark blue suit and his bemused smile. But for the life of me, I don't remember what his chin looked like.

I start to stack the pictures to put them back in the box, scanning the four-by-six glossy prints for my dad's clean-shaven face. I shuffle through photos of him and Mom dressed up for events or date nights, pictures of him with a twin on each knee, a few pictures of me and my dad, dozens of posed photos with me and the twins. More pictures of the twins. More pictures of my parents.

"Awww," Margaux says beside me. "Look how cute you were."

She hands me a rare photo of Mom and me after a mother-daughter charity fashion show. I must have been five or six. Her arm looks unnatural around me, her smile forced. My smile, however, is stretched across my face, revealing the missing tooth I was so proud of. It's the smile of a girl who hadn't yet realized that no matter how hard she tried, she would never be the daughter her mother wanted.

I turn back to the stack in my hands, flipping through one memory after the other. Photo after photo that isn't the one I'm looking for.

"Oh." Margaux's voice is breathless. My eyes lock with hers, and she offers me a smile before handing me a photo. *The photo.*

I inhale a deep breath and take in the image before me. My eyes are drawn to my dad's face, the sparkle in his eye and the dimple in the middle of his chin.

A tear slides down my cheek as I bring a finger to my own chin, smooth and dimple free. A shiver runs through me, and I quickly stand, knocking over a stack of photos.

I push the chair back toward my desk and sit down in front of my laptop, where the chat window is still open.

USER: Are you 100% sure there's no mistake here?

Three dots appear; Lisa F is typing. A lot, considering how long it's taking. I cross my ankles and two fingers on both hands, wishing harder than I've ever wished for anything in my whole life that she'll come back with a different answer.

LISA F: We are quite sure, but our test is not an official paternity test, so to speak. Most parent/child relationships share a very large amount of DNA in common, around 3,400 centimorgans, roughly half of the DNA. You share this amount with the match. Because of the sheer volume of DNA in common, a parent/child relationship is one of the easiest to determine.

I remember the question Maks told me to ask, part of it at least. Something about probability and comparing our DNA.

USER: So this is based on his DNA test and mine? Not on probabilities?

LISA F: Yes, that is correct. We compare new users' DNA to all the other DNA tests in our database of approximately 4 million people, and we provide matches based on how much DNA you share in common with any of them. And you directly share 3,400 units of DNA with this particular match.

USER: That's not what I wanted to hear, but thanks for the information.

LISA F: We're sorry for the unexpected turn of events but hope this turns out the best for you. Please let us know if we can help in any other way.

She can't help. No one can. I rest my head in my hands and let the flood of hot, angry tears fall. I don't hear Margaux walking up behind me, but I feel her hand on my shoulder. Her gentle touch makes me cry even harder, and I'm grateful she doesn't ask me to say the words out loud.

I can't even begin to wrap my mind around the enormity of it all. My mom lied to me. Probably lied to my dad, too.

The hole in my heart doubles in size, like I'm losing him all over again. Although it seems he was never mine to lose.

Chapter Six

Now

Hi, Mom!

I delete the exclamation point.

Hi, Mom.

That doesn't feel right, either.

Hey, Mom.

   Did you cheat on Dad in college?

Delete.

Hey, Mom.

   So I just got an email from FamilyTree.com that says Dad isn't my father. DID YOU CHEAT ON HIM???

Delete.

I close my eyes and focus on breathing, trying to center myself, but there's no use. I should feel validated for all the times I felt like an outsider in my family. My stomach churns at the thought of another family out there, another life where I might have grown up knowing how it feels to belong. My mother took that from me.

One more deep breath, and then I crack my knuckles and start typing.

Hi, Mom.

I got an email from FamilyTree.com. They said a man named Andrew Abrams is my father.

Paige.

Not bad, I think, rereading the words. Direct, straightforward, and not accusatory. Before I lose my nerve, I hit send.

It's just after three, so she's probably out having coffee with one of her girlfriends. I can picture her, glancing at her phone as the email comes in, her face growing pale, her jaw literally dropping.

"Elizabeth, what's wrong?" one of her girlfriends will ask. She'll put a perfect smile on her face and either say nothing at all or make some comment about "Paige being Paige." Because Elizabeth Meyer would never tell anyone anything that might reflect poorly on her.

My mother was still scarred from her original sin—getting knocked up when she was in college. While Aunt Sissy and most of their friends were out partying and having fun at University of Kansas fraternity parties, my parents were sitting in their off-campus apartment, Mom crying as much as her colicky baby. That's one story I wouldn't mind never hearing again.

Margaux walks back in my room, finished with whatever work call she had to take. She looks flustered—something that can usually be said about me but never about her.

"Why do you look nervous?" she asks.

I glance at my laptop, then back at her. "I emailed my mom."

Margaux sighs. "I thought we agreed it would be best to wait until you had some time to reflect and process all this."

"Have you met me?" I ask. The sound of an incoming email calls our attention back to my computer just as the box with the preview alert disappears. "She wrote back."

Margaux wordlessly sits on the arm of my chair, and we both read my mother's one-line response:

MARK MEYER WAS YOUR FATHER AND YOU SHOULD BE PROUD!!!!

I laugh, even though there's nothing funny about her all-caps words or her use of four exclamation points.

Margaux asks if I'm okay, but I don't answer, because I'm honestly not sure. I read the email a third time, and then a fourth, trying to find some meaning between the words.

"Either she's lying to me," I say, "or my DNA is."

"It's more an omission of fact than a lie," Margaux says, letting her law degree show. "She didn't say this new guy isn't your father; she said that Mark *was* your father. DNA aside, that's the truth."

"DNA aside?" I laugh. It's a little thing—but it's the biggest little thing. And as much as I might want to, there can be no pushing DNA aside. Not now that I know.

"You know what I mean," she says.

I look down at the picture of me and the man I spent forty-three years of my life calling Dad. "I don't know anything anymore. I don't know who I am."

Margaux stands up and looks down at me with her hands on her hips. "You are Paige Meyer," she says in her courtroom voice. "No blood, no chromosome or genome, can change that."

When I don't respond, Margaux redirects. "What if your mom is telling you the truth?" My ears perk up, desperate for any logic that would make my dad be my dad. "I mean, your dad's been gone for two years—it's not like she has to hide the truth from him anymore. What reason would she possibly have to lie?"

I feel a spark of hope, lighting the way for another explanation.

Margaux's phone rings again, and she sighs. "I've got to take this."

"It's okay," I tell her, meaning it. "Go back to work—I'll meet you and Maks at Dublin's at five." She gives my shoulder a squeeze before walking out.

I wait until I hear the front door close before pulling up the FamilyTree.com browser one last time. I type what feels like a Hail Mary to the stranger who has my life, my identity, in her hands.

USER: Me again.

USER: One more question—has there ever been a mistake? I mean, is it ever wrong, the DNA match or percentage? Because my mom's still saying that it's not true.

The dots appear on the screen as Lisa F starts writing back, if it's even her that I'm talking to. Lisa F might not even be a real person—

she might be a chat bot that's just programmed to sound human. But I hope not.

For some reason, I'm desperate to believe there's a real, live person with DNA, with her own mother and father, on the other side of the screen. A person who understands just how important this information is. It's not just science. It's my life.

LISA F: We have not come across any situations where such a close match was incorrect.

I shiver. *Such a close match.*

I'm not sure what to do next, but I know I have to stop staring at the screen with the words that changed everything I thought I knew about myself.

I close the laptop and walk into the bathroom. As I stand in front of the sink, my eyes stay glued to a smudge on the white counter, remnants of my eye shadow. I wipe it away with my thumb, aware I haven't been this afraid to look in the mirror since the mall makeover incident when I was in seventh grade.

Slowly, I lift my head until the eyes in the mirror are lined up with my own. I study my reflection. The anomaly of my blue eyes and red hair, unlike anyone else's in my family tree.

When I was in fifth grade, we did a project about our ancestors for history class. I remember looking through old family albums, turning the thick yellow pages and searching the photographs behind a layer of clear acetate, desperate to find signs of myself in the people who came before me. Even back then, I knew I didn't belong.

Dad found me sitting at the kitchen table, crying. He pulled me onto his lap even though I was at least two years too old for that. He told me everything was going to be okay, and part of me believed him, even though he didn't know what I was upset about.

Eventually, he got it out of me that I thought I had been adopted or switched at birth like that movie with Bette Midler and Lily Tomlin. "Sweet girl," he said. "The only person you need to look like is yourself. That's what makes you beautiful."

For some reason, his words made me cry even harder.

"Come with me," he said, standing up. I followed him into the living room to the shelf where the pink album that held my baby photos sat next to the three volumes that held photos from the twins' first year. "Did you know I was the first one to see you? Even before Mom."

I shook my head and sat next to him on the couch, leaning my head on his shoulder as he turned the pages. I listened as he told me the story behind all the photos, starting with the first one of him holding me, my face as red as my tuft of hair. He kissed the top of my head before he went on and whispered, "See? You've always been mine."

Even though I know it'll make me feel worse, I reach for my iPhone and pull up the last voicemail he left me. There was a time I listened to it constantly, wearing it out the way my teenage-self overplayed my favorite Debbie Gibson cassette.

There it is: Dad, cell, 07/21/16, 00:07.

I hit play and close my eyes. I slow my breathing and focus on his voice.

"Paigey," he says, and I mouth the words I know by heart. "Just thinking about my favorite girl. Call your old man when you get a chance. I love-love you."

Eight hours after that call, I got another one from Aunt Sissy. I was at the office on a deadline and I didn't answer. She didn't leave a voicemail, but when she called back a few seconds later, I picked up. That was the moment I learned pain can knock the breath out of you.

It's not that different from the way I feel now. How I imagine he would feel, if he knew. I hope he never found out I wasn't his, or that my mother, the supposed love of his life, cheated on him.

Chapter Seven

Then

"SHABBAT SHALOM," SISSY SANG OUT AS THEY WALKED INTO THE multipurpose room at the Hillel on campus.

Betsy elbowed her best friend as several people turned and gave them strange looks. Sissy always took this stuff too far. They were Jews every day of their lives, they didn't need to act differently just because they were at a Jewish event.

The whole point of asking Sissy to go along was so Betsy wouldn't have to walk into the party alone—but that might have been better than making a spectacle. Not that she should've expected anything less from her boisterous best friend. Betsy sighed, aware the whole conundrum could have been avoided if her boyfriend had picked her up instead of volunteering to be there early to set up.

Across the room, Mark caught Betsy's eye and winked. She smiled but wondered if her best friend would add winking to the list of Mark's attributes that weren't "cool."

Sissy wasn't wrong—Mark Meyer was a bit nerdy. But he was also handsome with his warm brown eyes and dark brown hair. She had even gotten used to his beard. The first time they kissed, almost a year ago, she had laughed, tickled by the rough hair. She'd worried it would scratch her face, that everyone would be able to tell what they'd been doing just by looking at her. But now, Betsy could hardly remember what it was like to kiss someone without a beard.

Not that she'd kissed a lot of boys before Mark, which had been Sissy's point. She thought Betsy was too young to settle for someone so boring—Sissy's words, not hers.

Betsy, on the other hand, thought it would be good for her best friend to settle on one guy, although she knew better than to hold her breath. She glanced back at Sissy, who was not-so-subtly scanning the room for a boy to flirt with. Betsy knew it wouldn't be hard for Sissy to find one.

There was a fire inside her best friend that instantly attracted members of the opposite sex. They loved her passion for life, and Sissy loved the attention, until she got bored and cut the poor boys loose.

Fire made Betsy nervous. She preferred someone like Mark, with a good head on his shoulders, smart and sweet, more of a man than a boy. He didn't just have a five-year plan; he had a plan for the rest of his life: graduate college and then law school, get married and start a family, spend as little as possible and invest as much as possible, so he could retire early to Israel or Arizona, depending on the political climate.

It was true he wasn't the most romantic—on their first date he'd gotten her a house plant instead of flowers because it would last longer. Betsy didn't mind, though. She knew from watching her mom chase one man after the next that relationships based on romance never lasted. Some ended in a whisper, others in thrown dishes and harsh words, but they always ended.

Betsy hoped that Sissy wouldn't suffer the same fate—never satisfied, always chasing the next thrill, until she woke up one day to find herself bitter and alone. Betsy wasn't going to let that happen to herself. Not in a million years.

"He's here," Sissy whispered as she adjusted her shirt to reveal even more cleavage.

Betsy followed her best friend's stare to see which "he" she was talking about. Confused, Betsy looked back at Sissy. She'd been staring right at Mark.

"Who?"

"The only attractive man in this room." Sissy licked her lips before applying another layer of her cranberry-red lip gloss.

Betsy followed her gaze again, and again, it landed right where Mark was standing.

"Don't tell me you only have eyes for your dork." Sissy brought a manicured finger to Betsy's chin, pushing her face a scooch to the left.

"Is that . . . ?"

"Andy Abrams," Sissy said. "The myth himself."

Of course Betsy had seen Andy Abrams around; she'd even admired him from a safe distance. He was easily one of the best-looking guys on campus. With his broad shoulders, thick chestnut-brown hair, and ice-blue eyes, he single-handedly took the hot factor of the AEPi fraternity up at least ten degrees. His role as the kicker on the KU football team had become a source of pride for all the Jews on campus—it wasn't often that one of their own climbed the collegiate athletic ranks.

"Let's go talk to him," Sissy said. "It's perfect—he's talking to Mark."

"So you *do* know my boyfriend's name," Betsy said, only half-teasing. If Sissy knew how much it bothered her, she wouldn't make fun of Mark—or at least, not as often.

"Don't be silly," she said, grabbing Betsy by the hands. She turned and walked backward, dragging Betsy across the room to where Andy stood with Mark. When they were just a few steps away, Sissy threw her head back in an exaggerated fit of laughter, as if Betsy had just said something hilarious, and bumped right into her target.

"I am so sorry," Sissy said, turning around with a flourish. "I didn't see you there." She rested her hand apologetically on Andy's arm.

Andy's muscular arm, Betsy noticed.

"This is Betsy," Mark said, momentarily breaking the spell. "My girlfriend."

Betsy nodded hello, surprised to find herself at a loss for words. There was something enchanting about Andy Abrams. He smiled, one side of his mouth tilting a little higher than the other, and Betsy wondered how someone's imperfections could seem so perfect.

Mark gently nudged her shoulder, and Betsy realized that Andy had extended his hand. She blushed and took his hand in hers, wishing his grip wasn't so firm. For one brief, beautiful moment, she imagined how it would feel to have those arms wrapped around her, his strong hands on her bare skin. Betsy shivered, embarrassed by just how much she enjoyed the thought of it.

"Nice to meet you," she said. "And this is Sissy." Betsy turned toward her friend, hoping Andy would shift his attention to someone else so she could stop focusing on him.

"Sissy," Andy repeated, a questioning lilt to his voice. "What's that short for?"

"That's a story that needs to be told over a drink," Sissy said, her

LITTLE PIECES OF ME

voice oozing sexuality. "Something other than kosher wine—no offense, Mark."

Betsy looked from Sissy to Andy, accidentally locking eyes with him. A charge pulsed through her, a glimmer of the sensation she was still waiting to feel with Mark. He did all the right things in all the right places, but there was never that electricity Sissy described when she told Betsy about the things she did in the top or bottom bunks of the AEPi and ZBT houses.

"None taken," Mark said. He draped his arm around Betsy's shoulder, and she flinched at the unexpected touch. His arm felt insignificant after imagining Andy's. She recovered quickly and leaned into his side, willing the inappropriate thoughts of Andy Abrams out of her mind.

"So, what do you say?" Sissy asked Andy.

"Why not?" he agreed, then glanced over to Betsy and Mark. "You guys coming, too?"

Betsy bit her bottom lip to stop herself from saying yes, even though every fiber of her being wanted to.

"We've got to stick around here," Mark said, and Betsy felt herself stiffen. Mark was the one on the board of Hillel, not Betsy. *She* didn't have to stay until the end. But of course she would.

Betsy let out a quiet sigh and slipped her arm around Mark's waist, accepting her role as the supportive girlfriend. She thought she saw a flash of disappointment cross Andy's face, but she dismissed it as her active imagination.

"Don't wait up for me," Sissy said, kissing Betsy's cheek on the way out.

Betsy smiled and said a little prayer that tomorrow morning, she wouldn't be hearing about what an amazing kisser Andy Abrams was. With those full lips, he had to be.

Not that she had anything to complain about—Mark wasn't a bad kisser. To prove it to herself, she turned and hooked her free hand around Mark's neck. She locked her lips on his, right there in the middle of the room, in front of everyone like she was as carefree and confident as Sissy.

Forgetting himself for a moment, Mark kissed her back before pulling away. "Let's save that for later," he said. "It's time to light the candles."

And just like that, he was off to help Deborah find the matches. Deborah always seemed to need Mark's help, whether it was something with the candles and wine or how to pronounce a Hebrew word.

Betsy wished she could look at Mark the same way Deborah did. Although she wondered if Deborah would still be that starry-eyed after spending a night in Betsy's shoes. Because Betsy knew that tonight would be like all the other nights at Mark's apartment.

If his roommates weren't home yet, they would kiss for a while on the couch before moving to the bedroom. There, Mark would take off his clothes and climb into bed, his back respectfully turned toward Betsy as she did the same. Once they were both under the covers, they would kiss some more, until Mark would reach for a condom from the box in his nightstand drawer before he rolled on top of her.

And just like every other night, Betsy would lie there, looking up at him with his eyes closed tight, grunting and biting his lip as if this act that was supposed to be the most natural thing in the world needed all his concentration.

Once, he made a face so funny that Betsy had to laugh. Mark's eyes flew open, and he looked so worried that Betsy tried to cover the laugh with a moan. It was believable enough, Betsy supposed, because Mark leaned down to kiss her before closing his eyes again and continuing to hump her with a renewed enthusiasm that Betsy quite appreciated.

It wasn't that she didn't enjoy herself. She did, sometimes more than others. But she didn't have any other experience to compare it to, which would have been fine if she didn't have a feeling there was something more out there.

ANDY ABRAMS HADN'T had high hopes for the evening when he let his fraternity brothers talk him into attending the Shabbat mixer at Hillel. He had planned to stay long enough to be seen but ended up having a fascinating conversation with Mark Meyer about the conflict of being a patriot while avoiding the draft. It was the closest Andy had come to expressing his own internal struggle since first admitting it to himself.

But then Sissy Goldberg bumped into him; on purpose, he suspected. He only agreed to go for a drink with her because he assumed Mark and his girlfriend would be part of the equation. By the time he realized that wasn't the case, it was too late to back out.

Cursed with a gentleman's conscience, Andy stayed with Sissy all evening, walking her home to the Sigma Delta Tau house after last call at the Crossing. She'd had one too many drinks for him to be confident she could get back safely on her own.

"Good night, *Melissa*," Andy said as they walked to the front door. It hadn't been easy to get her real name out of her, but Andy liked a challenge.

Sissy leaned back against the door with bedroom eyes that were unfortunately wasted on him. "I told you not to call me that."

Andy laughed. Sissy would be a fun girl to take to the Fall Fling in a few weeks. She was different from the other girls Andy went out with—girls who made it painfully obvious they were only at college for their MRS degree, looking for a guy who was looking for a wife.

Those girls, Andy went on one date with, maybe two. Never three. He always ended it before that, citing one thing or another when his fraternity brothers asked. Julia chewed too loudly, Rachel wouldn't stop talking, Leah wouldn't say anything.

He dated enough that no one questioned him. If anything, it left him with a reputation as a ladies' man, a picky one at that. The girls considered him a challenge to conquer, and his brothers enjoyed living vicariously through him.

Andy had gotten the breakups down to a science. He managed to introduce some of the girls to his single fraternity brothers, and he'd become friends with a few of the others. He hoped Sissy would fall into the latter category—she was crazy but fun.

"I had a good time tonight," he told Sissy, meaning it.

"The night doesn't have to be over," she slurred. Before Andy could stop her, Sissy lunged for him. A petite girl, she propelled herself up on her toes, so she was nearly Andy's height. Her breasts felt firm and full against his chest, her lips were soft, and she tasted like tequila. Kissing her was nothing like kissing William.

William.

Andy pulled away, but Sissy wasn't having it.

"Not on the first date," Andy said, awkwardly laughing as he turned his face away from her hungry lips. "I'm a gentleman."

"Lucky for you, I'm not much of a lady."

Andy lifted his chin up and away from Sissy, which she took as an invitation to start kissing his neck.

"Oh, Sissy," he sighed.

Again, she misread his intentions and carried on, slipping her hands underneath his shirt.

Andy took a step back, but Sissy followed as if she were initiating a dance. Her hands felt cool against his skin as they traveled up to his shoulders and back down, flirting with the waistline of his jeans.

Not even the sound of an approaching car dissuaded Sissy, but Andy stepped back just as two headlights illuminated them. Sissy laughed and fell forward into Andy, clutching his shirt for support.

The car pulled up to the front door, and the driver rolled down his window. "Don't let us interrupt."

It was Mark Meyer from Hillel.

"No problem," Andy said, trying not to sound as grateful as he felt. "I was just about to leave. Good night, Sissy."

Mark got out of the car and walked around the front of his powder-blue Pinto to open the door for his pretty girlfriend with the sad eyes. They kissed quickly before she rushed to the front door, where Sissy was slumped against the wall.

Andy watched as Mark's girlfriend helped her friend inside. As fun as Sissy had been at the bar with her wild stories and antics, Andy knew he couldn't risk a second date with her.

"Want a ride, man?" Mark asked as he started his car.

"I'm good walking," he said. "But thanks."

Mark waved before driving off, leaving Andy alone on the dead-end street. There was a bite in the September air as he started to walk. When he reached Jayhawk Boulevard, he turned left instead of right, away from his fraternity house.

There was a calm to the campus at night, as if the streets themselves were taking a collective breath, enjoying peace and quiet without the bustle of students. The way Andy felt in the art studio.

Around school and at the fraternity house, he was Andy the athlete, the student, and the brother. But once he crossed the threshold where the air was filled with the sweet smells of paint and chalk and clay, he became Andy the artist, the painter, and the lover. He became himself.

It wasn't just the effect of being around William, although that certainly helped. Andy had always felt like there was art living inside of him. From the moment Mrs. Clifton put the finger paints in his kindergartner hands, Andy had been hooked.

Soon he was stealing his older sister's crayons, wearing them down to colorful nubs. He loved drawing his interpretation of places he'd been and people he'd seen. Even without training, Andy had an ability to capture something not just by the way it looked but by the way it made him feel.

His mom understood. She wasn't artistic, but she had an appreciation for self-expression. Andy's dad pretended not to mind as long as the "artsy-fartsy stuff" didn't get in the way of the things that mattered, like sports and school. In that order.

Andy enjoyed the regimen and discipline that went along with team training, but his interest in athletics stopped there. He didn't have the competitive drive that motivated the rest of his teammates. What kept Andy going was the way his body felt after a long run, sweat coming out of every pore, his muscles aching as evidence of the hard work. Mostly, he did it for the connection with his dad. And, of course, the scholarship.

As Andy approached the art and design building, he slowed his brisk pace. He glanced to the left, then quickly to the right, to make sure no one was watching before he jogged along the side of the building.

His heart swelled in anticipation as he knocked three times on the first-floor window toward the back. The glass was frosted so he couldn't see inside, but the warm glow of yellow light let him know someone was still there. And that someone, Andy hoped, was William Palmer.

SECOND SEMESTER OF his freshman year, Andy's life had changed when he saw a flyer for open hours at the art studio, inviting any student to come and explore their artistic talents.

Until that fated moment, Andy hadn't really considered whether his art was any good. It was something he created for himself, not for others to see. But when a certain teacher's assistant started circling around him, Andy realized he might actually be good. He couldn't have known, not then, that the TA had an interest in more than just his brushstrokes.

Before long, Andy was spending every spare minute at the art studio. When he wasn't on the football field, in class, or fulfilling a fraternity obligation, Andy was in front of an easel, a paintbrush in his hand.

William, he later found out, was a terrible student but an inspiring teacher and a brilliant artist. The things he could do with a blank canvas left Andy in awe. He was eager to learn everything he could from William—how color is relative, defined not by what it is but what it's next to; how a simple shift of perspective could change everything; and how a flick of the wrist and a little pressure could take a brushstroke from a whisper to a scream.

The art studio officially closed at ten on weeknights, but one of the perks of being friendly with the TA was that William had a key, and the two would spend hours together, working side by side on their separate canvases.

Andy was amazed how differently they both saw the exact same object. When Andy painted an apple, it looked real and delicious. When William painted the identical piece of fruit, it looked luscious and tempting. Like the one Eve gave to Adam.

As they painted, they talked about things that mattered, like war and politics and music. They talked about Stonewall, and William told Andy about his life after coming out. His parents had kicked him out of the house, and he'd had to learn how to live on his own, traveling from city to city and lover to lover until life brought him to Lawrence, Kansas.

Mostly, Andy listened. But one night he'd had enough wine and had enough courage to share something, too. He told William that he wasn't attracted to women, either. It was the closest he had ever come to saying the words out loud.

Andy thought the confession would change their relationship. And it did, but not in the way Andy had hoped. William seemed to withdraw into his own private world, leaving Andy alone and more confused than ever.

Until one night weeks later. Andy had been there for hours, trying to get a crosshatch technique right with little success. His movements were too cautious and controlled.

He stiffened when William came up behind him, reaching for his hand that held the paintbrush. William guided Andy's hand, showing him how to get the angle just right.

When William's lips finally grazed his neck, Andy inhaled a deep breath and let the paintbrush fall to the ground. Andy turned to face him, studying the mix of passion and danger that flared in William's eyes. He felt understood, maybe for the first time in his life.

Once the line had been crossed, it was like William had unlocked an insatiable hunger in Andy. One that he didn't allow himself to satisfy outside the studio or the tiny apartment where William lived off-campus.

The sound of the lock sliding into the open position brought Andy back to the moment. William was already halfway across the room by the time Andy opened the door and let himself in.

"Sorry I'm so late," Andy said, closing the door behind him.

"Late is ten or fifteen minutes. You said you'd be here three hours ago." William's voice was cold and distant, but Andy wasn't too concerned. He was used to the dark space William sometimes immersed himself in to get to the real, raw emotion in his art.

"I know," Andy said, even though he hadn't promised he'd be there by eight. He'd just said that he thought he'd be able to get out of the Hillel event by then. But he hadn't expected Sissy to happen.

"There's wine on the counter," William said, the gruff gone from his voice.

Andy relaxed and walked to the corner of the room where they kept the record player. He flipped through the stack of records until he found *A Night at the Opera*, the new Queen album William loved.

He set down the needle on the B side a few centimeters from the edge so William's favorite song, "Love of My Life," would play. As the first melodic notes floated from the speaker, Andy saw William's shoulders relax as he moved the brush against the canvas like a seductive dance.

"I really am sorry," Andy said, sliding up behind William. He rested his chin on William's shoulder, studying the image of a cabin in a forest clearing that had been slowly coming to life over the last few weeks.

As Freddie Mercury sang, begging his love not to leave, Andy thought about how empty his life would be without William, who was as lanky as he was tall, all knees and elbows. His golden hair hung past his shoulders, the tips often colored by whatever paints he'd been using that day.

Tonight, Andy wanted to lose himself in William and erase any trace of Sissy from his lips. He wrapped his arms around William's torso and nuzzled his neck.

"What was her name?" William said, stiffening beneath Andy's touch. "I can smell her fucking perfume on you."

Andy took a step back, caught off guard by the hurt and anger in William's voice.

"What. Was. Her. Name?" William repeated, each word its own sentence.

"Sissy." Andy said her name like an apology.

William turned and stared at Andy for a torturous moment before taking wide, purposeful steps toward the bottle of wine on the counter. Andy watched as William filled an empty glass to the brim and took a long, angry swallow.

"Sissy." William spat her name.

"It didn't mean—"

The sound of glass shattering on the concrete floor made Andy's next words freeze in his throat.

"Don't you even think about telling me it didn't mean anything."

"But it didn't," Andy protested. This wasn't the first time they'd had this argument. As traumatic as William's own coming-out experience had been, Andy thought William, of all people, should have some patience with him. "Nothing happened. I don't know what else I can say to make you understand."

"You're the one who doesn't understand!" William yelled, his pale face flushing red. "You're a fucking coward. And you won't get it until you stop living this pathetic charade."

Andy stared at his feet, afraid to face William and the truth. "This isn't easy for me, either," he finally said.

William laughed, a sharp, biting sound. Andy looked up at him, afraid of what he might see. "You have no idea what it's like to know you're out there with someone else," William said. "While I'm here, alone, waiting for you to come back smelling like one of your cheap whores."

"If I didn't have to, I wouldn't," Andy said. "If they find out, they'll kick me out of the fraternity. I'll lose my house, I'll lose my scholarship, my father—I'll lose everything."

"Better off just to lose me, then," William said. "Get out of here—I don't want to look at your fucking face."

"Please," Andy begged, but William was already across the room. He turned the record player as loud as it would go, nodding his head in perfect time to "Bohemian Rhapsody." His long dirty-blond hair flew wild, covering the wounded look on his face.

"I'm sorry," Andy said once more, before letting himself out the back door and retracing his steps through campus. The quiet that had just minutes before felt calming now felt ominous as Andy made his way back to his house of lies.

Chapter Eight

Now

I'M CURLED UP ON THE COUCH WITH A PINT OF BEN & JERRY'S AND my laptop is balanced on my knees as Maury Povich reruns play on the television. "Who are you, Andrew Abrams?" I ask out loud as I type his name into the Facebook search bar.

A list of more than one hundred Andrew Abramses populate the screen. Some are "Drew," others are "Andy"; there's even one "Andrea." At least I can count her out.

I open a new window to search Google but realize I don't know anything other than his relatively common name. I go back to the email that started this whole mess, hoping to find something that makes him a little more cyber-stalkable.

Andrew Abrams hasn't uploaded a picture or answered any of the other optional profile questions on the FamilyTree website that might help identify him. The only information listed is his name and his date of birth: January 5, 1955. The same year as my mom. I shiver, knowing it probably isn't a coincidence.

Back to Google, I type in his name and date of birth. The first two results are links to LinkedIn profiles for an Andrew Abrams and an

Andrew J. Abrams, but I assume I'll have the same luck there as I did on Facebook. The third result is an obituary.

I close the browser without clicking to find out if it's him. It couldn't be—he had to be alive recently enough to spit in a test tube and send it in to FamilyTree. And if he's gone, then the answers to who I am and where I came from might be buried along with him.

I'm filled with a sudden urge to find him, to see if there's a connection between us. I hover the cursor over the "Send a Message" hyperlink beneath his avatar on the FamilyTree website. If I don't reach out, that's all he'll ever be: a generic dark blue outline of a man. And I'll never know if there was a family somewhere where I would have belonged.

I take a deep breath and click on the mail icon to send Andrew Abrams a message.

Instead of an empty message screen, a pop-up invites me to register for a free thirty-day trial. I scoff at the word "free"—it already cost me part of my identity.

Before I lose my nerve, I reach for my purse and take out my credit card to enter the information so they can charge me $12.99 next month when I no doubt forget to cancel the free trial. Once the transaction has been approved, the message screen appears.

I crack my knuckles and start to type. I'm surprised how much easier it is to find the words to write this stranger than it was to write my own mother.

Hi, Andrew.

According to FamilyTree.com, we're related. Seems unlikely on my end, but I thought I would reach out to say hello just in case. So, hello.

I consider adding a smiley face, but I'm not sure I want to be that friendly. All I really want is for him to write back and give me a reason he couldn't possibly be my biological father—that he's sterile, or gay, or that he's never even been to Kansas or St. Louis or any other place where he could have come in contact with my mother.

I hit send before I can overthink the message any more.

The instant I do, my email dings with an alert. My heart leaps, and I clutch my chest. Afraid, even though it couldn't possibly be him. He'd barely have had time to read the message, much less reply. But it could be from Mom—maybe she's changed her tune now that she's had some time to think it over.

I exhale a sigh of relief when I see the message is from Maks.

TO: Paige Meyer
FROM: Maksim Boyko
SUBJECT: Your predicament

P—

I did a little research.

Seems like this has happened before.

Other people with DNA matches that don't compute.

There's a whole support group full of people in the same ship.

Read this <u>article</u>.

See you at the bar.

M

I click on the link and quickly scan the *Atlantic* article about a woman who found out through a DNA test that her brother was only her half brother. My skin erupts in goose bumps as I read about the familiar way this woman looked in the mirror and didn't know who she was.

The story goes on to explain how the woman had posted about her situation on Facebook, and someone else commented that she'd had a similar experience. The two exchanged messages, which led to her eventually starting a Facebook group, DNA NPE Friends—NPE standing for "Not Parent Expected." According to the article, the group now has more than a thousand members.

I click the link to join, not sure whether I feel better knowing I'm not alone in this, or worse, knowing this is an actual thing that happens often enough to warrant an entire Facebook group.

Before they'll grant my access to the group, I have to answer a few questions. It feels weird, typing out my story in black and white for strangers to read before I've even had a chance to tell Jeff.

Luckily, I don't have to wait long for approval to join the group. Once I'm in, I get sucked into the wormhole, reading posts of people with stories not that different from mine.

The first post I read is from a woman who says she felt like her entire family died on the very same day. I haven't even thought about my dad's extended family—aunts and uncles and grandparents I may no longer have any claim to. The next post is a picture of a woman and her biological father—her DNA Dad, as she calls him—along with a brand-new extended family.

After a few minutes of scrolling, I realize there is no "normal" scenario. There are plenty of happy endings, but I find myself looking for the less-than-happy ones. Either I'm a masochist, or I'm trying to prepare myself for the worst-case scenario.

Morgan from Wisconsin told the story of her family disowning her after the truth came to light. Caroline from Seattle was devastated to learn about her biological father six months after he passed away. Larry from Omaha's parents got divorced after thirty years of marriage when the news came out.

My phone buzzes with a text from Maks in the group chain—letting Margaux and me know he's leaving the office and we better be at the bar or on our way. I glance at the time, shocked that almost two hours have passed.

Since I can't very well go to Dublin's looking like this, I close my laptop and walk back into the closet, where I expect the floor to be covered with the mess of my forgotten family photos. I smile and make a mental note of yet another thing to thank Margaux for.

If only she were still here to help me figure out the mess that is my wardrobe. I survey the half of the closet where my clothes hang, mostly black, white, and denim. I wonder what kind of clothes Paige Abrams would have in her closet if she'd been me, if I'd been her. It strikes me that she's as much of a stranger as I am.

Chapter Nine

Now

WALKING DOWN STATE STREET, I SEARCH FOR MYSELF IN THE face of every sixtysomething-year-old man I see. I feel pathetic, like that little bird in the children's book *Are You My Mother?*

Of course, statistically speaking, I know enough to know that this man, my "father," wouldn't randomly be walking down the same Chicago street at the exact same time I am. Although, before this morning, I wouldn't have imagined there was a chance in all the statistics in the world that I would get an email from FamilyTree.com, telling me my father isn't who I thought he was. That I'm not who I thought I was.

The windows at Dublin's are open, and sounds of cheer spill out onto the sidewalk. If I didn't know any better, I'd think it was a Saturday, not a Monday.

Scarlett waves from behind the bar and nods toward the booth where Maks and Margaux are waiting—a tall Tito's and soda with just a splash of cranberry ready for me. Maks frowns when he sees me, but I don't take it personally. I know I've looked better.

I slide into the booth next to Margaux and grab the tall glass, draining almost half of it in one big gulp.

"Easy," Margaux says at the same time Maks says, "You go, girl. Drink to forget."

"That's the last thing she needs," Margaux tells Maks. "Alcohol is a depressant."

"And a lubricant," Maks says, lifting his glass toward mine. I clink mine against his before taking another sip.

"Thank you both for being yourselves," I tell my two best friends. "I may not know who I am, but I know who you are."

I lift my glass to take another sip and catch them trading glances.

"I'm fine," I tell them, but they don't believe me any more than I do.

"So, what did Jeff say when you told him?" Margaux asks.

"I haven't," I admit. "He called, but he was so excited and nervous about his presentation tomorrow. I can't be the reason he's off his A game—and it's not like there's anything he can do from California."

"Provide moral support?" Margaux suggests.

"I've got you guys for that."

We clink glasses in a sad little cheer, then Maks asks, "Have you heard anything else from Elizabeth?"

I shake my head before sucking down more of my drink. "Nothing else for her to say, she's denying it."

"What do you think?" Margaux asks, tracing a finger down her wineglass.

"Honestly"—I pause—"I don't know what to think. On the one hand, my dad is my dad."

"Of course he is," Maks says in an attempt to placate me. He reaches for my hand, but I pull it away. I don't want anyone's sympathy right now. Not until I know for sure. Maybe not even then.

"But on the other hand," I tell them, "it's DNA. Science can't lie, but my mom could have."

"What I don't understand is why she would now," Margaux says. I can see her mind working, like she's trying to solve a case. "Your dad is gone. What's the worst that can happen if the truth comes out?"

I laugh dismissively. "You know how my mom is—Elizabeth Meyer cares more about how things make her look than how they actually are. We're talking about a woman who had her makeup professionally done *in the hospital* after she delivered the twins."

"Speaking of the Whoopsie Twins," Maks says, using his nickname for my sisters, "are you going to tell them?"

"I think this situation proves that I was the whoops—not them." I finish what's left in my glass. "And it's not like there's anything to tell. At least not until I hear back from him."

"*Him*-him?" Margaux asks.

I nod and signal our waitress for another drink.

"I'll have another, also," Maks says as she walks up, even though his glass is still half-full. "Cheap whiskey with your most expensive ginger ale."

The waitress laughs even though she hears the same joke every time Maks orders.

"How'd you find him?" Margaux asks.

"I didn't exactly find him. I looked on Facebook, but his name is too generic."

"Did you look to see if there was an Andrew Abrams on your mom's friend list?" Margaux asks.

I give her a dirty look for failing to give me that advice earlier when it would have been helpful. "I didn't think of that," I admit. "I ended up just emailing him through the FamilyTree site—will one of you remind me to cancel my membership before the free trial runs out in thirty days?"

"Girl, don't get me started on how many charges like that I've had to fight." Margaux looks annoyed, but we all know there's nothing she loves more than a good argument.

The waitress returns with our drinks and a round of Fireball shots from Scarlett, who's probably wondering why we're sitting at a table instead of up at the bar.

I lift the shot glass to my lips, but Maks stops me. "Wait, a toast."

I lower the glass, waiting for Maks to scroll through his mental Rolodex of quotes. The amount of information he keeps in his brain never ceases to amaze me.

"Pain makes you stronger," he says. "Tears make you braver. Heartbreak makes you wiser—and whiskey makes you not remember any of that crap. *Bud'mo!*"

"*Bud'mo*," Margaux and I repeat after him. It was the first Ukrainian word either of us learned after our first night out with Maks more than a decade ago.

I'd been sneaking out of the office where we both worked at seven o'clock, even though I was supposed to be working late on a pitch. Maks spotted me leaving and I thought he was going to bust me, but instead, he asked if he could come along. I'd been going to meet Margaux, who I'd recently become friends with because the guys we were dating happened to be roommates. We dumped the guys but kept each other—and Maks perfectly rounded out our little trio.

"So what did you find out about him?" Margaux asks after we've all downed the shots.

"Nothing. I tried Googling him after the Facebook fail, but I just got overwhelmed."

"You probably didn't do it right," Maks says. "No offense."

I have to laugh—everything Maks says should come with an implied "No offense." We wouldn't be friends if I were easily offended. "Is there a wrong way to Google someone?"

"You're so pretty," he says, petting the side of my face. "Did you just use his name?"

"I put quotation marks around it," I say, trying to defend myself. "And I added his date of birth. What else should I have done?"

"You've got to get creative," he says. "It's like the keywords on a stock photo search. You can't just type in exactly what you're looking for."

I nod—he's got a good point.

"Think about it," he says, leaning in. "Where was Mommy Dearest forty-three years ago?"

"She was in college," I answer, then gasp. "A sophomore at the University of Kansas."

Maks smiles, proud of himself. "It's a good place to start."

I open the Internet browser on my phone and search for "Andrew Abrams" and "Lawrence, Kansas." I quickly scan the results. None of them make sense.

"Nothing," I say, trying not to sound defeated. "There are no Andrew Abrams in Lawrence, Kansas."

"Babe," Maks says.

"What?" I ask. "And don't tell me I'm pretty again."

"But you *are* pretty," he says, trying to get back on my good side. "And you're also not thinking clearly. I'd bet at least eighty-seven percent of students who went to UK move to a different city or state after they graduated."

"It's KU," I correct him. "And you've got a point."

Maks smiles. He loves being right almost as much as he loves other people being wrong.

I type "Andrew Abrams," "Alumni," and "University of Kansas" into the browser and hit search.

My stomach feels queasy, the way it did when I got called back to the doctor's office for a second mammogram last fall. Everything turned out okay back then, I remind myself, so who's to say it won't now? I close my eyes and prepare myself for the worst, even though the worst already happened the day Dad died.

When I open my eyes, I see a list of articles that might be about him. The man who quite possibly gave me half of my DNA.

Impatient as ever, Maks takes the phone from my hand, clicks on an article, and starts to read.

"'Distinguished alumni Andrew Abrams returns to the University of Kansas for a one-night-only lecture,'" he reads. "He's distinguished."

"What does that mean?" I ask, leaning forward enough to make our table shift.

"Patience, grasshopper," Maks says.

Margaux laughs and I frown, not sure what part of that exchange could have been funny. I quickly realize she's making eyes with a cute guy at the bar, not paying attention to us.

Maks rolls his eyes toward me, then goes back to reading silently. He raises an eyebrow in that know-it-all way I know all too well.

"He's an artist," Maks finally says, looking up with a knowing smile.

"That doesn't mean anything," I insist, even though the goose bumps on my arms tell me otherwise. I've always been the only artist in my family. Dad was a financial planner, and Mom worked at a bank—even the twins had been business majors.

The signs were everywhere. It shouldn't have taken me forty-three years to figure out there was a reason I was the one thing not like the others.

"What kind of artist?" Margaux asks, focusing on our conversation again.

I glance behind me, and, sure enough, the cute guy from the bar is gone.

"A painter," Maks says. "Realism."

I nod, grateful it isn't abstract. That's one flavor of art I just don't get.

"'Abrams visited the campus from Naples, Florida,'" Maks reads out loud, "'where he lives and owns an art gallery that features his work, as well as pieces from marginalized artists.'"

"How altruistic," Margaux says. "At least you know he's a good person."

I shrug. Good, maybe. But my dad was a *great* person. One of the best.

"Looks like he graduated from UK—from KU," Maks says, correcting himself, "in 1977."

The same year as my dad.

"He was a member of AEPi," Maks says.

My dad wasn't a member of the Jewish fraternity, but my mom was in Sigma Delta Tau, the Jewish sorority on campus. The queasy feeling is back in my stomach. He had to have known my mom. And my dad. They all had to have known each other.

Maks gasps, and we both turn to look at him.

"What?" he asks, downplaying his reaction with faux innocence.

"Let me see." Margaux reaches for my phone. I watch her eyes widen as she looks back and forth from me to the screen. "Whoa."

I want to take my phone back, but I'm scared, so I reach for my glass instead. I lift it to my lips, but my hands are shaking so badly I have to put it back down. I slide the glass toward the edge of the table and lean forward to take a long, slow sip through the straw.

"Paige," Margaux says. Her voice is so soft, I can barely hear it over the pounding of my heart in my ears. "Look."

She sets down the phone, faceup in front of me. I keep my head held high and lower my eyes toward the phone, just for a second, then back up to her. Margaux's smiling, and I try to smile back, but my lower lip is quivering. I don't want to cry, not here, not now.

Maks puts his hand on my knee under the table, and as much as I hate being coddled, it calms me. I slow my breathing and look again. *It's just a photo.*

My eyes focus on the face smiling back up at me. He doesn't look the way I expected him to. His hair is brown, not red like mine, and he doesn't have a beard like my dad. He's a stranger. A stranger with a familiar crooked smile, a chin that's dimple-free, and eyes that are the same shade of blue as mine.

"You've got his eyes," Margaux says.

"Maybe not." I flip over the phone so the familiar eyes are no longer staring at me. "We still don't know if it's true."

I don't have to see Maks or Margaux to know they're looking at each other, exchanging worried glances. I know what they're thinking. I saw what they saw. I just can't.

"I have to go to the bathroom," I say, slipping out of the booth and making a beeline for the ladies' room. I just need a minute. I'll be fine in a minute.

For once, there isn't a line. I throw open the door and lock it behind me, sitting down on the toilet seat. I prop my elbows on my knees and lean my head against my hands. My heart is racing, and my chest is heaving with breaths that are coming even faster than they did after that stupid 5K I ran with Margaux. "I'm okay," I whisper to myself. "I'm okay."

Except I'm not okay. I'm having a panic attack in a bathroom. In a bathroom at a bar. At a bar where I know people. This isn't helping. *Breathe! Just breathe.* I inhale slowly and exhale even slower, but my pulse is still racing.

There's a knock on the door.

"Just a minute!" I yell.

"Paige." It's Margaux. The concern in her voice is familiar; it sounds the way it did after my dad died. *My dad.* Mark Meyer. He's my dad. Not this stranger with my eyes and my smile. "Paige." Margaux knocks again.

"I'm fine," I tell her, raising my voice so she can hear me through the door. "I'll be fine. I just need a minute."

The knocking stops, and I know she listened to me. It's one of her better qualities. Maks, on the other hand, would have forced the door open, even though this is the women's bathroom.

Outside, someone tries to open the door. I hear a girl laughing and talking with her friend. I don't want to hog the only ladies' room all night, so I stand and try to pull myself back together. As I wash my hands, I stare at the woman in the mirror. She looks different with her traitorous eyes. She's not me, not anymore.

Chapter Ten

Now

Back at the table, Maks and Margaux are huddled around my phone. They look at each other, then back at me. A round of fresh drinks are on the table in front of them.

"What now?" I ask, even though I'm not sure I want to know.

"I did a little more Googling," Maks admits.

"And?" I ask impatiently, sliding back into the booth.

"You, my dear, might have hit the daddy jackpot," he says.

I raise an eyebrow, giving him a doubtful look. No one wins the lottery twice.

"I found your dad's address and Google Earthed his house, and it's huge. Like, *Hi, I have a billion dollars and live in a ginormous mansion* huge."

"He's not my dad." My voice sounds flat and void of emotion, and I wonder if I have any feelings left.

"You might change your song when you see it," Maks says, sliding the phone over to my side of the booth.

"Aren't artists usually starving?" Margaux asks.

"They're supposed to be," I say with a shrug. I don't believe anything I thought I knew anymore.

"Maybe the whole artist thing is a cover, and he's really in the Mafia or something," Margaux teases.

Maks's eyes light up. "You kid," he tells Margaux, "but did you know there were actually a lot of Jews in organized crime? They called it the Kosher Mafia. And come to think of it—" He grabs my phone before I can get a closer look at the house, which I'm not sure I want to see anyway. I watch as he types something into my phone, his brow furrowed in concentration.

"I was right," he says, smiling proudly. "There was an Abrams. Hyman Abrams was a mobster during prohibition and was involved with some casinos in the nineteen fifties."

"Who knew you were such a badass," Margaux says with a wink. "A real-life descendant of the Jewish Mafia."

"I don't know what I am," I tell them, "but I'm not a badass."

I drop my head into my hands, my mind spinning with all the possibilities that didn't exist yesterday.

Margaux moves to wrap her arm around my shoulder, but I sit back up and lean away. "I'm okay."

"Are you, though?" Margaux asks. "I mean, it's completely okay not to be."

I sigh and take another sip of my drink. "I'm not not-okay," I tell her. "It's just, I don't know. I don't know how I'm supposed to feel. It doesn't make sense, but it also makes total sense. I never felt like I belonged in my family."

"Girl," Margaux says. "You don't have to explain to us how it feels not to belong."

Maks nods in agreement. "You wanna talk about growing up in

the uber-Catholic Ukraine, having a crush on Fred Savage instead of Winnie Cooper?"

"Or being the only black family in a super-rich white neighborhood?" Margaux adds.

"I know having a distant mother doesn't really compare," I tell my best friends. "But it's just—I thought it was my fault that I was different. But now I know it was my mom's fault; she cheated on my dad. It's like my foundation has been rocked."

"You think she cheated?" Margaux asks, back in lawyer mode.

"I could see it," Maks says. "I always had a feeling Elizabeth had a wild streak in her. I bet she was a party animal back in college."

I shake my head. "She wasn't, though. Every story I've ever heard about my mom in college was of her being the good girl who kept my aunt Sissy in line. Sissy was the wild child."

"Maybe Sissy's your real mom?" Maks says, his eyes growing wide with the thought of something even more scandalous.

"No way," I tell him, even though it would be a childhood dream come true.

"You're sure your mom didn't have a wild streak?" Margaux asks. I can tell the wheels of her mind are working.

"Positive. Aunt Sissy has told me a dozen stories of her having to practically drag my mom out to the bars and parties. She and my dad started dating halfway through her freshman year, and they were married by the end of her sophomore year."

Margaux looks nervously at Maks, then back at me.

"What?" I ask. "Don't hold back on my account."

"I just wonder," Margaux says. "Do you think it could have been sexual assault?"

My stomach flips. The thought hadn't even crossed my mind. It's so easy to think of Mom as the bad guy—but what if she was the victim? I take another sip, but the vodka tastes metallic in my mouth.

"Interesting," Maks says, drumming his fingers on his chin.

"Some things would certainly make more sense," Margaux says.

"Like what?" I ask, desperate to find some logic in this mess.

"I mean, you've always said your mom resented you for being born," she says. "You thought it was because you ruined her college years, but what if it was more than that?"

Maks brings a hand to his mouth, then looks at me. "What if every time she looked at you, she saw a reminder of the night she was raped? *Ow!*" Maks glares at Margaux. "Don't kick me for telling the truth."

"You can tell the truth without being an ass," Margaux says.

I feel sick at the thought, along with a surge of sympathy for my mom.

"It would explain why she didn't want to tell you the truth," Margaux says. "She wouldn't want you to know that."

I take another sip of my drink, wishing I could erase the thought from my mind.

"I know you don't care about this guy's money," Margaux says, "but if it was something rapey, you could make him pay. I don't know what the statute of limitations are in Kansas, but you can sue him for back child support. He should pay for what he did to your mom."

"It could have been consensual," Maks says. "Weren't the seventies about free love and drugs?"

Before I can think too much more about it, our waitress is back with another round of shots. This time, I don't wince as the Fireball goes down.

Chapter Eleven

Then

As the sun came up on Saturday morning, Betsy was already awake. Possibly *still* awake. She'd barely slept the night before thanks to the scene that kept playing over and over in her mind. Sissy with her hands and her lips all over Andy Abrams.

On the other side of the room they shared, Sissy let out a solitary snore and shifted under the covers. Betsy held her breath, afraid to make a sound until Sissy started snoring again.

Once she was certain her roommate was sound asleep, Betsy slipped out of bed. She got dressed as quietly as she could to save herself from having to hear a play-by-play of how wonderful Sissy's night had been.

Betsy tried not to be jealous of her best friend, but sometimes it just wasn't possible. She could feel the envy weighing her down like stones in her pocket. She wasn't about to walk into a river and give up like Virginia Woolf, although part of her worried that was exactly what she was doing by staying with Mark.

She would give anything to trade places with Sissy. For a night, not forever. Just long enough to feel that reckless spirit and wild abandon that her best friend lived by. But that kind of passion was reserved for the young at heart, and Betsy's heart had never really been young.

She tried not to feel sorry for herself and instead to focus on all the positive attributes that came from having to grow up at such a young age. She was responsible, having had to keep an eye on the clock to make sure she didn't miss the school bus, since her mom was usually upstairs, either asleep or hungover. She was resourceful, having learned how to cook so she wouldn't go to bed hungry on the nights her mom went out on dates. And most importantly, she'd learned how to do laundry and mend her own clothes so her appearance never gave away her troubles at home. As long as things looked okay on the surface, she could pretend they were. But sometimes, she wished she didn't have to pretend.

Downstairs, the main floor was still and quiet, but the basement light was on, which meant that Kathy, their house mom, had already set out the bagels for breakfast.

Betsy hesitated, but she realized Kathy was the one person in the house she wouldn't mind running into. The other girls didn't appreciate having a house mom to care about and look after them as much as Betsy did, but most of the other girls had their own caring moms back home.

The kitchen was unfortunately empty, so she grabbed a bagel and wrapped it in a napkin before tucking it into her book bag in case she got hungry later at the library.

Betsy didn't have much studying to do, but the library was one of her favorite places on campus. She loved everything about books—the heavy feel of them in her hands, the musty smell of the paper, and the whispery sound of the pages as she turned them. But most of all, she loved the way books could transport her to another time and place.

A book was just what Betsy needed to get out of the funk she was in. As she walked through the stacks, she tried to put her finger on what it was about last night that had gotten her so upset. It wasn't really about Andy Abrams, she knew that. It was what he represented. Everything her boyfriend wasn't.

Whenever Sissy pointed out how dull Mark was, Betsy had to stop herself from agreeing. She knew her best friend was right, but she didn't know why being dull was such a bad thing. Especially when it also meant he was safe and kind and predictable. He wasn't the kind of man who would leave, like her own father had. Mark was the kind of man who would stay, the kind of man who would think to celebrate his girlfriend's birthday.

Betsy had tried not to get too excited when Mark mentioned plans to celebrate her birthday the following weekend. A lifetime of forgotten birthdays had taught her it was better to expect nothing and be pleasantly surprised than to hope for something and be let down.

But she didn't think Mark would let her down. And if Betsy had to choose between the passionate sex Sissy seemed to be having and being with someone who cared enough to celebrate the fact that she was born, she was pretty sure she'd choose the latter.

Turning the corner into the *S* stacks, Betsy wondered if her approaching birthday was the reason for her sour mood. No matter how old she got, she still felt like that brand-new six-year-old girl who had come downstairs hoping for hugs and kisses and happy birthday wishes. Instead, her mom had asked her to take out the trash.

Betsy did as her mother asked, convinced that when she walked back inside there would be a wrapped gift and maybe pancakes waiting on the kitchen table. But there was nothing on the table or the counter when she returned—and instead of wishing her only daughter a happy birthday, her mom told Betsy that she had a date that night with a man who didn't know she had a kid, so Betsy would be spending the night at Sissy's house.

Birthdays at the Goldbergs' became a tradition, the one thing about the day Betsy could look forward to. Every year, they did something special for her—but nothing would ever be as special as that first year, when Mrs. Goldberg put a birthday candle in Betsy's chocolate pudding at dessert, and Mr. Goldberg had slipped her a five-dollar bill.

Over time, she'd learned to hide her disappointment, but Betsy had never been able to forget the way her own mother made her feel unwanted.

Out of habit, she went to reach for the red spine of her favorite book, *The Catcher in the Rye*, but there was an empty space on the shelf where it should have been. It seemed nothing was going her way.

HALFWAY ACROSS CAMPUS, Andy Abrams was lying on his bed, staring up at the ceiling. He held his breath every time the hallway phone rang, allowing himself to hope, even though he knew William wouldn't be calling.

Andy knew the next move was his to make. It had been his mistake, showing up there late and smelling like perfume. He wouldn't blame William if he never wanted to see Andy again, although the thought of making it through the next two and a half years without him seemed a crueler punishment than death.

As soon as the thought had formed into something as tangible as words, Andy knew they held his truth. He would rather die than live alone, without love.

Andy grabbed a pencil from his nightstand and reached for the sketchbook he always carried with him. It was his version of the journal he longed to keep but couldn't. If he did, it would just be an-other lie. He couldn't risk putting his real feelings into words for fear of the damage they would do if someone found them.

Instead, he drew.

No one could use a drawing against him the way they could use his words. Sometimes, he drew the way he felt, lost and alone. Misunderstood and insignificant. More often, he drew the world the way he wanted it to be. A place where he could walk down the street, holding William's hand. Where he wouldn't have to worry about the jeers and stares, the disgust in the eyes of passersby. The same expression he saw when he looked in the mirror.

Andy turned to a fresh page, channeling his anger and sadness into the drawing. The lines were dark and heavy, he could feel his pencil digging into the soft fibers of the page. It wasn't until he was finished that Andy realized he had drawn a self-portrait, his head hanging low, shoulders slumped in shame.

In the hallway, the phone rang. This time, he didn't bother wish-ing it was William. If he was going to wish for anything, he knew he should wish to be like everyone else. He should wish that he could be attracted to any of the girls who were interested in him. His life would be so much easier if he were.

Andy looked down at his notebook one more time before shoving it under his bed. He didn't want to see himself the way William did.

The phone rang again, and Andy sighed. He didn't believe in wishes anyway.

Chapter Twelve

Now

T HE NEXT MORNING, I'M STILL IN THE HAZE OF SLEEP WHEN the world's loudest noise comes from my phone. I reach for it, accidentally hitting the answer button before I see who's calling. I clear my throat in case it's a call from one of the dozen recruiters I'm waiting to hear back from. "Hello?"

"Morning, beautiful."

My heart swells, and I feel both instantly better and so much worse at the sound of Jeff's voice. "I miss you."

"I miss you, too. Just called to see how you were feeling this morning. You sounded pretty out of it last night."

"We talked?" I roll onto my side and put the phone on speaker so I can look at my recent call list. Sure enough, I called Jeff at 11:43. He laughs, and once again, I wish he were here. "What did I tell you?"

"Some crazy story about finding your dad on Facebook?"

"Not Facebook, it was Google."

"Is someone using his name?" Jeff asks, rightly confused.

"I wish." I sigh, then tell him everything.

There's silence on the other end of the line when I finally finish talking. I glance down at the screen to make sure there's still a connection. There is.

"Jeff?"

"Sorry—just wow," he says. I ache for him and wish he were on the other side of our bed, not the other side of the country. "I can catch a flight out this afternoon if you need me, Ross can cover the rest of the meetings."

"No!" I say a little too quickly.

Jeff exhales a long breath, and I can picture him running his fingers through his hair. We have an unspoken agreement that he doesn't complain about Maks, and I don't complain about Ross. Except he's the only one of us who holds up his end of the arrangement.

"I didn't mean it like that," I say, trying to recover. "It's just, this is your big opportunity, and I'm not going to let you blow it on my account."

"You don't have to protect me," he says. "And for the record, you're more important than any job."

"Easy there," I say through a laugh. "Let's try not to have both of us unemployed at the same time, okay?"

He sighs, and I can tell he's softening. "Okay," he says. "I just wish you would have called me first."

"I did," I protest, even though I know I should let it go. "You were my very first call."

"Dammit, Paige," he says, but I know he's more upset with himself than he is with me. "I would have called you back if you said it was important."

"I know," I tell him, and I do. I know he would have dropped everything for me, which is exactly why I didn't tell him. "But you had to focus on your meeting, and I had Maks and Margaux."

"And you have me," he says. "I want to be the person you turn to."

"You are," I tell him.

He exhales another deep breath. "What are the chances?"

"That I'd find you?" I ask. Based on all the bad dates and swipe rights I had before meeting him, it was one in a million.

"No," he says. "That this guy even exists, much less that he signed up for the same DNA test that you did. The odds have to be astronomical."

"Maybe I should start playing the lottery." I laugh but stop when I remember something Maks said about Andrew Abrams being filthy rich.

"And your mom denied it?"

"Yup," I tell him. "I wish I could, too—but I can't be someone who literally marched for science last year and then turn my back on it when it tells me something I don't want to hear."

"I just can't believe your dad isn't your dad."

His words sting, and I inhale sharply at the truth behind them. It's crazy how one phrase can be so wrong and so right at the same time.

"I keep telling myself he's still my dad," I say softly.

"Oh, babe." Jeff's voice is soft, barely above a whisper. "Of course he is, he's your dad in all the ways that count. I didn't mean it like that."

"But you aren't wrong," I tell him. "He's not *really* my dad. It's just, I don't know. It's like I exist in two universes. In one world—"

"In a galaxy far, far away?" Jeff teases, and I smile again.

"Exactly," I tell him. "There's the world where my dad is my dad, and I'm who I've always been. But then there's this other world where this other guy exists. And now that I know he's out there, that part of me is tied to him. It's like . . . ." My stomach feels like it's turning inside out, and I don't know if it's from the Velvet Taco I ate late last night or because I'm about to voice what exactly has gotten me so upset. "It's like everything I thought I knew about myself isn't true anymore. I was never supposed to be Paige Meyer."

"It's not too late to be Paige Parker," he teases, a smile evident in his voice.

I laugh, but my heart's not in it, and I can't shake the thought of Paige Abrams. I wonder how different she would be. What career she would have, if she'd be married already with kids. I can't imagine my life if I'd been her.

"No matter what your name is, you're still you," Jeff says with such conviction that I almost believe him. "You may have half of this guy's DNA, but you've got all your dad's heart."

"I just wish he were here," I whisper into the phone, as the tears I've been holding back break free.

"I wish I was there," Jeff says, his voice full of concern. "Are you sure you don't want me to catch a flight?"

"No," I say, brushing away the tears. "I'm okay. I'll be okay."

We're both quiet, and I'm grateful I finally found the person I don't have to fill the empty moments with.

"I know you'll think I'm being dramatic," I tell him, "but it feels like my past has been erased, like I've been living the wrong life story and I have to start over."

"A blank Paige," Jeff says. "Your dad would have loved that one."

I smile. One of my biggest regrets is that I hadn't met Jeff one month sooner, so he could have met my dad. But when he says things like this, I realize that in a way, he does know him, thanks to the stories I tell and how intently he listens to and loves me.

"He did love a good pun," I say.

"Like jumbo shrimp."

"That's not a pun; it's an oxymoron."

"Who are you calling a moron?" Jeff says, a playful edge to his voice.

I smile again, my eyes prickling with more tears. "I can't wait for you to get home," I tell him.

"Me too," he says. "If you change your mind—"

"I know, but I'll be fine. And you have a deal to close and a promotion to get." I decide not to tell him the bit about Andrew Abrams being wealthy. At least, not yet.

"I love you," he tells me. "Whoever you are."

I FEEL MORE human after a shower, and almost like myself once I get coffee and a bagel in my stomach. Then, and only then, am I ready to sit down in front of my laptop. I glance at my daily to-do list—Jeff's idea to help me stay motivated and feel productive.

Today's list includes looking for a potential hobby and emailing contacts under the guise of saying hello, while casually mentioning that I'm available for freelance or full-time opportunities. Although I can't imagine working to create a brand's identity while I'm struggling to find my own.

The Facebook NPE group is still open on my screen, and I spend a few minutes scanning the latest posts.

Gail from Orange County posted about a fight she had with her birth mom; Teddy from Texas wishes he'd never opened Pandora's box, saying he was happier when he didn't know who his father was. Candice from Ohio always knew her two moms had used a sperm donor, but she hadn't expected to find almost sixty siblings. Apparently her DNA Dad had been a hot commodity at the sperm bank.

When I've read all that I care to read about other people's stories, I open my email to see if FamilyTree has lobbed any more "new leaf" bombs my way. An aunt or an uncle, a half brother or a half sister. I realize with a start that the twins are only my half siblings. It explains so much.

There are two emails from FamilyTree in my inbox. The first one is an automated email, asking about my satisfaction with their customer service department. Other than the news they were delivering, it was fine, I guess. I delete it without submitting feedback and move on to the second one. My breath catches as I realize it's the email I was equally dreading and hoping for. A response. From *him*. New message from Andrew Abrams!

The copywriter who wrote that generic subject line wouldn't have had any way of knowing the email could be carrying life-altering news. The subject lines should be dynamic in response to the tone of the message inside. This one should probably read: Prepare yourself, you're not going to like what Andrew Abrams has to say.

Before I can talk myself out of it, I click to open the email. There's only one line:

Seems unlikely on my end, too.

My stomach sinks, and I'm not sure how I feel. Relieved? A little. Confused? Absolutely. I reread the six words, analyzing each one to try to find some hidden meaning. "Seems" is an unsure word, so noncommittal. And why "unlikely" and not "impossible"?

I call Maks, hoping he'll be able to talk me off the ledge.

"Hello?" His voice is groggy, and he sounds like he just woke up.

"Why aren't you at work?" I ask. It's almost eleven o'clock.

"I took a sick day."

"Are you sick?" I ask, waiting for an answer before I decide how much sympathy he deserves.

"I should have gone home when you guys did," he groans.

"Do you need me to bring you a Gatorade?" I ask. "I could use the distraction."

"No," Maks says. "I'm feeling better already."

I hear the rustle of sheets and a cat's sharp meow. Maks doesn't have a cat.

"Maks," I say, drawing his name out like a parent who knows her son is up to no good. "Where are you?"

He sighs audibly, knowing he's busted. "John's house. It seemed like a good idea at the time."

"No idea is a good idea at three a.m.," I tell him. I stop myself from turning this into a teaching moment, reminding him that it's impossible to have a casual hookup with someone you have actual feelings for. It might be thrilling in the moment, but the emptiness you feel afterward isn't worth it. A lesson that unfortunately took me an entire semester junior year at college to learn.

"I don't want to hear about it," he says. "Tell me the news with you."

"I heard back," I tell him. "From Andrew Abrams."

"What'd he say?" Maks says, sounding more alert.

"Nothing."

"He sent back an empty email?" he asks, and I remind myself that American euphemisms sometimes slip past Maks.

"No, but it might as well have been."

"Let me be the jury of that," he says. "Read it—actually, first read what you sent."

I scroll to the bottom of the message to find my original note. I'm about to start reading when I hear Maks whisper something in a bedroom voice.

"We can do this later," I tell him.

"Read," he says, giving me no other option. And honestly, if I'm keeping him from making yet another mistake with John, it's probably for the best.

"Okay." I clear my throat. "'Hi, Andrew. According to Family Tree.com, we're related. Seems unlikely on my end, but I thought I would reach out to say hello just in case. So, hello.'"

Reading my message out loud, I realize Andrew was just parroting my words back at me. His note means even less now, if there's anything less than nothing.

"Okay, now, what did he say?"

I read the line back to Maks.

"Hmm."

"Right?"

"I said I need a minute," Maks says, talking to John again. There's a bite to his voice that makes me frown.

"I'll let you go," I tell him.

"No, no, sorry. John was just being John," he says. "Back to you—what a bullshit, vague answer. Do you think she reached out and told him not to tell you anything?"

"Who, my mom?"

"No, Olivia Newton-John. Of course your mom."

"I don't know. I mean, maybe? I'd be surprised if she'd kept in touch with him all these years—how would she even contact him?"

"Sweetheart," Maks says in that condescending tone I know all too well. "Anyone can be found if you really want to find them. Especially if it means keeping your deep, dark secret."

"Maybe." I roll the idea around in my head, even though the

thought that I'm her deep, dark secret makes me queasy. And this is my mom we're talking about. "You have to remember we're talking about the woman who Googled 'How to Google something.' She and technology are like . . . me and fashion."

"Good point."

I dismiss his dig since I'm the one who brought it up. "And what if it was sexual assault like Margaux said?" I ask. "Do you really think she'd reach out to the man who did that to her?"

I shudder at the thought of my origin story coming from something so vile. If it's true, if she was a victim in all of this, it would completely change the way I think of her. It would make a lot of things make more sense: why my mom has always been so rigid, why she's pushed me away. Maybe I remind her of the worst night of her life.

The thought makes me nauseated, but I know it might not be true. I pull up the photo Maks found online and stare into the face of a sixtysomething Andrew Abrams. His eyes look friendly, his smile sincere. I can't picture someone who looks so nice doing something so cruel to my mom. Of course, isn't that what people usually say in hindsight about serial killers and rapists? *They seemed so nice.*

"Are you going to write him back?" Maks asks.

The cursor in the body of the reply message is blinking at me, as if it's daring me to make a move.

I hear a loud sigh, followed by the low rumble of John's voice. "Sorry," Maks says. "Can I call you later?"

"Don't worry about it—tell John I said hello and not to break your heart."

He hangs up and I make the picture of Andrew Abrams as big as it can get without looking distorted. Next to it, I drag a photo of myself. I look from his eyes to my own. His nose, my nose. His crooked smile, mine. Both of us with the left side of our mouths angled a little higher than the right.

It can't be a coincidence. This isn't something he can lie to me about. It's my life. Who I am. I have a right to know the truth.

Thanks for getting back to me so quickly.

I sit back and stare at the words, worried they feel too formal. It's not like I emailed him asking if he would pass along my résumé and portfolio. I continue.

Interestingly enough, it looks like you went to the University of Kansas the same time my parents did. My mom's name is Elizabeth Meyer. She would have gone by Betsy Kaplan back then. She was a member of the Sigma Delta Tau sorority.
My dad . . .

I hesitate. Not sure if it's okay to use the word "dad" about my dad when I'm talking to my DNA Dad. Since he clearly doesn't seem interested in claiming that title, I keep writing.

My dad was Mark Meyer. He passed away a few years ago.

I delete the last line, so he doesn't think I'm looking for a replacement.

My dad was Mark Meyer, he wasn't Greek, but he was really active in Hillel.

I sit back and read the message once more and then a third time. It sounds okay, but I don't know how to end it. "Love" is all wrong, but "sincerely" isn't right, either. I think through all the traditional sign-offs, but none of them seem right to end a message to a man who's denying our biological connection. I sigh, aware I'm over-thinking it.

I read the message a final time and end it with the first thought that comes to mind. An apology of sorts, so he knows I mean no harm.

I hope I didn't disrupt your day too much.

—Paige

I hit send and close my laptop, knowing I'll keep refreshing my inbox to check for a reply if I sit there any longer. I go one step fur-ther and silence the ringer on my phone so I don't jump every time the email alert dings.

Before I put my phone back down, I open the camera in selfie mode and wonder if somewhere in Naples, Florida, Andrew Abrams is looking at himself and seeing little pieces of me.

Chapter Thirteen

Then

MUCH TO ANDY'S SURPRISE, THE WORLD WAS STILL TURNING after his long and lonely weekend. The days seemed to go on forever without the promise of time with William or the release that painting brought him. But he wasn't about to go to the studio.

His limbs felt heavy as he forced himself out of bed for his Monday morning class. It was like the worst kind of hangover—only instead of alcohol, the toxins lingering in his bloodstream were regret and disappointment.

Andy knew he couldn't let himself go down that black hole again. He needed to keep going, playing the part that life had cast him in. He knew it would just take one wrong move—a slip of the tongue, a glance too long or a failed class—and the facade he'd so carefully built would come tumbling down. There were landmines everywhere.

To make matters worse, he had to start his day with his academic nemesis: Algebra 201. Andy didn't have a problem with numbers, and he would go as far as saying he had a strong affinity for letters—he just didn't think the two should comingle. Unfortunately, it was a required class for the business major he had chosen to please his father.

As Andy took his usual seat in the last row of the lecture room at Strong Hall, he debated which would disappoint his father more: that he had fallen in love with art or with a man. Of course, Andy knew neither would be acceptable in his father's eyes.

"Hey, man."

Andy looked up just as Scott Lawson, one of the AEPi pledges, slid into the seat next to him.

"I mean, good morning, sir." Scott extended his hand to shake with Andy, the way pledges were instructed to do when greeting members before they were officially initiated.

"'Man' is fine," Andy said. He studied Lawson's face, round where William's was thin, smooth where William's always had a day or two of stubble. Andy wondered how it would feel to kiss him, if it would make his cells stand at attention the way they did when he and William kissed.

Of course, Andy would never find out. Because no one in his fraternity was like him. They probably wouldn't allow him to keep living in the house if they knew. Another reason to keep his mouth shut.

"Rumor around the dorm is you left that mixer on Friday with Sissy Goldberg."

Andy shook his head. "If who I go home with is on the radar of anyone at the freshman dorm, I'm a little concerned you guys aren't doing college the right way."

"So, it's true?"

Andy shrugged and gave Lawson a noncommittal look. He never lied about anything that had or hadn't happened with a girl, but he didn't actively deny anything, either.

There had never been a shortage of women who were interested in getting to know Andy better. It helped that he showered regularly and put some effort into his appearance, unlike most of his fraternity brothers. The bar they set was pretty low.

It also didn't hurt that Andy had inherited his father's thick hair and angular face, along with his mother's striking eyes. Even as a young boy, he had a way of charming women. The ladies at the grocery store would often sneak him an extra cookie, which always drove his older sister, Rebecca, crazy.

"So?" Lawson asked, still pushing for dirt to take back to the dorm.

"We went out for a drink," Andy admitted.

Over the years, he'd developed a talent for revealing just enough information so people could twist whatever details they had into a narrative that lined up with whatever they wanted to believe.

"You are one lucky man," Lawson said, taking his notebook out of his backpack. "Everyone knows Sissy Goldberg puts out."

Andy smiled a smile that he hoped left little to the imagination before turning back to face the front of the class so he could pretend to care about the Pythagorean theorem.

Fifteen minutes into the lecture, Lawson nudged Andy's shoulder.

"Brother," he whispered. "Babe at three o'clock is checking you out."

Andy nodded as if he already knew and turned his attention back to the chalkboard so he could figure out why the professor had to bring a y into the equation when he was still worrying about x.

Andy didn't know why it was so important to solve made-up problems. It would be better if there was meaning behind the letters and the numbers. If William was the x and Andy was the y, then he'd be interested in finding a mathematical way to bring them together. Although he'd probably screw that up, too.

Lawson nudged him again; he wasn't letting it go.

After the third shove, Andy gave in and looked toward the right side of the lecture hall, where, sure enough, a pretty blonde was staring at him. She smiled and flipped her hair in that way girls did before turning back to the front of the class.

Andy already knew how their story would go. He would get her number, call her eventually, they'd go out on a date, maybe two. He always ended things before feelings got involved. Otherwise, it wouldn't be fair to the girls. *Or to William.*

Andy's stomach twisted at the thought of William's reaction the other night, how hurt and angry he had looked. He wished there was a way to ease William's pain without risking every other part of his collegiate life. He hated pretending, but if the roles were reversed and William had been the one spending time with a woman, Andy would understand.

A piercing screech brought Andy's attention to the front of the room, where a cloud of chalk dust turned the green board gray. *Gray like William's eyes.* He willed himself to focus, but the words coming out of the professor's mouth didn't even sound like English.

He had to start paying attention. If he kept letting his pathetic love life distract him, Andy's grades would suffer as much as his relationship.

Now that he thought about it, the threat of failing a class might be the answer to fixing things with William.

He pictured the problem laid out before him like the one scribbled in his notebook. He could say his grades were falling (which they weren't), and that he might get kicked off the football team and lose his scholarship (which he wouldn't) if he didn't get his GPA back up. Then he could tell everyone he needed to focus on his classes, that he wasn't going to date for the rest of the year.

Of course, he'd still need a girl to take to fraternity events—he couldn't get out of going to those. William would have to understand that. Andy could take a friend and ask her not to wear perfume. He could say he was allergic, like William was with cologne.

Andy smiled and leaned back in his chair. Maybe life could be solved like a math problem if you just thought about it the right way.

AFTER CLASS, LAWSON wouldn't let Andy out of the row until the pretty blonde made her way to the back of the classroom where they were obviously waiting. It was no wonder the freshman boys had nothing better to do than talk about who Andy Abrams was out with. They had no game.

Lawson stepped into the aisle just before the girl walked past.

"I'm Scott," he said. "And this is Andy."

"Tricia," the girl said. She smiled, and Andy was struck by the perfect symmetry of her face. She would make an interesting subject—even William could see that. Maybe he could start his no-more-dates rule after one with her. Two, if it took that long to convince her to sit and pose for him.

But then she flipped her hair and laughed in a sickly sweet way that made Andy realize an evening with her might be too high a price to pay. He would ask for her number so he wouldn't have to explain himself to Lawson, but he wouldn't call.

Andy pushed through the heavy doors of Strong Hall, holding it open for Tricia, who brushed against his arm as she walked past, swinging her hips in a way that was meant to be admired. He didn't look away, watching more in amusement than in interest. But his smile quickly faded when he saw the protest under way out front.

Students were chanting, "Gay rights are human rights!" and holding up homemade signs in every color of the rainbow.

Andy looked to his left, where his fraternity brother and this girl he didn't even know stood waiting for him to react, but he froze. Lawson leaned over and pushed the door closed behind them, giving Andy a curious look. "Freaks," he said, nodding toward the growing crowd.

Andy felt like he was stuck in a hyperreality. He could hear his heart pounding in his ears, and he felt a single drop of sweat making its way down his forehead. He had to get out of there. He could pretend he forgot something in the classroom, go back inside, and slip out the back door. There had to be a back door.

Before Andy could make a move in either direction, the crowd parted. A man with familiar golden hair hanging in front of his face, with the mustache that tickled Andy's nose when they kissed, walked toward him. The eyes that had been so cold and angry just a few days before were now pleading with him.

William walked up to the bottom step, holding a bright yellow sign with royal-blue words in a beautiful script that read, "My sexuality is my business." He tilted the sign toward Andy, offering it like a truce, challenging him to cross another line.

Andy stuck his fisted hands into his pockets and held William's stare. He wanted to be the kind of person who was brave enough to let himself be who he was. But he knew he wasn't. He glanced down at the broken concrete, then back up to William, who was still holding out the sign for him to take.

William's lips narrowed into a hard, thin line. They stood, staring at each other, until Tricia reached past Andy and took the sign from William's hand and joined the protest. Andy watched in awe as this girl so easily became one with the crowd. Maybe he'd been wrong about her.

Andy could feel Lawson watching him, waiting for him to react the way he should. To walk away. But William was still standing before him. His hands were empty, but his arms were open, a pleading look in his eyes.

Andy felt as if he were standing on the edge of his two lives, afraid to make the wrong move. Making no move, he knew, would be just as damning. But he couldn't bring himself to say or do anything.

"Fucking homo," Lawson said as he shoved William out of the way, harder than necessary.

Andy lowered his head and followed his fraternity brother, feeling sick to his stomach. He walked straight through the group of strangers protesting for the rights of people like him. He kept walking, past Lawson, toward the house where he lived with people who were nothing like him. Or maybe he was nothing like them.

"You okay, man?" Lawson asked, rushing to keep up with Andy's pace.

"I'm fine," Andy said, not slowing down.

"Seriously," Lawson said, a little out of breath. "Do you know that faggot?"

Andy stopped abruptly and turned slowly so his eyes met Lawson's. He swallowed the truth that was on the tip of his tongue, but his silence now and his lack of action back there had already said too much.

He could see Lawson's mind working, putting all the half-truths together to reveal the lie Andy had been living.

It was the one equation that could be the end of him—one popular frat boy plus an angry gay protestor, minus all the girls Andy wouldn't date, divided by the seconds he stood there, saying nothing. It didn't add up.

"I'll see you later, man," Lawson said, shaking his head. "I mean, sir."

Chapter Fourteen

Now

LATER THAT AFTERNOON, AFTER A WALK TO THE GROCERY STORE and an hour spent following up with recruiters, I reward myself with a little time on the NPE Facebook group. It's addicting, reading these real-life stories of people who are going through the same thing I am.

I try not to spend too much time dwelling on the sad stories, the ones where people found their biological fathers only to end up disappointed or rejected, or stories where people have discovered they're related to people they've dated in the past, or those who have been told troubling things about their new health history.

I'm reading the story of a Christian minister who found out that his biological father was Jewish when I hear the *Jaws* theme start to play. I look from my phone to the screen and back again. I know she can't see what I'm doing, but I minimize it anyway.

The phone is still ringing. *Duh-dun. Duh-dun.* She's the last person I want to talk to right now, but if I don't answer, she'll think I'm avoiding her. *Duh-dun. Duh-dun.* Then I'll have to call her back, and she'll be the one to decide whether she picks up, and—*shit*. It's about to go to voicemail.

"Hi, Mom," I say, answering the call.

"Paige." She sounds surprised that I picked up. "I know you don't want to talk about this," she says.

I inhale a quick breath in surprise. My mom puts the "passive" in "passive-aggressive." I had assumed she'd want to ignore this DNA bombshell the same way we've ignored all the problems we've ever had—like the time she overheard me on the phone wishing that Sissy was my mom, or the day she walked in on me and Cory Verblen "studying" in my room.

"Did you hear me?" Mom asks, an annoyed lilt to her voice.

"Sorry, I got distracted."

She sighs audibly. Elizabeth Meyer does not like to repeat herself, which she had to do at least a dozen times a day for the last forty years since my dad is so forgetful. *Was* so forgetful.

"I got a call from Barb at the country club," she says. "We really need to settle on a date for the wedding—they can't hold both Saturday nights for us much longer."

I let out a guffaw before I can stop myself. She really is going to act as though nothing's wrong, as if I'm not in the middle of an identity crisis after learning that she lied to me every single day of my life.

"What were the dates again?" I ask, playing along with her charade.

She sighs, even louder than before. "Paige, I swear, sometimes I wonder if you even want to get married."

I bite my lip to stop myself from starting a conversation I won't want to finish. As much as I wish I could be a normal daughter talking to her normal mother, I know we're not. And I can't tell her what I'm really worried about. That I'm not the same woman Jeff proposed to seven months ago. Back then, I had a job and I knew who I was. Not to mention the small detail that every time I think about the wedding, I feel like an old maid playing the part of a young bride.

"Of course I want to marry Jeff," I insist. And because I can't stop myself, I add, "But you heard what Annabelle said about brides over forty."

"Oh, Paige." Mom's voice sounds softer this time. "She's a child. You can't take what she says seriously."

"She's almost thirty."

Mom laughs, and I hope it's not directed at me. "Sweetheart, you were an adult by the time you were thirteen. But Belle, well, let's just say I'm happy she has Frannie to help ground her. You really shouldn't let her get to you."

I'm not sure how to react to my mom actually being mom-like. Maybe I could try to be more daughter-like and share my feelings instead of burying them. I take a deep breath and go for it, hoping I won't regret it later.

"Except she's not wrong," I tell her. "The whole bridal industry was designed for girls in their twenties. The big white dresses, the pomp and circumstance—I'm too old for all that. I want to marry Jeff, I'm going to marry Jeff, but the thought of me as a bride, it just feels silly."

"You listen to me, Paige Meyer." Her voice is shaky but firm. "I don't care how old you are—love is worth celebrating. Believe me, I know how lucky you are to have found the great love of your life." Her voice cracks, and my stomach sinks with the realization that I don't know whether she's talking about my dad-dad or my DNA Dad. "So push all the naysayers, including your sister, out of your mind and just tell me what day you want to get married."

I hesitate, wishing I'd written down the dates. "I'd pick one if I remembered what they were."

She laughs—and if I didn't know I was talking to my uptight, perfectionist mother, I wouldn't believe that a sound so real and genuine could come from her. It's contagious, and soon I'm laughing, too.

Maybe Maks was right. Maybe the distance between us for all these years hasn't been because she hated or resented me but because of the weight of the huge secret she was carrying alone.

"You're just like your father," she says after the laughter has died down. There's an awkward silence as she realizes she just brought up the subject she'd been trying so hard to avoid. "We have September eighth on hold—it's the weekend after Labor Day—and October thirteenth. It's a Saturday, so you don't have to worry about it being unlucky. At this point, we're only two months from September . . ."

"Let's do the October date," I tell her. "The thirteenth."

"Don't you want to talk to Jeff about it?" she asks.

"He won't mind."

"Okay, then October thirteenth it is."

I scribble down the date on a Post-it note and smile, realizing it's not just one date but a series of days Jeff and I will celebrate together for the rest of our lives.

"I'll call Barb and let her know; then the fun stuff can begin," Mom says. She's quiet for a moment, and I can feel the distance growing back between us, now that we've wrapped up the one thing she called to talk about. It's hard to believe I came from this woman, that she carried me below her heart for nine months. "And, Paige?"

"Yeah?" I ask, my voice full of false hope.

"I just want—I just— Don't let Belle get to you. You are going to be a beautiful bride, and you deserve all the love and happiness in the world. I hope you know that."

"Thanks, Mom."

There's another awkward silence, so different from the comfortable silence I have with Jeff.

"Okay, then," she eventually says. "We'll talk soon. Toodles!"

Toodles? I shake my head before saying, "Bye, Mom."

I sketch a heart around the date on the Post-it note and take a picture and text it to Jeff.

We would have had ten months to plan our wedding if we'd picked a date right after the engagement. At least I thrive on short deadlines after more than two decades in the advertising industry. And I have twice the life experience as brides in their twenties have, so it should take me half the time to plan.

It can't be that hard; neither of us want anything fancy. I'd honestly be fine eloping if I didn't know it would kill my mother.

There are few things Elizabeth Meyer likes more than getting all dressed up and throwing a party. It wouldn't be right stealing her chance at another wedding, since my impending arrival was the reason she'd had to settle on a courthouse ceremony. Well, maybe Andrew Abrams was the reason.

I glance down at my phone, as if it's still buzzing with the energy from the phone call with my mom. It's true she didn't bring up the elephant in the room, but neither did I. I could have told her that I reached out to him. Twice, now.

The FamilyTree site is minimized on my laptop, so I bring it up to full view. The inbox is still empty. It was stupid of me to think I'd get a reply after he basically wrote me off in his first note. I should have known better than to think he might be just as curious about me as I am about him.

I close the FamilyTree window and open LinkedIn instead so I can focus my new sleuthing skills on finding myself a job.

Chapter Fifteen

Then

W HAT DO YOU THINK OF THIS DRESS?" BETSY ASKED SISSY, who was lying on her bed, her hair still wrapped in a towel. Sissy's head was buried in one of the romance novels she was always reading, the kind with a half-naked man on the cover.

Betsy would be embarrassed to be seen holding a book like that, but she had flipped through a few pages once or twice when Sissy left them laying around. She didn't consider herself a prude, but some of the words she stumbled upon in those pages made her blush.

"It's nice," Sissy said without looking up from her story.

Betsy frowned and turned back toward the mirror, studying her reflection. The pastel pink made her skin look a little on the pale side, but she liked how the bodice hugged her waist and the way the pleated skirt moved when she walked.

"I don't think I've ever seen you this excited for a date," Sissy said, finally putting down the book. "Is there someone new? Surely you can't be getting this worked up over your nerd."

"Oh, stop." Betsy tried to make her voice sound playful, but today of all days, she didn't want to hear Sissy's negative comments about Mark. Betsy had been looking forward to this night all week, ever since Mark first brought up her birthday, and she wasn't going to let anything ruin it. Not even her best friend.

"No, seriously." Sissy sat up and tilted her head as though she was studying Betsy, who squirmed under the pointed stare. "What's going on?"

"We're just going out to dinner"—Betsy paused before adding the words that took their plans from ordinary to special—"for my birthday."

"Shit," Sissy said. "Did I forget again?"

"It's not until Thursday," Betsy assured her. "But Mark wanted to celebrate early."

Sissy looked relieved and went back to her book. She hadn't forgotten yet, but Betsy had a feeling her friend still wouldn't remember when the time came.

Fully committed to the dress, Betsy sat down at her desk chair to put on her pantyhose, careful not to tear the thin fabric as it slipped over her toes, painted pink for the occasion.

"I thought you hated your birthday?" Sissy asked, looking up from the book again.

"I used to." Betsy smiled as she stood and wiggled the pantyhose past her hips. "Before I had a boyfriend who wanted to celebrate it with me."

Betsy's smile faltered when she saw Sissy's furrowed brow and pursed lips. So much for not letting Sissy's negativity get her down tonight. She perched on the edge of her best friend's bed.

"Why don't you like Mark?" she asked softly, afraid she wouldn't be able to unhear the answer.

"I never said I didn't like him," Sissy protested.

Betsy sat quietly, knowing that Sissy would keep talking if given the space and opportunity.

"I just don't want you to settle." Sissy closed the book and sat up.

"Settle for what? Being happy?" Betsy wondered if Sissy would like any guy that Betsy dated. They'd been best friends since kindergarten, and this was the first time Betsy truly had something in her life that Sissy wasn't a part of.

"*Are* you happy?" Sissy asked. "Does he make you really, truly happy?"

Betsy frowned, afraid her best friend had a different definition of "happy." Having grown up with two loving parents, a big brother, and a dog in a house where there was always enough money and food on the table, Sissy hadn't known sadness or loneliness the way Betsy had.

"Did I ever tell you why I don't like my birthday?" Betsy asked.

"Did you not get the Barbie DreamHouse you were pining for when you were nine years old?" Sissy teased.

"I didn't get a Barbie DreamHouse or a Barbie. I didn't even get a 'Happy birthday' from my mom."

Sissy sat up straighter, her smile fading. "Your mom never wished you a happy birthday?"

"Not *never*," Betsy said, looking down at her hands. "Just not most years. I don't think my birthday was such a happy memory for her. My dad was engaged to someone else when my mom got pregnant with me, and her parents had kicked her out. She was all alone, and things weren't always easy for her. She had a lot going on, and she—"

Before Betsy could finish her thought, Sissy lunged across the bed, wrapping her in a giant hug.

"It's okay," Betsy said, wiggling out of the embrace.

"No, it's not," Sissy said, her voice full of empathy.

Betsy wondered if her friend was thinking back to her own extravagant birthday parties—one year, there had even been ponies in the backyard for all the kids to take rides on. It struck her now as odd that in all the years of their friendship, Sissy hadn't noticed that Betsy never had a birthday party, other than her annual sleepover at Sissy's house.

"It's sweet that Mark's doing something special for you," Sissy said. "He really is a good guy."

Betsy smiled at the quasi-compliment. A good guy was a step up from a boring one.

"So the dress is good?" Betsy asked.

"The dress is perfect," Sissy said, although her face suggested otherwise. "But your face and hair could use some work."

Betsy frowned and looked in the mirror. Her wavy brown hair looked the way it always did, and she had never been that adventurous when it came to makeup.

"To the bathroom," Sissy said, jumping up from the bed.

"Don't you have to get ready for the AEPi party?"

Sissy shook her head. "It doesn't start until eight, so I'll probably go around ten."

"Two hours late?" Betsy asked. The thought of being just a few minutes late anywhere gave Betsy hives. Sometimes she wondered how she and Sissy could be so close when they were so very different.

"Two hours late is early when you're talking about a frat party." Sissy smiled and turned to head toward the bathroom. "C'mon, let's get you dolled up, birthday girl."

NOT EVEN HALFWAY through his four years of college, and Andy had already ruined everything.

Pretending to be someone he wasn't would have been hard

enough on its own, but he had to go and complicate things even more by attempting to live two different lives at the same time. It had been selfish and stupid of him to even try.

It didn't matter that Andy was pretty sure he loved William. Or that Andy felt more like himself than he'd ever felt before when they were together. What mattered was that Andy had been careless, and he was going to ruin everything he'd so carefully built.

Stupid, he was stupid.

And now, on top of it all, Andy was probably going to fail Algebra. He had skipped both the Wednesday and Friday classes this week—the first classes he'd ever missed on purpose. But he couldn't bring himself to go. Not after the way Lawson had looked at him, disgusted, like the pieces were falling together, suddenly making sense.

Andy knew he couldn't talk himself out of this one, and he couldn't avoid talking to Lawson if he went to class. It wasn't like he could suddenly switch seats and sit on the other side of the lecture hall without making it even more obvious.

There was nothing he could do, unless Professor Matthews taught the same class another day or time. He could figure out a way to explain the switch—mandatory, early-morning workouts or something. He could say the coach was stepping things up because of their lackluster performance the last few games.

That would solve the problem of his grades, but he still had Lawson to worry about. The kid could single-handedly bring Andy's entire world crashing down around him. He couldn't just sit by and let that happen.

Tonight at the party, he would give it his all. Andy would show Lawson that he really was the ladies' man the freshman guys envied and gossiped about. He would find a girl and make sure everyone, not just Lawson, saw them together.

This time, Andy wouldn't just pretend to be a straight version of his normal self; he would pretend to be someone else completely. He'd be as cool as Elvis, as confident as David Cassidy, and as smooth as Donny Osmond. If he'd thought of that when he'd first gotten to campus, maybe he wouldn't be in this mess.

The phone in the hallway rang, and Andy's heart sank with the realization it wouldn't be William. He stared up at the ceiling, wondering if this shell of a life was even worth living. The loss of their relationship had been compounded by all the empty hours—hours he used to spend at the studio. His fingers were itching to hold a paintbrush, and William's hand.

Andy had thought about going to the open-studio sessions in the morning when he knew there would be no risk of running into William. But he'd gotten so used to their evenings, Andy wasn't sure his muse would find him during daylight. His best work had always been done in the late hours when it was just the two of them.

The phone rang again, probably one of the parade of girls asking questions about the party tonight. It wasn't going to be any different from all their other parties: a few kegs Andy was supposed to help carry inside, music with a beat strong enough to keep the dance floor going and loud enough to make it impossible to have a conversation. Girls would be drinking and dancing, flirting and teasing and giving Andy's fraternity brothers hope for a little action. Most of the guys wouldn't get any, but that didn't stop them from trying.

Andy flinched at the sound of someone banging on his door.

"Abrams!" David, the fraternity's social chair, hollered on his way downstairs.

"Coming," Andy said, getting up from his bed. His limbs felt stiff. He hadn't spent this much time alone in his room since he was a teenager hiding from the girlfriends his sister always had sleeping over.

He steadied himself before opening the door, almost like he was walking onto a stage instead of the second floor of his fraternity house.

"Action," Andy muttered under his breath as he stepped into the hallway, bumping into a half-naked Jared Evans.

Jared's skin was still slick from the shower, and the contact, however brief, made Andy physically ache for William's touch. He stepped back and accidentally glanced down to where Jared's towel was starting to slip off his hips.

"Sorry, man," Jared said, wrapping the towel tighter around his hips. "You're not my type."

Fear paralyzed Andy, and he couldn't move, much less come up with a quippy retort. Hell, it didn't even have to be clever, he just had to say something. Do something. But he couldn't. He just stood there, watching Jared—Lawson's "big brother" in the fraternity— turn into his room.

"Your breasts aren't big enough for my taste anyway," Andy said as the door closed in his face. He was too late, and he should have said "tits."

"Abrams!" David yelled again from downstairs.

He took the steps down two at a time to where the scrawny social chair was waiting.

"The kegs are out in the bed of the truck—need my help?" David asked.

Any of the other brothers would have made a snarky comment about David's lack of muscle tone, how he was more equipped to carry a cup than a keg, but Andy had to draw the line at pretending to be like the other guys somewhere.

Besides, Andy knew he would be the target of their cruel jokes as soon as they found out about him. Only then, it wouldn't be fun and games. They'd really mean it.

"I got it," Andy told David. "Just hold the door?"

He grabbed the first keg out of the truck and carried it effortlessly into the house. The physical exertion felt good. After he carried the fourth one inside, his adrenaline was pumping and he wished there was a fifth.

Andy realized with a start that painting wasn't the only way he could release tension and blow off steam. He felt a sudden urge to run, to feel the wind in his hair and the pavement beneath his feet. Andy glanced down at the watch his father had given him for his high school graduation. It was almost six thirty. The party started at eight, which gave him plenty of time to go for a run and get back to shower and change.

Unless he decided to fully embrace the role of "one of the guys" and skip the shower, spraying on some cheap cologne and calling himself ready instead. Andy chuckled at the thought as he ran upstairs to change into his running shorts and shoes. He could pretend to be a lot of things, but filthy would never be one of them.

Chapter Sixteen

Now

Longtime reader, first-time poster, I type into the text box on the NPE Facebook page. I found out last week that a man I'd never heard of is my biological father. My mom is denying it, but there are too many coincidences for it not to be true. I reached out to the man, and he said it didn't seem likely. I wrote him again with more "proof" but haven't heard a word.

I stop typing and read the post, wondering if I sound desperate or naive. There's an option to create a poll on the page, and I consider doing that.

Should I:

OPTION A: Ignore facts and science and pretend none of this is real.

OPTION B: Force my mother to tell me the truth.

OPTION C: Force this man to tell me the truth, even though he might have been a rapist.

I delete the post, knowing I've answered my own question. As much as I wish I could take option A, I know I won't be satisfied with the bits and pieces of information I've figured out on my own. I need someone, my mom or Andrew Abrams, to fill in the gaps.

I have the right to know about this man I'm biologically connected to: what his relationship or non-relationship was with my mother, any red flags in his family's medical history, and the big question—if he'd known that I existed.

As much as I would like to hear all these things from him, I know it isn't likely. He still hasn't answered my last email, and I'm not about to force myself on someone who clearly has no interest in getting to know me. A man who doesn't seem to be the least bit curious about who I am.

Which leaves Option B. *Mommy Dearest.*

Over the forty-three years we've been mother and daughter, I can count the number of tough conversations we've had on three fingers. She usually outsourced those to one of her two stand-ins: either my dad or Aunt Sissy.

Dad was the one who told me Mom was pregnant with the twins, and she had Aunt Sissy give me the sex talk. Which, in hindsight, was a good thing. There were definitely perks to being the only twelve-year-old in my class who knew what a Brazilian and a vibrator were.

But this is one conversation my mother has to have herself. She can't keep avoiding me, and I can't keep letting her.

I go to pick up my phone but realize I'm way too tense to call her now. It's a little after three on a Wednesday—close enough to the time that's socially acceptable to drink. I grab a Truly from the fridge and pop the lid. The bubbles tickle going down my throat.

I'm not sure what form of alcohol is in these spiked seltzers, but they're light and tasty and easy to drink.

I take another sip, wondering if half a can has enough liquid courage for me to force my mother to talk to me. I take one more can from the fridge just in case and go back to the desk in my bedroom.

I'm about to pick up the phone when it rings. Not the *Jaws* theme, thank goodness. Just the regular ring. I look down at the screen and see Frannie's face on the caller ID. My stomach drops.

"Frannie?" I say, answering the phone in a panic. "Is everything okay?"

"What?" she says. "Yeah, of course. It's fine."

"Thank goodness." I rest my hand on my chest in an attempt to calm my pounding heart.

"I was just calling to say hi," Frannie says, even though neither of my sisters has ever called just to say hi.

Our thirteen-year age difference would have been enough of a reason for us not to be close, but the fact that the twins looked like my dad and acted like mini versions of my mom made me more resentful of them than they probably deserved.

There has to be a reason she's calling. My stomach feels queasy with apprehension at the thought that she knows, that *they* know. The idea that Mom could tell them when she can't even talk to me about it makes my eyes fill with tears.

"Paige?" Frannie asks, and I realize I haven't said anything back.

"Sorry, I was distracted. A lot of stuff going on," I say, giving her an opening to tell me that she already knows, that she heard Dad wasn't really my dad.

"Yeah," she says, her voice sounding cheery and bright. "Mom told me you picked a date for the wedding."

"The wedding," I say slowly. "Yeah, it's not a lot of time to get everything done."

"It's so exciting!" Her enthusiasm seems forced, and I'm more curious than ever about the real reason behind this call. "Mom can't stop talking about you."

"Really?" I ask, trying not to sound too surprised.

"Oh, yeah," Frannie says. "She's telling anyone who will listen about how wonderful Jeff is and that she's so happy you've finally found your soul mate."

"Finally," I repeat, feeling the tension creep back into my shoulders.

"I didn't mean it like that," Frannie says, trying to backpedal. "I just, I don't know, you know how Mom is. I think she's lonely without Dad, so it's nice, you know, that she has something good to focus on."

I frown. I hadn't thought about Mom still being lonely. The first few months we all checked in on her a little more than usual, but she seemed to have adjusted to her new normal. Not that I could imagine her letting anyone, even her daughters, see otherwise.

"Anything new or exciting with you?" I ask, both to change the subject and to get on with whatever it is she really wants to talk about.

"Not really," she says. "Mom and Belle are driving me a little crazy with all the birthday party planning."

I laugh, surprised to hear Frannie say something less than glowing about her twin—or Mom, for that matter.

"That sounds like Annabelle," I say.

"Why do you still call her that?" Frannie asks.

"Because it's her name," I say. "And it drives her crazy."

Now it's Frannie's turn to laugh. "It does do that."

"So you really just called to say hi?"

"Is that so strange?" Frannie asks. "I was thinking about you. And about Chicago."

"Are you thinking about coming to town?" I ask. She's casually mentioned coming to visit before but has never followed through. Although neither have I.

It could be fun having Frannie in town for a weekend—less so if she insisted on bringing Annabelle along with her. Which I assume would be the case. The two have been roommates since they were wombmates; they do everything together.

"Something like that," Frannie says.

"Frances Meyer," I say, playing the part of the big sister I never really was to her. "What do you have up your sleeve?"

"Nothing, really. I promise," Frannie says. "I've just been feeling a little stuck lately. Like there's more out there. You know?"

"Believe me, I know." I decide not to tell her that some things out there aren't worth discovering.

"Do you think Dad liked his job?" she asks.

"He liked it enough," I say, surprised by the turn in our conversation. "I don't think he was super passionate about financial planning, but he was good at it."

"Yeah," Frannie says, and I can tell there's more behind her words.

"You're good at it, too," I remind her. She and Annabelle both got internships that turned into full-time jobs at the company where Dad used to work.

"I know," she admits. "It's just, I don't know, making rich people richer. I feel like there's more I could be doing."

My eyes well up, and I smile, wondering if my little sister realizes just how much she sounds like Dad. "That's why Dad volunteered and did all that pro bono work for people who were just starting out."

Frannie sighs, and I wish I could reach through the phone to give her a hug. "There are companies that do that, you know," she tells me. "Like, for charity, or people less fortunate."

"Are there?" I ask.

"Shoot, I have to go," Frannie says before she can tell me more. "Hey, Belle, come on in."

"Why was your office door closed?" I hear Annabelle ask.

"Maybe we can talk again soon?" Frannie says, a professional tone to her voice. She clearly doesn't want her twin to know what she's up to.

"Call me anytime," I say, surprising myself with how much I mean it. Just because we only share half our DNA doesn't mean that I can't start acting like a real big sister to her. Now that I know she's interested.

I decide to keep the family phone chain going and call my mom before I chicken out. The idea of her being lonely unsettles me, and I feel a little guilty for not doing more, not trying harder. Just because she won't reach out and start the conversation doesn't mean that I can't. That I shouldn't.

The phone only rings twice before Mom answers.

"Paige!" she says in lieu of hello. I hear a familiar door chiming in the background—she must be helping Aunt Sissy at her boutique today. "Everything okay?"

She sounds worried, probably as surprised to hear from me as I was to hear from Frannie. But I can't backtrack now that I'm finally being brave enough to talk to her, to ask her for the truth.

"Things haven't really been okay in a while," I tell her, being more honest and vulnerable than I'd expected. There's a sharp inhale on the other end of the line. "Nothing's wrong-wrong," I tell her, and she releases a long, slow breath.

"Goodness, you scared me."

"Sorry, I just meant, I thought we should talk about everything that's going on."

"The wedding?" she asks.

I laugh, wondering how everyone on the planet seems to be more concerned about my wedding than I am. "No, not the wedding."

"Then what, dear?" Mom asks, oblivious.

"Oh, I don't know," I tell her. "Maybe we should talk about that other thing—about me and who I am. About you and Andrew Abrams?" I let his name hang there between us, waiting for her to say something. Anything. But she doesn't. "Mom?" I ask.

"I told you your father was Mark Meyer," she says, her voice low and stern.

"I know you did, but my DNA is saying otherwise."

"A customer just came in," Mom says with false cheer. "Can we talk about this later, Paige?"

"Can we?" I ask. My voice wavers, and I don't think I realized just how much I need to have this conversation until now. "I mean it, Mom. I don't want to just brush this under the rug. It's too important."

"Bye, dear," she says in full performance mode. "Talk soon!"

Chapter Seventeen

Then

ONCE SISSY DECLARED HER PROPERLY READY FOR HER BIRTHDAY date, Betsy went down to the living room to wait for Mark. She caught her reflection in the mirror and smiled.

Sissy had said she looked like Marie Osmond with her hair so silky and straight. While Betsy wouldn't go that far, she did like the way the eyeliner and mascara made her deep-set eyes look so much bigger. She worried the orangey-red lipstick was too much, but Sissy insisted that a girl only turned nineteen once.

Headlights illuminated the front windows of the sorority house, and Betsy felt butterflies take flight inside her. She laid her hands over her stomach in an attempt to calm herself down.

There was no reason she should be nervous. She and Mark had gone out to dinner on dozens of Saturday nights, and this one wasn't any different—although Betsy hoped it would be. She hoped it would feel more special, that there would be a present. And cake. There had to be a cake—what was a birthday celebration without cake?

At seven sharp, she heard a knock on the front door and waited for one of her sisters to answer.

"Betsy," someone called. "Mark's here."

She stood and smoothed the skirt of her dress and resisted the urge to touch her hair, not wanting to mess up Sissy's handiwork. Betsy took her time walking toward the entryway to where she secretly hoped Mark would be waiting with flowers.

As she turned the corner, she tried not to be disappointed when she saw him standing there with empty hands but a big smile on his face.

"You look beautiful," he said, kissing her cheek.

"So do you." Betsy felt her cheeks blush even deeper than the rouge Sissy used to accentuate her cheekbones.

Outside, Mark opened the car door for her like he always did. Betsy sat with her hands folded in her lap, waiting for him to get in the other side. The queasy feeling in the pit of her stomach was a new sensation for Betsy. Despite the missing flowers, she was almost giddy with excitement, full of anticipation for every perfect moment.

"Where are we going?" Betsy asked as Mark settled into the front seat.

"I thought we'd swing by my place first," he said.

Betsy nodded and forced a smile, even though there wasn't anything special about going to his place—they went there almost every night they saw each other. She hated to think that Sissy had wasted so much time on her hair and makeup for nothing.

"I have a little something for you there," Mark said. "A birthday present."

Just like that, the fluttery feeling was back. Betsy could hardly follow the conversation during the rest of the ride, she was so distracted thinking about all the possible gifts Mark could have picked out. For her. For her birthday.

She hoped it was jewelry—something simple, not too expensive.

After all, it was the thought that counted, and no matter what it was, she would gush and say it was the prettiest thing she'd ever seen. And it would be, if it came from him in celebration of the day she was born.

A necklace would probably be best. Something with a charm, a blue charm, since that was her favorite color. A simple necklace she could wear every day.

Betsy smiled, imagining the compliments she would receive when she wore the necklace around campus. She could picture herself gently touching the charm, saying, "Thank you, it was a birthday gift from my boyfriend." That might even be more wonderful than the gift itself.

A bracelet would be nice, too. That way she could see it every time she looked at her wrist. She already decided that whatever it was, she would never take it off.

Betsy touched the simple pearl earrings she had borrowed from Sissy. She would love to have her own pair of nice earrings, although she wouldn't be able to admire them unless she was looking at herself in the mirror.

There was one other type of jewelry Betsy had yet to consider. She looked down at her bare ring finger. It was too soon to start thinking about marriage, but she could see herself getting used to a lifetime of birthdays being celebrated with presents and wine and fancy dinners.

"So, what do you think?" Mark asked as he pulled into the parking spot outside the off-campus apartment where he lived with a few other guys from Hillel.

"Sorry," Betsy said. "About what?"

Mark laughed and got out of the car without telling her what she was supposed to have an opinion about. She was going to have to do a better job at focusing on what Mark was saying. She was usually so interested in the things he talked about—politics and religion and history—but tonight, nothing could get her mind off this mystery gift. Once she opened whatever it was, she wouldn't have to pretend to be present.

Although she did wonder why he had to give her the gift at his apartment. Surely a jewelry box would be small enough that he could tuck it in his pocket.

"Why don't we just pick it up and I can open it at the restaurant?" Betsy suggested as Mark opened her car door. She usually shied away from attention, but the idea of people watching her open a present from her boyfriend made the whole thing feel more like the momentous occasion it was.

"It wouldn't fit under the table," Mark said.

Betsy paused before walking up the steps to his second-floor apartment. She couldn't imagine a gift that would be that big.

Mark smiled as he unlocked the front door, looking almost as excited as Betsy had been at the start of the evening. Inside, he nodded toward the living room, where a giant box was wrapped in balloon-covered wrapping paper.

"What did you do?" Betsy asked through a nervous smile.

The box was way too big to hold a tiny piece of jewelry. But maybe he was teasing her, and this box would lead to a smaller one, which would lead to a smaller one, until she got to one that would fit in the palm of her hand like those Russian nesting dolls.

"Go ahead," he said. "Open it."

Betsy heard herself squeal as she rushed toward the box. She slowly peeled away the tape, being careful not to rip the paper. She went slowly, wanting to savor this moment and remember every detail so she could tell Sissy all about it the next morning.

Behind her, Mark laughed. She gave him a smile, then turned back to her gift. The last bit of wrapping paper fell away, revealing an ordinary brown box. She opened the lid, prepared to see a second box, maybe even wrapped with a different kind of wrapping paper.

But there wasn't a second box inside. There was a big blue roll of fabric.

She looked back at Mark, confused. The slight frown on her face was in direct contrast to the huge grin on his.

"Do you like it?"

"What is it?" Betsy asked, trying not to sound ungrateful.

"It's a sleeping bag," he said, clapping his hands together like a little boy who had just gotten a shiny new toy truck.

"But, why?" Betsy asked. She wasn't trying to be rude; she was just terribly confused and inexplicably sad. She'd been so foolish to think about necklaces and bracelets, to put all of her hopes in a silly gift. Her eyes filled with a rush of tears.

"I thought we could go camping together," Mark said. His smile was still big and bright, unlike Betsy's, whose was falling more and more by the second.

"But I don't like camping," Betsy said, her voice barely above a whisper. They had talked about this, on more than one occasion. Whenever Mark brought up camping together, Betsy had told him that she didn't like the idea of sleeping or going to the bathroom outdoors like an animal. "This is a gift for you," she said.

"No, I've got one of my own. This is a sleeping bag for you," Mark insisted, his smile faltering. "Wait— Betsy, sweetheart. What's wrong? I thought you'd like it."

Betsy wiped her eyes and turned away so Mark wouldn't see how hurt she was. She told herself she ought to be grateful that he had gotten her a gift at all. She should just smile and tell him it was the thought that counted—but the thought *did* count, and his thought had been all wrong. Either he had disregarded her feelings, or he hadn't been listening to her.

That was what hurt the most, what caused the tears that were now freely falling. After almost a whole year together, Mark didn't even know her.

Betsy's stomach turned as she realized she'd been all wrong. She had been settling, and now it was obvious that she and Mark weren't right for each other.

If he wanted a girl to take camping, he needed someone else. And Betsy needed someone who saw her for the woman she was, not the woman they wanted her to be.

With a sinking feeling in her stomach, Betsy knew she had to end things. It wouldn't be fair to either of them to pretend they had a future together.

She thought of what Sissy might say if she were here, that it was about time. That Betsy should stop wasting the best years of her life with a guy whose punny jokes she didn't find that funny and whose kisses didn't make her toes tingle with desire.

"Bets?" Mark rested a hand on her shoulder, but she flinched away from his touch.

"I don't feel well," she said.

"Do you want some water?" He looked so concerned that Betsy almost considered giving him another chance. But then the sleeping bag caught her eye, and she felt the fury rise up again.

Betsy shook her head. "I think I just need to go home."

"Maybe if you lay down for a bit?"

"I said I want to go home," Betsy snapped. The sound of her voice scared her, taking her back to a place she never wanted to return.

Betsy could hear her mother's tone in her words, and she realized she'd had it all wrong.

She had been so focused on not being like her mother with a line of men rotating in and out of her bed that she missed the fact that she had already turned into her. Sad and alone, using men—in her case, one man—to desperately try to fill the void inside. A void, she feared, that would be impossible to fill.

BETSY DIDN'T SAY a word the entire car ride back to the Sigma Delta Tau house. She just sat in the front seat and crossed her arms over her lap, staring at the road ahead. All of her energy was focused on holding back her tears. She didn't want Mark to see her cry.

When he pulled up in front of the house, Betsy opened the door and climbed out before he could open it for her. She didn't want to look at the sad and confused expression on his face. The idea of explaining to him how much it hurt her to realize that he didn't know or understand her was too much to bear. And it wouldn't make a difference. As far as she was concerned, it was too late. They were over.

"Bets," Mark called after her.

She shook her head and let herself inside without saying a word. The TV was blaring in the living room, and Betsy stood there a moment with her back against the door as she heard Ali MacGraw tell Ryan O'Neal that love meant never having to say you were sorry.

Betsy caught a sob in her throat. She didn't want the girls to see her cry. She couldn't handle seeing their sad faces when she told them things with Mark were over. Especially not after they had all seen her acting so excited—so naive—as Sissy helped her get ready for what was supposed to have been such a special night.

She cupped her hand over her mouth to silence her cry as she rushed up the stairs to the second floor. She flung open the door to the bedroom she shared with Sissy, grateful that the room was empty. Betsy collapsed on her bed and let nineteen years' worth of tears pour out. Tears for the birthdays she had pretended not to care about, and the future ones she now imagined would be just as bleak.

Betsy knew she should pull herself together and stop being so melodramatic. It was just a sleeping bag, and she was used to her birthday being a disappointment. But Mark had gotten her so excited, and it wasn't really just a sleeping bag. It was a symbol, proof that she had spent almost a year of her life with someone who hadn't bothered to listen to the things she had to say, who hadn't cared enough to truly get to know her.

As the tears fell, Betsy's shoulders shook. She felt her nose running but didn't care enough to wipe it. She should have listened to Sissy. Her best friend, it turned out, could see what Betsy hadn't. Not until tonight.

Looking back, Betsy wondered if she had ever been in love with Mark or if she'd just been in love with the idea of being in love. Of having someone be in love with her. Sure, Mark was someone. But he clearly wasn't *her* someone. Her someone would know her, inside and out.

Betsy had wasted the last year of her life on a relationship that was going nowhere. And college was almost halfway over. She was running out of time, a thought that brought on a flood of new tears.

"Forgot something!" Betsy heard a familiar voice call from the hallway. "Be ready in a second!"

It was Sissy. On her way to their room.

Chapter Eighteen

Then

ANDY FOUND COMFORT IN THE RHYTHM OF HIS FEET POUNDING the pavement, keeping a steady pace through the streets of campus. The campanile chimed as he ran past the bell tower, downhill toward the football stadium, which was empty thanks to it being a bye week, then right toward Potter Lake.

He didn't run because he was good at it; he didn't do it to be fast. He ran because it helped clear his mind, allowing his worries to fade away. Letting himself forget about the note Lawson left for him at the house. "Stopped by to chat," the note had read.

Sure, his fraternity brother could have stopped by to give him notes from the classes he'd missed this past week. But Andy knew that wasn't what Lawson wanted to talk about.

He pushed himself to run faster, leaving thoughts of the mess his life had become in his dust.

When his muscles started to burn, Andy slowed to a stop. He bent over to catch his breath, and it was only when he stood back up that he realized he was standing at the corner of William's street.

His pulse started to quicken again, and he tried to calm himself, slowly breathing in and out.

Andy knew he couldn't just stand there doing nothing like a lost fool, so he started to stretch. He twisted his body and brought his left arm across his chest, trying to decide whether fate or habit had brought him here. And what he wanted to do about it.

Of course Andy wanted to see William more than he wanted anything, but it would crush his soul if William refused to see him. Still, Andy knew he had to try. Especially if his gut feeling was right and he was going to be outed soon.

Once the truth was out, Andy would no longer be welcome in his fraternity. He would be brotherless and homeless. He'd probably be kicked off the football team, too. And without a scholarship, he'd have to leave college and go home—if his parents would even take him back, which he knew was unlikely.

The only bright spot was that if he lost everything, there would be nothing left to come between him and William. As long as Andy could convince him to be patient a little longer, to give their relationship another chance. He had to try.

Andy started to jog down the street, toward the square, brown, nondescript building where William rented a studio apartment on the third floor.

The buzzer had been broken for two months, so someone had folded an old pizza box under the door to keep it from locking. Andy had worried about William's safety, knowing anyone could simply walk into the building. But that day, he was grateful to have one less hurdle.

Andy let himself in and ran up the first flight of stairs, pausing before the second to collect himself and his breath. He took the last flight one step at a time, torn between anticipation and dread.

He stood in front of apartment 3C and raised his hand to knock, tentatively at first. After a few torturously long seconds, he knocked again. This time, louder and with purpose, committing to his decision no matter how flawed.

The door flew open, and William stared at him with unfocused eyes. Andy couldn't tell if he was half-asleep or high. Maybe both. William's lips were set in a straight line, neither a smile nor a frown.

Andy's eyes trailed down William's bare chest to the thin line of hair that disappeared beneath his flannel pants. He looked back up to William's face, trying to find forgiveness in his eyes.

"I . . . " Andy started, but he didn't know what else to say. He hadn't thought past what would happen once William opened the door. He didn't know what he'd been thinking, showing up like this. "I," he said again.

Andy looked down at the stained carpet in the hallway, a cacophony of colors from decades' worth of spilled messes that had never been cleaned up.

He soaked in every detail in case this was the last time he stood at this threshold. Andy couldn't believe he was being sentimental about such a filthy place, but he ached for the person who was inside it, and the person he was inside those four dirty walls.

Just like that, Andy knew what he had to say. He looked up at William, but before he could deliver the apology from his heart, William's hands were clenching Andy's sweat-soaked shirt, pulling him inside. He slammed the door closed with more force than necessary and backed Andy up against the wall.

Andy opened his mouth to speak, but William's lips were already on his. William's hands were under his shirt, kneading his back. William briefly broke the kiss to slip Andy's shirt over his head.

Before his shirt even hit the floor, Andy closed the distance between them, hungry for those lips, for the man he thought he'd lost forever. William's tongue tasted like wine, and Andy felt drunk with pleasure. He pushed off the wall, and they stumbled together toward the mattress on the floor.

AFTERWARD, ANDY LAY on his back, looking up at the ceiling. He stared at the brown stain that looked like a rotten apple and smiled, relieved that things with William were going to be okay. As long as Andy had William, he'd be able to face whatever was waiting for him back at the house. He'd be strong enough to go back to math class, inspired enough to paint again.

William, he realized, was his muse. The word fit him perfectly—more important than a partner, more intimate than a lover. He was the one who had unlocked Andy, opening his heart and his eyes to the artist, the person he could be. Andy smiled and looked over at him, his muse. William was facing the wall, his back toward Andy.

More relaxed than he'd been all week, Andy slipped an arm around William's waist and curled up against him. Andy wished they could lie together all night, but he knew he wouldn't be able to come up with a reason for his unexpected absence if he stayed.

"I better get going," Andy said. "I need to show my face at the party, but I'll be back before you know it."

He felt William tense in his arms.

"If you leave, don't bother coming back," William said, his voice cold and distant.

"I'll just be gone an hour," Andy said. "Maybe less. Thirty minutes? You won't even miss me."

William's silence said more than any words could, and Andy knew it wasn't worth pressing his luck, not when he'd just gotten

William back. The party would be crowded, and people would be drunk. He could say he'd been there, even if no one remembered seeing him.

"You know what?" Andy said, leaning down to lay a kiss on William's shoulder. "It's just a dumb party. I can stay right here with you."

"Get. Out," William said.

"But we just . . . I thought we . . ."

"It was just sex," William said, still facing the wall. "That's what you came here for, wasn't it? A quick fuck before you go back to your fucking fraternity brothers and the slutty girls you tease and take out on your stupid fucking dates?"

"No, I—" Andy didn't know what to say. "I just told you I'd stay."

"You're just like them," William spat. "Fucking breeder."

"I am not a breeder," Andy said. "That's not what I want. I want you." He wished his voice didn't sound so shaky. He knew it made him sound unsure, but he was more sure than he'd ever been about anything. He didn't want to be a coward anymore. He wanted this life and whatever it looked like, as long as he was with William. He didn't just want William; he *needed* him. They needed each other.

"Look at me," Andy pleaded. "I just need time. I'm not as brave as you are."

William didn't answer, and he didn't move.

Andy sat up on the thin mattress, trying to put a name to the sensation he felt building up from the pit of his stomach. It wasn't fear, and it certainly wasn't love. It was rage.

He was angry that William had opened his arms just to push him away again. He was furious that William couldn't forgive him, that he wouldn't understand that Andy was only doing what he needed to survive.

As soon as Andy graduated, as soon as he was on his own, he would be and do anything William wanted. He wasn't asking for forever; he was just asking for a little patience. If William couldn't give him that, then maybe Andy had been wrong about how true their love was.

Andy stood in a rush and found his boxers in the tangled pile of sheets. He slipped them and his running shorts back on and looked down at William. The man he thought was so strong and unbreakable was lying in a broken heap on the floor.

"Call me if you decide to grow a heart," Andy said before turning to walk out the door for what he knew would be the last time.

Chapter Nineteen

Then

JUST HAVE TO GRAB MY LIPSTICK!" BETSY HEARD SISSY YELL.
She was getting closer to their room by the second.

There was no way Betsy would be able to hide the fact she'd been crying, but maybe she could pretend to be asleep. If she could just avoid talking about what happened until the morning, she'd be able to make something up about coming home sick; she could say something she'd eaten hadn't agreed with her.

Sissy was never one for details, so maybe she wouldn't realize it had only been an hour—that Betsy couldn't possibly have gone to a restaurant with Mark, gotten back, and already fallen asleep.

She could hear Sissy's steps in the hallway and quickly pulled the covers around her. Betsy turned her face toward the wall just as Sissy opened the door. She could feel her heart pounding wildly in her chest, but she tried to slow her breathing to a sleep-like state. She wanted to make it look as authentic as possible, but she had no clue what she looked like when she was asleep. She didn't think she snored but couldn't know for sure.

The heavy door slammed behind Sissy, a sound that normally would have woken Betsy, a relatively light sleeper. But she couldn't worry about being that authentic since it would defeat the whole purpose.

She could only hope that Sissy would be so caught up in the rush of getting ready for the party that she wouldn't notice Betsy lying still beneath the covers. Maybe she would—

"Bets?" Betsy felt the mattress shift as Sissy sat down. "Are you okay?"

Sissy gently rubbed Betsy's back as she spoke, mimicking the soft tone and touch she likely gleaned from all the years of being comforted by her mother.

Instead of making her feel better, the tender gesture only reminded Betsy that she'd never experienced that kind of maternal love before. Betsy squeezed her eyes shut tighter and tried to keep her breaths steady, but she could feel the bed shaking beneath her with the force of her quiet sobs.

"Bets," Sissy said again. "What happened?"

"Sissy!" one of their sorority sisters yelled up the stairs. "You coming or what?"

Betsy felt the mattress shift again as Sissy got up and opened their bedroom door. "Go ahead without me!" she yelled back. "I'll meet you there."

"No." Betsy's voice was muffled by the pillow, so she turned her head and said it again. She wasn't going to let her heartache ruin Sissy's night, too.

"What's that?" Sissy asked, back in her nurturing voice.

"Go," Betsy said between sobs. "Don't miss the party on my account."

"I'm not going anywhere," Sissy said. "Especially not until you tell me what happened."

Sissy placed a hand on Betsy's shoulder and attempted to get her friend to turn and look at her, but Betsy knew she would crumble at the sight of Sissy's worried eyes.

"I don't want to talk about it," Betsy said, brushing away the stubborn tears that refused to stop falling. "You should go."

Sissy sat still for a moment, and Betsy didn't have to see her friend to know she was tilting her head with a finger resting thoughtfully on her chin, playing through the options of the best thing to say or do. But Betsy knew there were no good options, nothing could help her feel better.

The phone in the hallway rang once, twice, three times before someone answered it.

"Betsy!" someone called from downstairs. "It's Mark for you."

A new set of tears stung her eyes, this time from embarrassment. Now everyone would know she was home, not with Mark on the romantic birthday date that she should have never mentioned in the first place. Now she'd have to add utter humiliation to her list of troubles.

"I don't want to talk to him," Betsy whimpered into her pillow.

"It's okay," Sissy said. "You don't have to."

Sissy got up and walked out into the hallway, where she picked up the house phone.

"I've got it," Sissy called down. There were a few beats of silence as Sissy waited to make sure the line downstairs had been hung up. Her voice was firm and resolute as she spoke. "She doesn't want to talk to you."

Betsy heard the crash of the receiver against the phone cradle as her best friend hung up on what she supposed was now her ex-boyfriend.

"I got rid of him," Sissy said as she walked back into the room. "Now sit up and tell me what happened."

There was an edge to Sissy's voice that hadn't been there before, and Betsy realized the longer she held out, the longer she would be keeping Sissy from the party. Betsy knew her best friend would eventually get the story out of her, so she might as well get it over with.

Betsy took a deep breath and sat up, keeping her eyes on the paisley pattern of her comforter. The comforter had been a gift from Sissy's mother, so the two girls could have matching bedding. And probably because Mrs. Goldberg knew that Betsy's own mom wouldn't think or care enough to take her daughter shopping for school.

After a moment, Betsy looked up at Sissy, whose face fell at the sight of her. Sissy handed Betsy a tissue from the nightstand, which Betsy used to dab the corners of her eyes, which were probably streaked with remnants of mascara. She hoped she hadn't ruined her beautiful pillowcase.

"What happened?" Sissy asked, resting her hand on Betsy's knee.

The tears started again, but Betsy managed to get the story out—from her naive hope for a gift of jewelry to her visceral reaction when she saw what was in the giant box.

"It's not about the sleeping bag," Betsy admitted.

"Of course it's about the sleeping bag," Sissy said. "You told him no both times he asked you to go camping with him."

Betsy nodded, grateful to have Sissy's support. "It just—it feels like he should have known that after almost a whole year together. I wasted all that time on him."

"Good riddance," Sissy said. "He was a boring excuse of a boy-friend anyway."

Betsy narrowed her eyes, a reflex from all the times she'd had to defend Mark.

"I never told you this," Sissy said, "but I wasn't the biggest fan of his."

Betsy laughed. "That was hardly a secret."

Sissy shrugged and took a cigarette out of her purse, twirling it around her fingers since she knew Betsy didn't like it when she smoked in their room. "Would you rather I lie?"

Betsy shook her head.

"You could have done worse for a first boyfriend," Sissy admitted. "He was decent-looking, just lacking a little in the personality department. Was he at least good in bed?"

Betsy felt her cheeks blushing. It was one thing listening to Sissy go on and on about her conquests, but Betsy preferred to keep private things private. But it was just Sissy, and it wasn't like she had to protect Mark anymore. So, Betsy shook her head no, hoping Sissy wouldn't press for more details.

"I figured," she said. "Although you'd be surprised to know that some of the most boring people are actually freaks between the sheets."

"Not Mark," Betsy said. The tears, she hoped, were over, having dried and left salty tracks on her cheeks. She dabbed her eyes again with the crumbled tissue. "I must look like a mess."

"I've seen you look better," Sissy admitted. "But that dress is still killer. You should come with me."

"No way." Betsy shook her head and tucked the comforter tighter around herself to make her point.

But Sissy had her own point to make. She stood and put a hand on her hip in a pose Betsy assumed was trying to be intimidating. "Don't tell me you'd rather sit around here and mope all night."

"What if I would?" Betsy asked.

Sissy huffed in frustration. "You're single now, and you're supposed to be celebrating your birthday tonight."

"I'm not in much of a celebrating mood."

"Not yet, you aren't," Sissy said. She tilted her head and rested her finger on her chin. "Come to the AEPi party with me for an hour. One drink, one dance, and if you aren't having fun, we can come back home."

"I really don't want to," Betsy said.

Sissy frowned, and Betsy knew that she had won this battle. She smiled to herself in victory, looking forward to a night alone in her bed, maybe with a book.

"Okay," Sissy said, slipping out of her party shoes. "If you're not going, neither am I."

Betsy sighed. One downside of having a friend who was more like a sister was how well Sissy knew her. And Sissy knew there was no chance Betsy would let her bad mood ruin Sissy's night.

"Fine," Betsy conceded with a sigh. "But you're going to have to fix my face first."

"Happy to," Sissy said brightly, helping Betsy out of bed.

Betsy's face fell at the sight of her reflection in the mirror. Her dress was wrinkled, looking as out of sorts as her face and her hair.

"I have a steamer," Sissy assured her. "Now let's go make you beautiful again."

BY THE TIME Andy got back to the fraternity house, the party was in full swing. No one, it seemed, had been aware of his absence, and he was able to slip upstairs unnoticed.

He grabbed a towel from his room and headed straight for the shower, where he stood, letting the hot water pound his back. He turned and lifted his face toward the showerhead, closing his eyes and opening his mouth, letting the hot water erase the taste of William from his lips.

Andy turned back around and reached for the soap, scrubbing his skin until it was red and raw. He wanted to wash away William's fingerprints and any remnants of their mingled sweat. He knew it wouldn't be easy to wash away the anger, the shame, or the hurt, but he was damn well going to try.

When the water turned cold, Andy turned off the shower, shivering and unsatisfied. Maybe this party was exactly what he needed. He could get mind-numbingly drunk and forget that the one beautiful thing in his life had tarnished along with the rest.

He wanted to be sad, but he was just so angry.

Andy walked down the empty hallway, back toward his room. It was too early in the evening for his brothers to be bringing girls upstairs, trying to beat their roommates to the punch so they could be the one to leave a tie on the door, calling dibs on the private space.

Andy didn't have a roommate. It wasn't common for a sophomore to get a single room, and at first, he worried it was because they suspected the truth about him. Then he realized it was a benefit to his position on the football team. Even though the team wasn't any good.

As the kicker on special teams, Andy's time on the field was directly related to how well the offense played, which meant he didn't get to play much. But Andy didn't complain. The amount of work he put in wasn't proportional to the benefits awarded him in and out of the house.

Back in his room, Andy took his time getting ready. He put Vitalis in his hair before it dried so his brown locks would fall in just the right way without getting frizzy. He slipped into his favorite jeans, trying to forget that they were William's favorite, too. He chose an orange shirt and light plaid jacket that girls always seemed to like. He laughed at how obvious they could be, touching his lapel or trying to adjust his collar when he knew it was already perfectly straight.

A defiant spritz of the cologne he'd stopped wearing because William was allergic, and Andy was ready to go. He studied his reflection in the mirror, satisfied that he looked the part of a single guy looking for a girl to make the night a little less lonely.

Tonight, he would put on a performance worthy of an Academy Award. He would dance with any girl who looked his way. He would spin them around and maybe, if he drank enough, he would have the nerve to kiss one—right on the dance floor, where everyone could see. Lawson would have a hard time getting others to believe his suspicions after that.

As Andy made his way down the stairs, he surveyed the room and tried to ignore the hollow feeling in the pit of his stomach. He should have taken a swig of the whiskey he kept under his bed to give him a head start. He usually needed a drink or two before he could start to flirt back with the girls who made eyes at him.

Andy stopped at the landing to straighten his jacket when he saw her walk in. Mark Meyer's girlfriend. Her sad eyes looked even sadder tonight, but she smiled at him in recognition as Sissy dragged her toward the kitchen.

Sissy hadn't seen him, and Andy wasn't sure if that was unfortunate or lucky. That girl was a lot, but he knew she'd be game to help him put on a show. It could help that there were already rumors about the two of them. And based on her reputation around the house, the odds were pretty good that she was just looking for a good time. He wouldn't have to worry about feelings getting involved.

That was the biggest thing holding Andy back—other than the fact he wasn't attracted to women, he knew it wasn't fair to play with people's emotions.

Andy took the last few steps down and smiled at a girl he didn't recognize before making his way to the kitchen through the living room so he wouldn't have to bump into Sissy quite yet. He needed a few drinks before he was ready for that hurricane.

At the memory of how forceful Sissy had been the other night, almost aggressive, Andy second-guessed his decision. He had a feeling it would be nearly impossible to get Sissy to stop once they started going. And if any of the brothers saw him resisting a sure thing, it would only help prove Lawson's suspicions. He'd be better off playing it safe with someone new tonight.

Andy was surveying the room for available girls and not paying attention as he turned the corner into the kitchen, bumping right into Jared. Beer sloshed out of Jared's cup, leaving a burnt-orange puddle in the middle of Andy's shirt. He cringed, knowing he'd have to resist the urge to go upstairs and change.

"Hey, man," Jared said, hooking his arm around his girlfriend's shoulder. "We've got to stop running into each other like this. I told you, you're not my type."

Andy laughed and tried to play it off like the joke it was meant to be, until he realized Lawson was standing right behind Jared. They hadn't seen each other since the incident on Monday morning. Andy started to take a step back but stopped himself. He had to play it cool in case his suspicions had been wrong and Lawson hadn't figured out his truth.

"Lawson," Andy said, giving his younger fraternity brother a smile. Lawson nodded curtly in response before moving past him, back toward the living room. *Shit*.

With the sinking feeling back in his stomach, Andy glanced behind him in time to see Lawson whispering something in Jared's ear. He watched, as if in slow motion, as Jared turned and looked back toward Andy. The expression on Jared's face was burned into his mind so clearly he could paint it. It was a look of disgust.

Andy filled his cup with beer, downing it in one gulp before filling it back up again. He knocked the second one back and did the same with two more before he felt calm enough to go back to the main room.

If he was going to go down, he might as well go down drunk. Who cared anymore? He didn't. He couldn't. He didn't have any feelings left.

Chapter Twenty

Now

B ABE?" JEFF CALLS FROM THE KITCHEN.
"Mmm," I answer from the warm cocoon of our bed. In my world, Saturday mornings are made for sleeping in. Jeff, on the other hand, lives on a planet where time spent sleeping is wasted time you could be up and living life.

Since moving in together, we've learned to compromise—he wakes up early and I sleep in. Not much of a compromise, I know, but I really like my sleep. And last night was Jeff's first night back home since this whole mess began. We stayed up until almost two in the morning with one too many bottles of wine, going over all the facts and possible outcomes, debating whether the no-contact-after-three-days rule of online dating was also true when it came to reaching out to one's DNA Dad.

I had a feeling it was, and I was slowly coming to terms with the fact that I would not be hearing back from Andrew Abrams. I was disappointed, of course, but part of me was a little relieved that I wouldn't have to worry about anyone trying to replace my dad.

"Breakfast is almost ready," he says, leaning against the open bedroom door.

"I can't hear you," I say, turning back into my pillow.

I don't have to see him to know he's smiling at me. One of the many things I love about Jeff is that he knows my games but plays them anyway. I slide over to make room for him on my side of the bed.

Even though the mattress doesn't move, I sense him sitting beside me. "Breakfast," he whispers, leaning so close his breath tickles my ear, "is almost ready."

"What was that?" I tease.

"I've got eggs scrambling," he says in a voice too slow and seductive for the words he's saying. "Bagels toasting and bacon . . . baking?"

"That sounds good," I say, rolling onto my side to face him. "But you know what sounds even better?" I raise an eyebrow and try to keep the corner of my mouth from lifting into a smile.

"What?" Jeff asks, even though he already knows. He tucks a wild strand of hair behind my ear, and I roll with his touch, pulling him closer.

"You." I kiss his neck, the stubble of a few days' growth rough on my skin. I move to his lips, and he's almost a lost cause.

"But breakfast," he says between kisses.

"Breakfast can wait." I lift the covers for him to climb inside. This is my kind of compromise. "We can work up an appetite."

"Less talking," he says, nuzzling my neck. His hands slip under my tank top as I slide his pajama pants down over his hips. He props himself above me. I look up into his blue-gray eyes and remember why I'm willing to put up with all this wedding crap. It's worth it, if I get to spend forever with him.

"I can't wait to marry you," I tell him. I can feel how excited he is, so I reach for him.

Knock, knock.

He hears it, too.

"Are you expecting someone?" he asks.

I shake my head no and run my hands over his broad back, feeling his muscles contract under my touch. "Wrong apartment?" I guess. "They'll go away."

I arch my back, closing the distance between us when we both hear it again. Louder, more insistent this time.

Knock, knock, knock.

He looks at me, his eyes giving me permission to ignore our would-be intruder.

Knock, knock.

You've got to be kidding me.

I slide out from underneath him and reach for my robe. "You've got the wrong apartment," I say as I yank open the door, prepared to unleash my pent-up frustration on our uninvited visitor.

"Darling," Aunt Sissy says, walking past me and into the living room.

"Aunt Sissy," I say, loud enough for Jeff to hear. "Babe, Aunt Sissy's here."

"Hi, Sissy," Jeff calls from the bedroom.

"Not that I'm not happy to see you," I say, "but what are you doing here?"

"I'm here to see my favorite girl, of course." She peers over the island that separates our kitchen from our living room. "Your bagels are burned."

"We got distracted." I tighten the belt of my robe and look away so she doesn't see me blush. I know I don't have anything to be ashamed of—I'm a grown woman, an engaged woman—and besides, who doesn't call before coming over? "How did you get up here? The front desk didn't call."

"I have my ways," she says, batting her eyes.

"Good morning," Jeff says as he comes out of the bedroom, redressed in his plaid pajama pants and my favorite gray shirt of his that's just the right amount of worn. "What brings you to Chicago?"

"I came to have a heart-to-heart with my best girl," she says, glancing at me. She looks almost nervous, which is not a trait I would associate with my mom's lively best friend.

Suddenly I understand.

Sissy might look innocent and cute with her petite frame and perfectly coifed blond hair, but she can be ferocious when it comes to protecting my mother. It figures Mom would send Sissy to do her dirty work, to have yet another conversation she can't handle.

My heart races, and I don't know whether to be relieved or terrified. This is what I wanted: answers. They aren't coming from the person I wanted them from, but I can't afford to be picky. I also can't unknow the truth once it's out there.

"We need to talk," Sissy says, and this time her tone is firm, her resolve absolute.

I look back toward Jeff, but he's disappeared into our room. Moments later, he's back, fully dressed, wearing jeans and sneakers.

"Where are you going?" I ask, my voice cracking with concern. He can't leave me alone with her; she's like a well-groomed pit bull.

"Just going to walk the dog," he says, giving me a kiss on his way out.

"We don't have a dog!" I call after him. Damn Jeff for being supportive and giving me space.

"Love you," he says before closing the door, leaving me alone with Aunt Sissy and the conversation I've been both dreading and hoping for.

"Can I at least get dressed first?" I ask.

Sissy smiles and nods, as if this were all part of her plan.

"Make yourself at home," I tell her as I walk back into the bedroom. I glance at our unmade bed, the sheets that would have been more rumpled if we hadn't been interrupted.

I trade my robe for yoga pants and one of Jeff's old T-shirts and pull my unruly hair into a messy bun. Before I go back out there, I send Jeff a text: Not cool.

Aunt Sissy is sitting on the couch with her legs crossed, displaying the perfect posture I used to try to imitate when I was a kid. She looks like she's waiting for a meeting with the Queen. I should have put on a nicer shirt.

She pats the seat beside her, inviting me to sit down on my own couch. I do, of course, folding my legs beneath me. I feel like my fourteen-year-old self, the one who knocked on Sissy's door almost thirty years ago, wanting to run away from the terrible-two-year-old twins who had taken over my house and my life.

"Did she send you?" I ask.

Aunt Sissy purses her lips, making a face I know all too well. Her allegiance to me doesn't run as deep as it does to my mother.

The sun is shining through the windows, highlighting every speck of dust on the furniture and the floor. I should close the blinds; it's too bright in here.

I look out the window at the apartment building across the street. If someone over there is looking in here, I wonder what they'll see. A woman about to have her world knocked off its axis.

"I want to tell you a story," Aunt Sissy says.

Chapter Twenty-One

Then

A S THE TAXI PULLED UP IN FRONT OF THE AEPI HOUSE, BETSY felt a combination of nerves and excitement for the night ahead. It was almost like getting a do-over, a completely different evening than the one she'd been planning on with the person she was trying not to think about.

Sissy was halfway up the sidewalk before Betsy even closed the taxi's door. She felt bad for making Sissy even later than she'd planned to be. Betsy had been to a few fraternity parties freshman year before she met Mark, but even back then, she didn't feel like she belonged there. Not like Sissy did.

Betsy hurried to where her best friend was not-so-patiently waiting and decided that tonight, she was going to pretend to be more like a normal sorority girl. She would act confident, carefree, and cool. Like she had a wild streak that couldn't be tamed, a charming sense of humor, and eyes that could seduce with one come-hither look. Tonight, she would pretend to be Sissy.

It shouldn't be hard to do; she knew her best friend almost as well as she knew herself. And if she was being honest, being Sissy would probably be easier than being herself. It would certainly be more fun.

She followed Sissy through the open door where the party was in full swing, as it should be since it had started almost three hours earlier. It was almost eleven o'clock—if Betsy had stuck with her original plans, she would be standing by what had become her side of Mark's bed, unceremoniously stepping out of her pretty party dress.

But she was here. And as she crossed the threshold into the crowded entryway, Betsy forced away her lingering sadness and focused on the excitement and glimmer of possibility. Her transformation was almost complete.

As if it were a sign she'd made the right decision, the first person Betsy locked eyes with was none other than Andy Abrams. Her stomach fluttered with the memory of their brief handshake the other night, the two of them palm-to-palm. She smiled, then looked away in embarrassment. They'd met so briefly, he probably didn't even remember her.

"Where's the keg?" Betsy asked, surprising Sissy, who probably expected her to act like a wet blanket or a wallflower.

Sissy's smile lit up her face. She grabbed Betsy's hand and led her deeper inside the fraternity house, toward the kitchen and the promise of beer. This was going to be a good night for them both.

Betsy pushed thoughts of Mark firmly out of her mind as a cute boy pumped the lever of the keg before handing her a plastic cup, thick with foam at the top.

She took a timid sip before remembering she was supposed to be acting more like Sissy. She raised the glass a little higher and tilted her head back. The bubbles tickled her throat, but she kept going until the glass was almost empty.

Betsy wiped her lips with the back of her hand. A tiny burp escaped her mouth, but instead of looking disgusted like he ought to be, the boy pumping the keg looked impressed.

"Ready for another?" he asked.

Betsy nodded and handed her cup over for a refill. She smiled at Sissy, who was watching the scene play out with fascination, before leading the way back toward the main party room.

The beer was already going to Betsy's head, and she kind of liked it. Her limbs were loose, and her head felt like it might float away at any moment, like a balloon tethered to her neck.

She closed her eyes and moved to the left and the right, back and forth, trying to keep in rhythm with the beat. She felt almost like she was part of the music, her body just another instrument in the band.

The song changed to another, and she changed her rhythm right along with it. She'd missed dancing. Mark wasn't exactly a let-loose-and-dance kind of guy. She decided then and there that she liked fraternity parties and would start attending more of them.

Betsy's eyes flew open as someone grabbed her hand and pulled her onto the makeshift dance floor.

The guy—she thought his name might be Bobby—was dancing a little too close. His hands were roaming a little too freely, moving up and down her back, resting occasionally on her hips before taking off again.

Betsy put her arms around his neck but regretted it almost instantly. The boy took it as an invitation to move even closer. She could feel his hot breath on her neck as he started grinding his body against hers, thrusting as if they were having sex right there on the dance floor.

Betsy dropped her hands; this wasn't what she wanted.

"I'm sorry," she said, rushing away from the sweaty boy, away from the dance floor. The room seemed to be swaying a bit, and she couldn't find the exit through all the people.

Dancing was too much—she wasn't ready for that yet. But she was definitely ready for another drink.

ANDY WAS RIGHT on the edge of the good kind of drunk. He'd stop drinking soon so he could keep his wits about him. It wasn't a good idea to completely lose control in this company.

He refilled his cup from the keg and walked back into the living room, which had been transformed into a dance floor.

Sissy, he noticed, was performing some kind of sexual dance act on one of his fraternity brothers. The kid looked like he was a few degrees away from ecstasy; his eyes were wide, and it was obvious he didn't know what to do with his hands.

Andy smiled at him, then at Evelyn Green, who looked like she would rather be having a root canal than dancing with Tiny Blumberg. Poor girl, maybe he should cut in.

Across the room, Andy noticed Lawson huddled in a corner, talking to two guys who lived in the house. They all turned to stare at him, and Andy felt the energy of the room shift.

He tried to take a casual sip of beer but missed his mouth, and the cold liquid dribbled down his chin. He wiped it away, then turned to leave when he saw Jared and a group of three other brothers looking at him with their eyes narrowed, an expression of dismay tinged with disappointment written all over their faces.

Andy turned again, realizing his only way out was through the dance floor. He downed the rest of his beer, dropping the empty cup on the ground before trying to disappear into the crowd, jostling people in various stages of rhythmic groping as he went.

Andy's pulse quickened, and he could feel sweat starting to drip down his forehead. This wasn't his imagination. Everyone was staring at him. They all knew. He needed a plan, but he couldn't think straight. He needed to calm down; he needed another drink.

There wasn't a line for the keg, so he walked right up and pumped the lever harder than he needed to, but it felt good. The physical exertion gave him a place to focus his nervous energy.

"Keg's tapped," Eric Freedman said. "There are a few six packs in the fridge, though."

"Thanks," Andy muttered. He let go of the lever just as Mark Meyer's girlfriend walked into the kitchen. She smiled, and Andy noticed again how pretty she was. A natural kind of pretty, not forced and fake like a lot of the other girls. He would like to draw her, he decided. If he ever felt inspired to bring pen to paper again.

"Betty, right?"

"Betsy," she said, correcting him.

"That's right, Betsy." He liked that name; it suited her. She smiled at him and raised her eyebrows as she turned her empty cup over in her hand, clearly waiting for him to offer her another. "Keg's empty," he said.

Her face fell a little, and she looked disappointed, her sad eyes back. Andy liked it better when she smiled.

Behind her, two brothers were walking toward the kitchen. They stopped in their tracks when they saw Andy, as if they were surprised to see him still there if the rumors were true.

The room felt like it was getting smaller, the floor seemed to be on an incline, and everywhere he looked, people were staring at him. He needed to get out of there. His eyes landed on Betsy, beautifully there, right in front of him.

"I've got more in my room," he told her.

He watched as Betsy bit her lip, uncertain. She didn't seem like the kind of girl to go up to a guy's room at a frat party—she had a boyfriend, for Christ's sake. He clearly wasn't thinking.

Andy looked around for other girls he might be able to bring upstairs, but he didn't have the energy to talk to anyone else. He didn't want to talk to anyone else; there was something about this girl that intrigued him. He had a feeling he wouldn't have to pretend with her.

"Okay," she said, surprising Andy. "Let's go."

She gave him a sweet smile, then looked down at the empty keg for a brief second. When she looked back up, she seemed different. More confident.

Andy smiled and extended his hand. She took it and allowed him to lead her out of the kitchen. Andy felt more eyes on him as they walked back to the front hall. Jared Evans was standing in the entryway, looking right at them. Andy stopped abruptly, and Betsy bumped into him.

"I'll be right back," he said. "Just going to grab another cup."

BETSY COULDN'T BELIEVE her night was going so well. It hadn't been that long ago that she'd been fantasizing about a scenario that started a lot like this. She knew she shouldn't get ahead of herself— they were just going upstairs for another drink. *Upstairs to Andy Abrams's room.*

Betsy felt a tingling sensation in her belly. She leaned into the feeling, finally able to understand the appeal of drinking beer and going to fraternity parties. Sissy had been right about this, like she'd been right about Mark. Betsy had been missing out on an essential part of her college experience. But she wasn't now, not anymore.

Being Sissy was so much better than being herself. If she were acting like boring old Betsy, she'd be at home alone, crying herself to sleep instead of standing in the middle of a party, waiting for Andy Abrams.

She looked around the room at all the girls who would surely kill to trade places with her. And she was going to enjoy every moment of it before she had to go back to being herself.

Betsy wasn't naive enough to think she could have a real relationship with Andy—everyone knew he was the pickiest boy in AEPi. He'd gone on a few dates with most of the girls in her sorority, and while they all genuinely liked him, the feelings, it seemed, hadn't been reciprocated.

Now it was her turn. She was about to go up to Andy Abrams's room. For a drink. Maybe even a kiss or two. She wouldn't let things go too far—she was only pretending to be Sissy. Beneath the makeup and the hair and the pretty dress, she was still her responsible self, and she'd only been single for a few hours.

"Sorry," Andy said, joining her again. He put his arm around her shoulders, and Betsy smiled and walked beside him.

At the base of the stairs, Andy stopped. Betsy's smile faltered, worried she had accidentally broken character or done something to change his mind.

"Everything okay?" she asked.

"I just love this song," Andy said.

Betsy strained to hear it, but she couldn't recognize the lyrics through the muffled speakers.

"One dance first?" Andy asked.

Betsy happily agreed, and Andy set down their cups before leading her into the living room, where a slow song was playing. Bolder from the beer, Betsy didn't hesitate to hook her arms around Andy

Abrams's neck. She rested her cheek on his broad chest, swaying back and forth.

She was grateful Andy danced like a gentleman, not like the horny toad she'd danced with earlier. His hands felt solid on her waist, as big and strong as she'd imagined. She closed her eyes and sighed. It wasn't even officially her birthday yet, but it was already turning out to be a good one after all.

ANDY HAD ALWAYS enjoyed dancing. His mother had insisted that he learn when he was a teenager. There was nothing worse, she said, than a man who couldn't dance. She'd promised back then that the ladies would flock to him once they found out he could spin them around a dance floor. She'd been right—what little good it did him.

He appreciated the choreography—the give and take, gliding across a polished floor, counting the beats under his breath. Of course, there wasn't much use for that kind of dancing at a frat party. But with Betsy in his arms, the way she sighed so softly, he wished he could twirl her and make her pleated skirt spin around her. But guys his age weren't supposed to dance like that, so he just held her in his arms as they swayed back and forth.

Andy considered kissing her right then and there, but Betsy had a boyfriend, and he didn't want to risk scaring her away. Besides, he knew his brothers would be more impressed by Andy taking a girl upstairs than they would be by a chaste kiss on the dance floor.

When the song ended, Andy took a step to the side, so his arm was around Betsy's shoulder. "Ready?"

She nodded and smiled, leaning in closer to him. Andy hated himself for making a big show of leaving the room together, but Betsy didn't seem to mind.

As they turned the corner at the landing, Andy wondered if William had been right about him. If there was a deeper reason he hadn't been able to stop taking girls out.

If he was being honest with himself, Andy could picture a companionable life with a girl like Betsy. He wondered if he could go on pretending, if he could fully embrace the role he'd been playing most of his life. Not everyone had to have a great romantic love. A pretty girl with a sweet smile who smelled nice could be enough for him.

Maybe he should just try to see what would happen. Life would certainly be a lot easier if he could be attracted to women. If he could trick himself, his body, into loving a woman like Betsy, then maybe he'd be able to let the other part of himself go. Let William go.

"Nice room," Betsy said. "I didn't think the bedrooms in frat houses would be so clean."

She looked nervous, and Andy realized his plan had ignored one crucial factor: Betsy was in a relationship. She wasn't interested in him; she just wanted another drink.

Andy smiled and decided to enjoy the moment for what it was, an opportunity to get to know a sweet girl better while helping to dispel the rumors about himself. He grabbed a tie and, before closing the door, hung it around the doorknob. It wasn't necessary for privacy since the room was his alone, but it was necessary if he wanted his brothers to jump to the intended conclusion.

When Andy turned back around, Betsy was flipping through the book on his nightstand, a book he checked out from the library after William had made a joke about him being like Holden Caulfield.

"Have you read it?" Andy asked.

Betsy smiled and flipped to the front of the book where the names of everyone who had previously checked it out were listed. Betsy's name was written in at least half the spaces. "Once or twice," she said.

Setting the book back down, Betsy moved to inspect the canvases Andy kept stacked against the wall. He thought of it as his precoital collection, all the artwork he created in the studio while waiting, hoping, for William to make the first move.

Everything, all of his artwork and his creativity, was tied to that man. Andy realized with a sinking feeling that he owed William almost as much as he resented him.

"People talk about you," Betsy said coyly.

Andy felt the hair stand up on the back of his neck. "It's not true," he insisted.

"Oh, I think it is." Betsy lifted up the last painting from against the wall. The one he'd thought about getting rid of more than once. Or hiding, at the very least. It was a charcoal drawing of a nude figure, a man, from one of the first classes he'd taken.

"It's n-not what you think," Andy stammered. He'd been kidding himself to think he could make it through four years of college without people finding out who he really was.

His fraternity brothers were one thing—they didn't think that much about each other—but girls talked to and about each other and the boys they dated. Someone in the sorority had obviously figured out why none of them were "good enough" for Andy Abrams. They saw right through him, just like Lawson had.

"It's exactly what I think," Betsy said. "You're . . ." She hesitated, and Andy felt his face turn red as he prepared himself to hear the name, the label, he'd been hiding from. ". . . amazing."

"I'm what?" he asked, not sure he'd heard her correctly.

"You're amazing."

Andy looked down at Betsy, who was looking up at him. Her big brown eyes looked like they were hiding a secret, too. She broke his stare and glanced down at the drawing before meeting his eyes again.

"I mean, seriously. You're obviously talented," she said, nodding toward the canvases. She kept talking, her words tumbling out as if she'd been storing them up and they'd finally broken free. "You're smart and nice, all the girls say so, even Sissy, and you're athletic . . ." Her words trailed off, and Andy watched her eyes slide down to his chest.

"Please don't ask why a guy like me is still single."

"I won't," Betsy said. "As long as you don't ask why a girl like me would come up to a guy's room she barely knows."

Andy smiled. He hadn't expected Betsy to be so forward, so much like her best friend.

"For a drink, of course," he said, remembering the reason they'd come upstairs. "Whiskey okay?"

Betsy nodded. "I usually stick to wine or beer," she admitted. "But I'm up for trying anything."

Andy reached under his bed for the bottle of whiskey he kept for days when his mind was racing and needed help calming down. It was a little more than half-empty, or a little less than half-full, if he was looking on the bright side, which thanks to Betsy and all the beer, he might actually be doing.

He lifted the bottle toward Betsy, but her eyes were focused on something else—the sketchpad sticking out from under the bed.

"May I?" she asked, gesturing toward the book.

Andy hadn't let anyone, not even William, look inside. But there was something about Betsy that made him feel safe, so he nodded, giving her permission.

Andy felt his muscles tense as she sat down on his bed, slowly flipping through the pages. She didn't compliment each one, but she did tell him when and why she liked something.

Her favorite was his favorite, too. A young couple sitting on a campus bench, looking at each other. There was something intimate about the drawing, like he had captured the pull of attraction between them, in spite of their distance.

Andy watched her as she turned the pages with care, sitting on his bed as if it were the most natural thing in the world. He liked her being there, he realized. He liked her very much.

Betsy looked up at him and smiled. He smiled back, and they were just smiling at each other, until she finally spoke.

"Aren't you going to give me a drink?" she asked, nodding toward the bottle in his hand.

"Yeah, of course, sorry." He poured three fingers into both cups and handed one to Betsy.

"To new friends," she said.

"To new friends."

BETSY TOOK A small sip of the whiskey. It burned going down her throat, and she didn't care for the taste. Still, she took a second sip, and then a third. She looked up at Andy, leaning against the wall, looking handsome in an effortless way, like David Cassidy.

She took another sip. The taste was growing on her, and there was a warm feeling growing in her belly that she quite liked. Betsy looked back down at the sketchbook on her lap and turned to the next page.

This one was different from the rest—empty except for a few harsh lines. It felt raw and angry, incomplete. She looked up at Andy, about to ask for the story behind it, when she noticed his face seemed to close up. Flipping to the next page, she hoped his smile would return. But the following page, like his face, was blank.

Betsy wished Andy was as easy to read as Mark had been, but she also knew that mysteriousness was part of his appeal. She had a feeling there were depths to Andy Abrams that none of the other girls had managed to reach yet. Maybe she would be the one to unlock him.

"What are you going to draw on this one?" she asked, looking from the empty page back up to him.

Andy smiled before taking a slow sip of his whiskey. "It depends," he said. "I don't really plan ahead, just wait for inspiration to strike."

"How does that happen?" she asked.

Andy laughed and finished the last of his whiskey. "I wish I knew. This might help," he said, filling his cup again.

He took a few steps toward the bed, and Betsy held her cup up, even though there was still plenty of whiskey left. His eyes locked with hers as he tilted the bottle down, filling her cup. Everything he did was sexy. She blushed, embarrassed by the thought.

"How about you?" he asked. "What inspires you?"

"Me?" Betsy laughed. "I'm not a very inspired person. I'm pretty boring, actually."

"I beg to differ," Andy said. "I find you very inspiring."

There was a fire in his eyes, and Betsy realized he was looking at her like a work of art. His gaze left hers for a moment, landing on the sketchbook. When his eyes found hers again, she smiled permission.

Andy sat down on the bed beside her, taking the sketchbook in his hands. She inhaled his musky cologne as he reached over her to get a charcoal pencil from the nightstand.

"Lean back a little," Andy said.

Betsy scooted back against the pillows at the head of his bed. Her feet were dangling off the mattress, still in her shoes. She wasn't sure what to do with her legs or her arms.

"Like this?" she asked.

"More on your side," Andy said. "May I?"

She nodded, aware that she would do anything this man asked of her. He hadn't even kissed her, yet her body was responding to him in ways it never had with Mark.

Her breath hitched as Andy took her foot in his hands, slipping one shoe off and then the other. He continued to move her, to pose her like she was a marionette and he was the puppeteer.

Andy moved one of her hands so it was resting against her chest, the other flat on her hip, her legs crossed at the ankle. He sat perched at the foot of his bed, facing her. She felt his eyes on her, taking her in from head to toe, seemingly satisfied.

Once the pencil hit the paper, it was as if Andy came to life. They were in the same room but separate hemispheres.

Although she was fully clothed, Betsy had never felt more naked. She could feel his eyes drinking her in, capturing every curve, every flaw and imperfection. She'd never felt more vulnerable or more turned on.

Betsy didn't feel like she was pretending to be Sissy anymore. She was being herself. A new self, or maybe one that had been inside her all along, waiting for someone like Andy to set her free.

Here in Andy Abrams's room, on his bed, under his artistic gaze, she wasn't her mother's daughter, Mark Meyer's girlfriend, or Sissy Goldberg's best friend. She was Betsy Kaplan, a wanton woman.

Time seemed to stretch on in the best possible kind of torture. Her limbs were stiff from laying still, and the room felt thick with their sexual tension. He hadn't even touched her yet, but Betsy knew this was the feeling Sissy chased. This was it, and it was everything.

Andy's hands slowed down, and Betsy could tell he was almost finished. He looked back up at her, then down at the drawing a few more times before he tucked the pencil behind his beautiful ear. As far as Betsy was concerned, every single part of him was beautiful.

"Can I see it?" she asked, breathless.

Andy wordlessly handed over the sketchbook, and Betsy couldn't believe her eyes. The girl on the page was her, but she wasn't her. She was soft and lovely; she was captivating. The girl's eyes, Betsy's eyes, made her shiver. Somehow Andy had managed to capture the essence of her, a lost girl full of hope and sadness.

"It's beautiful," Betsy finally said.

"That's because you are." Andy looked up from the drawing to meet Betsy's eyes, and she couldn't control herself. It might have been the whiskey, or maybe a small part of her was still pretending to be Sissy, but she wanted to kiss him more than she'd ever wanted anything. So, she did.

The kiss was brief and awkwardly one-sided. Andy didn't move a muscle, and Betsy was reminded of the practice kisses she'd place on the back of her hand as a young girl.

She pulled back, afraid she had misread the situation. But then their eyes locked, and Andy closed the distance between them, his mouth hungry on hers. He tasted like whiskey and bad decisions.

ANDY HADN'T BEEN expecting Betsy's kiss, and he wasn't prepared to reciprocate. But she'd looked so sad and disappointed when he hadn't kissed her back. So, he did.

With other girls he'd kissed, Andy had just gone through the motions. He wasn't trying to feel anything. But this time, he tried to focus on Betsy's soft lips, the way she tasted like bubble gum and whiskey. Andy closed his eyes and tried not to think about how what they were doing was both completely different and exactly the same as what he'd been doing earlier with William.

The kiss wasn't bad. It might have even been nice. But he didn't feel the same pull as he did with William.

Andy didn't want to think about William right then. He had a beautiful girl in his bed, and his body was reacting to her touch. His life would be so much easier if it turned out William had been right about him. Maybe it just took the right girl for him to realize it. That, or he'd gotten so good at pretending that he'd even fooled himself.

Andy knew there was only one way to find out. The music was reverberating through the walls, and it felt like his heart was beating outside of his chest. He tuned out the voices in the hall, doors closing, girls laughing. It was just the two of them.

Andy reached behind Betsy's back and slid the zipper of her dress down, slowly, so she could stop him at any moment if she wanted to.

BETSY DIDN'T KNOW how she could be both inside and outside of her body at the same time. Every inch of her seemed to come alive under Andy's touch in a way she'd never felt before.

She heard herself moan as his hands made contact with the skin on her back, and she wasn't sure if she would die first from pleasure or embarrassment. This was already so different than it had ever been with Mark.

Andy slipped off his jacket without breaking their kiss, reminding Betsy how much more experience he had than she did. Her fingers fumbled with the buttons on his shirt, eager to see the broad chest she knew was hiding underneath.

The buttons on his shirt weren't any different from the ones on her own blouses, but Betsy couldn't make her hands work to unfasten them. She felt Andy smile through their kiss. He leaned back, looking at her with those eyes that saw the woman she wanted to be.

Betsy shrugged her arms out of the sleeves of her dress and watched as Andy unbuttoned his shirt. She wanted to touch his chest, to run her fingers over the contours of his muscles, so she did. He was strong and solid where Mark was soft.

Stop it, she told herself. It wasn't kind or fair to compare them. They were like two different species. And she definitely preferred whatever species Andy was.

Betsy wanted to quiet her thoughts and banish any trace of Mark, so she reached for her cup on the nightstand and drank what was left of the brown liquid. It burned her throat all the way down and she realized too late that it might not have been the best idea to drink so much so quickly, especially on an empty stomach.

Andy was looking at her, a smile on his face that made his blue eyes shine even brighter. She couldn't believe how much her luck had changed in the course of one evening. Betsy set the cup back down and slid closer to Andy, so close she was practically sitting in his lap.

Their mouths connected again, and Betsy tensed at the feel of his strong hands on her bare skin. They kept kissing as Andy fumbled with the clasp on the back of her bra. When he couldn't get it after the third try, she reached her hands back and did it for him.

He looked down at her as if he was seeing a woman in his bed for the first time, taking her in like she was a sculpture, not a person.

Betsy took advantage of the pause in the kissing to stand up and slip out of her dress. Andy shifted so his feet were on the floor and she was standing before him, wearing nothing but her underwear.

Andy's cup was empty, so he took a swig straight from the bottle. When he finished, she took the whiskey from his hands and set it on the nightstand. She pulled him up, so they were standing face-to-face, chest-to-chest.

Betsy shivered in anticipation, and maybe a little bit of fear, as she reached down to unfasten his jeans. She kissed his collarbone, grateful this button was easier to undo than the ones on his shirt had been.

She started to slide the jeans down over his hips when Andy grabbed her hands. Betsy stepped back, afraid she'd done something wrong.

"I'm sorry," she said, even though she wasn't sure what she was apologizing for.

"No," Andy said. "You didn't do anything. It's just, I don't have any protection."

Betsy looked up at him in disbelief. She hadn't met a single man in college who didn't have a condom on him at all times, just in case he got lucky. But Andy didn't have a single one in the whole room? He couldn't be serious.

Her face fell; she was more disappointed than she had any right to be.

"I could see if someone else has one?" Andy suggested.

"No!" Betsy said, a little too loudly and a little too quickly. She didn't want whatever this was between them to be tarnished by other people knowing what they were about to do—especially since no one but Sissy knew she and Mark had broken up.

"It's okay," Andy said, pulling his pants back up.

"No, it's not." Betsy reached for his hand to stop him. "Just pull out before . . . you know."

Andy didn't look so sure about the idea, but Betsy had never felt this turned on, and he'd barely even touched her yet. She wasn't going to let anything stop them. Betsy was tired of being the careful, thoughtful girl everyone believed she was. She wanted to be wild and feel alive.

Betsy stood up on her toes to kiss him. She could feel his hesitation slip away as he undid the top button of his jeans. She smiled and ran her hands down Andy's broad, smooth shoulders before lying down on his bed, giving him what she hoped was like a come-hither look. She decided right then and there that having him for a birthday gift was better than any necklace or earrings could ever be.

MORNING-AFTER RUMBLINGS IN the hallway woke Andy at half past nine on Sunday morning. His head was pounding, his mouth was dry, and his arm was tingling, asleep beneath Betsy. He looked down at her, not yet awake. Her hair was a bit tousled, but other than that, she looked just as she had the night before, laying on his bed with those come-and-get-me eyes.

Anyone could see she was beautiful, but as much as Andy wished otherwise, he didn't feel attracted to her. The only thing he felt was a dull ache for William.

William, who hated him, who had pushed him away and accused him of being a "breeder," as if it were the worst thing he could be. The human race needed people to breed—their parents were breeders, otherwise they would never have existed to meet in an art studio and fall in love.

The thought of a world where William didn't exist crushed Andy. It threatened to extinguish the little spark of life he had left. The spark that had been put out by the same man who had started the flame.

Betsy made a noise that sounded like the mewing of a cat. The way she smiled in her sleep made Andy sick to his stomach with guilt.

He wished he could blame it on the whiskey, but he had known what he was doing. He was naive to think that one night could change who he was, and he was an asshole for bringing Betsy into his web of lies. No feelings, that was his rule. He'd never let anything get even close to that far before. And to make things worse, he genuinely liked Betsy. Andy knew he deserved everything bad that was coming to him.

"Hi," Betsy said from her spot in the crook of his arm. She moved a little, still catlike, looking up at Andy, who was relieved to finally be able to move his arm.

"Hi," he said back, but his voice was all wrong. He was doing all of this wrong.

Betsy frowned and pulled the sheet up to her neck. "Would you hand me my dress, please?" she asked.

Andy sat up and bent to get the pink dress from where it lay crumpled on the floor. "Listen," he said, "last night was . . . We were both drunk."

"Very drunk," Betsy agreed.

"And you're with Mark," Andy said. He knew he should stop trying to make excuses for his mistake—if he was looking for forgiveness or absolution, he was looking at the wrong person.

"Not anymore," she said. A quiver in her voice let him know how hurt she was, either by him or by Mark. Maybe both. Betsy turned away from him and slipped the dress over her head.

"I'm sorry," Andy said to her back. "I just went through a breakup, too."

Andy's stomach revolted as soon as he heard the words come out of his mouth. It had been a mistake to let his walls down around Betsy. One wrong word could bring his whole world crashing down around him.

"I didn't know you'd been dating anyone," she said, turning back to face him. "Is that your ex?"

Andy turned to see what she was looking at, praying it wasn't a sketch or drawing of William. But it was the framed photo he kept on his desk, his arm thrown around Rebecca's shoulders.

"That's my sister," Andy said.

"She's pretty."

Andy smiled fondly in agreement. His sister hated her bright red hair, but he loved the color—as fiery and untamable as she was.

Betsy looked from the photo back to Andy, and he could imagine the chain of thoughts running through her mind. If the picture was of his sister, then who was the mysterious ex that no one on campus knew about?

"It's complicated," Andy finally said, breaking the uncomfortable silence.

"With your sister?" Betsy looked confused, and Andy realized he had misread her once again.

"Oh, no," Andy said. "With my ex. I'm still getting over it. But if I wasn't, I mean, you're a great girl."

"Oh, please," Betsy said. "Don't give me one of those 'it's not you, it's me' lines. Just be honest with me."

Andy wished he could be honest with her. He imagined how freeing it would be, to share his burden with someone else. But it would be too dangerous. If Betsy told one of her sorority sisters, then they would tell another and another and another until everyone on campus would know who and what Andy Abrams was.

When he didn't answer, Betsy climbed over him and out of his bed.

"It's okay," she said, reaching for the door. "I knew the kind of guy you were when I agreed to come upstairs with you. It's fine, I'm fine."

Andy could see the hurt in her eyes, and he knew she wasn't okay. Just like he knew he was a terrible person for putting her in this position. But he couldn't just let her walk out the door believing his half-truth.

"Wait," Andy said, as her hand rested on the knob.

He imagined all the worst-case scenarios—her entire sorority house hearing that he'd just ended a relationship. A relationship none of his fraternity brothers knew anything about. They'd have questions, and he wouldn't have answers.

Andy looked at Betsy looking back at him. There was no way out, Andy realized. He wondered for a brief moment how it would feel to say the words out loud. To confess everything. Of course, he wouldn't. He couldn't. It was too big of a risk.

Betsy sighed and turned back to the door. The knob was turning, and he knew he had to say something to stop her from leaving.

"Your dress," Andy said.

Betsy looked both relieved and disappointed. Relieved that she wouldn't have to run out of the AEPi house with her dress unzipped and, if Andy had to guess, disappointed that he wasn't asking her to stay.

Resigned, Betsy walked toward him and turned so her back was facing him. He reached for her, pulling the zipper up, slowing as it got halfway up her back. He brushed her hair out of the way so it wouldn't get caught, and he felt her shiver as his fingers made contact with her skin.

Andy hated himself for breaking her heart. He wished he could return her feelings, that he wasn't the way he was. He couldn't give her that, but, he realized, he could give her something he'd never given anyone else. The truth.

He brought the zipper up the rest of the way, and with her back still toward him, Andy spoke his name.

"William," he said. "My ex, his name is William."

Chapter Twenty-Two

Now

"YOUR MOM HAS ALWAYS TOLD ME EVERYTHING, BUT I DIDN'T hear a word about this whole Andy Abrams business until you called her the other day," Aunt Sissy says, sounding a little wounded herself. "When she got off the phone with you, she burst into tears like I've never seen. That's when she told me what happened with Andy."

What happened. I replay the story Sissy just told me: that Mom was upset because she hadn't liked the sleeping bag Dad had gotten her for her birthday. She broke up with him over it—which seems like a silly thing to me, but it does explain why my dad always went so overboard for my mom's birthdays. That night, she went to a frat party and slept with Andrew—Andy, they called him—who was apparently a hot commodity in college, one Sissy herself had gone out with. Now that I know there was no sexual assault involved, I don't have much compassion for her.

"I can't believe she cheated on my dad," I tell Sissy.

"It was a onetime thing—and they were broken up," Aunt Sissy reminds me.

"Yeah, they'd been broken up for what? A few hours?" I say, my stomach twisting with sympathy for my dad. I can picture him picking out a sleeping bag, planning a camping trip for his girlfriend, then being totally bewildered when she broke up with him. "She was clearly heartbroken over it."

"She was," Aunt Sissy insists. "I had to drag her out of bed to go to the party with me. And believe me, Andy Abrams was hard to resist."

I shake my head. "So my DNA Dad was a player."

Aunt Sissy doesn't defend him. "He took almost every girl in our sorority out at least once. Even the annoying ones."

"And you don't think my dad knew?" I asked, afraid for the answer. I hate the thought of my dad—the most honest and trustworthy man I've ever met—being hurt by this deception.

"Your mom didn't even know, not for sure, until she got your email," Aunt Sissy says. "Your parents were back together before she found out she was pregnant, and she hoped the baby—that you— were your father's."

"She's not the only one." I take a sip of my now-cold cup of coffee.

"Come to think of it," Aunt Sissy says thoughtfully, "there was one girl in our sorority. Lauren, she was a real bitch. Your classic 'Jewish American Princess' from New York. She was convinced that something was going on between your mom and Andy. She asked me once if the baby could be Andy's, and I yelled every curse word in the book at her." Aunt Sissy sighs. "I guess I owe her an apology."

I shake my head and look down at what's left in my coffee cup. "I need something stronger."

My legs feel stiff from sitting so long, but I shake them out and walk to the kitchen, where all the ingredients I need to make a

Bloody Mary are thankfully in the fridge. If Jeff hadn't left to walk our imaginary dog, he could be making them for us. They taste better when he makes them for me.

"Want a Bloody Mary?" I ask.

"Have you ever known me to turn down a drink?" Aunt Sissy says. She moves to the other side of the kitchen island and watches as I work, pouring Zing Zang mix into two cups filled with a little bit of ice and a lot bit of vodka. I add a splash of Worcestershire sauce in each cup and toss in a few of the fancy blue-cheese-stuffed olives Jeff buys from Whole Foods.

As I stir, I consider the convenience of this story. I have no reason not to believe Sissy, college in the seventies was a crazy time, and it's not like I've never had a one-night stand. But what I don't buy is that Mom didn't know.

Even if she wasn't sure, she had to suspect that I was Andy's. I could tell from just looking at the picture—we have the same eyes and the same smile. And then there's the inconvenient fact that I'm the only one in the family who has an artistic bone in her body. It all finally makes sense.

I hand over one of the glasses to Aunt Sissy and take a long drink of mine, remembering one morning when I was fourteen or fifteen. Mom had put one of the twins' unrecognizable scribbles on the fridge, covering up my latest drawing, a lifelike representation of Beary, the well-loved teddy bear I'd slept with since I had been a baby.

At the time, I used that as proof that she loved the twins more than she loved me, but now I wonder if she didn't want to see another reminder of the man who had impregnated her. She couldn't have not known.

I take another sip, and the ice cubes knock against my teeth. I look into the glass, surprised to see it's almost empty.

Aunt Sissy laughs. "You do you, sweetheart."

"I don't know what or who I am anymore," I admit.

"Paige Meyer," Aunt Sissy says, a stern tone to her voice. "You take that back."

I raise my eyebrows, feeling like a teenager again, testing limits. "Don't you mean Paige Abrams?"

The words sound wrong coming out of my mouth. The two names don't belong together; they don't belong to me.

"You are Paige Ann Meyer," Aunt Sissy says, still in her mom voice. "You are the daughter of my very best friend in the world and her husband—the love of her life." Her voice starts to waver, and I wonder if she feels like Mom betrayed her, too. "Mark Meyer is still and will always be your dad. No DNA test can change that. It doesn't change who you are."

My new friends in the NPE group would disagree. Just last night, a woman said that telling a person with a parent not-expected that it didn't change who they were was just as bad as telling a parent who lost a child that they were "in a better place."

I don't have the energy to make Aunt Sissy understand that it's less about my dad and more about me. How it feels to know that part of myself—half of me—is completely unknown.

"So, when are you going back to St. Louis?" I ask, desperate to change the subject.

"Itching to get rid of me already?"

"Of course not," I tell her. "Just wondering how long I have you for."

"I'm on a flight back tomorrow afternoon," she says. "Tonight, I'm taking you and Jeff out for dinner and drinks—pick someplace good. And tomorrow, maybe a little shopping?"

"Sounds great," I tell her, meaning it. My mom may not be open or honest with me, but at least I have Aunt Sissy. "Thanks for coming, for telling me the truth."

Her face softens. "Oh, honey, come here."

I walk back around the kitchen counter and step into Aunt Sissy's open arms, as grateful for her as I'm sure my mom must be. As much as I wish Mom had been the one to tell me, I can't imagine having such an open and honest conversation with her. Not now, after all these years. And not for something this big.

The front door opens, and Jeff quietly closes it behind him. Nervous, I'm sure, to see what he's about to walk into. He steps apprehensively around the corner, smiling when he sees us.

I give Aunt Sissy one last squeeze before letting go. I may not know who I am, but I know I'm lucky to have her.

"Where's the dog?" I ask Jeff.

He looks around him and shrugs. "Must have lost him, but I've got donuts from Stan's."

"Bloodies and donuts," Aunt Sissy says. "I may never go home."

AFTER AUNT SISSY leaves to do a little window-shopping and freshen up for dinner, I lay down and close my eyes, hoping to quiet my racing mind. I'm dizzy from everything Aunt Sissy told me, how and what it means for me.

Andrew "Andy" Abrams is a real person. I knew that before, of course, but hearing Aunt Sissy talk about him made him less hypothetical and more human.

"Want to talk?" Jeff asks, leaning against our bedroom door, the same spot where he stood a few hours ago.

I shake my head and pull the covers tight around me. The only person I want to talk to is the only one I can't. "I miss my dad," I tell him.

Jeff's quiet for a moment, before lying down beside me. He curls his body against mine and wraps his arms around me. "Want to not talk?" he asks, nuzzling my neck.

I sigh, wishing it would be that easy to let myself forget. "Aunt Sissy thinks Mom didn't know until I told her."

"Hmm," Jeff says. I can tell from his tone that he doesn't believe that, either.

"I know she knew," I tell him. "There's no way she couldn't have. But I really don't think my dad knew."

"Even if he did, it doesn't change the fact that he loved you," Jeff says.

"But here's the thing," I tell him. The memory has been niggling on my mind the last few days. "Four or five years ago, he found out he had some genetic heart condition, and he insisted that the twins and I go for a stress test. He was adamant about it—but if he knew, he wouldn't have been worried about me. Just the twins."

"Hmm," Jeff says again. This time I'm not sure if it's an affirming "hmm" or a *you're delusional* "hmm," so I turn around to face him.

"Maybe he didn't want to see the truth," Jeff says. "Maybe he wanted to believe you were his. Can't blame the guy."

He kisses my forehead, and the realization that I'll never know the real truth knocks the wind out of me.

"He was your dad in all the ways that matter," Jeff says.

In all the ways but one.

Chapter Twenty-Three

Then

BETSY'S FACE BURNED AS SHE HURRIED DOWN THE STAIRS AND out the front door of the fraternity house. She couldn't believe she'd been so stupid. She could pretend to be like Sissy all she wanted, but Betsy was still her boring old self. She knew better than to think Andy Abrams might like her—but never in a million years would she have imagined that he liked boys.

It wasn't that Betsy had a problem with homosexuals—she didn't. She even had a friend in high school who she was pretty sure was gay. He had been more feminine than masculine, spoke with a lilt, and loved musical theater. He fit the stereotype to a tee—but Andy hadn't. He was masculine and athletic. And he had slept with her. She had slept with him.

A shiver ran down Betsy's spine at the thought. What did that say about her? She wished Andy had just let her leave. That she could go on thinking that she'd been dismissed like all the other girls in her sorority. But he hadn't.

When Andy first said the name, Betsy thought she'd heard him wrong. That he'd misspoken, that maybe the girl's last name was

Williams. But when she turned and saw the look of terror on his face, she knew. There was no mistake. It took everything she had to stay calm.

Betsy was numb as she sat back down on his bed and let Andy tell her the story of a young boy who knew he was different from the others. He hadn't known how just then, but he knew he didn't belong.

She listened as he told her about the moody TA who had unlocked his passion for art and for life, who had broken his heart. He apologized for not being honest with her and pleaded with her to keep his secret. He'd looked terrified that he would lose everything.

Betsy knew how it felt to have nothing and no one, so even though he had deceived her, Betsy promised to keep his secret. It was her secret now, too. She didn't want anyone finding out how foolish she'd been, what she'd done.

Before she left, Betsy made Andy promise he would stop taking her sorority sisters out on dates. It wasn't fair to them or to her.

As Betsy walked through campus, she kept her head down, concentrating on the dancing shadows the sun cast on the sidewalk through the trees. She'd spent her whole life feeling invisible, but now Betsy wished she was.

Anyone who saw her would know she had been out since the night before. She was embarrassed of being dressed this way so early in the morning, with leftover makeup on her face. She also felt guilty. Because even after all she'd learned, a small part of her didn't regret what she had done with Andy Abrams. How he'd made her feel.

If she hadn't gone to the party with Sissy, Betsy would have never known what she'd been missing. How desire could build with torturous anticipation that turned into sparks. There had been actual sparks.

Now that Betsy knew that kind of passion existed, she was devastated to realize that she might not feel that way again. Surely Andy had felt it, too. That kind of attraction couldn't be faked.

Betsy flushed at the memory of the things she'd said, the things he'd done. *Had his arousal been an act, too?* Betsy wondered how he could have made his body do the things it had done to hers if he'd just been pretending.

She was a piece of work, just like her mother always said. In twenty-four hours, Betsy had managed to break up with a guy who loved her and throw herself at another who didn't even like women. She was becoming more and more like her mother every day.

Betsy let herself into the sorority house, grateful it was early enough that most of her sisters would still be asleep. For all they knew, she was just coming back from her birthday celebration with Mark. She could have gone back out with him after he called. That was totally plausible.

Sissy wasn't in the room when Betsy walked in. She was probably still at the fraternity house, in another boy's room, in his bed, getting a much better morning-after reaction than Betsy had gotten. She didn't want to be bitter, but it was hard not to be jealous—especially now that she knew what she'd been missing. If it was always like that for Sissy, it was no wonder her best friend was so loose and easy with her heart.

Betsy slipped out of the dress she knew she'd never wear again and wrapped herself in a towel. She walked down the hall toward the bathroom, going through the motions of her morning routine, even though she didn't feel like herself anymore.

As the hot water hit her shoulders, Betsy came undone. The water mixed with her unstoppable tears and she clasped a hand over her mouth to quiet the sobs.

The tears weren't for Mark, and they weren't for Andy, either. No, the tears were for herself. What she'd had, what she'd lost, and what she worried she might never find again.

IT WAS NOON by the time Andy showed his face downstairs. The house was a wreck, with plastic cups and cigarette butts scattered around the floor.

He grabbed a trash bag from the kitchen to start cleaning up. The smell of stale beer made him sick to his stomach, but it was better than sitting alone in his room. He'd already stripped and remade the bed, but it couldn't erase what he'd done.

"Bro," Jared Evans said as he made his way down the stairs, his girlfriend steps behind him. "You and Betsy Kaplan, huh?"

"No way," his girlfriend said. Andy balked, afraid that he was too late. "She's dating Mark Meyer. They're practically engaged."

"Well, she wasn't calling Mark's name last night," Jared said, humping the air and making grunting noises.

"You're disgusting," his girlfriend said, giving him a kiss before turning to go. Jared swatted her behind, and she shot him a playful, dirty look before slipping out the door.

"So, how was she?" Jared said, leaning against the bannister. "I bet she was an animal in bed—the quiet ones always are."

Andy balled his fist around the trash bag in his hands. He wanted to punch that condescending look off his fraternity brother's face, but he knew he had to keep playing the part, even if it chipped away another tiny piece of his soul.

"A gentleman doesn't kiss and tell," Andy said. He hoped Betsy would forgive this last betrayal as he added, "But let's just say there were no complaints."

"Bro!" Jared slapped Andy's shoulder. "I knew you had it in you."

Andy forced a smile even though he'd never been more disgusted and disappointed with himself. Jared looked as if he was waiting for more details, but Andy couldn't bring himself to say anything, not even a lie. He'd already done enough to hurt Betsy.

"If you're just going to stand there," Andy finally said, "you should help me clean."

"Wish I could stay," Jared said, walking back up the stairs. "But I've got to get some sleep. My lady's an animal, too. Kept me up all night." He howled like a wolf as he dragged himself up the stairs.

Once Jared was out of sight, Andy let himself deflate, thinking again of the broken look on Betsy's face before she'd left.

Andy hated himself for what he'd done, and he hated that the person he hurt held his future in her hands.

Chapter Twenty-Four

Now

S ISSY LEFT, AS PROMISED, ON SUNDAY AFTERNOON, AFTER SPOIL-ing us with dinner and drinks on Saturday at Ema, one of our favorite restaurants down the street, and dragging me up and down Michigan Avenue the next day until I conceded and let her buy me a dress for the rehearsal dinner. It was the kind of mother-daughter-like day I hadn't realized I needed until it was over—although I'm still not sure whether I'm going to keep the dress.

As grateful as I am that she took the time to come and tell me the sordid story of my conception in person, I still don't have all the answers. Some only Mom can give me: Did she love my dad? Did she love this other guy? Does she love me? Others, I need to hear from Andy Abrams. And he still hasn't replied to my last message.

Which brings me a mile down State Street, where the Blick Art store is relatively empty. It shouldn't surprise me, seeing as it's the middle of the afternoon on a Wednesday, but it does. Other than having to call the toll-free unemployment line every two weeks, and moments like this, it's easy to forget the rest of the world is sitting at their desks, not shopping.

The reminder casts a shadow of guilt over me. I should be looking for another job or posting an article on LinkedIn instead of spending money I'm supposed to be saving. But Jeff has been on me to pick up a new hobby. Maybe this is exactly what I need.

"Do you need help finding anything?" a young saleswoman asks.

"I'm okay, thanks," I say. The words feel false, but she wasn't asking about my mental health or my strange motivation for coming here.

I know I should be relieved to finally understand where my artistic roots come from, but I can't stop focusing on how things would have been if my talent had been nurtured. If I'd gotten a degree in fine arts, instead of in design. Sure, advertising is a more stable career choice, current situation notwithstanding, but what if I had the potential to be something more? What if I'd been encouraged to try my hand at painting instead of the sketches I was always drawn to?

I walk down an aisle where a wall is filled with three times the amount of brushes as they have at the Sephora in Water Tower. Some look like the ones Margaux talked me into buying so I could properly blend my eye shadow. Another looks like my tiny eyeliner brush, and there's a whole row that remind me of the blush and foundation brushes I sometimes mistake for each other. Much to my mother's chagrin, I have never been that into makeup.

I pick up a long, slender brush and hold it between my hands like a pencil. I close my eyes and wait for whatever feeling it's supposed to awaken inside of me. I switch hands, rubbing the soft bristles between my fingers, but there's still nothing. It was stupid of me to think that holding a paintbrush would trigger some feeling, like my DNA would instinctively know what to do.

My eyes fly open when I hear the familiar notes of the *Jaws* theme song, and I fish my phone out of my pocket.

"Hey, Mom," I say, trying to sound as casual as possible. I quickly put back the brush and turn to leave the store, empty-handed and empty-hearted.

"Hi, sweetheart," she says, her voice as insincerely sweet as it always is. "I wasn't sure I'd catch you," she says—code for *I was hoping you wouldn't answer so I could just leave a message.*

"Well, you did," I say, pushing through the double doors. "What's up?"

"I was just making a mental to-do list of all the things we have to do for the wedding—it'll be here before we know it."

"If the date is too soon . . ." I start to say.

"We are not pushing it back," Mom insists. "Nothing is impossible. It just helps to be organized."

"Okay," I say, a little apprehensive. "Well, I have one thing we can cross off the list. Aunt Sissy talked me into getting a dress for the rehearsal dinner when she was here."

I hear Mom inhale sharply. I shouldn't have mentioned Aunt Sissy's visit. For one thing, I have a feeling we're supposed to be pretending the conversation never happened, and I also forgot that Aunt Sissy said the shopping trip should stay just between us.

"Well, that's nice," Mom says in the voice she reserves for strangers and Dad's old business associates. I detect a note of jealousy in her voice, which doesn't make sense. I've wanted her to care enough to do all the typical mother-daughter things with me my whole life, and she's never seemed interested. With the twins, yes. But never with me.

"I still have to find the actual wedding dress," I say, trying to make amends. I might be upset with her, but I don't want to hurt her feelings. Especially if what Frannie said was true, that she's still lonely without Dad.

"I'm afraid the selection might be limited to sample sizes," Mom says, still in her polished voice. "Most brides pick out their dresses a year before the wedding."

I flinch, wondering if she knows just how much her words hurt. "Yeah, well, most brides are also in their twenties or thirties," I snip back. The twins could probably fit into sample sizes.

"Not that again," Mom sighs. "I shouldn't have said anything— I'm sure you'll find something lovely. I would say you should come home and we can look here together, but I assume there's a better selection in Chicago."

There's so much to unpack in her sentence. In the same breath, she invited and uninvited me to go to St. Louis to shop with her.

"You're probably right," I tell her. "I'm sure I can get Maks and Margaux to go with me."

"Oh," she says, not hiding the disappointment in her voice, and I wonder if I was supposed to invite her to Chicago instead. I sigh, missing my dad fiercely. It was so much easier to communicate with her when he was there to be the go-between.

"You can always come too, if you want," I tell her. "We could make a weekend of it."

"That would be really nice," she says, and I can feel my hopes lifting just the tiniest bit.

Until now, I've only been thinking of the consequences that came along with the news of my paternity, but I wonder if something good could come from it, too. Maybe carrying such a big secret acted like a clog, blocking the motherly love she'd always wanted to give me.

If forty-three isn't too old to have a wedding, maybe it isn't too old to start having a relationship with your mother, either.

"Although," she says, bringing my hopes crashing down, "I'm not sure it's a good idea to wait much longer. If your friends can go with you this weekend, that would probably be best."

My eyes prick with tears, and I nod, forgetting she can't see me. It was stupid of me to expect her to change.

"Paige?" she says when I don't respond.

"I'm here," I tell her. "There will still be plenty for you to help with."

"Plenty," she says, sounding like her bright and cheery self again. "I was thinking that if you come home for Rosh Hashana a bit early this year, we could do the menu tasting at Westwood and meet with the florist. And of course you still have to decide whether you want a DJ or a band."

"The Rosh plan sounds good," I tell her. "And I'll talk to Jeff to see what he thinks about the music."

"Okay, now, let's see." I can hear her rustling papers on the other side of the line. "Rosh Hashana is on a Monday this year, so maybe you both can come in that Saturday, and I can schedule appointments for Sunday."

"Perfect," I say, meaning it. I'm grateful she's taken such an interest in the planning part of the wedding. While I have plenty of time on my hands these days, the details just stress me out. And I know she loves it. In some ways, it's like she's getting a chance to plan the wedding she never got to throw for herself.

"Okay, I'll let you go, then," she says. "It sounds like you're somewhere fun?"

I look behind me, where two chattering girls are walking out of the art store. "Just out for a walk and a little window-shopping," I tell her, settling on a half-truth.

"That sounds lovely," she says with a sigh of relief, as if I've suddenly transformed into a daughter she can relate to. If she only knew what I was shopping for.

HAVING CHICKENED OUT of the art supply experiment, I decide to keep walking. It's a beautiful day, and it's not like I have anywhere else to be. Maybe I'll stop by Whole Foods on the walk home and pick up some cheese, olives, and prosciutto to make a charcuterie board. Jeff loves them, and it's pretty much the extent of my cooking abilities.

As I make my way through the swarm of tourists on State Street, I can't get the phone call with my mom out of my head. In the moment, it felt different from our normal conversations, but now I realize it was exactly the same. We talked around everything without talking about the one thing we should have been talking about.

I wonder if we'll ever be able to have a real conversation. Or if they'll all end up being the same—either empty and tense or full and fake. If we're going to have a relationship in this new world where Dad is gone and the idea of Andy Abrams exists, we're going to have to be honest with each other.

As I turn right on Madison toward Michigan, I realize it's never going to happen if I wait for her. If I really want answers, I have to be the one to start the conversation. Feeling somewhat emboldened, I reach for my phone and pull up the Recent Calls menu. I tap the "Mom and Dad" label that I really should change, but that can wait. This can't.

She answers on the second ring. "That was fast," she says. "Let me guess—DJ?"

"What?" I ask, thrown off guard.

"Oh, I thought you'd maybe talked to Jeff."

"No, I haven't talked to Jeff," I say, feeling my brief bout of confidence slipping away. Before it's gone completely, I say, "But I did talk to Aunt Sissy, as you know."

"Yes, I'm aware," she says, the chill back in her voice.

"And I just thought, I don't know, that maybe we should talk about it?" I cringe at the sound of my voice and wish I sounded like a mature woman, not a timid teenager desperate for her mother's approval. Although I guess some things never change.

Three hundred miles away, my mom sighs. "Honestly, I don't know what there is to talk about, Paige. Sissy told you everything there is to tell."

The closer I get to Michigan Avenue, the more crowded the streets get, filled with pedestrians looking between the map and the street signs, no doubt trying to figure out which direction to go to get to the Bean. I cross the street with hordes of them, hoping to find a quiet square of grass in the park where I can sit and have the first truly honest conversation I've ever had with my mom. If she'll let me.

"You really don't think there's anything else to say?"

"What do you want to know, Paige?" she asks, resigned.

"Did you love Dad?"

It seems like a natural question to me, but she sucks in a shocked breath. "Your father was the love of my life," she says, her voice starting to waver. "This hurts my heart, too, you know. I wanted you to be his."

I nod and brush a tear from my eye. I may have questioned my mom's feelings for me, but I shouldn't have questioned her love for my dad. Even when he was driving her crazy, the love between them was evident. But I still have more questions.

"Are you going to reach out to him? To Andrew? Andy Abrams?" I ask.

"Of course not," she snaps, as if the thought were ridiculous. "He doesn't matter—he's no one, just a man I made a mistake with a very long time ago. A mistake I've regretted every day since."

Her words hit me like a slap in the face and I inhale sharply, even though they just confirm what I've always known. But thinking your own mother regrets your being born is different from hearing the words come out of her mouth.

"Oh, Paige," she says with an exasperated sigh. "You know I don't mean it like that. I don't regret having you."

I don't say anything, because there's nothing left to say.

"I knew nothing good would come from talking about this," Mom says. "I regret what I did to your father—I hope Sissy told you we were broken up at the time, but still. I regret the action, not the result. I . . ." She pauses to take a steadying breath. "I don't want to talk about this, Paige."

My throat has closed to the point where I'm having trouble swallowing. I know this must be difficult for her, but it's not easy for me, either. She keeps pushing me away when all I want is the honesty that could bring us closer together. But there's no point if she won't try.

"I shouldn't have bothered," I finally say.

"It's your right to want to know," Mom says. "But it's also my right to not want to talk about it. It's in the past, Paige. It doesn't change anything. Your dad is still your dad, and I'm still your mom."

She's still my mother, but she's wrong about this not changing anything. And the fact that she doesn't understand why this is important makes it even worse. I swallow down the anger and try to speak calmly.

"If there's nothing left to talk about, then I guess I'll let you go. Bye, Elizabeth."

I hang up without giving her a chance to respond with more empty words. My heart can't handle it. She may not want to say any more, but I don't want to hear any more, either.

Chapter Twenty-Five

Then

B ETSY FELT LIKE SHE WAS COMING DOWN WITH SOMETHING. She'd never been one for naps, but the last two weeks, she'd taken one nearly every day. She was attempting to take one now, but there was too much noise coming from downstairs.

She opened one eye at the sound of her name.

"Betsy!" one of her sisters called a second time. "You got another delivery!"

She closed her eyes again, embarrassed by what she could only imagine was another over-the-top gesture from Mark. Her desk was already covered with vases full of flowers. There were daisies and tulips and lilies—he clearly didn't know what her favorite flower was. The smell of them was so overpowering that it was starting to make her sick. As far as Betsy was concerned, it was too little, too late.

There was a knock on her door.

"Come in," Betsy said, propping herself up on one arm.

Evelyn, a sweet girl in her pledge class, opened the door, a bouquet of red roses and baby's breath in her arms. "Where do you want me to put these?"

"In the trash," Betsy said.

"Oh, don't be silly, they're beautiful."

"You can have them," Betsy told her. "I don't want to look at them."

"Do you mean it?" Evelyn's eyes lit up at the thought. She was a girl who was more comfortable with books than boys, and Betsy wasn't sure if Evelyn had ever been on a date outside of organized sorority parties. She deserved to have beautiful flowers, and the flowers deserved to make someone happy.

"Of course," Betsy said. She lay back down so she wouldn't have to look at the flowers anymore, hoping Evelyn would take the hint and leave her to get some sleep. "They're yours."

"Thank you!" Evelyn said. "But here, at least take the card."

The bedroom door closed softly as Evelyn walked all the way inside. She gently lay the card on Betsy's bed before taking the roses back to her own room, where Betsy never had to look at them again.

Betsy's eyes welled with tears. She hated how much she'd been crying lately. She didn't have the right to be sad—she was the one who had ended things with Mark. If the flowers were a sign, he would gladly take her back if she wanted.

But Betsy didn't want him back. She didn't want the kind of future that a life with him would look like. It would be so much easier if he'd been the bad guy and done something really wrong. But it was pretty much the opposite.

Betsy had to admit she missed him: the way he'd call her on the house phone to say good night after he got back home from dropping her off. She missed the way he laughed at his own silly puns even though no one else did. And she especially missed watching the news with him, the conversations they would have when it was over. He talked to her like she was smart and her opinion mattered. Not everyone cared what a girl like her thought about politics and issues of the world, but Mark did.

In spite of all that, she couldn't forget the awful way he'd made her feel that night—like she hadn't been important or special enough to notice, that she didn't matter. And as hard as dealing with the loneliness was now, she knew it was better than settling on a lifetime with someone who didn't care enough to really get to know her.

And then there was Andy.

Her head and her heart clearly weren't on the same page where he was concerned. She was still upset with him—but the week before, when she saw him on campus, Betsy felt a physical yearning for him. In spite, or maybe because, of that, she'd crossed to the other side of the street.

Betsy knew she couldn't handle making fake small talk with Andy, that she wouldn't be able to see his eyes, his lips, his hands, without thinking about the way they'd explored her body. The way he'd brought her to life, only to crush her spirit.

She couldn't have Andy, and she didn't want Mark. Her future was bleak, and all Betsy wanted to do was sleep. She flipped over the pillow to the cool side and lay her head back down. The tiny envelope from the flowers was so close to her face that it poked her nose.

Betsy opened the envelope and read Mark's words, another way of saying the same thing he'd said in every card, every letter, and every message he'd left with one of her sisters:

Betsy,

    Please, talk to me so I can understand what I did, so I can try to make things right.
    I'm sorry. I love you.

Mark Meyer

Betsy had to laugh at the way he signed his full name on what was supposed to be a romantic gesture. As if there could be another Mark sending her apologies by the dozen.

She put the card on the nightstand with the others and closed her eyes. It wasn't fair for him to spend so much money on her when there was no chance at reconciliation. She wished there was a way to let him down without having to see or talk to him again. Maybe she could send Sissy to do it for her. She was used to breaking boys' hearts.

Of course, Betsy could never do that. In spite of everything that had happened, she liked Mark too much to sic Sissy on him. Maybe she would write him a letter. Then she wouldn't have to look at his sad expression when she told him goodbye.

Satisfied with the idea, Betsy yawned and pulled the covers up to her chin before drifting off to sleep. She would solve the Mark problem later, and then everything would be okay. It had to be.

ANDY'S DAYS HAD never felt longer. Every second seemed slower than the one before, as he tried to come up with ways to pass time between classes and football practice. He was in better shape than he'd ever been thanks to the long runs he took outside of practice—always in the opposite direction of William's apartment.

The rest of the time, Andy spent in the library. Other than dropping in when he needed to check out a book or when one of his study groups had research to do, Andy hadn't spent much time there. But after the past few weeks, he had a new appreciation and respect for the grand old building.

He found solace in the quiet, not having to fill the empty spaces with words. At the library, a smile could replace a conversation, and it played rather nicely into his latest lie. Andy had told his brothers that Coach Fambrough put him on a dating ban outside of official fraternity events until his grades picked up. Between that and the rumors about him and Betsy, he'd been granted a small reprieve.

When he wasn't studying, Andy read. Fiction and nonfiction, books on art and art history. He filled his creative well with inspiration, studying the work and techniques of the greats. It was the closest he had gotten to actually painting since his failed attempt during the morning open-studio session a week earlier.

In the crowded studio, Andy had flinched at every sound: the door opening or someone breathing too loudly. He couldn't focus, and he felt as empty as the blank canvas in front of him. The lack of inspiration made him frustrated, which made him angry. He'd left without his brush even touching the canvas, and he was afraid that his artistic days were over.

When Andy's eyes got tired from reading, his other companion was his sketchbook. He'd started to draw a collection of people in the library—men and women—as they sat and studied. He called it: *A Study on Studying.*

His charcoal pencil scraping across the paper was the only sound other than the occasional turning of a page. Already that morning, Andy had captured a pretty girl biting her lip in concentration as she studied, and he'd just finished a sketch of a kid, no doubt a freshman, who had nodded off, using his history book as a pillow.

He was thinking about calling it a day and going for another run when he saw her.

Betsy.

She didn't see him—if she had, Andy knew she would have quickly left the room in search of another, the way she'd crossed the street when she saw him on campus the week before. He had pretended not to notice, in part because it was easier—but mostly because he was still ashamed of the way he'd treated her. Ashamed, and terrified that she would change her mind and spill his secret.

Betsy seemed content as she cozied up in one of the plush red chairs near the stacks and opened her book. *The Catcher in the Rye.* He wondered if it was the same copy he'd returned, the one with her name written so many times on the checkout card.

Andy opened his sketchbook and started to draw. The curves and lines of Betsy's face were more familiar than they had a right to be, and he brushed away thoughts of his night with her. If he hadn't been so stupid and selfish, she could have been a friend. A good friend, a real friend. He didn't have many of those, and he had lost his chance with her.

Betsy's cheeks looked flushed, and Andy wondered what part of the story she was reading. Maybe the scene where Holden was in his hotel room, observing strangers across the way: the man wearing pantyhose and the couple engaged in some strange kind of foreplay, spitting their drinks into each other's mouths.

He wished he could go over and talk to her about the book and ask what about it made her read it over and over again. If she could see herself in Holden, too. Or if it was his sister, Phoebe, she related to. But of course he couldn't.

The sleeping guy at the table in front of Andy's picked that inopportune moment to wake up. Startled and disoriented, he flailed his arms, knocking his thick textbook on the floor. It echoed like a shotgun in the quiet room. Everyone looked up, including Andy. And Betsy.

Her eyes met his, and Andy gave her what he hoped she knew was a genuine smile. She didn't smile back. Andy didn't want her to have to leave when she had looked so happy, so he closed his sketchbook and went to find another spot, another way to escape.

Chapter Twenty-Six

Now

"DOES THE BRIDE CARE FOR ANY MORE CHAMPAGNE?" MARGAUX asks, walking into the dressing room where a dozen white dresses are discarded on the chairs around me.

I nod a little too enthusiastically, and she laughs as she fills my glass. "This is supposed to be fun, right?" I ask.

"It is fun!" she says with the enthusiasm of a woman who can look drop-dead gorgeous in anything she tries on. And it is a lot more fun than it had been in the beginning with the saleslady hovering around us. I don't know how Margaux managed to ditch her, but I'm grateful she did.

I'm too stressed to handle the saleswoman's false cheer, especially because it turns out my mom was right. Without the months usually allowed for alterations, it wasn't going to be easy finding the perfect dress. Although at this point, after three failed stops on our wedding-dress-shopping crawl, I'd settle for something that's better-than-okay.

"Try this one," Margaux says, holding up the second-to-last dress on the rack.

I cringe at the sight of it. "It's so . . ." I flip through my inner thesaurus to find the word that matches my level of disgust. "Girly."

"Most wedding dresses are, my dear," Margaux says with a wry smile. "Just try it. You might be surprised how much you like it."

The line is an echo of a memory that comes rushing back. One I had almost successfully blocked out: shopping for a prom dress with my mom. The twins were in tow as they always were, and I was at an awkward stage where I hated everything about the way I looked—my curves, my curls, my breasts.

Mom insisted on making me try on frilly dress after frilly dress. I hated them all, and I resented her for making me continue to try them on. The last straw had been a bright pink dress with poofy sleeves and a narrow waist. The color clashed against my red hair, and I burst into tears at the sight of myself in the mirror.

I remember looking back to my mom for sympathy, but she just stood there with her arms crossed and her lips in a thin line. It was obvious she didn't know what to do with me—her daughter who was more artsy than feminine, who wanted to blend in, not stand out.

We didn't buy a dress that day, and I'd cried to Dad, saying I'd rather skip the dance than go shopping with Mom again. In the end, I agreed to go the next weekend with Aunt Sissy. Thanks to her patience, her fashion sense, and her industry connections from owning a clothing boutique, we were able to find a classic but pretty black dress we could all agree on.

"My glass is empty," Maks calls from outside the dressing room.

"Hold your horses," Margaux yells back.

"I don't want horses," Maks whines. "I want champagne."

Margaux ignores Maks and slips the dress off its hanger, holding it out for me to step into.

"Speaking of horses—did you know Queen Victoria was the first one to wear a white wedding dress, back in the eighteen hundreds?" Maks says.

"What does that have to do with horses?" Margaux whispers.

I shrug and shout back to Maks, "Who knew!"

We share a smile, and I pull up the dress easily, but the tulle underneath tickles my legs. If I can't stop myself from laughing before the dress is all the way on, there's no way I can make it through an entire night with it. "Take it off," I plead through uncomfortable laughter.

"Just let me see it first," Margaux insists.

"I'm parched," Maks says. "Cover your bits, I'm coming in."

He pushes through the curtains, grabbing our second complimentary bottle of champagne from the side table. Before taking a swig straight from the bottle, he looks at me with an expression that sums up how I feel about the dress.

"Right?" I hold my arm out toward him, as if his face can make the point for both of us.

"It's a little 'Barbie gets married,'" he agrees. "Although Jeff does have a Ken vibe about him."

I shoot Maks a dirty look, and he smiles before leaving the room, the bottle of champagne still in his hand. I wish the two men in my life could love each other as much as I love them both. Margaux thinks they're both jealous of the other, which is just ridiculous.

"Don't even think about it," I tell Margaux, wiggling out of the dress before she can snap a picture to send to my mom. So far, Mom has responded with a heart-eyed emoji to every single dress—including a hideous one we sent to her as a joke.

"Last one," Margaux says, reaching for the final dress. "And if you don't like it, we're going to have to go to another store."

Outside the curtain, Maks groans, and I'm sure I don't look happy at the prospect, either.

"You're going to have to accept that most wedding dresses are girly," Margaux says.

"A little girly is okay," I tell her. "I just hate tulle and taffeta and things that are poofy."

"You're the bride," Margaux says, resigned.

I'm happy to see the last dress doesn't have any of the offending fabrics and actually has cute capped sleeves. Finally a happy medium between the dozens of strapless dresses and the occasional few that have full-length sleeves.

I step into the new dress. The fabric feels smooth and cool against my skin as I pull it up.

"It feels nice," I tell Margaux, which is the most positive thing I've had to say about any of the dresses we've tried. As she fastens the tiny buttons that run up the back, I study my reflection in the trio of mirrors before me.

The bodice has a lace overlay that dips down just past my waist, falling into an A-line skirt. *Flattering*. The neckline scoops low enough to be a little sexy without looking like I'm trying too hard. And the capped sleeves are the cherry on top.

I find Margaux's smiling face in the mirror.

"Well," she says.

"Let me see." Maks opens the curtain again. "Oh, wow."

"Good wow or bow wow?" I ask, hoping he picks the right answer. I don't have it in me to go to another store.

"Good wow, holy wow," he says. "Turn around."

I spin on the small platform, and the dress swooshes perfectly around me. When I complete the circle, I look back in the mirror. Suddenly, I can picture myself walking down the aisle toward Jeff.

"I think this is it," I say, as a smile creeps onto my face.

"She said yes to the dress!" Margaux shouts, giving Maks a high five. "Let me get a few pictures before you take it off."

I don't have to try to smile for this picture—my happiness is finally real. Until I notice Maks standing off to the side, scowling down at his phone.

"O.M.G.," he says, pronouncing every letter as if it's its own word.

"What?" I ask. He looks up as if he's just remembering Margaux and I are in the room. He looks down at his phone and then back up at me, a *don't kill me* look on his face.

"WHAT IS MAKS doing with a Google Alert for your dad?" Jeff asks for the third time since I started telling him about what happened that afternoon.

"He's Maks. Who knows why he does half the things he does," I say. "And he's not my dad; he's my DNA Dad."

Jeff nods an apology before turning to put the purple cauliflower and smashed hazelnuts into the oven. He checks the Blue Apron recipe card before setting the timer on his phone.

We decided it would be nice to do one of those meal-delivery services to help us commit to cooking together a few times each week. In reality, Jeff cooks while I sip wine and watch—or, like tonight, help him by designing the deck for the latest request from the tech giant he's pitching. And I thought advertising clients were tough.

After a smashing week of presentations in San Francisco, where everyone was properly happy and impressed, they are still asking for additional case studies before officially awarding the contract.

"So, what are you going to do?" he asks, wiping his hands on a dish towel.

I shrug. When Maks read the Google Alert out loud, I thought he was joking. I mean, what are the chances my biological father would be coming to Chicago for a one-weekend-only showing of his art the same weekend Frannie is coming to visit—on her own, which I still can't believe. If it were any other weekend, I wouldn't hesitate. But it's not like I can bring Frannie with me to get a glimpse of my DNA Dad.

The gallery apparently has visiting artists a few times each month, but it still feels like too big of a coincidence that he'll be here. In Chicago. Less than a mile from where I live. This could be my one and only chance to make him give me the information I have a right to know. He can't dodge me in person the way he did with my email.

"What do you think?" I ask, genuinely serving the question back to Jeff.

He pours the prepackaged noodles into the fancy pasta-boiling pot with a built-in colander—one of his contributions to the relationship. He stirs it before turning back to me.

"I think . . . that's not something I can answer for you."

I frown and take a sip of the red wine the recipe card suggested pairing with our dinner. I want him to tell me what I already know: that of course I have to find a way to go.

"It is a pretty amazing coincidence he's going to be in Chicago," Jeff says.

"Right?" I agree, not-so-subtly trying to steer him in the right direction.

He turns back to look at me, raising an eyebrow. "Babe, this has to be your decision. I can't make it for you."

"Why not?" I playfully pout.

"I can help you talk it through?" Jeff offers.

I sigh, and he gives me the most adorable *go on* expression as he stirs.

"I have to go, I want to go," I tell him. "But Frannie."

"What if we say I have a work thing that night?" Jeff suggests. "Maks and Margaux can take her out for a drink while we go to the gallery, and then we can meet them after for a late dinner."

I frown. It could work, but I'm still not sure I'll be brave enough to go.

"It's not just Frannie," I admit. "He didn't respond to my last message—what if he doesn't want to meet me? What if he's there with his *wife*?"

"It's possible," Jeff agrees. Sometimes I love the way his business-minded brain attacks problems so logically. Other times, I wish he could be a little more impulsive and go with his gut, so I didn't have to wait so long for him to make whatever decision he was deciding for us.

"I don't know," I say. "When I see him, I'm not sure I'll be able to hold my feelings back. He has a right to his privacy and not to be accosted in the middle of an art gallery."

"True, but you also have a right to know where you came from," Jeff says, and I inwardly swoon. I proudly call myself a feminist, but I still love it when he sticks up for me, especially when I'm having trouble sticking up for myself. "There's nothing wrong with being curious—this guy, he can't be that bad if you're a part of him."

"You really think so?" I ask.

He leans across the counter and answers me with a kiss just as the timer goes off. His lips linger on mine before he turns back toward the stove.

While he works, my mind rolls over what he just said. What if the pieces of me that came from Andrew Abrams are the worst parts of me? The selfish part, the part that can hold a grudge for years and is terrible at math?

"What are you thinking?" Jeff asks.

"I just," I start. "What if I don't like him? What if he doesn't like me? What if—"

"No matter what 'ifs' end up happening, you'll be okay—and you won't have to deal with it on your own."

"Does that mean you'll go with me?"

He volleys the question back to me. "Does that mean you want to go?"

"How can I go?" I ask.

"How can you not?"

I know he's right. I can't pass up this opportunity to be in the same room with my DNA Dad. To look him in the eye and make him finally give me the half of my story I'm missing.

Chapter Twenty-Seven

Then

Friday night, Betsy let herself into the sorority house, physically and emotionally drained from another long week. She was grateful the weekend had arrived, and she had no plans other than to relax and maybe paint her nails. Several girls were going to an event at Hillel that night, where she would have been if she were still living her old life.

But she no longer had to go to those boring events with their cheap wine and stale small talk. It made her angry to think of all the hours she'd wasted playing the good girlfriend. Angry and a little sad.

Betsy closed the door behind her, aware her moods were all over the place lately. She was tired of being tired, and as much as she wanted to go up to her room and lay down, she knew she had to at least try to be social for a while.

The night before, Sissy had told her that several of the girls had asked her if Betsy was all right. The thought of people talking and worrying about her made Betsy uneasy, so she vowed to start acting as if everything was normal, even though they were anything but.

A few girls were watching television in the living room, and Betsy put on a smile before joining them.

Jeopardy! was on TV, but no one was really paying attention. Even the girls who were usually trying to guess the question before Art Fleming revealed it seemed distracted. Betsy noticed they were all dressed nicer than usual—instead of sweatpants and pajamas, they were wearing nice slacks and dresses. Even Evelyn was wearing makeup.

Before she could ask what was going on, the smell of roasting garlic and tomatoes wafted upstairs and into the living room. Kathy, their house mom, must be cooking something especially pungent for dinner.

The smells that usually whet her appetite were now playing tricks with Betsy's stomach. She needed to get some fresh air.

"Excuse me," she said, holding her hand over her nose. She ran toward the back door, letting herself onto the porch, which looked down over Edgehill Road. She leaned against the closed door and shut her eyes, taking deep breaths of the crisp fall air.

Betsy's eyes flew open when she heard one of her sisters clearing her throat. It was Lauren, a junior from New York City, who acted like she was the best thing since sliced bread.

Most of the girls in her pledge class were enamored with the upperclassmen, but Betsy wasn't impressed.

Her sorority sister was standing in an unnatural position, leaning against the railing like she was Lauren Hutton instead of Lauren Rosenbaum. She looked more silly than sexy, wearing a crop top so short it could have been a bra, and jeans so tight they probably had to be peeled off.

"Can we help you?" Lauren asked through her forced smile.

We?

Betsy looked to the right, where Andy Abrams was standing in front of an easel as if it were the most normal thing in the world for him to be standing there, outside her sorority house. He waved an awkward hello, and Betsy had a feeling he was as uncomfortable as she was.

"Can we help you?" Lauren said again.

"I-I just . . ." Betsy stammered. "I just needed some fresh air."

"There's plenty of fresh air out the front door," Lauren not-so-subtly hinted.

"It's okay," Andy said, coming to the rescue. "I could use a little break." He wiggled the fingers of his right hand—the right hand that held the power to awaken a part of Betsy that had been dormant her entire life. "Gotta give my hand a rest."

Lauren dropped her pose. "We can take a break," she said. "Want a tour of the house? I can show you my room?"

"Actually, I'm a little parched," Andy said.

Lauren looked at Betsy as though it were a matter of seniority, and Betsy should be the one to go get Andy a glass of water. She would have gladly taken the opportunity to leave if it hadn't meant going back inside, where the smell of dinner, she imagined, was even stronger now.

When Betsy didn't make a move, Lauren huffed and headed inside—but not before giving Betsy the evil eye. Once the door closed behind her, Andy spoke.

"Hi," he said.

"Hello." Betsy was determined to stay calm, cool, and collected. Which lasted for only about ten seconds. "What are you doing here?" she asked.

"Lauren saw me with my sketchbook at the library and asked me to do a painting of her, a gift for her parents."

"Her poor parents," Betsy said, quickly realizing her mistake. "I don't mean you, I mean . . ."

"It's okay." Andy gave her that crooked smile that made her insides melt, and she was relieved to realize he wasn't upset with her. Betsy wasn't really mad at him anymore, either. She was mostly sad. "It's my first paid commission," he said, looking proud.

"A real, professional artist," Betsy said. "It'll be worth real money one day."

"It probably wouldn't sell for a quarter," he said with a self-deprecating shrug. "I'm not great with people's faces."

"I'm sure it will be beautiful," Betsy said.

They were both quiet for a moment, and Betsy wondered if Andy was thinking back to the other night when he sketched her, face and all, and somehow managed to make her look beautiful.

"I saw you the other day," Andy said. "At the library."

Betsy pursed her lips. She hoped he wouldn't ask why she had so obviously been avoiding him, because she couldn't answer with a straight face.

Hopefully he knew it wasn't because of what he was, that he was gay. She wasn't like all the others who thought it was unnatural, a sin, or a crime. She wished he wasn't that way, but only for selfish reasons.

Mostly, she was embarrassed that he had seen a side of her no one else had before. A side she hadn't even known existed.

"Anyway," he said, eyeing the door in case Lauren was listening in, "I just wanted to say I'm sorry, for everything. And thank you for . . . you know."

"I know," Betsy said. She looked at Andy standing there, looking just as sad and lonely as she was. She wished things were different, that they could have at least been friends. Of course, it was too late for that now. "I keep my promises," she told him. "But you need to keep yours, too. No more dating my sorority sisters—it's not fair to them."

"Of course," Andy said.

A calm quiet settled around them, the only sound coming from the rustling leaves as the wind blew through the trees. Betsy shivered.

"You know, it wasn't all an act," Andy said. Betsy felt her cheeks blush. "I really do like you. I just—"

The back door opened, and Lauren stood there with two glasses of ice water. Betsy considered reaching for a glass and thanking Lauren. It was what Sissy would have done, but acting like her best friend had already gotten Betsy into trouble once.

"Good luck with the painting," Betsy told Andy.

He gave her a sad, secret smile before she turned to go inside and join her sisters in pretending to watch what was left of *Jeopardy!*

Chapter Twenty-Eight

Now

I NEVER WEAR HIGH HEELS. I DON'T KNOW WHAT IN THE WORLD I was thinking when I put them on tonight. Okay, I know what I was thinking. Frannie said the outfit would look even better with heels, that they'd make my legs look "hot."

Even though that's not the look I was going for to meet my DNA Dad, it was fun having her help me with my outfit, almost like we're real sisters. She's only been here for a day, but it's already been great getting to know her as herself, and not her sister's shadow.

But now that we're here, I'm suddenly regretting every decision that led to this moment. I sigh and pick up my left foot, rolling it. "I want to go change my shoes," I tell Jeff.

"Now?" A flash of annoyance crosses his face, and I don't blame him. He has been as patient as a saint through all my mood swings this past week. I'd be annoyed with me too if I were in his shoes—although my feet would be so much more comfortable.

"Yes, now."

I know it would have been better to realize my shoes were

uncomfortable before we got into the Uber, not when we got out of it. But my feet didn't hurt then.

"Babe, you look great," he says, trying to placate me. "You don't need to change a thing."

"Not all of my wardrobe choices are about looking good, thank you very much," I snap. "It's about how I feel, not how I look."

I know I don't need to be telling him any of this—he's a bigger feminist than I am—but my skin itches and my feet hurt, and I don't think this was a good idea anymore. What if Andrew Abrams takes one look at me and it just confirms that he doesn't want anything to do with me?

Jeff pulls me in for the hug I didn't realize I so desperately needed. "No pair of shoes is going to help you feel any better right now," he says, planting a kiss on top of my head. "But it's okay. You're okay."

"I don't think I am," I admit.

"We can always go home if you want," he says. "We don't have to do this."

"Yes, we do," I tell him. "I do."

I take a deep breath and grab Jeff's hand as we walk toward the gallery.

He opens the door for me, and I step inside. It's a cute space, tucked among the giant office buildings on Wacker Drive. The front window looks out on the river, and the walls are filled with paintings—his, I assume. A few are framed, but most are in raw canvas form.

"Welcome to the Second City Gallery." I turn to see the curator, a thin, angular woman. Her hair, her glasses, her sleek dress and even her nail polish is a shade of black so deep it's almost purple. "I'm Victoria," she says, extending her long, thin arm.

"Margaux," I say, shaking her hand. "And this is Jeff."

Jeff raises an eyebrow at me but thankfully doesn't give me away.

"Nice to meet you both," she says. "Please sign in here—just your name and email address so we can let you know about future events."

My hand shakes as I bring the pen to the page. I manage to write down Margaux's name and her email address before handing the pen to Jeff.

"Help yourself to some champagne, and everything you see here is for sale. Oh, and please fill out a name tag, if you don't mind. The artist's request."

Jeff thanks the woman and leads me toward the corner with the champagne and name tags. "You can breathe now," he says. "*Margaux*."

"I panicked," I admit.

He smiles and hands me a glass of champagne. "This will help."

I bring the flute to my lips and drain the glass. The bubbles tickle my nose from drinking too quickly, but that doesn't stop me from trading my empty glass for a full one. Next, we move to a high-top table where "My Name Is" stickers and Sharpies are laid out. I don't attend many events at art galleries, but this doesn't seem like a standard practice.

Jeff takes a sticker and scrawls his name, with a single line connecting the *f*'s, like he always does. I, however, take my Sharpie and write out Margaux's name carefully, as though I'm going to be graded on my penmanship.

All labeled and semi-liquored up, I grab another glass of champagne, and I'm ready to see the art created by the man who had a part in creating me. A new kind of panic settles in my stomach—what if I don't like his work?

"Here," Jeff says, handing me a glossy five-by-seven card. "A memento."

The same photograph Maks found online is smiling up at me. On the other side of the card, there's a bio and a few thumbnails of his work. I read the bio:

Andrew Abrams has been an artist since his mother (my grandmother) *gave him his first acrylic paint set when he was just eight years old. It wasn't until his college years at the University of Kansas that he became committed to his art.* (At least he was able to commit to something, if not any of the girls he dated.) *He now lives in Naples, on Florida's west coast, where he owns and runs a small gallery. Critics have compared Abrams to a modern Edward Hopper, but the artist describes his work as looking at life through smiling eyes.*

I frown, wishing I had inherited his glass-half-full look at the world.

"Ready?" Jeff asks, offering his arm.

I link mine through his and tuck the postcard in my purse as we turn the corner to see the exhibit. I wish I knew more about how to appreciate fine art, but I know enough to know the first painting we see is beautiful. It's lifelike, just slightly more stylized.

The painting features a woman, standing on the beach, looking out at the ocean. The waves look so real I can almost hear them crashing against the sand, but there's something haunting about the woman. You can't see her face, but based on the way her arms are wrapped around her torso, it looks like she's trying to console herself.

So much for smiling eyes.

"How funny, you're the second Margaux tonight," I hear the curator say.

I turn to see Maks and Margaux walking in the gallery, my littlest sister trailing behind them. I should have known they wouldn't be able to stay away.

"Hey, Paige," Frannie says, giving me a hug. "I hope you don't mind we crashed Jeff's work thing—Maks said you wouldn't mind."

"Of course not," I say, hoping she can't hear the panic in my voice.

Her eyebrows furrow as she notices my name tag. She looks up at me questioningly.

"It's just something Margaux and I do for fun sometimes," I tell her. "You know, I was always jealous when you and Annabelle pretended to be each other." I look at Margaux and pretend to scold her. "You didn't want to be me tonight?"

"Whoops," Margaux says through an awkward laugh. "Hey, Frannie—want to come with me to get some champagne?"

My sister nods, and I exhale a deep breath as soon as they're out of earshot. "You're not supposed to be here," I whisper to Maks.

"Hey, your sister said she likes art, too!" he says in his defense before leaning in close. He cups his hand around his mouth in an attempt to whisper, but it just amplifies the sound. "Did you meet him yet?"

I cringe at the volume of his voice and shake my head no. The art of whispering is something Maks has yet to learn. He blames it on English being his second language, but I'm sure people whisper in Ukraine, too.

"The artist?" the curator asks, joining our small circle. "Andrew is just over there if you'd like to meet him—"

"No!" I say a little too loudly. Everyone's eyes are on me, and beads of sweat start to form on the back of my neck. Thank god I ended up wearing my hair down. "I mean, no need to bother him."

The chime of the front door opening saves us all from another awkward exchange, and the curator excuses herself to greet the next group of patrons.

There's a pretty big crowd—either Andrew Abrams is more well-known in the art world than I realized, or maybe I'm not the only one who recently found out he was their biological father and decided to come confront him tonight.

"Paige," Jeff says, steadying me with his hand on my elbow as Frannie and Margaux rejoin us. I hadn't realized I was shaking.

I quickly pull myself together, and we walk toward the next painting. It's a small canvas with a bowl of fruit, Andrew's take on an image as old as time. There's something about how vibrant the colors are or his use of depth and shadow that makes me want to reach out and touch the apple.

The next painting is of a small room with a single mattress in a corner. There aren't any people in it, but I can sense the presence of someone. It's heartbreaking and has a sense of loss and longing that I wouldn't expect from an image of an empty room.

Jeff and Frannie have moved on to the next painting, but I can't take my eyes away from that mattress on the floor.

"He's good, huh?" Maks says, coming up behind me.

"Not bad," I admit.

"I've heard worse," a man says behind me. His voice is deep and smooth, and I know it's him before I turn around. My stomach flutters, and I'm afraid I might throw up. I count to three and turn to face the man I came to meet.

Andrew Abrams.

He's got a thick head of hair, more brown than gray, and his blue eyes seem to shimmer, bright against his tanned skin. He's taller than my dad was, with wide shoulders and a trim waist. He's handsome, and I imagine he was quite the catch in college. It's easy to see why Aunt Sissy and my mom both fell for him all those years ago.

My eyes dart away from his, searching for Frannie. I'm relieved to see she's halfway across the room, in what looks like a deep conversation with Jeff and Margaux. Looking back to Andrew Abrams, I open my mouth to say something, but no words come out. I'm not sure whether I should apologize to him or demand that he apologize to me—for what, exactly, I'm not sure.

"Margaux," he says. I'm confused for half a second, until I follow my DNA Dad's eyes to my name tag. "That's the French spelling, right?"

I nod, still unable to form a sentence. Standing this close to him, it feels like the air is charged with electricity. My arms are covered in goose bumps, all the tiny hairs standing at attention. I want to reach out and touch him—whether to hug him or slap him, I'm not sure. Although I have a feeling neither would be appropriate.

I wonder if he feels something too, if there's an invisible connection between us, or if it's just my overactive imagination. I look into the eyes that look like mine, then down to his familiar half smile. It's faded from warm to polite now, as if he's ready to move on.

"Well, thank you for coming," he says before turning to talk to someone who will probably tell him how much they like his art, or at least say something, instead of just standing there like an idiot.

I watch as he walks away, then look down at what's left in my glass of champagne. My eyes find Jeff, across the room, who gives me a smile that lifts my fragile heart. My eyes fill with tears, knowing he won't judge or blame me for chickening out. For not having the nerve to say anything.

Beside me, Maks is shaking his head.

"What?" I ask.

"So she does speak," Maks says.

I look away from him, toward a painting where a goldfish in a bowl is staring longingly out at the ocean just outside its window.

I can relate to its conundrum—the bowl is safe and familiar, but there's no feeling like freedom. Even if there are predators waiting outside.

The gallery walls feel like they're closing in on me, so I leave Maks and head outside for some fresh air. On the way out, I set my empty champagne glass down and take another full one.

I sit down on a bench overlooking the river, slipping out of my ridiculous heels. My feet hurt, my head hurts, and I'm pretty sure my heart hurts, too. It was stupid of me to come here, to think I'd be brave enough to talk to him, to think I wouldn't need to say anything—that Andrew Abrams would see me, and he would just know.

But then I hear his voice, coming from the gallery door.

"I'll just be a minute," he says to someone inside. "Need to get some fresh air."

His voice echoes through me, in my ears and down my throat, around my heart to the pit of my stomach, and down to my aching toes. I freeze as if he won't be able to see me if I sit still enough. I'm barely breathing when I hear him walk up behind me.

"Beautiful night, isn't it?"

I turn and look at him, standing there, looking at me as if we're just two ordinary people with no connection other than the fact that we both chose the same moment to step outside. I nod, still not trusting myself to speak. I look back toward the river, away from the eyes the same shape and shade as mine.

"Mind if I join you?" he asks. "Margaux, right?"

I offer a crooked smile of my own, and the man who gave me half of my DNA sits down on the other side of the bench.

"Are you originally from Chicago?" he asks, his question only a smidge less generic than one about the weather.

"St. Louis," I tell him.

He nods, and I don't know why I expect him to say something like, "I used to know a girl from St. Louis," or something equally Bogarty. Except he doesn't, and he wouldn't. Betsy Kaplan probably doesn't even register as a ghost in his memory—she's just one of the many, many girls, according to Aunt Sissy, who he fooled around with in college.

"You?" I ask, even though I know he's from Minnesota.

"The Twin Cities," he says. "But Florida's home now. Couldn't handle the cold anymore." He shivers at the thought, and I wish I weren't wearing the wrong name tag. I wish I were brave enough to tell him who I am and ask him who he is. What I am to him, if anything.

We continue to sit side by side, watching the river below us. The reflection of the moon sparkles on the water, and a few boats pass silently by. I wonder how he might paint this scene we're living, but, of course, he has no idea there's any significance to this moment. For all he knows, I'm just a stranger on a bench who accidentally insulted his art.

I try to think of questions I can ask him without revealing my identity. I consider asking something about his art, where he studied. Of course, then he'd bring up the University of Kansas, and I could casually mention that that's where my parents went to school.

But then he'd ask their names, and I wouldn't be able to lie, and then I'd have to explain why I was wearing a fake name tag, pretending to be somebody else.

The silence between us is heavy with all the questions I'm not brave enough to ask. There are so many things I want to know about him, but I don't know where to start.

"Do you like pizza?" I ask. The question catches me as off guard as it does him. He laughs, and it sounds familiar even though I've never heard it before. "I mean Chicago pizza," I quickly add. "We're famous for deep dish."

"Ahh, yes," Andrew says. "I've never met a slice I didn't like, but I do prefer thin crust. It has a better bread-to-cheese ratio."

"Me too," I admit, wondering what else we have in common.

"How about—"

"Babe?" I'll never know what he was going to ask, because I turn around and see Jeff. Andy turns too, and I can see the pieces falling together in Jeff's mind as he looks between us on the bench and Frannie, who is standing beside him.

He stops in his tracks, and Frannie looks confused.

"Sorry to interrupt," Jeff says.

"Nothing to be sorry about," Andy says, standing back up. "I should get back inside, anyway. Nice to meet you, Margaux from St. Louis."

I wave a pathetic goodbye and watch as my chance to get to know my biological father walks away. I take a deep breath, knowing I can't fall apart quite yet. I have to show my half sister a night out on the town.

Chapter Twenty-Nine

Then

THE NEXT WEEK PASSED IN A BLUR FOR BETSY AS SHE WENT through the motions that were her life. She went to her classes, sat through chapter meetings at the sorority house, smiled and nodded as people around her talked about things that didn't matter. But she wasn't really present, not for any of it.

Her sorority sisters assumed she was still in a funk because things with Mark had ended. She was grateful for the convenient excuse because she couldn't quite put into words how she felt, like a balloon that had become untethered. It felt like she was floating above herself, directionless.

She wished she could talk to Sissy about all the emotions flooding her, but she couldn't explain it without telling her everything. And it wasn't her secret to tell.

Besides, Sissy didn't even know that Betsy had gone upstairs to Andy Abrams's room during the party. As far as she knew, Betsy had come back home at a decent hour and gone to sleep alone like the good girl she was. The good girl she used to be.

The door to their bedroom opened, and Betsy looked up from the book she was pretending to read.

"Are you sure you don't want to come with me?" Sissy asked. She was stalling, taking her time getting ready to go to another party at the AEPi house, wrongly convinced that Betsy would go with her if she asked enough times.

"Never been more sure." Betsy smiled before looking back down at the same page she'd been on for the past twenty minutes.

Betsy wished she could flirt and date and kiss guys as if it weren't a big deal. But it was a big deal for her. Especially now that she didn't trust her own intuition anymore. If she'd been that wrong about Andy, how would she ever know if a guy was really into her or just pretending? Besides, she didn't think her heart could handle being rejected again so soon.

"I don't get it," Sissy said. "You had fun last time."

Her best friend was relentless, but Betsy couldn't blame her for what she didn't know.

"I'm just not feeling up to it," she said, trying to be both nonchalant and convincing.

"You haven't been feeling up for anything in weeks," Sissy said, studying her. "You know, you can always go back to Mark. If he makes you happy."

"I told you it's not about Mark," Betsy said sharply. "I just don't want to go to a dumb frat party."

Sissy flinched, as startled as if Betsy had slapped her.

"I'm sorry," Betsy said, her voice back to normal. "I'm just not feeling like myself these days."

"You're not acting like yourself, either," Sissy said.

"I said I'm sorry," Betsy snapped. She'd never talked to Sissy like that before, and she wasn't sure the dynamic of their relationship could survive it. But Betsy couldn't help herself; it was like a mad scientist was off in the wings, controlling her moods.

Sissy leaned close to the mirror to put on another layer of lipstick. She pressed her lips together before turning back to Betsy. "Whatever's going on, I hope you get over it soon. I want my best friend back."

Betsy offered a sad smile that Sissy returned before opening the door to go.

Once she heard Sissy's footsteps heading down the stairs, Betsy lay back on her bed. She hated being this miserable, but she knew a party wasn't the answer—especially not an AEPi party.

The other day she had walked past an open window at a bar, and just the smell of whiskey made her gag. She'd gotten sick that night and the next morning. She didn't think she'd ever be able to taste or smell whiskey again without thinking of that night and the way she felt afterward.

Betsy's stomach flipped again, and she wondered if she was PMSing—that would explain her foul mood and the uneasiness of her stomach. She climbed off her bed and opened her desk drawer to get the little calendar where she marked the dates of her period.

The whole month of October was empty. She flipped back to September and saw that her last period had finished on the fifteenth. She remembered now how disappointed Mark had been that she wouldn't go back to his place after the Rosh Hashana party at Hillel.

She flipped back to the current month. It was October 23—she should have gotten her period two weeks ago. She was two weeks late. Her schedule normally fluctuated a few days here or there—that's why she kept track. But she'd never been this late before.

Maybe the breakup with Mark had affected Betsy more than

she realized. She did feel more stressed than normal. It had to be stress—she and Mark were always careful. Careful to the point it frustrated her sometimes. They never, not even once, had sex without protection. The only time she ever—

Betsy made it to the bathroom just in time to lose the minimal contents of her stomach. She continued heaving even after there was nothing left. This couldn't be happening. She wasn't that unlucky. One time. It had just been one time, and he'd pulled out. He didn't even like girls.

She retched again before going back to her room and climbing into bed, where she planned to stay for the rest of her miserable life.

THE HARD PLASTIC chair was cold on the backs of Betsy's legs as she sat in the waiting room. Just two days earlier, a visit to the medical center on campus had confirmed her worst fears. The doctor had droned on, discussing her options.

Options.

Betsy scoffed at the word that made it sound like she had a choice in any of this. This wasn't her choice. She didn't belong here in this depressing waiting room, where no one was making eye contact with each other. The other girls looked like she felt, embarrassed and ashamed.

She supposed they had that in common, but Betsy wasn't like them. She wasn't supposed to be there. Even when Betsy thought she and Mark had a future together, children weren't a part of their plan for at least five years.

The door opened, and a nurse with a severe face walked into the waiting room. "Sarah Smith?"

The girl who stood up didn't look like a Sarah Smith any more than Betsy looked like a Jane Johnson. She watched as "Sarah" took slow and cautious steps toward the open door where the nurse was impatiently waiting.

This was the right decision for her future, Betsy told herself. The doctor had said she had three months to decide, but she didn't want to give herself a chance to change her mind. It would be crazy to try to raise a baby on her own. She didn't have the right to be anyone's mother, and it wasn't like Andy would want to be involved with her or their baby.

If the baby were Mark's, Betsy wouldn't be there. She'd have another choice. She wished the baby was his. A child needed someone like Mark—boring was good when it came to raising a family. She certainly would have preferred a boring parent to the one she ended up with, unreliable and emotionally unavailable.

Betsy swallowed the sob she felt rising. She wouldn't let herself cry in this cold, sterile place. What a waste it had been, spending so much energy trying to be different from her mother when she was fated to end up in the same situation.

Not exactly the same situation, she realized. When her mother had gotten knocked up, she had made a different choice. She decided to keep and raise Betsy herself, even though she clearly hadn't been equipped to do so, emotionally or financially. Betsy didn't know if that had been more or less brave than the choice she herself was making now.

Betsy felt a flutter inside her stomach—she wasn't sure if it was nerves or the baby. *The baby*. She couldn't wrap her head around the fact that there was a baby inside her—or, at least, the possibility of one. An actual human being who would have called her "Mother." It could have been a chance for Betsy to be for someone else what she never had.

Betsy placed her hand over her stomach and sent a silent apology down to the baby who would never be. In a little less than an hour, she would no longer be pregnant.

Betsy felt a pang of sadness at the thought, which surprised her. She should be feeling relief. This was what she wanted. *Wasn't it?*

The door opened again, and the nurse called out the next name on her list. "Jane Johnson."

In that moment, Betsy made a decision. Whether it was out of strength or fear, she didn't know. But she couldn't do this. So instead of standing and following the nurse down the hall, she held her breath and looked around the room as if she too was wondering who Jane Johnson was.

The nurse pursed her thin lips before reading the name again. She waited a few more seconds, and when no one got up, she called the next name.

As soon as the nurse disappeared behind the door, Betsy grabbed her purse and hurried out of the room. Outside, she gasped for air as if she'd been suffocating.

"I'm sorry," she cried to herself and her baby. "I'm sorry, I can't."

Her fingers fumbled as she unlocked the door to the car one of her sorority sisters had let her borrow. She locked the door and sank low into the driver's seat as if she was hiding from someone chasing her. But she was only running away from herself and the bad decisions that had brought her here.

Betsy was supposed to be the good one. She was the one who dated the boring guy, who settled for average, who was average herself. She wasn't the one who had one-night stands. She wasn't the one who was supposed to get knocked up. But she had, and Betsy knew she had no one but herself to blame. It wasn't the baby's fault, and she couldn't bring herself to undo what she'd already done.

Betsy lay her hand on her stomach again, and a wave of nausea washed over her. She opened the door and leaned out, getting sick all over the packed brown dirt of the parking lot. She wiped her mouth with the back of her hand, popped a piece of Doublemint gum in her mouth, and started the car.

Heading back toward campus, Betsy hoped that she'd made the right decision. She still had options, even though none of them were good. She would give anything for Mark to still be one of them. He wasn't exciting, but he was safe. He was good, and Betsy knew he loved her—even if it wasn't the way she wanted to be loved.

Betsy didn't realize she was crying until she felt a tear slide off her cheek, leaving a dark, wet spot on her skirt. She wasn't sure if the tears were for herself, for her baby, or for Mark.

Chapter Thirty

Now

O H, I THOUGHT YOU WERE JEFF," MOM SAYS, LOOKING UP FROM the plates she's setting on the table.

"Just me," I say, not bothering to hide my disappointment. Although I'd rather hang out with Jeff than with me, too. It's been a long two days of wedding appointments, and as usual, I've reverted to my teenage self around my mother.

But after all the talk and all the obsession over little decisions that don't really matter—pink flowers or yellow; plated dinner or buffet; napkins on the plate or beside it?—I'm tapped. And a little resentful that with all that talking, all those wasted words, there wasn't a single mention or reference to the one thing we should have been talking about.

Of course, I didn't bring it up, either.

"Want to grab the glasses and fill them with ice?" she asks.

I nod and walk into the kitchen, toward the cabinet where Mom keeps the nice glasses she uses only for company and special occasions. Tonight being the latter, Rosh Hashana, the Jewish new year. I take down one glass for each of us—myself, Jeff, Mom, Annabelle, and Frannie. I'm looking forward to seeing Frannie tonight. We've been texting a bit since her trip to Chicago, and it turns out she's a pretty cool kid when her twin's not around.

As I fill each glass with cubed ice from the fridge, I can't help but think how happy it would make Dad to know that we're still doing the Jewish holidays together. He was by far the most religious one in our family. The rest of us always went through the motions, mostly for his benefit, but he really believed in it all.

Two at a time, I carry the glasses back into the dining room. On my third trip, I realize there's an extra place setting at the table. I wonder if Mom set it for Dad, out of habit. I smile at the thought of saving a seat for him at our holiday table, like for Elijah at Passover.

I'm about to ask Mom if that was her plan when the doorbell rings. *That's odd.* Annabelle and Frannie both have keys—they wouldn't ring the bell.

I look at Mom, expecting her to be as confused as I am, but she seems to light up from the inside. She smiles nervously and smooths out her dress before walking to answer the door. I watch her, as if I'm seeing a scene play out in a movie, not my life. She pauses briefly to fluff her hair before opening the front door.

"Joel," my mother says in the voice she usually reserves for babies and people she's trying to impress. "So glad you could make it."

"Thanks for having me."

Joel Levy walks into my mother's house, kisses her on the cheek, and hands her a bottle of white wine.

"I hope you found the house okay?" she says, a little louder than necessary.

Joel looks confused but quickly recovers, nodding and mumbling, "No problem at all."

"You remember my daughter Paige, don't you?" she asks. "Paige, Joel Levy."

"Of course, hello," he says.

Joel extends his hand, and I reluctantly take it since my hands are unfortunately empty. Compared to my dad's, his grip is on the weak side. I guess no one taught Joel Levy the importance of a good, solid handshake when he was a kid, the way Dad taught me.

"I'm going to put this in the fridge," Mom says. "This way, if you want to join me."

Joel gives me a smile that's laced with an apology before following my mom into the kitchen. This is a good thing, I remind myself. Dad wouldn't want her to grow old all alone. But it would have been nice to have a little heads-up. *And Joel Levy?* I gag at the thought of him touching my mother with his weak, clammy hands.

I glance longingly upstairs, where Jeff is hopefully finishing up his conference call. I desperately need him down here to help me try to act normal. Hopefully he'll have good news—everyone, myself included, is eager to get this contract sorted out and signed. I can't wait until we can officially celebrate, but Jeff doesn't want to jinx anything until it's a done deal.

The sound of Mom laughing in the dining room startles me—it's not the fake laugh I usually get, but the real belly laugh Dad always got out of her, and sometimes Annabelle. Maybe Joel Levy could be good for her, clammy hands and all.

I take the back way into the kitchen, so I don't have to fake awkward small talk with the two of them. I take my time, reaching for another fancy glass and filling it with ice, one cube at a time. With nothing left to procrastinate, I walk back into the dining room just as Jeff comes downstairs.

"Dinner smells amazing," he says, stopping suddenly when he realizes there's company.

He gives my mom a kiss on the cheek before extending his hand to Joel. "Jeff Parker."

My mother's boyfriend shakes my fiancé's hand, and I honestly don't know what to do with myself.

The front door opens again, and Annabelle and Frannie walk in, bickering about something or another. Probably about their upcoming birthday party, which Annabelle hasn't stopped obsessing over. I fear the day she gets married.

It sounds like Annabelle is in the middle of a diatribe about their guest list and the number of couples who should be invited compared to the number of single girls and single guys.

"You cut your hair," I say to Frannie, stating the obvious, as they turn the corner into the dining room.

For the twins' entire lives, they've had the same long, brown, perfectly straight hair. When one gets it trimmed, the other does, too. When one got bangs, they both got bangs. This is the first time I've ever seen them look anything but identical.

Annabelle huffs, clearly not a fan of her sister's new short do. Frannie brings her hand shyly to her hair, which falls just below her chin.

"Do you like it?" she asks. "Margaux said a short cut would accentuate my cheekbones."

"I love it," I tell her, meaning it. "And Margaux is almost always right."

More than the haircut, I love that Frannie is doing something for herself that doesn't involve her twin. She's finally stepping out from her shadow.

I think back to how much fun we had on her visit and wonder if Frannie is going through a little reinvention of her own.

"Girls," Mom says, calling the attention back to herself. "You remember Joel."

"Of course, hi, Joel," Frannie says.

Annabelle waves a quick hello before glancing down at her phone as if anything and everything else is more important than being present with her family on a holiday.

"Okay, everyone, take a seat," Mom says. "We've got to get this meal rolling if we're going to make it to Temple on time."

"Temple?" I ask. I assumed the family meal would be the extent of our celebration this year.

Mom nods, as if the idea of not going to the evening Rosh Hashana service would be a crazy thought. "Of course, you know I love it when they blow the shofar."

Annabelle looks up from her phone just long enough to laugh before turning back to whoever she's snapping or chatting with.

I've never seen Mom this out of sorts and nervous, so I take the high road and don't remind her that they only blow the shofar during the morning service. Instead, I decide to act like the good daughter I imagine she wants Joel to think I am.

It's a holiday, after all. And it's what Dad would want me to do.

AT TEN PAST eleven that night, with Jeff snoring softly beside me, I give up on sleep.

For a nonreligious person, I was pretty moved by the service at Temple Israel tonight. It was equal parts reflective and restorative, with hope for the year ahead. God knows it's got to be better than the last year has been.

The year started off on the right foot, with Jeff proposing. But from there, it's been a slow, sad decline. I lost my job and sense of self-worth, I found out my dad wasn't really my dad, and I discovered my mother had been lying to me for my whole life. Piece by piece, parts of myself have been chipped away.

I look over at Jeff, grateful he's sticking by me for better or worse before he legally has to. I may not be the person he proposed to anymore, but I'm going to do my best to try to be the kind of partner he deserves.

Careful not to wake him up, I slip quietly out of bed and tiptoe across the carpeted hall, down the steps, and into the kitchen. Maybe a cup of Mom's Sleepytime tea will help.

I'm too lazy to boil water the normal way, so I fill a mug a little more than halfway and stick it in the microwave. I stand in front of the window, watching the red mug spin around and around. The movement is mesmerizing, and I can't take my eyes away from it. I'm already getting sleepier when I notice the timer is about to hit zero. I open the door quickly to avoid the loud beep.

Mom has ears like a hawk, and the last thing I need is her padding down here to have another empty conversation. I reach in the microwave to grab the mug, forgetting how hot the mug itself has become. "Ouch!" I whisper.

"Can't sleep?"

Startled, I practically jump at the sound of my mother's voice. I turn to find her standing there with her hair in a perfect ponytail, wearing leggings and one of my dad's old silk pajama tops.

I feel an unexpected pang of sympathy for her. She misses him, of course she does.

Once my heart rate has settled back to normal, I shake my head in answer to her question, hoping she doesn't press for details on why I wasn't able to fall asleep. I don't think she wants to know all the things running through my mind.

"Jeff's been out for hours," I tell her instead.

"Men." She laughs and pulls out a chair at the kitchen table. "Your father was the same way—he never had a problem falling asleep. Never, no matter what."

I smile at the thought of him, sleeping in his recliner, sleeping on the couch, even falling asleep at the kitchen table once or twice. I grab a dish towel from its hanging spot on the oven door and use it to bring the still-steaming mug out of the microwave.

"Do you want me to make you a cup?" I offer. "I can use the kettle."

"I'd love one," she says with an unfamiliar smile to her voice. "And the microwave is fine."

I put the tea bag in the mug I'd made for myself and set it in front of her. "Careful, it's hot."

I take another mug out of the cabinet and repeat the process. It feels weird with her sitting there, quietly watching me, so I focus on the microwave as the seconds tick down.

When it beeps, I use the hand towel to remove it and carefully set it down across from my mom.

"Do you want any sugar? Or honey?" I ask. It strikes me that I don't know how my mom takes her tea. I know how Dad took his coffee—three little creams and three sugars.

"This is perfect." She takes a sip and smiles, as if I've done something more than sticking a tea bag in hot water for her.

We sit there in uncomfortable silence as she sips her tea and I wait for mine to cool down enough to do the same. I don't have trouble talking to anyone—strangers, kids, clients, salespeople. Yet

I can't figure out how to talk to my own mother when she's sitting right across the table.

"So, what was keeping you up?" she asks, and I wonder if she's as nervous to hear the answer as I am to tell her.

"A little bit of everything," I say, chickening out.

She nods as if she understands. Maybe she does. Maybe the high holidays make her a little introspective, too.

Even though I don't know what most of the Hebrew words mean in the prayers we recite, it's almost like a part of me deep inside understands them anyway. There's something beautiful about the chorus of people repeating words in harmony that lifts my heart and my spirits.

The rabbi's sermon tonight really spoke to me as well. In addition to the talk about new beginnings and moving into the new year as the best version of ourselves, she talked about being present in every moment. And despite all the upheaval I've had to deal with lately, there have been a lot of wonderful moments. Lazy mornings in bed with Jeff, spending time with Maks and Margaux, getting to know Frannie in a new light—if I try hard enough, I can even find gratitude in all the wedding errands this weekend with Mom and Jeff.

"Westwood did a nice job yesterday with all the tastings," I tell her.

She nods. "Funny to be having your wedding in the same room where you had your bat mitzvah."

"Becoming a woman and becoming a wife," I say.

There's a faraway look in Mom's eyes, and I wonder what part of that special day she's thinking back to. I have so many favorite parts—my sparkly dress, the dance with my dad, the poem Aunt Sissy presented on a piece of cardboard, where certain words like

"Snickers" and "Good & Plenty" were replaced with the actual candy.

"The twins were just babies then," she says. "Not even a year old."

I stare at my tea. I can't deny it hurts that her first memory of a monumental moment in my life is about the twins, not me. I know I shouldn't let it bother me, especially after everything I've learned about in the last two months. There was a reason she kept me at arm's length, a reason, I now know, that had more to do with her than with me.

When the rabbi spoke about the Ten Days of Awe between Rosh Hashana and Yom Kippur, she talked about the importance of asking forgiveness from the people you have wronged in the past year with your thoughts, your words, and your actions, for what you did and what you didn't do. I kept looking over at Mom, wondering if she was thinking about all the things she had to apologize for. It's too late for her to tell Dad how sorry she is, but I'm right here.

I know my mother well enough to know that I shouldn't hold my breath on that happening any time soon, but maybe I don't need an apology to forgive her. I look across the table to where she's slowly sipping tea and try to picture the young girl in her sophomore year in college who just found out she was pregnant, not quite sure who the father was.

If that young girl were anyone but my mother, if that baby were anyone but me, I would have sympathy for her. But because she is who she is, and I am who I am, I've been holding it against her. That's not the kind of person I want to be.

Across the table, Mom looks up from her mug and gives me a small smile. I take that as a sign to follow the spirit of the holiday.

"You know, Mom," I say, "I just want to tell you that, well, I forgive you."

Mom coughs a little and wipes the corner of her mouth before putting down the mug.

"You forgive me?" she asks. "For what? Was the brisket too dry?"

"The brisket was perfect," I say, already flustered. I should have slept on this, or at least thought through what I wanted to say before opening my big mouth. "I'm talking about everything else, what Aunt Sissy told me, all the stuff I found out about."

"You forgive me?" she repeats. Then she laughs—a sinister laugh I've never heard from her before.

I take a sip of my tea and stare a hole into the table, feeling like the fifteen-year-old girl who got caught cutting her sisters out of a family picture.

"There are things I did that I'm not proud of, and yes, there are people I owe an apology to," Mom says. "But I don't need your forgiveness for things that happened before you were born."

I glance back up to see if she looks as angry as she sounds. She does. "I just meant—"

"Oh, I know what you meant." She holds my gaze for a moment before standing to empty the rest of her tea in the sink. "It's getting late," she says.

As I watch her leave, I realize the error of my words. She might owe me an apology for keeping the truth from me, but she doesn't owe me anything for the event that gave me life. And suddenly, I'm the one who should be asking her for forgiveness.

Chapter Thirty-One

Then

FOR ONCE, THE UNIVERSE SEEMED TO BE WORKING IN BETSY'S favor. The Hillel House was hosting their monthly Shabbat mixer, and she knew Mark would be there. It had been two weeks since her failed appointment at the clinic, over a month since she had seen or spoken with Mark. He'd stopped trying to get in touch with her after the sixth bouquet of flowers went unanswered, but she hoped he would still be happy to see her.

The plan had come together slowly, piece by piece. At first, she thought maybe she could convince Mark that the condom had broken one of their last times together, but she knew he was too careful. He wouldn't believe her.

Betsy knew this was the only option she had left. And if it worked, if Mark took her back, then everything would be okay. But if even one small detail was off, then—well, she hadn't thought much about what would happen then. But if that was what it came to, Betsy would figure something out. She could give the baby up for adoption. But she couldn't go back to the clinic.

The moment she'd walked out that door, the baby became *her*

baby. She already felt a deep connection to the tiny human growing inside of her, which was all the more reason why this plan had
to work. It just had to.

Standing outside the Hillel House, Betsy went over the plan
again. She was ready; she had rehearsed it to the point of exhaus-
tion, going over what she would say word by word.

It was almost ten o'clock. The last stragglers would be leaving
soon, and Mark would be there alone, cleaning up and making
sure everything was back where it belonged. That was when she
would walk in and pour her heart out. If things went the way she
hoped, Betsy would be back where she belonged, too.

The front door opened, and two girls Betsy recognized walked
out. She bent down as if she were tying her shoe, even though her
shoes didn't have laces. She didn't want to see anyone, didn't want
any small talk to cloud her mind. She had to stay focused on her
goal, on her baby, and on their future.

Betsy looked through the front window and saw Mark walking
across the empty room. Now was her chance.

She walked up the sidewalk and opened the front door. Mark
was standing a few feet away from her, the cabinet where they
kept the Shabbat candles open before him. He turned and looked
at Betsy, who shivered under his blank stare.

She opened her mouth but couldn't find the words she'd been
so sure of just moments before. She had planned what to say if he
was happy to see her, if he was angry or upset. But she didn't know
what to do with this nothing.

"I found the trash bags— Oh, hi, Betsy," Deborah said. Unlike
Mark, her expression was easy to read. Pure disappointment. "I'll
just leave these with you," she told Mark. "Have a good night!"

Betsy watched as Deborah grabbed her purse and gave Mark

one last look that was so full of longing that Betsy felt a pang of guilt.

She'd convinced herself that what she was doing to Mark was okay because he'd be getting what she knew he always wanted: a family. But maybe she was keeping him from finding an Andy of his own. Not Andy, exactly, but a person whose touch was like electricity. A person, maybe someone like Deborah, who got that tingly feeling from just looking at him.

Betsy hesitated, not knowing what to do anymore. At the sound of Deborah closing the door behind her, Betsy turned and looked at Mark, who still wore the same empty expression. He wasn't helping matters, but she knew this was her mistake, and it was her responsibility to make it right. She rested her hand on her stomach for a fleeting moment as if summoning courage from the tiny seed of a person she was doing all this for.

"What are you doing here?" Mark asked, breaking the uncomfortable silence.

"I-I . . ." she stammered. "I'm sorry."

Mark nodded, patiently waiting for her to say something more. When she didn't, he sighed. "Is that all?"

"No," Betsy said, taking a small step toward him.

"I tried calling," Mark said. "Several times. I sent flowers."

"I know," Betsy said. "I'm sorry." She was starting to hate those two pathetic words.

"I can return the sleeping bag," he said. "You can pick out something else."

"It wasn't about the sleeping bag," Betsy said. She took another step closer, so she was standing right in front of him. She looked at him, really looked at him, and his face finally revealed what he was feeling. It was clear in his kind eyes, which were glimmering with tears, that he was hurting—and she was the one who had caused his pain.

Betsy hated herself for that. He was a good person, a good man, and he'd be a good husband and a good dad. A great dad. He'd never have to know.

"Then what was it?" Mark asked, his voice cracking. "I don't understand."

Betsy reached for his hands. They were damp with sweat. He was nervous, too. "Can we go somewhere and talk?" she asked.

"I have to finish cleaning up."

Betsy looked around the room. There wasn't much left to do. Together, they could have it finished in ten minutes. Five if they hurried.

"I'll help," Betsy said. Mark looked surprised—and Betsy felt a twinge of regret for not helping him more in the past. "Just give me the bag," she said.

Mark did, and he rewarded her with the smile she hadn't realized she'd so desperately missed.

TWENTY MINUTES LATER, Mark pulled into a spot in front of his apartment. The same spot where they'd parked the last time. It had just been a month ago, but Betsy felt like an entirely different person. So far removed from the girl who had been so naively excited, waiting for some big, romantic gesture she knew would never come naturally to a man like Mark.

Betsy scolded herself as she unbuckled her seat belt. She needed to stop thinking of Mark as a consolation prize—he was a good man, a kind man, and she cared for him. And he clearly cared about her, too. She hadn't expected it to be quite so easy to convince him that they should go back to his place to talk.

Mark was already out of the car, and Betsy opened her door before he had a chance to do it for her. They weren't back together yet, and Betsy knew she didn't deserve his kindness.

She followed behind him as he walked up the stairs to his second-floor apartment. They stood there for a moment, the keys in Mark's hand. He looked at her with what felt like trepidation, and Betsy was nervous that he could sense that he was walking into a trap. But then he smiled and unlocked the door, holding it open for her.

Inside, her eyes were immediately drawn to the sleeping bag—blue, her favorite color, a fact she'd overlooked—sitting in the corner of the living room.

Mark's eyes followed hers toward it.

"I would have put it away if I had known you were coming over."

Betsy smiled an apology—for what she'd done and for what she was about to do—and sat down on the couch where they'd sat dozens of times, watching TV before they retired like clockwork after the evening news.

Mark sat down beside her, his knees turned toward hers. One small move and they'd be touching. Betsy looked from his knees up to his eyes, which were pleading, waiting, hoping. His raw emotion tugged at Betsy's heartstrings, and she knew that it wouldn't be "settling" to be with Mark.

She had loved him once, and she could find it again. He wasn't just a good person; he was good for her. Maybe this was how things were supposed to work out after all.

"So?" Mark said. He'd already been more than patient.

Betsy opened her mouth to start her speech when she realized she'd forgotten a crucial part of her plan. "Just a minute," she said, standing up and tucking her purse beneath her arm. "I have to use the restroom."

Mark nodded and watched her go into his bedroom, toward the connected bathroom. But instead of going into the bathroom, she walked toward the dresser where she knew Mark kept his condoms. She quietly opened the drawer and reached for the box. There were four left. She emptied them into her purse and put the box back in its place. She prayed he didn't have an extra one hidden somewhere.

Betsy let out a deep breath and went to the bathroom. She went quickly, flushing and washing her hands, trying to ignore the way her stomach seemed to be turning inside out.

Mark stood up as she walked back toward him. It seemed like he was as nervous as she was. They both sat back down, and Betsy turned toward him, this time close enough that their knees were touching, hers between his. She took his hands in hers and started to talk.

The words weren't hard to say because they were all true. She told Mark about her childhood, about growing up with a woman as detached and depressed as her mother had been, of all the disappointments that filled her early years, on her birthdays and all the days in between. She told him that he had been the first person in her life to make an effort, to really care about her birthday. And she had gotten her hopes up, which wasn't his fault. She apologized for running away without explaining herself and for shutting him out afterward.

"I won't get you another sleeping bag for as long as I live," Mark promised. His eyes were wide, and she knew he meant it. That he'd really heard her.

Betsy smiled. This was where things got a little trickier. "It wasn't just that," she said.

Mark took his hands back, folding them in his lap.

"I mean, it started there," Betsy told him. "But the more I thought about things, the more I realized I wasn't happy."

Mark's face fell at her words, and he looked away, twirling his class ring the way he mindlessly did when he was nervous.

"But I want to be," she said, reaching for his hands again. Betsy knew she had to be as close to honest as she could if this was going to work.

Mark nodded and looked up at her, his expression still unsure. "I want you to be, too. What can I do?"

His voice cracked at the end, and Betsy's heart broke a little. She never imagined she could have so much influence over another person. And now that she had it, she wasn't sure how she felt about using it. But this wasn't just for her. There was someone else counting on her, too.

"It's not just me," Betsy said. "I want you to be happy, too. Are you? Were you?"

"I was," Mark said, and she knew he was telling her the truth. "You make me happy. How can I make you happy?"

"There was a time you did. It's just, I don't know, I feel like we got stuck in a routine. Like we were an old married couple or something."

"What's so wrong with that?" Mark asked, confusion clear on his face.

"Nothing, eventually. But we're young. I want passion and excitement. A little romance."

Betsy looked at Mark, hoping she wasn't laying it on too thick.

He was nodding, taking her words in, but she didn't think he understood. She knew it was now or never.

Betsy swung her leg around so she was sitting on Mark's lap, facing him. She scooted close so her chest was pressed against his.

"I want that passion and excitement from you," she said. "*With* you."

Betsy took his face in her hands and kissed him, holding him still so he couldn't fall into their old routine. It already felt different, better, taking control and asserting herself.

She didn't expect to feel as good as she had with Andy—Betsy blushed at the thought of how she'd surrendered herself to him. But if she could do that with someone who wasn't even attracted to her, then there had to be a way to get there with a man who actually loved her.

She wanted to be the one to show Mark how good sex could be.

"Wow," Mark said when they came up for air. Betsy smiled and leaned in for another kiss. She dropped her hands, letting them slide down Mark's chest. She kept the comparison out of her mind; she needed to stay focused. Mark was the one here. He was hers.

Her hands kept drifting, her fingers trembling as she found the button on his jeans. She undid it before moving down to the zipper.

"Whoa," Mark said. "Slow down."

"I don't want to go slow," she whispered into his neck.

Mark nudged her head back up and started kissing her again. She could feel him responding to her, his breaths becoming more ragged. She smiled. This was working.

Betsy felt Mark's hands slip up the back of her shirt. He was starting to get it. If he just followed her lead, he would see how much better it could be.

"Let's go back to the bedroom," he said between kisses.

"No," she whispered. "No one else is home—let's do it here."

"You're crazy." He laughed nervously. She could tell he was out of his comfort zone, but so was she.

"Please," she said, her lips pressed against his.

He was quiet for a moment before saying, "Just give me a second."

Betsy slid back onto the couch and watched as Mark walked into the bedroom. She waited for the sound of him opening the top drawer of his nightstand. Moments later, he came back, looking like a kid who'd just had his candy stolen by a bully.

Betsy hated knowing that she was the bully, but she pushed the thought away as Mark buttoned his jeans back up. "I just have to run to the store," he said.

"What? Why now?" Betsy looked up at him in a way she hoped looked sexy, not childish.

"I'm out of condoms," he said. "I could have sworn there were a few more—I'll be back in ten minutes."

"Don't bother," Betsy said, summoning every ounce of courage inside of her. "I should leave anyway."

"Wait—what?" She could see the panic in his eyes, but she pressed forward. "This is exactly what I'm talking about—no sense of adventure, everything always so safe and"—she hesitated—"boring."

Mark looked dumbfounded. "But—"

"I'm talking about this, living in the moment. I'm sitting right here, wanting you—*you*," she said again for emphasis. "And you're going to leave me here? I thought you wanted to make me happy."

Betsy hated herself for playing that card, but she had no choice. This was the only way. She was doing this for her baby, for their future.

"You can come with me?" Mark offered.

"Forget it." Betsy stood and reached for her purse. She knew—she hoped—he would stop her.

"Please don't go," Mark said.

"I'm not even in the mood anymore," Betsy told him, straightening her skirt. Purse in hand, she turned and looked at him. "Will you take me home, please?"

She waited for Mark to say something, to agree in the respectful way he always had. But he surprised her by folding her into his arms. His breath was hot on her neck before his lips found hers. They stumbled back toward the couch, and she felt Mark unbuttoning his shirt.

"No," Betsy said, stopping him. Poor guy looked hopelessly confused until Betsy leaned in to kiss him and started to unbutton the shirt for him. "Let me."

Mark smiled and let her undress him. She could tell he was getting as worked up as she was. Maybe Andy Abrams was the best thing that could have happened to their relationship.

Once Mark was undressed, standing before her, more than ready to go, she pushed him gently onto the couch. Betsy watched his face as he watched her, slipping out of her skirt. Betsy didn't want to wait any longer, so she pulled her shirt over her head and undid the clasp of her bra, letting it fall to the floor.

Mark's eyes got wide as she climbed onto his lap. The slow burn was new for him, and he didn't last long. But still, it was an improvement from their normal routine. Betsy smiled, feeling more optimistic about her future than she had since the moment she realized she had screwed everything up.

"Thank you," she whispered as she collapsed in Mark's arms. She started kissing his neck, wondering when he might be ready for another round. Once was enough for her plan, but it was also enough to convince her that maybe there was hope for finding the passion she craved with him.

"I should be thanking you," he said, letting his hands slide up and down her bare back.

They had been each other's first, and she was his only. Betsy hated herself for taking that title away from him, but maybe, if things worked, he could be her last. Her forever.

Betsy promised herself that if this worked, she would give Mark the best life she could. She would love him and let him love her. They would live a happy life, and it would be enough.

Chapter Thirty-Two

Now

"WHEN ARE YOU GOING TO TELL ME WHERE WE'RE GOING?" I ask Maks and Margaux for the hundredth time since they sprang this bachelorette weekend on me.

Instead of answering, Margaux looks at Maks, who is clearly the ringleader of this circus.

"When we get to the gate," he says, lifting the last suitcase into the back of our Uber. "Or maybe when we're on the plane."

Margaux and I climb into the back seat, while Maks takes shotgun.

"I don't get why you're so focused on the place," Maks says from the front seat. "We told you there would be sun, sand, and fruity drinks."

"And no penis paraphernalia," Margaux adds.

Maks shakes his head and makes a disappointed grunt. "Can you even call it a bachelorette party if there isn't a single penis straw?" he asks our Uber driver, who probably doesn't think you can call something a bachelorette party if there's a man in attendance, much less one who planned the event.

I had only a few mandates before agreeing to this little weekend away: I didn't want any of the silly props that young brides shared all over "the 'gram," and I insisted that I pay for my own flight. I had to Venmo Margaux the money since they wouldn't tell me where we were going. I didn't even know whether we were flying out of Midway or O'Hare until they called the Uber.

"You have the patience of a saint," Margaux whispers. I almost got the secret location out of her a few times, but I knew as well as she did that Maks would make us both miserable if she spilled. And I'd be lying if I said a small part of me wasn't enjoying this.

"How long is the flight?" I ask, still trying to get clues out of them.

"A few hours," Maks tells me.

"So, Hawaii is out," I tease. "And I didn't need to bring a passport..."

"Boo, please." Maks doesn't even bother looking back. "You'll know soon enough."

I smile and lean back into the seat, feeling grateful for my two best friends. I look down at my phone, wondering if it's too soon to text Jeff. He leaves tomorrow for the bachelor weekend Ross planned with a few of their old college buddies. A three-night rager in Vegas, which, knowing Ross, was more about an excuse to party rather than having a send-off to Jeff's single life.

When I found out about their plans, I told Maks we should just have our bachelorette weekend there, too. Then Jeff and I could go ahead and turn it into a surprise wedding right then and there. Elvis could marry us, and I could avoid the headache that planning a wedding with my mother has turned into.

She's been more distant than usual since our failed late-night bonding session two weeks ago, but she has not wavered in her desire to plan the wedding of her dreams. I thought she'd be happy if I let her make all the decisions, but apparently the fun comes from deciding *together* what shade of red we want the napkins to be.

I tried telling her that these details didn't matter at the end of the day. Her wedding didn't have any napkins at all, yet she and my dad had one of the strongest and most solid marriages I've known.

I've seen only one picture from my parents' wedding day. It's the first picture of all three of us—although Mom is holding an oversize bouquet to try to block her growing bump. Her smile is polite and measured, unlike Dad's. He's grinning from ear to ear, his white teeth standing out against his dark beard. Standing with his arm draped around Mom's shoulders, he looks like he's just been given everything he ever wanted.

If he only knew then what I know now.

I used to think I was the reason for Mom's subdued smile in the photo. I assumed she was embarrassed that I was inconveniently there, forcing her to abandon the carefree fun of college. Now, I wonder if a small part of her was grateful that Dad had agreed to marry her. Although I'm sure it didn't take much convincing based on the way Dad told it.

In his version of the story, Mom knocked on the door to his apartment close to midnight. Dad said it was a school night, and he was happily surprised to see her until he noticed her tear-streaked face.

He brought her inside and offered her a drink, which made her cry even harder. Eventually, she told him the news that he said made him the happiest man in the world. He said it didn't matter that they were doing things a little out of order.

He asked Mom to marry him that night, and she, of course, said yes. A few weeks later, they moved her stuff out of the sorority house, and his things out of the apartment he shared with two guys from Hillel, and into a small one-bedroom apartment even farther off-campus.

I wonder how the story would have changed if he'd known what she'd done while they were apart for that month. If he would have married her just the same. Knowing his big heart, I wouldn't have been surprised if he would have.

"What airline?" the Uber driver asks as we approach Midway.

"Southwest," Maks tells him.

He turns and gives me a look, as if daring me to try to figure out our destination from the airline. Two can play this game, so I give him a knowing nod as if my suspicions are confirmed.

"You wait here," he says, once we're out of the Uber. "Margaux can check your bag as one of her two."

I start to protest, but he and Margaux have already wheeled our bags over to the skycap.

Miss me yet? I type in a text to Jeff, adding a kissy-face emoji before sending.

New phone, who's dis? he texts back.

I send back the laughing-so-hard-I'm-crying emoji.

Your kidnappers are doing it wrong, letting you have your phone.

I'll text you when I land wherever I'm going, I text. And don't go marrying anyone else while you're in Vegas.

Never, he texts back. Unless she's really cute and employed. xx

Very funny, I reply before slipping my phone back into my purse.

Maks and Margaux are next in line, and as I watch them whispering with their heads bent together, I'm overcome with gratitude.

There's a reason people say that friends are the family you choose, and I would choose these two over and over again.

"Next stop, Nay—" Margaux stops short when Maks elbows her sharply in the side. "Ow."

"Zip your mouth," he says, shaking a finger at Margaux. "I should have kept you in the dark, too."

"Sorry," Margaux says, following Maks as he leads the way through the automatic doors and down the escalator toward security. "I've got a lot on my mind."

Maks scoffs at her excuse. "The only thing on your mind should be sun, sand, and piña coladas."

"I'm more of a Miami Vice girl," I tell him.

"You would be," he says.

I laugh, not sure whether I should be offended. "What's that supposed to mean?"

"Just that you can't ever make up your mind on one thing."

I nod because he's got a point. Part of the reason I agreed to their little plan was that it took the decision-making off my plate. I would have been fine having dinner and drinks somewhere in Chicago—but the idea of choosing a restaurant and deciding who to invite had given me hives.

Thanks to my two best friends, who accept this about me, the only decisions I'll have to make over the next four heavenly days involve which bathing suit to wear and what fruity drink to order.

The regular security line isn't long, but I'm still surprised when Maks follows Margaux and me to the regular lane instead of going to the one for TSA PreCheck. He must not trust Margaux to be unsupervised with me.

I don't see what the big deal is—the surprise has been fun, but I'm going to find out in a few minutes anyway.

"Aren't you PreCheck?" Margaux asks, a little slow on the up-take.

"I am," Maks says, giving her a sideways glance.

"Oh, please," Margaux sighs. "I'm not going to tell her we're going to Naples."

She clasps her hands over her mouth, but she can't take the words back, and I can't unhear them.

"You better be talking about Italy," I tell her. My insides twist at the thought of being tricked into spending the weekend in the same Florida town where Andrew Abrams lives.

Maks shoots Margaux a look that could, and might, kill. We're next in line for security, but I don't care. I look behind me toward the escalator.

"Ma'am," the TSA agent says, and Margaux steps up to show her license and boarding pass.

I take one more look at the escalator, but Maks grabs my hand. "You are going, and you are going to like it," he says in a harsh whisper.

"Next," the TSA agent says, and Maks practically pushes me forward before handing the woman my documents.

After the TSA agent circles and initials my boarding pass, I get in line behind Margaux. I know she was just going along with Maks's stupid plan, but she should have known better. She should have tried to stop him, or at least warn me. She should have known that I wouldn't want something this big sprung on me, masqueraded as a bachelorette party. Whether I tried to see or talk to my DNA Dad again had to be my decision, done my way. Not like this.

"Paige," Margaux says, her voice full of apology.

I shake my head, not ready to talk to either of them. According to my boarding pass, I still have a good forty-five minutes to decide whether I'm going to get on the plane.

"Don't be mad," Margaux says as she slides into the middle seat between Maks and me. "It'll be fun."

"Fun for you, maybe. Fun for him, definitely," I say, looking around her to where Maks is pouting in the aisle seat. Somehow, he turned this around and is mad at us both.

I left them after the security gate and went straight to the nearest bar—they were smart and didn't follow me. I needed my space, and I needed to think this through.

Going on a trip to Naples wasn't the worst idea in the world—and maybe I would have agreed to it someday under different circumstances. When I felt brave enough to try again. But this wasn't just a casual acquaintance they wanted me to drop in on. This was the man who impregnated my mother. The man who left my email sitting unanswered in his inbox for two months now, who looked me straight in the eye and didn't know who I was.

After the first beer, I was calm enough to log into the NPE group on Facebook. I've started commenting on other people's posts recently and am slowly becoming more comfortable with the group. It's easier to be honest around people who get it, who are living through the same experience—whether theirs have turned out to be a dream or a nightmare.

I posted my dilemma—to get on the plane or not—and the responses were mostly in the *you should go* camp. One woman, Maisie from Nashville, had a good point, that just because I was in the same city as he was didn't mean I had to meet him. Robert from

Oregon told me not to read into the lack of email response from my DNA Dad. Old people, he reminded me, aren't the best at technology. Only one person said that I shouldn't go, but I recognized the name as someone who had posted an awful story of a parental reunion gone wrong.

After a second beer, I decided to take Maisie from Nashville's advice and take things one step at a time. I would get on the plane, and I would focus on having fun with my friends on the beach as long as they agreed and understood that I would be the one to decide if, how, and when we did anything that even hinted at the idea of my DNA Dad. They would have to promise not to even mention his name or the idea of him if I didn't bring it up first.

"I'm glad you decided to come," Margaux says, buckling her seat belt. "We don't have to see him."

"Whether we do or we don't, it has to be my call," I tell her.

She nods, and I look over to make sure Maks agrees, too. He mumbles something under his breath, which I choose to take as an apology and a promise to keep his nose out of my business.

He doesn't have to understand my decision, but he has to respect it, whatever it ends up being.

I sigh and lean back into my seat, looking out the window as Chicago gets smaller in the distance. For Maks's sake, I hope he understands the only thing I plan to come back home with is a tan. Not a new daddy-daughter relationship.

Chapter Thirty-Three

Now

The resort Maks booked is beautiful. As its name would suggest, the Edgewater Beach Hotel is on the edge of the water, right on the beach. We have a view of it from our room, and it's gorgeous. I know we have the lake in Chicago, but there's just something about the ocean.

I felt the tension leave my shoulders as soon as I inhaled the salty air, and decided to park my frustration and deal with Maks and his lack of boundaries once we got back to Chicago.

As rough as the start of yesterday had been, it ended pretty perfectly. The hotel is giving us first-class treatment. We were greeted at check-in with complimentary glasses of champagne and were told there would be warm, freshly baked cookies set out every afternoon, which pleased my sweet tooth.

The concierge recommended a wonderful place for dinner, and after two martinis, I was finally able to let go of the worry that Andrew Abrams and his wife and children might happen to walk into the same restaurant.

After dinner, we went back to the hotel bar for a nightcap, which, of course, turned into one too many drinks.

Today, Maks and I are committed to curing our hangovers with a little hair of the dog by the pool, while Margaux, healthy human that she is, goes for a run.

The pool, it turns out, is actually two identical pools with a tiki bar and café between them. We find three chairs by the shallow end closest to the beach and settle in for a day of nothing but vitamin D and whatever vitamins are in piña coladas and strawberry daquiris.

This is the vacation I'd been hoping for. As long as I keep pushing away the niggling thought that somewhere nearby, Andrew Abrams is breathing in the same ocean air I am.

As we settle into our chairs, Maks is quick to wave down a handsome young waiter.

"Can I get you anything to drink?" he asks.

"Penis Colada for me," Maks says. He has more fun messing with straight men than should be legal. "And a Miami Vice for the bride-to-be."

"Do you need anything else?" the waiter asks.

"Only if you do backs," Maks says, nodding toward the sunscreen on the table between us.

"We're fine," I tell the poor kid, who looks tongue-tied.

I give Maks a look once the waiter has gone back to the bar. We haven't even been at the hotel for twenty-four hours, and I'm already worried he's going to get us blacklisted and we won't be able to come back.

"I'm never going home," Maks says. "Men love me here."

"Keep telling yourself that," I laugh.

TWO DRINKS LATER, Maks and I are attempting to lounge in the pool amid an intense game of Marco Polo. The second pool is kid-free at the moment, but neither of us has the energy to move.

One round of the game is ending and another is beginning when I realize Maks is being uncharacteristically quiet. He hasn't said a word since he told me about Marco Polo being the one to introduce Europe to the concept of paper money. He didn't even have a snippy comment when I brought up the twins' big birthday party next weekend.

"You okay?" I ask him.

"Hmm?" he says, clearly somewhere else. I wonder what, or who, he's lost in thought over. Hopefully not John.

"Just thinking," he says, before holding his nose and dunking under the water to cool off. The first time I saw him do that, I laughed because he looked so much like a child. Then I remembered how hard his childhood had been compared to mine. I don't think he even stepped foot in a pool until he moved to the States as a teenager.

"Remember when we went on that roller-coaster thing in LA? The free-fall one?" Maks asks when he comes back up for air.

I groan at the memory. We were on a work trip together in LA and had an off day, so the production company got us free tickets to Magic Mountain. Traditional roller coasters, I was fine with. But the one Maks wanted me to go on was anything but.

The ride featured a podlike contraption that took you all the way to the top of a tower, where a mechanical-arm-like object took you out over the edge and dropped you. Dropped you as in nothing between you and the ground, free-falling all the way to the bottom.

I was terrified, but Maks was insistent. He begged me to go with

261

him, and when I tried to turn back right before we got on, he literally blocked me from leaving. I thought I was going to throw up before the ride even started, but he held my hand from the moment the seat-belt-protector bar came down, until we landed safely at the bottom.

I loved it as much as I hated it—that time, and the other four times I made Maks go with me.

"How could I forget?" I ask, my stomach feeling queasy from the memory.

"You did not want to go on that ride," he says. "You begged me to let you go back down."

"But you wouldn't let me."

He smiles, clearly still proud of himself. "And you ended up loving it—you just needed a little push."

I nod, knowing where he's going with this. But while going on a roller coaster and meeting your biological father are both terrifying, they are two very different things.

"I know it's not the same," he says, before I can use the words on him. "I just wanted you to know where I was coming from. I thought you needed a little push."

"It's different," I tell him.

"I know," Maks says.

His favorite waiter to flirt with walks by, and Maks doesn't avert his eyes for even a second. He's focused on me, on our conversation, in a way I haven't seen since we had a heart-to-heart about why *Love Actually* is the best romantic comedy of all time.

"And I know I'm not supposed to bring it up unless you do," he says, "but time keeps moving forward even if you don't."

"Deep," I tell him.

He smiles in appreciation, but I can tell he's not ready to end the conversation. "We're here. What do you have to lose?"

"My self-respect?" I say. "You forget, I'm the one who reached out to him. Twice now. The day I got the email—which he replied to with a blow-off one-liner, and a second email that he never responded to."

"But you went to the art gallery," Maks says. "Clearly you wanted to meet him."

"I did," I admit. "It seemed fated, him being there. But I went, and he looked me in the eye and didn't know who I was."

"You were wearing the wrong name tag," Maks reminds me.

I frown, knowing he's right. There was a part of me that hoped Andrew would know it was me—either because he could sense it or, more likely, because he had Googled my photo the same way I had his.

"Anyway, you're here now, in the same city," Maks says. "Couldn't it be fated this time?"

I have to laugh at his earnest attempt to bend logic to fit the story he wants to tell. "This trip is less a coincidence of fate and more the butting in of a dear, but pushy, friend."

"I just—"

"Maks," I say, trying to stop him. "I love you, but I really don't want to talk about this anymore. He clearly doesn't want to meet me."

"But what if he does?"

"What if he doesn't?"

Maks purses his lips, and I know him well enough to know that he's thinking of what he wants to say in Ukrainian before attempting to find the words in English.

"You really don't think Elizabeth called him the second she knew that you knew and told him to leave you alone?"

I laugh. "You give my mom a lot of credit. According to my aunt Sissy, she barely even spoke to him after that one night. And I doubt

263

she could find him that fast even if she wanted to. He could have a happy family, a life he doesn't need interrupted by the forty-three-year-old bio-daughter he never knew he had."

"But we're not just talking about any bio-daughter," Maks says. "We're talking about you. He'd be lucky to get to know you, to have you in his life."

"Flattery will get you everywhere," I tell him. "Except for here. I've made my decision, and we both have to live with it."

"Got it," he says. "I'm listening, and I hear you. If you aren't curious and you really don't want a second chance to meet this guy—as *you* this time—I'll let it go. Especially for now, because I'm getting pruny."

He gives me a kiss on the cheek before lifting himself out of the water, taking the long way around the pool so he can pass the tiki bar where his favorite waiter is standing by.

My fingers are getting pruny as well, but I'm not quite ready to get out yet. Especially since the Marco Polo kids have moved their game to the other pool. I think back to that moment on the roller coaster: Maks holding my hand, my eyes shut tight, the rush of wind, and the sensation that I left my stomach at the top of the ride. The sweet relief when I opened my eyes and we were safe on the ground. To this day, it's the most terrifying and thrilling thing I've ever experienced.

Maks might not be right about everything, but he may not be wrong about this. And we're already here—when am I going to have another chance to casually be in the same city as Andrew Abrams? And if he really doesn't want to see me or get to know me, then at least I'll know I tried.

"Daddy, stop!" a little girl screams in delight as her dad grabs her and throws her high in the air. She lands with a splash, swimming back toward the edge of the pool. "Do it again, Daddy! Do it again!"

Growing up, we spent every summer weekend at the Westwood Country Club pool. Mom would sun herself in a lounge chair on the grassy lawn with her girlfriends, but Dad was like this guy, playing in the water, letting me swim through his legs, throwing me up in the air, and teaching me how to get the most splash from a belly flop.

The little girl shrieks as she flies through the air, landing in another splash. This one close enough to get me.

"Sorry," her dad says as his daughter swims back to the edge.

"No problem," I tell him. "She's a lucky girl."

I had been, too. The luckiest. And if the secret had come out before I was born or even when I was young, then it might have changed things with my dad while he was still alive. I never would have stopped loving him, but our relationship might have shifted, and I'm grateful it didn't.

I've always been the kind of person who believes things happen for a reason. And there has to be a reason all of this came out now. That out of all the DNA tests in the world, Andrew Abrams did the same one I did. That he did it when he did, after my dad was gone.

Before I chicken out or change my mind, I swim over to the shallow end, then get out and wrap my towel around me.

"Do you think the gallery is open tonight?" I ask Maks.

He smiles tentatively. "Until nine."

I nod and take the chair beside him. I'll never admit he was right, but maybe I did just need a little push.

Chapter Thirty-Four

Now

I THINK I'M GOING TO VOMIT," I say, stopping in the middle of the sidewalk as we turn onto Fifth Avenue. "Let's go back to the hotel. I changed my mind—I don't want to do this anymore."

I turn and find myself face-to-face with Maks. "We can go back if you want," he says uncharacteristically.

"No," I tell him. "That's not what you're supposed to say."

He and Margaux look at each other before coming around to either side of me, each taking a hand.

"There's no going back now," Maks says. "The only way out is down."

I turn to him, just like I did when we were next in line at Magic Mountain. "What if it crashes and we fall?"

"Then I'll be there to catch you," he says, giving my hand a squeeze.

I nod and take a deep breath before we walk toward the gallery where my DNA Dad has no idea what's coming.

The distance is short, but it feels like it takes forever to reach the front door. I drop my hands to straighten my dress, second-guessing my decision to go with the blue one, even though it brings

LITTLE PIECES OF ME

out the color of my eyes. The other dress I brought, a simple black maxi, is more timeless, more forgiving. I glance down at my flip-flops, grateful that I'm at least in more comfortable shoes this time.

"Do you want to go in alone?" Margaux asks when I don't make a move to open the door.

"No," I tell them both. I don't think I can do this without them.

Maks and Margaux stay close beside me as I reach for the door and wrap my hands around the handle. I hold on, steadying myself before opening the door I thought would always stay closed.

A chime sounds, and I practically jump out of my sandals. I feel Maks's hand on my shoulder, stopping me from turning back.

And then I hear his voice. Andrew Abrams's voice, calling from somewhere in the back. "Hello?"

His footsteps echo against the floor, the loudest sound in the room. He turns the corner, very real and very much in front of me. He looks more casual, more comfortable, than he did in Chicago. He's clearly at home here, in this town and in his gallery.

"Welcome," he says, as though we're just customers here to browse. "We're closing soon, but feel free to have a look around."

There's a flicker in his blue eyes that look like my blue eyes, and I think he might realize who I am. He walks closer, and I hold my breath, afraid I might vomit all over his Docker's.

"You look familiar," he says. "Have we met before?"

I open my mouth, but no words come out.

He stops right in front of me, his face lighting up in recognition. "Chicago, right? Margaux. I never forget a pretty face."

He thinks I'm pretty.

I'm so flustered by the compliment I don't correct him.

"I'm Margaux," Margaux says, clearly forgetting that I borrowed her name at the gallery.

Andrew Abrams frowns as he looks between Margaux and me. "That's funny, I could have sworn you were 'Mar-go find the girl with the pretty red hair.'" He chuckles to himself before explaining. "It's a trick my partner taught me to try to remember names."

Partner? I glance behind me at Maks to see if he picked up on Andrew's use of the word. He could be talking about his business partner at the gallery. Remembering customers' names must be important for business.

"You're not wrong," I tell him.

Andrew Abrams's head tilts the same way mine does when I'm confused. A shiver runs down my spine, and I'd consider turning and making a run for it if Maks wasn't between me and the door.

"I told you my name was Margaux," I admit. "Because I didn't want you to know my real name." I pause, gathering my strength, hoping he won't be able to reject me when I'm standing right in front of him. "It's Paige," I say, watching his eyes for understanding. "Meyer."

Andrew Abrams takes a small step back, and I watch his Adam's apple move up and down as he swallows. "Paige Meyer," he repeats.

"Your biological daughter," I tell him.

I watch the lump in his throat go up and down again before Andrew Abrams drops his head. His shoulders slump, and I realize how wrong it was to drop in on him unannounced. This was a mistake.

"I-I'm sorry," I stammer, bumping into Maks as I inch toward the door. "We shouldn't have come."

"No," Andrew Abrams says. His voice sounds soft and faraway, but I hear its meaning loud and clear: he thinks I shouldn't have come. My chest tightens and it's hard to breathe, but I won't let him see me fall apart. My instincts were right; I never should have let Maks talk me into this. He doesn't want me.

"Please," Andrew Abrams says as my hand reaches for the door. "Don't go."

I turn back and watch as my biological father walks toward me. The closer he gets, the more my skin tingles, as if my genes somehow recognize his.

He stops less than a foot away from me, looking me up and down in a way I haven't been looked at since I was a twentysomething partying in River North. His eyes are shining with tears, and I wonder if they're happy or sad, if he finds it as oddly comforting as I do, looking at a part of yourself in someone else. A familiar stranger.

He lets out a deep breath and extends his hand. "Andrew Abrams," he says. "It's so nice to finally meet you."

I reach out my hand, grateful he didn't go straight for a hug. His handshake is strong and firm. Dad would have approved. I shiver at the thought but manage to hold myself together.

"Nice to finally meet you, too," I say.

We both look at each other, equally unsure of what to say or do next. Behind us, Maks and Margaux walk around a corner, either to look at the artwork or to give us our space. Probably a little bit of both.

"Your work is beautiful," I say in a weak attempt to break the ice, hoping he doesn't remember my lukewarm response at the gallery in Chicago.

"Thank you," he says. "How's your mother? And your . . ." He stumbles before choosing the right word, the only word. "Your father."

"Mom's doing well," I tell him, aware that I sound like I just ran into one of my dad's old business associates at a cocktail party. "She's still living in St. Louis, working part time doing the books for a few small businesses."

"And your . . . How's Mark?"

My throat feels thick with emotion, and I swallow before answering. "My dad, he passed away a few years ago."

"I'm so sorry to hear that," Andrew says. "He was a good man."

"The best," I say, a little too loudly, a little too eager to defend his character, or his honor, or even his existence. "And just so you know, I'm not looking for a replacement dad or anything—I didn't go looking for you. I got that email, and it practically flipped my world upside down."

"I didn't know, either," he said. "And I'm sorry I didn't write you back. I don't have a good excuse—I was just scared. I started a dozen different times but couldn't find the words."

"Anything would have been better than nothing," I tell him, softening my words with a smile.

"Patrick, my partner, keeps telling me the same thing."

There's that word again.

"Your partner?" I ask. "In the gallery?"

"Oh, no," Andrew says. "Patrick is pretty much retired. He mostly fishes—at least that's what he tells me. He's never come home with anything big enough for us to eat, though."

"So he's— So you're . . ." I stop before I can put my foot any further in my mouth. I know it's not polite to straight-out ask, but surely social standards are different when said person is your biological father.

"Gay?" Andrew asks, as if it's a question he's asking me. "Didn't your mother tell you?"

I laugh. "She didn't tell me anything."

"Oh, dear." Andrew scratches his thick head of hair and walks past me to sit at the bench in the front window. "Does she know you're here?"

I shake my head. "This . . . You aren't a topic she wants to talk about. She sent her best friend, Sissy, to tell me what happened."

"Oh, Sissy." Andrew shakes his head and smiles. "Tell me—did she ever settle down? Get married?"

Now it's my turn to shake my head. I take a seat at the opposite end of the bench, turning slightly so I can see his face.

"That girl was a handful." Andrew Abrams laughs, and I try to find a piece of myself in the melody.

"And my mom?" I ask, desperate to understand how she could have been someone who had an affair, who would cheat on my dad.

"Betsy was a beautiful girl," Andrew says. It's strange hearing him use a name that doesn't fit my mother. Betsys are young and carefree, full of hope and life. My mom is definitely an Elizabeth now—reserved and stoic, proper and full of judgment. And regret.

I wonder if he's the one who made her stop being a Betsy.

"That night we . . ." He pauses and looks down at his hands, folded in his lap. I look down at my own lap and quickly unfold mine. "We were both broken," he says. "We were looking for something in each other to help fix us, but it wasn't right. We weren't right for each other."

I nod, wondering how different my life would have been if he'd been a part of it, with his thoughtful words and gentle presence. If he was anything like this in college, I'm not surprised Mom was drawn to him.

"So she knew? That you . . ."

"Not before," he says, catching my meaning. "I told her the next morning. Your mom was the first person I told. It was the first time I'd said the words aloud, and I didn't mean for things to go as far as they did. Like I said, we were both broken."

"Who broke you?" I ask, figuring this might be my one and only chance to get answers. I'm surprised how comfortable I feel around him—the idea of him was scarier than the reality.

Andrew takes a deep breath and stands from the bench. He looks back and nods for me to follow him, so I do. He leads me toward a painting on the right side of the gallery.

The canvas is hanging next to one I recognize from Chicago—the small room with the single mattress on the floor. But this one, I didn't see at the show. I would have remembered it. There's a man with long, shaggy hair standing in the middle of a protest. He's holding out a sign, as if he's handing it to the viewer. His eyes look angry and hurt, as if they are daring the person on the other side to take it.

"His name was William," Andrew says. His voice sounds sad and low, and I wonder if there's a part of him that's still broken.

The chime on the front door sounds as an older man and younger woman stumble in. They're clearly drunk, and their presence shifts the energy in the room, as if the bubble around us has broken.

"I'm sorry, we're closed," Andrew says.

"What about them?" the drunk man shouts, waving his arm toward Margaux and Maks, almost knocking a painting off the wall.

"Les' jus' get outta here, babe," his girlfriend slurs. "S'not that any good anyway." She laughs before they both stumble back out the front door and onto Fifth Avenue.

"We should probably get going, too," I tell Andrew, not wanting to overstay our welcome. He was closing up shop; he had a home, a partner, to get back to. "It was very nice meeting you."

"Wait," Andrew says, before I reach the door. "Do you like ice cream?"

Chapter Thirty-Five

Now

W HILE ANDREW CLOSES THE GALLERY, I WAIT OUTSIDE WITH Maks and Margaux.

"So? What do you think?" Maks asks as we take a seat on the bench in the little courtyard outside the gallery.

"Not here," I whisper, even though there's no way Andrew can hear us. I can't take my eyes off him, watching as he moves through the space. There's something about seeing him go through this nightly ritual that makes him feel even more real.

Before this moment, he's been like a character in a story that only existed in context of the past. I never pictured him here in the present, doing all the little things that make up a person's day: brushing his teeth, driving to work, watching the news, going out for ice cream with his biological daughter.

"It's this way," Andrew says as he joins us outside, leading us to the right. I walk beside him with my support team bringing up the rear. Neither of us talk at first, and I fill the empty space by looking in the windows of the shops we pass by.

"I hope none of you are lactose intolerant," Andrew says, breaking the silence. "My sister, your aunt, she has a love-hate relationship with dairy."

I nod, feeling the weight of an entirely new family tree on my back. Aunts and maybe uncles, possibly cousins. And grandparents. All of mine are gone, but what if I suddenly have grandparents again? What if I get them, only to lose them? My pulse quickens, and I can feel a panic attack coming on.

This is just ice cream, I remind myself. I'm not committing to the holidays or family reunions—just ice cream.

"Paige just has a love-love relationship with dairy," Maks says.

"She's definitely got a sweet tooth," Margaux chimes in.

I glance back at them, grateful they're here to be my voice.

"Patrick says all my teeth are sweet ones," Andrew says. "I'd have dessert with every meal if I could."

I laugh a laugh that's too loud and doesn't sound like my own. It's like I don't know how to be me around him.

"This is the place," Andrew says as we walk up to Regina's Ice Cream Pavilion. "They've got fifty flavors, puts Baskin-Robbins to shame."

"Kitschy cute," Maks says as we walk inside. "I like it."

It is cute in an over-the-top vintage way—the decor reminds me of a Cracker Barrel, with tchotchkes covering almost every surface. Between the life-size statue of Betty Boop and the classic car coming out of the wall with Howdy Doody riding in the back seat, I'm not sure where to look first.

"Hey, Andy!" a woman behind the counter calls out.

I wonder if he prefers Andy to Andrew. I haven't actually addressed him by name yet. "Dad" is out of the question—but I'll have to call him something.

He waves a greeting back to the woman, and we get in line behind two rowdy families. I wonder if anyone looking at us would think we were family. If they would see the similarities I see, the ones Mom couldn't have ignored.

It's no wonder she had such a difficult time with me. I can't imagine trying to raise and love a person who is proof of your greatest regret. I feel sorry for my mom—sorry for myself and the relationship we could've had if things had been different.

"The usual?" the woman asks Andrew as we get to the front of the line. Andrew nods, looking a little embarrassed.

She smiles at me, and at first, I think she must see the resemblance. Then I realize she's just waiting for my order.

"A scoop of mint chocolate chip in a waffle cup, please," I tell her.

"Two usuals," she says, and my stomach drops.

It's just a coincidence—mint chocolate chip is probably one of the most popular ice cream flavors in the world—but my heart feels like it's another in the long line of betrayals I've committed against the memory of my dad.

I almost change my order and ask for pralines and cream because that was his favorite, but I stop myself. It'll just taste like a reminder of how little we had in common.

"Here you go." The woman hands Andrew and me our matching cones of mint chocolate chip, and we smile our matching smiles. I can't decide if this feels all wrong or if this is just the way it feels to belong.

Maks gets something decadent and chocolatey, but I'm happy to see that Margaux also got mint chocolate chip. A cup with a double scoop, which she can get away with, since she's been going on all those long runs.

Andrew pays for everyone, then leads the way outside, where there's a small walkway between shops lined with two-top tables.

Maks makes a move to sit at a table farther back, but Andrew is already pulling up two extra chairs to a table in the middle.

"So, how long have you lived here?" Maks asks, as we crowd around the small table.

Andrew tilts his head back and scratches his chin as though he's trying to do the math. I add mathematics to the tally of my flaws that I can now blame on genetics.

"I've been in Florida for about forty years," Andrew says. "Thirty-five in Naples. I started out in Miami but eventually got tired of the scene."

"I can't remember some of the best nights of my life in Miami," Maks says.

Andrew laughs, and I hate myself for feeling jealous. I should be grateful for Maks's ability to make small talk with anyone, anywhere. But I want to be the one making Andrew laugh.

"It was quite the culture shock for me," Andrew admits. "Kansas was as conservative as it got, especially in the seventies. But in Miami, I was finally able to be myself."

"You think Kansas was bad," Maks says, "you should try being out in Ukraine."

Andrew shakes his head, and Maks nods. "Naples is quieter, more my speed."

Through their conversation, I find out that Andrew didn't have much of a relationship with his parents, my grandparents, after he came out, although he thinks it had more to do with the fact that he rebelled against having a traditional career than his sexuality.

I learn that Andrew would always be grateful that his mother introduced him to the world of art, but he couldn't forgive her for abandoning him for most of his adult life. They reconnected about five years ago, when his father was on his deathbed, but they were more like strangers than family.

I choke on my ice cream as he says those words—*more like strangers than family*—aware that the same could be said about him and me. He must realize it too, because he smiles an apology toward me before tearing an edge off the waffle cup and scooping a bite of his ice cream onto it.

When our ice cream is gone and Maks is in the middle of a story about the night Jeff and I met doing karaoke at Four Farthings, I get suddenly antsy and push my chair back to stand. It must have been more abrupt than I intended, because everyone turns and stares at me.

Andrew stands too, taking my cue that it's time to go. He gives me a shy smile, and I wish I'd stayed in my seat. If he has more to say, I want to hear it.

"This was nice," Andrew says. "Thank you for coming."

"You should thank Maks," I tell him. "I was just along for the ride."

"Well, then, thank you," he says to Maks before looking back to me. "I can't tell you how much this means to me. To meet you, to get to know you."

His words sound like a question, an invitation. He seems to be leaving the decision in my court, but it shouldn't all fall on my shoulders—even though I'm the one who caused this whole mess by being born.

The moderators of the NPE Facebook group would tell me that I'm not the problem, that I'm the result of a problem. But it doesn't feel that way.

I look at Andrew's face, waiting for an answer I'm not ready to give, to a question he didn't really ask.

"It was nice to meet you, too," I finally say. I extend my hand to shake his, the way my father taught me—although I'm sure he never imagined the politeness he instilled in me would be used in this exact scenario.

Our awkward goodbye continues when we realize we all have to walk back in the same direction, toward the gallery, where both our cars are parked.

We come to our rental car first, and Maks gives Andrew a hug before going around to the driver's side. Margaux waves shyly before climbing in the back seat, leaving me alone with him.

"Thanks again for the ice cream," I tell him.

"My pleasure," Andrew says. "Really."

I nod and open the car door. Before I climb inside, I turn back and tell him good night instead of goodbye. I'm not ready to fully open the door to whatever this is, but I'm not ready to close it yet, either.

As Maks pulls away, I look back. Andrew is standing with his hands in his pockets, watching us drive off. I look back at the road ahead, focused on where we're going. That matters more than where we're coming from.

WE'RE ALL QUIET on the car ride back to the hotel, but when we get there, I'm too wired to sleep.

"I need a drink," I announce, and Maks and Margaux are more than happy to oblige.

The hotel bar is too crowded for the mood I'm in, so we buy a bottle of wine, grab three plastic cups, and head down to the beach. The sand is cool without the warmth of the sun, and the water looks dark and ominous.

I sit there, staring out into the vast emptiness of the ocean, listening to the waves rolling onto the sand, contemplating life and my existence.

"Well, that was fun," Maks says, and for him, I know it was.

"Do you think you'll hear from him before we leave?" Margaux asks.

"I know I won't," I tell her.

"Why?" Maks asks.

"He didn't ask for my number," I tell them. There's no emotion in my voice, because I'm not exactly sure how I feel about it. I'm the one who said I wanted answers, not a relationship, so I can't very well be disappointed that he gave me what I wanted.

"Oh, for fuck's sake!" Maks says. "You're too old to play these games."

"You're older than I am," I protest.

He ignores my jab, even though he's usually quick to counter that months don't count when we were born in the same year. "This isn't some guy you met at a bar that you can ignore. He's your father."

"Enough!" I scream, startling us both. "He is not my father. He's just some asshole who screwed my mom. Who screwed up my life."

I look over at Maks, expecting him to say something in Andrew's defense since he seemed to be so smitten by him tonight. But Maks doesn't say anything, and neither does Margaux, so I keep going at a more respectable volume.

"If he wanted my number, he could have asked for it. I'm the one who reached out to him first, I came to meet him, I'm done. I'm not going to force myself on him. If he wants to get to know me like he says he does, then it's his turn to make a damn move."

"It's totally his move," Margaux agrees.

We both look at Maks, waiting for him to chime in.

"I'll only disagree with you on one point," Maks says.

I narrow my eyes, ready to pounce if he says that I should do one more thing to make any of this easier for Andrew Abrams.

"Yes?" I say, annoyed he isn't just spitting it out.

"He didn't screw up your life—your life isn't screwed up."

I sigh and lay back on the sand.

"My life is fine," I admit. "I just feel like it's not mine anymore. I promise I'm not trying to be dramatic, but it's like none of the things I used to hang my identity on belong to me anymore. I'm not my dad's daughter, I'm unemployed—"

"Not for long," Margaux interrupts, even though the prospects are few and far between for a senior art director in her forties.

"You are more than who your parents are or what you do for a job," Maks says, suddenly full of wisdom.

"God, I hope so," Margaux says. "Did I tell you guys I quit my job?"

"What?!" Maks and I both say at the same time. I sit back up and look at one of my best friends, feeling guilty for how self-absorbed I've been.

"Why didn't you tell us?" I ask.

Margaux shrugs. "Still not sure I made the right decision."

"Are you going to a different firm?" I ask. I know she hasn't been thrilled with her job for the last few years, but she made it sound like every law firm was more of the same.

"No," Margaux says. "I'm going back to school."

"For what?" Maks asks.

"Interior design," Margaux says.

"Goodbye, cushy lifestyle," Maks says with a flourish.

"You aren't moving, are you?" I ask, aware of how selfish that must sound. But our building isn't cheap, and I would miss having her live a few floors down.

"No. Not now, at least. I've got savings, but I just haven't been happy. And all this talk about what and who defines us over the past few weeks got me thinking."

"So this is my fault?" I ask, wondering if there's a way to pin this back on my mom instead.

"Not your fault," Margaux says. "Your credit, maybe. I think it's a good thing."

"What are you if you're not French or a lawyer?" Maks ponders.

"Exactly," Margaux says. "I'm still me. Right, Paige?"

I nod, processing all the things.

"But don't you worry," Maks says. "I'm still your devilishly handsome, smart, and talented friend."

"And who am I?" I ask.

"You're our second musketeer," he says.

"You're kind; you're funny and smart," Margaux adds.

"You hate the same people I hate—even if you don't know why," Maks says.

"You're like the glue that holds us all together," Margaux says. "You keep Maks grounded and push me to have more fun."

"Not that much fun," Maks says with a shrug.

"You're not just one thing," Margaux says. "It's like you're this one-of-a-kind amalgamation of everyone who made you, who raised you, and who loves you. You're little pieces of your mom, of your dad, and of Andy. You're Paige."

She pulls me into a hug, and we both tumble to the sand. Maks joins in, and for one beautiful moment, I know exactly who I am.

Chapter Thirty-Six

Then

BETSY STOOD OUTSIDE MARK'S APARTMENT, NOT BOTHERING TO shield herself from the rain. Her wet hair was sticking to her face and her dress was soaked through, but she didn't move. She was too afraid.

She and Mark had been back together for three weeks now, and things had been going better than they'd ever gone before. He was making such an effort to listen to her, to be romantic and even a little spontaneous. But every gesture she made in return was laced with the guilt she felt for deceiving him.

And tonight was the night she'd been dreading all along. She couldn't put it off any longer. Soon, she'd start to show, and it would be impossible to convince Mark that she was so newly pregnant. It would be hard enough when the baby came earlier than planned, although babies were born early all the time, she told herself.

Betsy lay her hand on her belly, trying to glean courage from the little bean growing inside of her. She had come this far; she had to see it all the way through. So she took a deep breath, tried to brush her wet hair off her face, and started the slow climb to the second floor.

She could hear the TV playing on the other side of the door, and she hoped Mark was home alone. She knocked on the door and took a step back.

Mark opened the door, and Betsy watched the shift of emotions on his face, from surprise and joy to worry and concern.

"Bets?" he asked, reaching to pull her inside.

His love for her was so evident that she was overcome by it. Betsy started to shake, shivering from the cold. Tears quickly followed, and she couldn't get a word out.

"Bets?" Mark said again. "Sweetheart? You're scaring me. What's wrong?"

Betsy shook her head, the gesture exaggerated with her shivers that were getting worse by the second. Mark grabbed the blanket his mother had crocheted for him from the couch and wrapped it around her. He pulled her close, rubbing her arms and her back in an attempt to warm her up.

His kindness made Betsy cry even harder—she didn't deserve to be so loved and cared for by him. But her baby did. Having Mark as a father would be the best gift she could give to her child. A gift she would spend the rest of their lives paying back.

"I have to tell you something," she said through hiccupping sobs.

Mark pulled back and looked into her eyes. Betsy saw a flash of fear cross his face, and she knew he thought she was ending things again. Betsy wanted to erase that thought, that possibility from his mind, so she let the words rush out.

"I'm pregnant," she said.

Betsy bit her bottom lip to stop it from quivering and watched his expressive face, waiting, hoping he would be happy. That he wouldn't question the baby's paternity, that he would tell her it would all be okay.

"Y-You're . . ." he stammered.

"Pregnant," she said, finishing his sentence. "I'm so sorry—that night a few weeks ago, you tried to be smart and I—and I . . ."

"Shhh," Mark said, pulling Betsy in for another hug. He kissed the top of her head, moving down to her cheeks, which were damp from both the rain and her tears. Then his lips found hers—it wasn't their best kiss, he was smiling too big, which made her smile, too.

"You aren't upset?" she asked.

"Upset?" Mark laughed, the big, deep belly laugh she loved. "I'm the opposite of upset. I'm the happiest man in the world."

He picked her up and spun her around like they were in a romantic movie, not in her sad, pathetic life. When Mark put her back down on her feet, he dropped to his knee.

"It might be a little out of order, but I love you, Elizabeth Kaplan, and I can't wait to have a family with you. Will you marry me?"

Betsy looked down at this man, this good, strong, kind man, who was handing her the world on a silver platter. She couldn't help smiling back at him, and she realized with a surge of love that not only would this be the best life for her baby, but it could be the best life for her, too.

"Yes," she said. "Yes, I'll marry you."

Mark was instantly back on his feet, kissing her with renewed passion. "I love you so much," he said. "I promise I'll make you happy every day of your life, both of you."

He slid down to her belly and rested his head against her. Betsy closed her eyes and forced herself to be present in the cacophony of her feelings: fear that Mark wouldn't be acting this way if he knew the truth, worry that she wouldn't be able to keep it from him—and most of all, gratitude for this man she loved.

ON THE OTHER side of town, just a few blocks from campus, Andy was locking the door behind him in his new closet-size studio space. It had been kismet—he'd seen the ad in the newspaper just a few days after Betsy's sorority sister had paid him for her portrait.

The portrait had turned out pretty well—he'd taken a few liberties to make Lauren look a little softer around the edges—and if she'd noticed, she hadn't said anything. A few other girls from the sorority had hired him to do similar portraits, and while it wasn't where his passion lay, it was an easy way to fill his time and earn a little cash.

And now, Andy could afford his own little studio, which had a lock on its door and a cabinet where he could keep his artwork away from prying eyes.

Andy came to the studio almost every night, painting scenes from his life. It was therapeutic, as if getting the pictures from his mind onto the canvas released them somehow, so they didn't lay as heavy on his conscience.

The first thing he painted was William's sad little apartment. He had the image committed to memory from the last time he saw it. The mattress on the floor, the crumpled sheets, the stain on the ceiling. He'd taken a little artistic liberty, painting the watch his father had given him, resting on the bed.

There was so much symbolism entwined in that one little watch—time itself, a gift from his father, and it represented the piece of Andy that he knew would always be among those walls where he first learned what love was.

That evening, Andy was painting another image he couldn't get out of his head. The sight of Betsy standing in front of his door with her back toward him in her pretty pink dress. The zipper was down, revealing the pale, soft skin of her back. Her face was in profile, turning toward him, the moment he stopped her from leaving.

This painting, this moment, was more beautiful than any portrait he could paint for her sorority sisters, and Andy wished he could gift it to Betsy. Of course, he knew he never would. Who would want a painting of a night they so clearly wanted to forget?

Andy would remember for them both. He would carry the hurt he'd caused Betsy like a scar on his own heart.

Looking at the painting-in-progress, the way Betsy was coming to life on the canvas, Andy wondered if he could paint the life he couldn't give her—making her look as if she were in love and content with her life, smiling so her sad eyes turned happy.

Chapter Thirty-Seven

Now

THE NEXT MORNING, THE LIGHT ON OUR PHONE IS BLINKING when we get back to the room after a walk on the beach. Margaux finally convinced Maks and me to get off our "lazy asses," as she so delicately put it, and join her.

My lazy ass was happy with the thought of parking it by the pool all day, but once she started talking about fitting into my wedding dress in a few weeks, I reluctantly agreed.

It ended up being more like a leisurely stroll for Maks and me. The two of us dillydallied along the shore, picking up shells and talking, stopping to take pictures of the water while Margaux ran up to the pier and back. She joined us again for her cooldown, and we finished the short distance back to the hotel together.

Our walk may not have burned many calories, but I did feel lighter somehow, more like myself than I have in months. I'll never admit it, but Maks was right. While it didn't go exactly as I'd hoped, I don't regret going to the gallery and introducing myself, this time as myself.

"I call dibs on the first shower," Margaux says, heading straight for the bathroom. She doesn't have to fight me for it. The only sweat

I worked up was from the sun, and the only way I want to wash it off is in the pool.

I look over at Maks to see if he's going to put up a fight for the fun of it, but he's on the phone.

"Thank you," he says. "I'll be right down to pick it up."

"Pick what up?" I ask. It can't be the bill; we don't leave until tomorrow, and they usually slide it under the door. Maybe it's champagne or something that Jeff sent. It would be just like him to do something so thoughtful and sweet.

"They didn't say," Maks says. "Something someone left at the front desk."

I raise an eyebrow. "Did you leave something in whoever's room you ended up in last night?" I ask.

"Only my dignity," Maks says. "It's not my fault there are attractive men crawling all over this place. I'll be back in a hot flash."

"Unless you run into one of your pool boys," I tease.

"You're just jealous I can still have sex with strangers," he says before closing the door and winning the last word.

I smile, happy for him. If anyone deserves a vacation fling, it's Maks. I only hope he can find someone who will make him realize there are good guys out there so he can stop crawling back to John. I used to get excited when they broke up—now I know it's only a matter of time before they fall back into bed together. Some bad habits are harder to break than others.

With Maks on his errand and Margaux in the shower, the room is blissfully quiet. I take my phone out to the balcony and settle into one of the Adirondack chairs. *I could get used to this.*

I send a quick text just to let Jeff know I'm thinking about him. We talked last night so I could tell him the latest, and it seems like he's having fun with the guys.

Next, I open the Facebook app to check in on the NPE group page. Someone has posted a selfie with their bio-dad, and the resemblance is striking. I wish I'd thought to take a picture with Andrew last night, but it would have made our goodbye even more awkward.

I switch over to the FamilyTree website, hoping that maybe last night gave Andrew the courage to write back, to take the next step. But my inbox is as empty as it's been for the last few months.

"Some help?" I hear Maks call from the hallway outside our room.

"Coming," I say—even though I can't imagine what he'd need help with, unless he left his key in the room.

I open the door and find Maks standing there, his arms spread as wide as they'll go, holding a tall, flat, rectangular package wrapped in brown craft paper. There's an envelope where the twine comes together in the middle, and it has my name on it.

"Are you just going to stand there?" Maks asks, awkwardly lifting the package.

I prop open the door with my hip and take one side of the canvas-shaped package. We carry it over to the couch, where we set it down carefully.

"Looks like he made a move," Maks says.

I shoot him a "not now" look and sit down on the couch to open the envelope. My name is written on the front in a beautiful cursive font. I wonder if his to-do lists are typeset this beautifully.

Paige,

I couldn't sleep last night. And when I can't sleep, I paint. I hope you'll accept this gift from me to you. There must have been something in the air that made me stop and pay attention that night. Because when I stood outside that gallery in Chicago, watching the beautiful girl with red hair watching the river, I had a feeling it was a scene I would want to paint one day.

Maybe I knew deep down it was you. I knew you were in Chicago—that's why I asked the gallery to have those silly name tags. I kept looking for a Paige, terrified you would show up and terrified you wouldn't.

When I saw you at the show, a beautiful young woman with red hair, for a split second I thought it must be you. You had to be mine. But then I saw your name tag and my heart sank. I think it was that moment that I realized how badly I wanted to meet you.

I know we only met last night, but I already can't imagine not knowing you. If it's not too much to ask, Patrick and I would love to invite you and your friends over to our house for dinner. Tonight at six. If you have other plans, I understand, of course. But Patrick is dying to meet you, and I would love the chance to get to know you better.

No pressure, just dinner.

Best,
Andy

Below his name, he left all of his contact information—the house phone, his cell phone, his home address and email address.

I read the letter two more times before handing it over to Maks. He oohs and ahhs as he reads. When he's finished, he looks up at me with pleading eyes.

"Can we go?" he asks, sounding like a little boy begging his parents to go to the toy store.

"Go where?" Margaux asks, walking out of the bathroom, a towel wrapped around her. She stares at the still-wrapped package and shakes her head. "And what's that? How long was I in the shower?"

"To Andy's house for dinner," Maks says. "A painting he left for her and about five minutes too long."

"Are you going to open it?" Margaux asks.

"If she doesn't, I will." Maks makes a playful move toward the canvas but stops short of opening it. He looks at me, waiting to be reprimanded. I can picture him so clearly as a little boy that sometimes I forget we didn't meet until we were in our mid-twenties.

"Go ahead," I tell him. His eyebrows shoot up in surprise. "I mean it, go ahead."

Maks looks at Margaux for confirmation that it's okay to listen to me. When she gives him the okay, Maks unties the twine, then releases the first fold of paper. I watch him opening the package more slowly and carefully than I'm sure he's ever opened anything in his life.

Margaux stands beside him, and I watch their faces as the sides of the craft paper fall away.

"It's gorgeous," Margaux says, looking back and forth between me and the painting.

"It's you," Maks says. "Come see."

I unfold myself from the corner of the couch and stand beside them. Sure enough, it's me, sitting on the bench outside the gallery. The sky is so dark blue it's almost black, except for where the moon has lit up the clouds. The buildings are dark, with just a few office lights on. It looks so real, as if he captured the moment with a camera, not a paintbrush and his memory.

You can't see my face in the picture, but I'm amazed he managed to capture how lost I'd been feeling, the way my shoulders are slumped and my head is tilted down. It's like he really saw me.

"It's amaaaazing," Maks says, drawing out the word.

"He even got the dress you were wearing right," Margaux says.

I take a closer look and realize she's right. I wonder again if he'd known, whether he would have paid such attention to a stranger if he didn't.

"So what do you think?" Maks asks.

"About the painting?" I ask, not sure I can put my feelings into words. It's both flattering and overwhelming.

"About dinner," he says. "At the mansion."

"It's a house, not a mansion," I tell him.

"Tomato, to-mah-to," he says. "Can we go? Pretty please?"

I look from the painting back to where Maks and Margaux are waiting for an answer. It's obvious they both want to go, and I admit I'm curious to see where he lives, to meet his partner. My DNA stepfather? I shake my head. But his note said it was just dinner. And we have to eat.

An hour later, Margaux and I are sitting by the pool while Maks is up at the bar, flirting with the servers who I'm sure won't be sad to see us leave tomorrow morning.

I pick up my phone and pull up the new contact I added earlier and type out a quick text. Thank you for the painting.

A moment later, I add, It's Paige Meyer, in case he's in the habit of gifting paintings to strangers.

The messages both say "delivered." I try not to stare at the screen, but I'm relieved when the three telltale dots appear seconds later.

He's writing back.

My stomach flips, and I can't believe I'm so casually texting my DNA Dad. Only one day ago, I was convinced he didn't want anything to do with me, and now we're texting. This whole thing has the cadence of a teenage relationship.

I'm so glad you liked it, he writes.

I'm about to type back that I hope I can find a way to get it back home when the dots appear again. They disappear for a moment before returning. This happens two more times, and I can't take my eyes off the screen. He must be writing a lot.

When the message finally appears, it's so short that I laugh.

And how about dinner tonight?

We would love to, I type, but delete it before hitting send. "Love" might seem too eager, and I don't want to come across too strong. But "like" doesn't feel right, either. This shouldn't be that hard.

I decide to answer his question with another question that implies my answer to his original question is yes.

What can we bring? I type, and hit send.

Just yourselves.

Another text comes moments later.

Can't wait!!!!

Four exclamation points. I guess he's not worried about coming across too strong.

I'm not sure how or if I need to reply since I already have the time and the address, so I settle on sending back a smiley face, then tuck my phone in my bag.

I lean back into my chair, and much to my surprise, I realize I'm smiling.

Chapter Thirty-Eight

Now

AFTER A NOT-SO-QUICK STOP AT PUBLIX TO PICK UP A BOTTLE OF wine—Maks took so long trying to decide between white and red that we ended up buying one of each—we're only a few minutes late to dinner.

Maks slows down as we pass Fourth Avenue on Gulf Shore Boulevard. "It's on the next street," Maks says, even though we all know that the numbers are going down, and three comes before four.

He puts on his blinker and turns right onto the small side street where the enormous house sits, holding court at the corner, taking up the whole block.

"That's the one," Maks says as he turns left into the driveway where the gate has been opened for us. "It looks even bigger in person."

"Please don't be creepy," I beg. I don't want Andy to get the wrong idea about my intentions, and the thought of Maks sizing up his house online doesn't feel right.

"Who, me?" Maks laughs as if there's no way he would ever do something to embarrass me.

"Has Margaux been the one practically cyber-stalking the man for the last two months?" I ask.

Maks puts the car in park and turns toward me. He cups my face with his hands and pouts his lips like he's talking to a baby. "I'm just looking out for you, boo."

"And the fact that they have a guesthouse out back has nothing to do with it?" Margaux asks. She knows Maks as well as I do.

"Oh, hush," Maks says. "You'll be thanking me once you see the inside."

"Inside the house?" I ask. "Last I checked, Google Earth didn't show the inside of people's houses."

"There may have been a photo spread on the place in *Better Homes and Gardens*," Maks says. He's out the door before I can reprimand him, and I'm reminded why there are no secrets between us. If I didn't tell him everything, he'd find a way to figure it out anyway.

I unbuckle my seat belt but don't move to get out of the car.

"I'm fine," I tell Margaux, who I can feel watching me. "I just need a minute."

Meeting Andy last night at the gallery had been a big deal, but tonight, having dinner at his house—the place where he lives, where he wakes up every morning and goes to bed each night, feels like an even bigger deal. It doesn't get more personal than this, and suddenly I'm not so sure I'm ready for it.

I look out the window, taking the house in from the safety of the car. Maks was right—this place is a mansion. The centerpiece of the circular driveway is a fountain with two white palm trees towering on either side. The house itself looks to be three stories with a patio on each floor. With its white stucco walls and red-shingled roof, there's a Spanish influence, but the pale blue, weathered

ALISON HAMMER

shutters are clearly one of the small touches that makes this an artist's home.

All the lights are on inside the house, giving it a warm glow. Their electric bills are probably more than my rent. But if you can afford to own a mansion like this, I'm sure the utilities are just a drop in the bucket.

"Need a little push?" Maks asks as he opens my car door.

I give him a small but grateful smile before stepping out of the car. He takes one hand and Margaux takes the other as we walk up the front steps. I imagine our trio looks like a scene from *The Wizard of Oz*, with the Tin Man and the Lioness holding up Dorothy as they approach the end of the Yellow Brick Road.

At the front door, Maks reaches out and presses the doorbell. I'm expecting some grand bells to ring, so I'm surprised to hear the chorus of Flo Rida's "My House" echoing inside.

Maks laughs. "DNA Dad's got a sense of humor."

I shrug and peer through the spotless glass windows on the front door. Even from the outside, I can tell this house is more than worthy of a magazine spread. An extravagant chandelier hangs in the entryway, casting tiny rainbows around the pristine room. I can't imagine growing up in a house like this, leaving my shoes and backpack by the front door, hanging my artwork—pathetic in comparison—on the fridge.

The pit in my stomach is getting deeper by the second, and I'm afraid I might vomit, but when I see Andy come around the corner, the smile that brightens his face sets my mind, and my stomach, at ease. It's hard to imagine this man hurting my mom all those years ago.

I realize with a sinking feeling that my dad isn't the only one I'm betraying by letting this stranger into my life. My mom might disown me if she ever finds out.

"Welcome to my house," Andy says, opening the door, his voice as bright as his smile. "The doorbell was Patrick's idea. I would have settled for a ding-dong."

I drop Maks's and Margaux's hands and step inside, meeting Andy's eyes for a moment before looking away. "Your house is beautiful," I tell him, even though "beautiful" is far too plain a word for something this magnificent.

I've never been one to think much about architecture, but the grand hallway or entrance or whatever this vestibule is called was clearly created to be admired.

"We brought these for you," Maks says, as he and Margaux both hand Andy a bottle of wine.

"Thank you," Andy says, taking the bottles and closing the door with his hip. The casual move seems out of place in such a formal room. He clearly doesn't have a problem feeling at home here.

"Should we take our shoes off?" I ask, my cheeks burning with the memory of the first time I made that faux pas, leaving my shoes on inside my best friend from third grade's house, tracking mud all over her mom's white carpet. I hadn't been invited back until halfway through seventh grade.

"We're not that kind of house," Andy says. "Leave them on—unless you're more comfortable with them off?" His nervous laugh lets me know I'm not the only one who realizes this dinner is more than just a dinner.

"We're fine with them on," Maks says, answering for all of us. I manage to smile at Andy, who leads us through the entryway, toward what looks like a sitting room. He turns left through an arched doorway, but I hesitate, looking instead toward the right, where a library catches my eye.

Andy must sense I'm no longer behind him. He stops and turns back, smiling when he notices what I'm looking at. "Do you like to read?" he asks.

I nod. Since I was a little girl, books have been my escape, my guilty pleasure. I devoured every single one of the Baby-Sitter's Club series. I especially related to Kristy, with the little sister almost ten years younger than she was. When I finished that series, I graduated to Sweet Valley High, and then I moved on to my mom's Danielle Steele novels. I was almost never without a book.

Andy changes direction and leads us into the library. I stop at the first bookshelf, but Maks and Margaux walk toward the back of the room, giving us the space they know we need.

There are bookshelves covering every inch of the wall, towering all the way up to the ceiling. It makes me think of *Beauty and the Beast*, and I can picture Belle herself sliding along the wall on a rolling ladder, singing about her love of books.

"I love to read, too," Andy says. He smiles, and I wonder how he feels about the similarities we keep uncovering. "Sometimes I wish I'd been a writer instead," he says. "You can't live inside a painting the way you can a good book."

I step closer to the shelves and run my hand along the spines. They seem to be organized by color rather than by title or subject matter. I glance up to a shelf just above my eye level and stretch to pull a familiar title off the shelf: *The Essential Ginsberg*.

"A poetry fan?" Andy asks with mild surprise in his voice.

I shake my head. "Not really," I admit. "But my dad loved Ginsberg. He had this book, too."

The air in the room seems to shift at the mention of my dad, as if his name doesn't belong here. I stiffen at the thought, because I don't want to belong in a place where he doesn't.

"That doesn't surprise me," Andy says. "Ginsberg seems right up his alley. I remember once we had an interesting conversation about whether it was possible to support the country without supporting the war."

"That sounds like him," I laugh. "He could philosophize just about anything."

We're both quiet for a moment, and I smile at the thought of my two dads talking with each other. I wonder if my mom was there too, if this conversation was Before or After.

Maks must notice the prolonged silence, because he walks toward us, saving the day again. "Which one of these is your favorite?" he asks.

I thank Maks with a smile before looking back to Andy, eager to hear his answer.

"That's like asking me to pick a favorite child," he says.

My expression clearly gives away my surprise at his response, and Andy laughs.

"Just teasing. I'm pretty sure you're the only one. Even if you weren't, I have a feeling you'd still be my favorite."

I blush at the compliment and wonder what he would think of the twins if he ever met them. Not that I can imagine a scenario that would have them together in the same place.

We're all quiet for a moment, looking at Andy. His smile falters when he realizes he never answered the question. "But my favorite book," he says. "The one I've read the most times would be . . ."

His voice trails off as he walks past me. My skin prickles as the soft fabric of his light sweater—cashmere, no doubt—brushes against my arm. He reaches up and pulls down a worn hardcover copy of *The Catcher in the Rye*.

"I always related to Holden Caulfield," Andy said. "The whole outsider wanting to belong, but hating the idea of belonging. I was a conflicted kid."

"Tell me about it," Maks says, acknowledging what I assume must be a shared experience. Although I imagine coming out in the nineties was quite different from coming out in the seventies.

"Have you ever read it?" Andy asks me.

"Ages ago," I tell him. "Junior high, I think."

"Here." He presses the book into my hands, and I look down, realizing that his fingers are as long and slender as my own.

"Oh, no," I say, lifting my hands as if the book had burned me. "I couldn't—you said it's your favorite."

"All the more reason for you to have it."

Reluctantly, I take the book and tuck it into my purse. "Well, in that case, thank you."

"Andrew, dear," a musical voice calls, echoing as it bounces around the walls. "Couldn't you at least offer our guests a drink before boring them with all your books?"

I turn to see the man behind the voice, his style as light and airy as he sounds. On anyone else, the Hawaiian shirt might look gaudy, but with his tanned skin, beach-blond hair, and husky frame, it works.

Patrick brings a manicured hand to his mouth as his eyes lock with mine.

"Oh, my," he says, stopping in the middle of the room. He quickly recovers his manners and steps closer. He wraps me in a hug before I can object or even say hello.

His embrace is packed full of emotion, and although I know even less about him than I do about Andy, I feel myself hug him back. I can already tell I like this man.

Patrick pulls back and looks at me, his eyes watering, showing so much emotion that one might think *he* was my biological father.

"Andy," he says, keeping his eyes on mine. "She's the spitting image of Rebecca."

Rebecca? This name is new to me, but after a lifetime of trying to explain where my red hair came from, I'm hopeful that this might mean I'm close to an answer.

"Patrick," Andy says, "meet Paige. Paige, this is my Patrick."

"We've already met," Patrick says, hugging me again. "I've always wanted a daughter to spoil."

I cringe a little at his use of the word "daughter," but then he hugs me tighter and I realize how good it feels to be accepted and loved so easily. He doesn't even know me yet. My eyes water at the revelation, but I quickly wipe the tears away. The last thing I want to do is scare them away, being too clingy.

"Patrick," I say, stepping out of his embrace.

"Oh, you can call me Paddy, all my friends do." His green eyes sparkle, and I have a feeling Paddy has a way of getting whatever Paddy wants, while somehow making the giver feel good about themselves for complying.

"Paddy," I try again. "These are my best friends, Maks and Margaux."

Patrick looks to the left, and his face lights up again, as if he's just noticing for the first time that we aren't alone in the room. He gives Maks and then Margaux the same warm greeting he'd given me. Margaux laughs uncomfortably at first, but she quickly softens, too.

Once all the hugs and greetings have been exchanged, we stand in an awkward semicircle, staring at each other. I look over at Andy, waiting for him to say or do something, but he just stands there, looking bemused.

We share a smile before both turning to look at Patrick, who's grinning like he just won the lottery. Although by the looks of their house, I wouldn't be surprised if he'd already won. More than once.

"These margaritas aren't going to drink themselves," a woman with a thick Spanish accent calls from somewhere in the house.

I glance back at Maks, who is grinning. I laugh to myself, grateful he didn't say anything out loud about winning one of the little wagers we had on the evening. Andy doesn't strike me as the kind of man who would have hired help, but Patrick certainly is.

"That would be Rosa," Andy says.

"Our Spanish Rose," Patrick adds, as he takes my hand and leads me toward the promise of margaritas.

Chapter Thirty-Nine

Now

ROSA, IT TURNS OUT, IS A FIRECRACKER WHO I INSTANTLY LIKE. She looks too young to be a grandmother, but with her quick tongue and never-idle hands, I can picture her managing a house full of loud, happy humans. She commands the kitchen as if it's her house, and both Andy and Patrick stay out of her way.

"When's the wedding?" she asks, nodding down to the ring on my left hand.

Patrick's eyes light up, and he grabs my hand, studying the diamond. "You're engaged?" His eyes tear up again, and I wish there were an easier way to fit them both into my life, a way that didn't have to involve my mother and the baggage between them.

"In a few weeks," I tell him. "October thirteenth."

Patrick drops my hand and brings his up to cover his heart. "That's not a Friday, is it?"

"Saturday," I tell him.

"Thank goodness." Patrick looks relieved. "Why tempt fate by bringing bad luck into it?"

"I don't want any talk of bad luck in my kitchen," Rosa barks, handing the first two margaritas to Margaux and myself.

While she mixes the next batch, I tell Patrick about Jeff. I know it wouldn't be a bachelorette weekend if Jeff had come along, but I wish he were here tonight. Jeff officially met Andy in Chicago, but that didn't really count. And I have a feeling he and Patrick would get a kick out of each other.

Once we all have our salt-rimmed glasses in hand, Patrick and Andy show us out to the veranda.

I almost bump into Maks and Margaux, who have stopped just outside the door, staring out into the distance. I turn to see what they're looking at.

"Whoa," I say before I can stop myself.

It's like one of Andy's paintings has been brought to life, and it's even more breathtaking in person. The sun looks bright orange as it sets, casting a symphony of colors along the water. It somehow makes every other sunset I've seen less spectacular, and I wonder if they timed our arrival outside to witness it. If this were my house and they were my guests, it's what I would have done.

"This view is the reason we picked this house," Patrick says.

"It's majestic," Maks says. With English being his second language, he doesn't always choose the right word to match what he's thinking—but then there are times like this, where his not-quite-right word fits the moment perfectly.

It's quiet as we watch the last sliver of sun disappear beneath the horizon. I stand there for another moment, soaking in the beauty of it all before turning to look at the veranda, as Patrick called it, which is as wide as my apartment is long. There's a full bar and four different seating areas, one on each end, with couches and chairs, one with a TV that Jeff would kill for and another in the middle with a long dining table, already set for a dinner party.

The decor, I notice, is the same shade of blue as the shutters around the house. The furniture looks nicer and more comfortable than what I have in my living room—it doesn't look like it's made for the outdoors like most patio furniture I've seen. Maybe because it's veranda furniture.

"Did you bring your suit?" Patrick asks, coming up behind me.

I shake my head, disappointed, especially when I notice the infinity pool between the house and the ocean.

"Next time," he says, and I smile, realizing I'd like there to be a next time. Hopefully, with Jeff.

"It's a shame you're leaving tomorrow," Andy says. "The pool doesn't get as much use as it should. And the beach is just a few steps away if you prefer that?"

"I usually stick to the pool," I tell him. I watch his face and imagine him stowing away that fact in a mental filing cabinet. I can picture the label written in his beautiful handwriting on a manila folder: "Things I Never Knew about the Daughter I Never Knew I Had."

"How about you?" I ask. I can't shake the feeling that this is like an awkward first date, all these basic get-to-know-you questions.

"I'm an equal-opportunity swimmer," Andy says. "Come on, let's sit. I want to know everything there is to know about you."

We sit down on the couch, joining Maks and Margaux, who are mid-conversation with Patrick. I steal a glance at Andy, who's unapologetically looking at me.

"So what do you do for work, Paige, dear?" Patrick asks.

My cheeks flush and I panic, not wanting their first impression of me to be that I'm unemployed, even though I know there's nothing to be ashamed of. Still, I don't want them to think I might need or even want their money.

"Paige and I both work in advertising," Maks says, answering for me.

Rosa walks out just then, shifting focus from my current lack of employment and toward the delicious spread she's setting down before us. There's a trio of bowls: one filled with a chunky guacamole, another with mango salsa, and a third with queso. There's also a basket of chips that are so thin and crispy you can almost see through them.

I dip a chip into the guacamole, which looks homemade, and take a bite. "Oh, my god," I accidentally say with my mouth still full. "It tastes like butter—and these chips—where did you get them?"

Rosa tsks, refilling my glass. "It's all handmade, *mi hija*."

I took only two semesters of Spanish in high school, but I remember the words we learned that go along with all the family members. Including that word. *Daughter.*

I'm struck by the thought that even their employee, for lack of a better word, seems so eager to welcome me into the family. I try to relax into the thought. For some reason, it's easier to think of myself as Andy's daughter than it is for me to think of him as my father. A man can have several daughters, after all, but most daughters only have one dad. And I'm not interested in replacing mine.

My eyes get misty at the thought of my dad. I know it's been two years, but sometimes I still feel his absence the way you feel a stomachache. It can come on out of nowhere—sometimes it's just a flutter of discomfort, and other times, it's so debilitating that all you want to do is curl up in bed and cry.

It's almost exactly like a stomachache—except it's my heart

that hurts, missing his smile, his laugh, his voice—which is getting harder and harder to remember. Yet his funeral, which I'd give anything to forget, is still fresh in my mind.

I close my eyes, and for one brief, horrible moment, it's like I'm back there: standing at the edge of a six-foot hole, a shovel in my hand.

The rabbi had explained that helping to cover a casket with dirt is one of the highest levels of mitzvah one person could do for another, because it is a charity that can never be repaid. Still, I couldn't bring myself to do it.

I set the shovel back on the ground and turned to go, but Mom stepped toward me and put her hand on my shoulder. I turned and looked at her, expecting a critical word or glare, but I was surprised to see love and understanding in her teary eyes.

With her standing beside me, I picked the shovel back up and scooped a small bit of dirt from the pile. I held the shovel out over the hole and tilted it ever so slightly, just enough to make the soil fall like brown rain. It landed softly on top of the mahogany casket where I couldn't picture my dad lying in the suit I'd helped Mom pick out. I insisted they leave the top two buttons of his shirt undone because he always said he felt like he couldn't breathe when it was buttoned all the way up.

My chest tightens, and just like that day, I'm finding it hard to breathe.

"Excuse me," I mumble.

I look for a coaster to put down my margarita, but there isn't one, and I don't want to ruin this evening or their table, so I bring the drink with me. I walk as fast as I can without looking like I'm running away, even though that's exactly what I'm doing.

At the end of the veranda, I set down my glass carefully on the stone ledge and place my hands beside it. My heart is racing, my head is spinning, and every breath hurts my lungs. It's not fair that I'm up here breathing when he can't.

I drop my head and close my eyes, counting breaths in and out. After a minute or so, my heart rate is back to normal and the mental picture from the worst day is replaced by the image of my dad's smile right before he pulled me in for a hug, whispering, "I love-love you" in my ear.

"Do you want to be alone?" Andy asks from a respectful distance behind me.

It shouldn't be a hard question to answer, but it is. With my dad's smile still fresh in my mind, as if he's giving his blessing, I shake my head no.

Andy steps beside me, close but not too close, and puts his hands on the ledge. I look at him, then back out at the ocean, now mostly dark with the light of the moon dancing across the water. The rhythmic sound of the waves crashing against the shore has a calming effect on me, and after a moment, I'm feeling brave enough to talk.

"Sorry about that," I tell him. "Was just thinking about my dad."

Andy nods. "Grief can hit you at the damnedest times," he says. "And your dad, he was a great guy."

"The best," I agree.

We're both quiet for a while in a way that feels more comfortable than it should, seeing as we're still not much more than strangers.

"What was my mom like?" I ask, partly to change the subject away from my dad and also because I'm curious who this *Betsy* was and how she could have gotten herself into the mess that made me.

"She was something," Andy says. His eyes have a faraway look, and I wonder if somewhere, a part of him actually cared about her.

"She wasn't like the rest of the sorority girls she hung out with. Maybe that's why we connected—we both played the part when we had to. But the rest of the time, it seemed like she was standing at the edge, observing from a distance instead of being in the middle of it all."

I nod, because in some ways, it seems like she's still just playing a part, going through the motions of life.

"How much do you know about . . ." Andy lets the words fall off, and I don't make him finish the sentence because I like him too much to make him say something like "the night you were conceived."

"Not much," I admit. "Just what my aunt Sissy told me."

He's quiet for a moment before letting out a sigh that sounds like he's been holding it in for decades. "Let's go sit down," he says, leading me toward the second seating area on this far end of the veranda. He sits down on the couch and I take the chair beside it. I sink into the soft cushions but try not to get too comfortable. I'm aware this is a once-in-a-lifetime conversation, and I want to make sure I don't miss a word of what Andy Abrams has to say.

He looks at me, and I shiver under his purposeful stare.

"My biggest goal in college was graduating without anyone finding out I was gay. And back then"—he pauses as if he's trying to find the words before he continues—"it's hard to be someone you're not when people are always watching. It can be hot under the spotlight."

Spotlight? He must read the surprise on my face, because he laughs before explaining.

"It sounds silly now, but that's how it felt back then. I was on the football team, just the kicker, mind you. But I was the only guy in either of the Jewish fraternities on campus who was on the team, and my house, AEPi, took a lot of pride in it. There were always eyes on me.

"So it may have looked like I was playing the field—I had a reputation for being very picky when it came to the girls I went out with—but I only went on as many dates as I needed to, to keep my cover. I always stopped before things went too far. Well, almost always."

He smiles a sheepish smile before going on. "There was only one place on campus where I could really be myself. The art studio, where I met William."

The faraway look is back in his eyes, and I wonder how often he talks about his past. If it wasn't a pleasant part of his life, I imagine it's one he doesn't revisit often. I give him a smile that I hope makes it easier because I don't want him to stop.

"He was the most talented artist I'd ever met," Andy says, "and the first openly gay person I had in my life. He gave me permission to be myself. He was a beautiful, tortured soul, and I thought I loved him. When we were together, it was like the world just made sense. I made sense.

"But with that talent came a dark side. William was angry at the world he thought was holding him back, and he was furious I wouldn't come out. It had nothing to do with him—I just wasn't ready—but he couldn't get over it. We had a big fight."

Andy looks down at the floor before looking back to me. He continues to talk, telling me about the fraternity party that night. How he was on edge—devastated from the breakup and terrified because one of his fraternity brothers was suspicious after seeing him and William together.

Then he saw my mom from across the room. There was a conversation, an empty keg, and the next thing he knew, Andy was inviting my mother up to his room for a drink. He only wanted his fraternity brothers to see them together, to help distract them from the truth.

Andy spoke in broad terms after that, telling me how one thing led to another, and he somehow convinced himself that his life would be easier if he could be the kind of man who could love a woman like my mom. The next morning, wrecked with guilt, he told her the truth. The real truth.

"What did she say when you told her?" I ask, hoping my mom hadn't said the wrong thing.

"She mostly listened, and then she left. She promised me she would never tell anyone—I guess she kept her word. Anyway, a few weeks later, I heard that she was back together with your dad. I didn't see her around much after that, and I honestly thought it was for the best. I didn't know . . ."

"It's okay," I tell him, in an odd reversal of roles.

When he looks back up at me, tears are shining in his eyes. "That night has always been one of my biggest regrets because I hurt your mother. After you contacted me, it brought it all back—all those regrets. But if it hadn't happened, you wouldn't be here, and I don't regret that you exist. That feels like a miracle to me."

I smile, and for the first time since my world got turned upside down, I don't regret it, either.

Chapter Forty

Then

WEDNESDAY WASN'T THE MOST ROMANTIC DAY OF THE WEEK to get married, but Mark didn't have class until eleven— and they figured there wouldn't be a line at City Hall. Sissy was there to be their witness and Betsy's emotional support, and Mark had asked Will Byington, a friend from Hillel who had a camera, to come and take a few pictures after.

Betsy clutched the marriage license in her hand like it was a life raft, which, she supposed, it was. She looked over at Mark, who looked nervous, too. He kept fidgeting with his tie, buttoning and unbuttoning the top button of his shirt. He caught Betsy's eye and took her hand in his, giving it a reassuring squeeze.

The marriage, she reminded herself, was more important than the actual day. She didn't need the fancy dress or the party; she had a good man who loved her and would take good care of her and her child. *Their child.*

She needed to stop thinking about the baby as Andy's. It was a secret she was going to take to her grave, along with the secret she was keeping for Andy. One secret *for* him and another *from* him.

At eight o'clock on the dot, a security guard unlocked the front door to the ugly brick building, letting the wedding party inside. It was so early, the building itself seemed to be just waking up. Betsy's heels echoed as they clicked against the floor. It brought to mind the image of a prisoner, walking toward their execution. She shook the thought from her mind.

Betsy knew there were many worse fates she could be embarking on. Even if she wasn't in love with Mark, she did love him, and she loved how he was trying so hard to be the man he knew she wanted. He had taken her words to heart, and she was trying to do her part by focusing on all the good things, remembering the reasons she fell for him in the first place.

Like the way his face lit up when he realized someone was up for a real conversation—not small talk, but real intellectual and philosophical debates. She felt proud to be by his side when he won an argument, or at least got someone to stop and think about things from a different perspective.

He would have made a great lawyer, Betsy thought, her stomach wringing with guilt. Mark told her the week before that he was delaying his plan to go to law school when he graduated. It made more sense to get a job right out of school so he could support their family. He had plenty of time to become a lawyer, he told her.

Betsy felt her eyes brimming with tears. She blinked them away and added his abandoned plans to the list of things she would spend her life making up to Mark.

"I think it's down here," Sissy said, leading the way downstairs into the basement of the building. There was a waiting room at the bottom of the stairs where they were told to take a seat until the judge was ready for them.

Betsy's stomach flipped, and she wasn't sure if it was due to nerves or the baby. Maybe both.

"How're you feeling, bride?" Sissy asked.

Betsy gave Sissy a smile that she hoped conveyed what she couldn't find the words to say out loud: that she was nervous but grateful. Both for Mark and her best friend. The night before, their last night as roommates, she and Sissy had stayed up talking until nearly two a.m. She made Sissy promise their friendship wouldn't change after the baby came, that they'd still talk and be there for each other, that Sissy wouldn't move on and forget all about her.

Sissy promised they would always be best friends, but deep down, Betsy knew it was unlikely. After today, there would be a clear divide between her life and the lives of all her friends. Sissy included.

"The judge is ready for you," a clerk said, opening the door to the waiting room.

Betsy stood and took a deep breath before following Mark, with Sissy and Will right behind her.

The ceremony, if it could be called that, was held in a room that looked more like an office than a courtroom. The judge wore traditional black robes, but he smiled brightly, clearly happy to be on the wedding circuit instead of in traffic court.

Instead of repeating the vows after each other the way they did in movies, the judge read the vows to them, and Betsy and Mark only had to take their turns saying, "I do."

Betsy listened intently to every word the judge said, inscribing them in her mind and on her heart. She promised to have and to hold, to love and cherish Mark for richer, for poorer, through sickness and in health. She added a few promises of her own—

that she would never take his love for granted, that she would give him love in return, and that she would try every day to make him happy.

When Betsy said, "I do," Mark's face lit up brighter than the sun. He leaned in for a kiss, but the judge stopped him.

"Not yet, son."

Mark nodded and took a step back, looking like a little boy with a grown man's beard. Betsy's heartstrings tugged at the realization their child wouldn't share any of Mark's features.

Before the judge got to the till-death-do-you-part section, Mark was already saying, "I do."

Everyone laughed, including the judge, who again said, "Not yet, son."

After the judge said his final words, he nodded at Mark, who loudly, with no uncertainty, said, "I do."

"*Now* you may kiss the bride," the judge said.

The words had barely left his lips when Mark took Betsy into his arms and kissed her like he couldn't wait to spend the rest of their lives together.

Sissy started whooping, Will snapped pictures, and the clerk tried to usher them out of the room so another couple could unceremoniously tie the knot.

"I love you, Mrs. Meyer," Mark said, a sparkle in his rich brown eyes.

"And I love you, Mr. Meyer," she told him, meaning it. She let out a deep sigh of relief, and Mark squeezed her hand, mistaking it as a sigh of happiness.

Perhaps it was a little bit of both. Her plan had worked, and she was officially married.

"Let's go get some real pictures," Sissy said, leading the way back upstairs.

Betsy smiled, grateful for her best friend and the bouquet of flowers that she could hold in front of her expanding stomach, covering up her shame, her secret.

ANDY HAD STARTED going for a run on the mornings he couldn't sleep. His legs had never been in better shape, and it was a shame he hadn't had more opportunities to kick field goals for his team. But the offensive line had to start scoring touchdowns—or at least avoid turnovers for that to happen.

This season, Andy was grateful to the team for more than his scholarship. Thanks to the hours spent on practices and games on top of his classes and his work in the studio, it wasn't a lie when Andy said he didn't have time to date.

Which also left him with less time to mope around and think about William, wondering if he was thinking about him, too.

Andy had started to look at graduation as the medal at the end of a four-year marathon. He just had to get through two more years. Once he had his degree, he could live his own life without being beholden to his parents or his fraternity. Andy would be free to be himself.

He could already picture his life, living in New York or San Francisco, maybe Miami. He would paint, he would play, he would sleep with beautiful men and no longer have to hide his desires.

Andy pushed the thought away, knowing the more eager he got, the further away the future seemed. Instead, he focused on the moment, the music of his run, the rhythm of his feet hitting the pavement, the haggard sounds of his breath, and the beating of his heart. He turned the corner down Sixth Avenue before circling City Hall to start the run back home when he noticed a bride and groom standing on the front steps.

A Wednesday morning was an odd time to get married, he thought. Andy slowed his pace to get a good look at the bride and the groom. He'd always loved weddings, but recently the realization he'd never be able to have one of his own made him feel sad.

Even from a distance, Andy could see the huge smile on the groom's face. He envied the man for being able to declare his love, loud and proud.

The closer he got, the more the groom looked like Mark Meyer. Andy's eyes drifted to the man's right, and he almost tripped over his own feet. The bride was Betsy.

Andy had heard they were back together—Jared Evans had been more than a little excited to deliver the news—but he hadn't heard they were getting married.

As he watched the bride and groom kiss for the camera, Andy felt a flood of unfamiliar emotion. He was jealous—not because he wanted to be marrying Betsy but because she was getting the love and life she wanted, while it still seemed like an impossible dream for him. Even so, Andy was happy for her, happy for them.

Picking up the pace, he ran until the wedding party was behind him. There was a trace of a smile on his face as he let himself imagine a day when he might find the man of his dreams, just like Betsy had found hers.

Chapter Forty-One

Now

LESS THAN A WEEK AFTER WE BOTH RETURNED FROM OUR BACH-elor and bachelorette parties, Jeff and I have to leave town again—at least this time, it's together.

"I promise I'll make this up to you," I tell Jeff, leaning down to give him a kiss.

"I'll take more of that," he says, pulling me down so I fall into his lap. "But you don't have anything to make up for. Family comes first."

I harrumph and stand to get my small suitcase from the closet. "We should be celebrating you this weekend," I tell him. "Not my sisters."

The contracts had finally been signed yesterday afternoon, and Jeff is now officially the lead candidate to replace his boss when he retires at the end of the year. Not Ross. The whole thing was a little anticlimactic because their new client had taken more than three weeks to dot the i's and cross the t's, but he still deserved to have his own celebration.

"They're going to be my sisters-in-law soon," Jeff says. "Besides, we have to go for the final wedding appointments your mom made for us."

I groan, overwhelmed at the thought of spending so much time with my mother, without letting it slip where I was and who I met last week.

"C'mon, how bad can cake tasting be?" Jeff asks. "There's cake!"

If only it was just cake.

We'd originally planned to drive up on Saturday morning for the party that night, then back home on Sunday, but Mom thought it would be a great idea to come in Friday night so we could squeeze in a few more wedding appointments.

We'd already tasted the menu, but cake, apparently, was an entirely different appointment. Mom had already booked the bakery, but she didn't want to choose the flavor without us. We were also meeting with the wedding coordinator, the rabbi, the florist, and the photographer.

The details are all so overwhelming, each one coming with a dozen different decisions. It's so exhausting, I can understand why people elope or go for simple courthouse weddings like my parents did. Although, theirs wasn't exactly by choice.

Not for the first time, I wonder how Mom felt before her wedding. Maybe she didn't feel trapped like I'd once assumed. Maybe she felt safe and proud of herself for securing a stable future for her child. For me.

It strikes me that I've been thinking about this all wrong. Everything she did, she did for me. Or at least the idea of me, since she hadn't met me yet. It was after *Roe v. Wade*—she had choices. And for some reason, she chose to keep me.

I remind myself to choose the high road this weekend, to try to be grateful and forgiving.

"We should get moving if we're going to make it in time for dinner," Jeff says.

I sigh and zip my suitcase, wishing I hadn't fallen in love with someone who was always so optimistic. Jeff grabs my bag and his, and we walk down the street to pick up the rental car.

"What if she asks how my bachelorette trip was?" I ask. Mom had called once during the trip, but I'd been at Andy's and silenced the phone. I know she wouldn't have known where I was, but I felt like it would be dishonest, talking to her without letting her know. Although not telling her I was there in the first place wasn't that honest, either.

"If she asks, then you tell her the truth," Jeff says. "Or at least part of the truth. Say you had a great time."

"What if I slip up and accidentally tell her the rest of it?"

Jeff laughs.

"I'm serious."

He sighs and turns to look at me. "Would it be such a bad thing? I mean, look where keeping secrets has gotten you both."

I know he's right, and I'll tell her eventually—just not this weekend. And not before the wedding.

THE BACK ROOM at Sub Zero, a trendy bar in the Central West End, has been transformed into a black, white, and silver spectacle for the twins' thirtieth birthday. My senses are in overload, and I'm grateful Jeff and I stopped to have a few drinks at a low-key bar around the corner first.

A DJ is spinning songs I'm not cool enough to know while kids I recognize from the twins' social media feeds get down and dirty. I blush on behalf of some of the girls, whose outfits leave nothing to the imagination.

I look around the room, taking it all in—including the ice sculpture in the shape of a "30" that doubles as an ice luge, and the photo booth, complete with life-size cardboard cutouts of the twins wearing the same little black dresses they have on tonight.

Frannie had mentioned that Mom wanted to help plan the party, but all Annabelle wanted was her checkbook. Her twin had a "vision," according to Frannie, and if this was it, then I'm glad I turned down her half-hearted offer to help with the wedding.

I glance at Jeff, who looks equally overwhelmed. He leans down to kiss my neck, just below my ear, and whispers, "More vodka will help." I follow him to the bar, smiling because other than the cake tasting—which he was right about—having forever with him is the best part of this whole wedding thing.

"Jeff! Paige!"

I smile at the sound of my mom's voice, thinking this could be a bonding experience that we suffer through together—until I turn to see her, wearing an over-the-top black-and-silver dress that perfectly matches the decor. Joel Levy is trailing behind her, looking about as happy to be here as I am.

I smile and wave before finishing my drink and setting down the empty glass.

"Another, please," I yell to the bartender.

By the time he hands me a fresh vodka soda with a splash of cranberry, Mom has reached our corner of the bar. She gives me the kind of hug that means we have an audience. I hug her back, then give an obligatory shoulder-pat-hug to the man she still hasn't admitted she's dating.

I'm grateful the music is loud enough that we won't have to talk much. I can finally relax without worrying I'll slip up and say the wrong thing. Carrying a secret is exhausting, I have no idea how she managed to pull it off so effortlessly the last forty-three years.

"So, what do you think?" Mom shouts over the music.

"Sorry?" I yell back.

"Brunch tomorrow sounds great," Jeff says, saving me. I flash him a grateful smile.

Mom's face lights up, and she says something else, but I can't make out her words over whatever loud song is currently playing. Instead, I give her what I hope looks like a heartfelt smile and raise my glass toward hers.

"Ready for another?" Joel shouts.

I glance down at my glass, surprised to see it's almost empty. Joel smiles, and I see a flash of understanding in his eyes. I smile back and realize that for the third time in her life, my mom has picked a genuinely nice man. That's one thing she and I have in common.

My ears perk up as the DJ plays a song I actually know. I grab Jeff's hand and lead him out to the dance floor. I hook my arms around him and pull him closer. Pressed together in the middle of the crowd, we keep the beat with our bodies as Camila Cabello sings to us about Havana.

The room is hot, and sweat is pooling on the back of my neck, making my hair frizz, but I don't care. The music pulses through my body, and I don't want the song to stop because the more I move, the more I let go of everything and everyone that's been weighing on my mind.

The song ends, and I drop my arms, ready to go back and join the grown-ups in our wallflower position, but three familiar chords from the next song stop me in my tracks. I look at Jeff, who is smiling right back at me.

People laugh that "our song" isn't a schmoopy love song, but this one is more us. It instantly takes me back to the moment that my life started turning right-side-up again. The night a cute guy at the bar caught my eye with his slightly off-key rendition of "Friends in Low Places."

Jeff grabs my hand and spins me around, and when I land back in his arms, I realize the crowd has parted around us. I look for Annabelle, worried she'll be upset that we're embarrassing her, but she's lost in her own world, with her arms thrown around little Adam Fogel, who isn't so little anymore.

My heart lurches for Frannie, who's had a crush on Adam since he moved next door when the twins were in third grade and I was getting ready to leave for my junior year in college. Frannie doesn't seem to mind, if she even notices. She's dancing, surrounded by a group of girlfriends, a familiar smile on her face. My dad's smile.

It's as if someone turns the light off in the room. My mood darkens that quickly. I've been so caught up in the idea of what the addition of Andy Abrams means to my life that I haven't let myself really feel everything I've lost. Until now.

I realize with a start that Annabelle and Frannie are the only ones who can claim any biological connection to our dad. They're the ones who have his smile, his eyes, his DNA.

I stumble and step back. Jeff reaches for me, but I don't move. I can't.

His face falls when he realizes something's not right. He takes a step toward me, but I shake my head. He can't help me with this. I turn and push my way through the crowd of drunk, happy people dancing; past my mom and Joel Levy; past Aunt Sissy and the elaborate photo booth, where Dylan and Alex Murray are posing with their arms around the twins' cardboard cutouts.

I keep walking, out of the private room, through the rest of the club, where another DJ is playing music with so much bass I can feel it reverberating through my bones. I push through the front door, gulping like a fish out of water. I turn the corner and lean back, my shoulders pressed against the brick wall.

I drop my head, grateful for the curtain of hair covering my face, making me feel invisible. Footsteps slow as people walk past and around me, probably thinking I was overserved, which I suppose I was. How many times do I have to learn that I shouldn't drink so much on an empty stomach? This all could have been avoided if I'd just agreed to go to dinner earlier with Joel and—

"Paige?" Mom's voice sounds far away, even though she's just a few feet from me, getting closer by the second. "Paige, honey, are you okay?" She brushes my hair away from my face and tucks it behind my ear. "Sweetheart?"

I look up at her face, full of the love and concern I've spent my whole life craving. Part of me wants to let her put her arms around me and tell me everything will be all right, but the rest of me knows that nothing will be okay until she knows what I did in Naples.

"I met him," I say, freeing the words that have been on the tip of my tongue all weekend. I feel light with the freedom that comes from speaking the truth, until the heaviness of guilt weighs me down.

Mom purses her lips and tilts her head as if she's not sure which "him" I'm referring to.

"Andrew," I tell her. "Andy Abrams. My father."

Her eyes grow wide, and she looks so vulnerable that for a brief second, I think I catch a glimpse of Betsy before her frigid Elizabeth mask returns. Her hand flies up, and I flinch in preparation for a slap that never comes. She catches herself and brings her hand down, gripping my arm like a vise, her perfectly manicured nails digging into my flesh.

"Your father was Mark Meyer," she says. Her voice doesn't show any hint of emotion other than anger, but I'm angry, too.

I want her to admit it, to acknowledge what I've lost. Not just my dad—for the second time—but half of my identity. I want her to realize the truth doesn't just belong to her; it's my truth, too.

Be easy on her, sweetheart, I imagine my dad saying. But he also told me to do the right thing, even if it wasn't easy. To be open and honest, because lies hurt more than the truth.

That's what secrets are. Lies we tell ourselves. I don't want to lie anymore.

"He's still an artist," I tell her. "A good one." I watch my mother's face for a sign that she feels anything, but her expression stays frozen. "I always wondered where my artistic side came from. But you knew. You always knew."

She stares at me, her lips stretched in a thin line. Her nose flares as she breathes in and out, and I can tell she's trying to stay calm—after all, we're standing in the middle of the Central West End, where someone she knows might see her.

"He has an art gallery in Naples and lives in a gorgeous house with Patrick. His partner. He's still very handsome, in case you're wondering."

I keep my eyes locked on hers like we're playing a game, and the first one who blinks will lose. But there are no winners here. Not tonight. Maybe not ever.

Mom opens her mouth but shuts it without saying a word. I

narrow my eyes, daring her to say something. To say anything. A small, sad sigh escapes her mouth, and I know it's a lost cause. Just because I've changed doesn't mean that she ever will. But I'm not finished, not yet.

"You'll be able to see for yourself when he comes to the wedding," I tell her.

That does it. The color drains from her face, and her eyes fill with tears. She starts to say something just as Joel turns the corner.

"I was wondering where you two went," he says, saving us from each other.

Joel looks back and forth between us, and I wonder what, if anything, he knows. If she's kept secrets from him the way she has from everyone else. From Andy, from my dad, from Aunt Sissy. From me.

"They're about to bring out the birthday cake," he says. There's empathy in his eyes, and it's clear he cares for my mom. Cares for me, in some removed way. I hope she does tell him, that she opens up and lets at least one person in. To really see her, flaws and all. "Ready to go in?" Joel asks.

Mom closes her eyes and nods. When she opens them again, she puts a smile on her face that's just for show. I know, because it's the same one she's been giving me my entire life.

Chapter Forty-Two

Now

THERE'S A KNOCK ON THE BATHROOM DOOR, BUT MY HEAD feels too heavy to lift from its resting spot on the closed lid of the toilet seat. I mumble something that's trying to sound like "Come in."

The door opens a crack.

"Babe?"

Jeff. *Thank god.* I don't know what I would have done if it had been my mom.

The rest of last night, after our one-sided conversation, is mostly a blur. I remember we all went back inside to sing "Happy Birthday" to the twins. My eyes kept darting toward my mother's, but she never looked at me. Not once. She was back to her usual self, poised and smiling, chatting with guests and dancing with Joel Levy.

Of course, I couldn't stop looking at her, desperate to see a crack in her facade. A hint, a clue that what I'd said had mattered to her.

From the looks of her, you never would have known that anything out of the ordinary had happened just moments before. She smiled that picture-perfect smile, clapping her hands like an excited toddler as the twins blew out the thirty candles on their giant sheet cake.

If the cake had been tiered instead of flat, the party could have passed for a wedding reception.

I groan at the memory of telling Mom that Andy would be at the wedding. Sure, I'd thought about it, but I wasn't actually going to invite him. I wasn't a masochist, and I wasn't trying to hurt my mom. I really wasn't.

"Feeling any better?" Jeff asks.

I shrug because words are too hard right now.

He walks inside and shuts the door behind him, stepping over me and taking a seat on the ledge of the bathtub. He reaches down and strokes my hair, which makes me feel a little better.

"I fucked up, didn't I?" I ask, turning my head toward him.

"It wasn't your best moment," he says.

I groan. "She must really hate me now."

"She's your mom. She doesn't hate you," he says. But he doesn't know her the way I do.

"I should go talk to her." I move to get up, but my head feels heavy, and I don't think my legs can hold my weight.

"She's not here," Jeff says, and I collapse back down on the floor. "She said she was going to help Sissy at the store."

"The store is closed on Sundays."

"Maybe they're doing inventory?"

"Doubtful." I pinch my eyes shut to try to keep the tears at bay. If I were my mom, I wouldn't want to see me, either. I ruined the twins' party just like I ruined her life.

My stomach lurches, and I feel a familiar grumbling in the pit of my stomach.

"Get out," I tell Jeff, lifting the lid of the toilet seat.

The only move Jeff makes is to grab my hair and hold it back as whatever's left in my stomach revolts. When it's over, I wipe my mouth with the back of my hand and look up at Jeff, who's still holding my hair.

"Are you sure you want to marry me?" I say, asking the question that's been on my mind for months. "I'm a mess."

"True," he says, letting my hair back down. "But you're my mess."

I look up and give him the biggest smile I can muster. "I'm definitely getting the better end of this whole marriage deal."

"Nonsense," he says. "If it weren't for you, I'd still be wearing socks with my sandals, I wouldn't know how delicious noodle kugel is, I wouldn't laugh nearly as much as I do now—and don't forget, your Keynote skills are probably the reason my presentation was such a big hit."

"You still wear socks with your sandals," I remind him.

"Hey, nobody's perfect," he says. "Think you're feeling up for the drive home?"

I nod, because the only thing that sounds worse than five hours in the car is still being here when Mom gets home.

WHILE JEFF BRINGS the bags out to the car, I scribble a note on the monogrammed notepad Mom has kept on the kitchen counter for as long as I can remember. I take the cap off her pen—all her pens have the correct caps on them—and hold it over the paper, waiting for words to come.

"I'm sorry" doesn't seem like quite enough, but I can't think of anything else.

Mom,

    I'm really sorry about last night.

I start to write that I didn't mean the things I said, but I stop myself because that wouldn't exactly be true. I think for a moment, the pen resting between my lips.

    I hate to leave without saying goodbye, but Jeff has to get back to the city tonight. Maybe we can talk soon when I haven't had too many vodka sodas?

I stare at the letter, not sure how to end it. I can't remember the last time I wrote her a note, but I usually just end emails with my name. Maybe with a couple of *x*'s and *o*'s. But that doesn't feel like enough.

"Ready?" Jeff calls from the front door.

"Be right there," I tell him.

I pick up the pen and add the three little words that used to belong solely to my dad.

    I love you.

The words stare back up at me, unfamiliar and out of context. But they're not a lie.

I leave the letter in the middle of the counter where I know she won't miss it. I read through it one more time, hoping it's enough. I'll give her a few days to call me, and if I don't hear from her by Wednesday, then I'll pick up the phone.

She may have started this mess, but who's to say I can't be the one to end it?

Chapter Forty-Three

Then

BETSY FELT LIKE A WHALE. A HUGE AND HIDEOUS BEAST. NO ONE would ever say she glowed the way they described other pregnant women. Her ankles were swollen, her belly was so big it blocked the view of her toes, her breasts had become unwieldy, and it was impossible to find a comfortable position.

Mark, of course, was being the perfect husband and doting on her, which only made Betsy feel worse. It seemed like he lived to take care of her, making sure every craving was satisfied, rubbing her feet when they ached, and loving her even when she snapped at him. Betsy knew she didn't deserve any of it, but she was too miserable to insist otherwise.

The one moment she let herself enjoy was when Mark talked to her belly. Her baby, their baby, was the one who deserved his love. He or she hadn't done anything wrong; only Betsy had.

When they lay in bed in their new off-off-campus apartment, with Mark curled up to her side, telling their baby about all the things he couldn't wait to show him or her, Betsy knew she'd made the right decision.

But other times, like today, there was nothing Mark could say or do that would make her feel better. Because today wasn't any old Saturday; it was the Saturday her old sorority was throwing their annual "C'mon I Wanna Lay'a" party—a luau with leis and tropical drinks and Caribbean music.

It had been one of Betsy's favorite events her freshman year, and she'd been looking forward to it again this year. But she wasn't welcome there anymore. Events were only for members of the sorority, and she was no longer a member. She wasn't even a student anymore. Betsy didn't know who or what she was. A wife, and soon to be a mother, she supposed. But those titles didn't feel like they belonged to her, either.

"You sure you don't want to do anything tonight?" Mark asked.

Betsy shook her head.

"We could go to dinner or a movie?"

"I wouldn't be able to fit in the theater seats," Betsy said. "And the last thing I need is food to make me even bigger."

"You're beautiful," Mark told her.

"And you need to get your eyes checked," she said, her own eyes brimming with tears. "You know, I think I just need to take a nap. That might make me feel better."

Mark looked hopeful, which broke Betsy's heart even more. She was failing miserably at her intended plan to make every day happy for him. So far, the only thing she'd made was a mess.

A FEW HOURS later, Betsy woke to the sound of voices coming from the living room. She dismissed it as noise from the television—Mark always had the volume up too high. But then she heard a familiar laugh, one she hadn't heard since her last week in the sorority house.

Sissy.

It wasn't her best friend's fault that they hadn't been spending as much time together. Sissy had a full schedule between classes and her busy social life—fraternity parties, sorority functions, and all of her dates. It wasn't Sissy's fault that Betsy had nothing but empty hours to spend sitting and waiting for her baby to arrive.

On the rare occasion they did get together, Betsy realized they barely had anything to talk about. Sissy didn't want to hear about her pregnancy woes, and it broke Betsy's heart to hear about all the things she was missing out on.

So she couldn't figure out what Sissy was doing there, in her living room with Mark, when she should be at the party.

Betsy heaved herself out of bed, breathless from the effort. She ran a brush through her hair and wished she had taken Mark up on his offer to take her shopping for more flattering maternity wear.

She hated the feeling of pants around her enormous waist, so day in and day out, she wore shapeless dresses that looked more like nightgowns than anything she could actually wear out in public. But it was too late for that now.

Sissy was laughing again. Mark wasn't *that* funny. Maybe they were watching TV together, although she still couldn't fathom why Sissy would be there in the first place.

Betsy opened the bedroom door and walked as quietly down the hall as she could, wanting to see what was going on before anyone realized she was awake. But when she turned the corner into the living room, Betsy gasped.

"What in the . . . ?" she said, her voice trailing off.

Mark's face looked bright with hope. "Do you like it?" he asked.

"I helped," Sissy announced, looking proud of their handiwork.

While Betsy had napped, the two of them had transformed her

and Mark's living room into a tropical destination. Mark was wearing a Hawaiian shirt, and Sissy was dressed to party with a grass skirt and bikini top.

"I-I . . ." Betsy stammered. "I can't believe you did this."

Mark walked toward her and placed a lei around her neck, kissing her cheek. "You seemed so sad that you were missing the party," he said.

"So we brought the party to you," Sissy said.

"You should be at the real party," Betsy told her former roommate. "Just because I'm missing out doesn't mean you should have to."

"Oh, I'll still go," Sissy said. "But you know I like to make an entrance."

Betsy frowned, looking at the two people she loved most in the world, who had gone out of their way to do something special for her. She didn't deserve their love, but she was grateful for it.

"Thank you," she finally said. "Both of you."

Mark breathed a deep sigh of relief, and Betsy felt a pang of regret. She was going to have to do a better job at pretending to be happy, for his sake.

The baby would be here in just about two months. Luckily, Mark hadn't done the math—and if he did, Betsy was prepared to say the baby was early. She'd already mentioned a couple of times that she herself had been a few weeks early, even though she'd actually been late.

Betsy used to think her mom had been exaggerating when she went on and on about how miserable she'd been during her pregnancy—that she had wanted to serve Betsy an eviction notice, but Betsy wouldn't budge.

She used to think her mother held a grudge, still resentful of Betsy for those two extra weeks in the womb. Now, Betsy understood.

For the first time in her life, she thought about apologizing to her mother.

"I made virgin piña coladas," Sissy said, coming out from the kitchen with a glass for Betsy.

"And I picked up a pizza," Mark told her. "Hawaiian."

"Ooh, and the music!" Sissy ran over to the record player and set down the needle. The music completed the picture, taking her to another place. She could almost smell the ocean and feel the sun warming her skin.

It was apparent now, the happier she seemed, the happier Mark was. Betsy felt her heart surge with love for him. It was a great responsibility, having someone's happiness on your shoulders. A responsibility she wouldn't take lightly.

This wasn't the life Betsy had planned for, but she was going to make the best of it. She was lucky, and she wasn't going to let herself forget it.

Chapter Forty-Four

Now

I'M CURLED UP ON THE COUCH WITH THE NPE FACEBOOK PAGE pulled up on my computer when Jeff walks in from work. There are hundreds of new people joining the group each week, and now I find myself among the seasoned members comforting the newbies, letting them know they're not alone. I never tell them things will be okay, because I know they might not be.

"I got the mail," Jeff says.

I nod and keep typing, finishing up a comment. "You can just put the wedding catalogs in the trash," I tell him. These days, most of the mail we get are bills and bridal things thanks to whatever vendor sold my name to a wedding mailing list.

"Already dumped them in the recycling bin," Jeff says. "What'd you do today?" he asks.

"Emailed a bunch of recruiters, wrote and rewrote my bio section for LinkedIn, did the laundry, and pondered my existence," I tell him.

He smiles, but it doesn't reach his eyes. "Are you still going to that happy hour thing tonight?" he asks.

I sigh and lean back into the decorative pillows. "I don't feel like being reminded that everyone else has a job, or at least freelance work," I tell him. "I've got nothing."

"So, you've got nothing to lose," he says, a little too brightly. When I don't respond he adds, "You won't find another job if you don't put yourself out there."

I sigh again; he's not wrong. "Maybe I can start walking dogs or something to help bring a little money in."

"It's not about the money," Jeff says. "I just want you to be happy."

I frown even though I know he's right. I didn't think it would be this hard to find a new job, but over forty isn't exactly a benefit in an industry that puts so much emphasis on being young and hip. "If I go, I'll have to wash my hair," I say, only slightly teasing.

"Don't do it on my account," he says. "And here, there was something in the mail for you."

My heart leaps at the thought of a letter from my mom. It's been two days and she hasn't responded—not by text, by phone, or by email.

Jeff hands me a brown padded envelope with my name carefully written across the front in familiar handwriting. But it's not my mom's.

I slide my finger beneath the flap of the envelope that's fastened by one of those fancy wax moldings that has his initials, AA, emblazoned on it.

Inside, I find a page that looks like it was torn from a sketchbook, complete with the little torn bits of paper on top. The side facing me is blank, but I turn it around and gasp. It's a drawing, of a woman who looks an awful lot like my mom. *Betsy*, I think, grateful for this glimpse into the woman my mom used to be.

In the picture, she's sitting in a deep chair in what looks like a library. She looks so young and innocent, biting her lip as she reads. I know it's impossible, but I wish I'd known her back then, before my arrival changed everything, changed her.

There's something else in the envelope. I slide out a sheet of ivory paper that's soft to the touch.

I unfold the letter slowly, as if I'm unwrapping a gift. Before I read the words, I take in his handwriting—his artfulness apparent in all the details, from the perfect loops in the letters to the lines so straight they could have been drawn by a ruler. I take a deep breath, then start to read.

Paige,

I got your thank-you email, and I apologize for not writing back right away. When it comes to communication that really matters and face-to-face isn't an option, I prefer a written letter. It really is a lost art—but I digress.

It took me a few days to grasp the gravity of our situation. I have a daughter. A daughter. You know how there are things in life you never knew you always wanted, but once you have it, you can't imagine how you considered the world any other way? That's how this feels to me.

I hope I'm not coming on too strong. While you're the only daughter in my life, I know you already have a dad. From what I can remember, he was a great man—he had to have been to raise such a lovely young woman.

I've been reminiscing a lot about those days, about the person I was, the person your mom was. She really was something special. I see a lot of her in you. I found this drawing in an old sketchbook and thought you might like to have it. She was already pregnant with you that day, although I obviously didn't know it at the time, and I'm not sure she did, either.

This is turning into a longer note than I intended, but I wanted to thank you. For coming to see me, for hearing me out, and for opening my eyes to a part of life I never thought would be possible for me.

I say this with love for you and the utmost respect for the man who raised you, but I would be grateful for any role you'd like me to play in your life. Again, it's not my intention—nor would it ever be possible—to replace your dad. I'd be happy to just be your Andy.

All my love,
Andy

I read through the letter again and then once more before handing it over to Jeff, who has migrated back in from the kitchen. I watch his face change, softening as he reads. The corners of his mouth lift in a smile, and he looks up at me, his eyes watering.

I'm waiting for him to say something, but he turns and walks into our bedroom.

"Jeff?"

How can he read that letter and not say something? Anything?

I'm about to get off the couch and follow him into the bedroom when he comes back into the living room. The letter from Andy isn't the only thing in his hand.

"You have to," he says, handing me one of our last wedding invitations. "He's your Andy."

My eyes well with tears, and I can't wait for my fiancé and my DNA Dad to meet. For real this time.

I take the wedding invitation from his outstretched hand and reach for a pen to address an envelope to Andy and Patrick.

Mom will forgive me; she'll have to. And even if she doesn't, I have to do it anyway. Because as much as I thought this was about her, it's not. It's about me, and getting to know the person who is half the reason I'm alive to walk down the aisle in the first place.

MAKING MY WAY to the second floor of Quartino's, I can feel butterflies going crazy in my stomach. It would be so much easier if Maks were here to do the small-talking for me. I wish Girlsday, the group for women in advertising hosting this event, allowed gay men to join.

Turning the corner, I remind myself that I have faced more in the last four weeks than I have in the last four years. If I can meet my DNA Dad face-to-face, then surely I can handle a little schmoozing and networking. Because rent isn't cheap, and Jeff is right: a new job won't find me if I keep camping out on the couch.

"Paige?" I smile, happy to see a friend from the Creative Circus, the grad school I attended after college. "It's so good to see you," she says. "Where are you working these days?"

And there it is: the career equivalent to *Why aren't you married?* or *When are you going to have kids?* I smile through the discomfort, reminding myself that people won't think of me for a job or freelance opportunity if they don't know I'm available.

"I'm in between jobs at the moment," I tell her.

A frown crosses her face for less than a second, but it's impossible to miss. Before she makes a sad comment to go along with her sad face, I say something that's almost guaranteed to turn her expression around. "It's actually been great," I lie. "It's given me a lot of time to plan my wedding."

I lift my hand to show the diamond that would be much sparklier if I'd actually gone to the jeweler's to have it cleaned instead of just talking about it.

"O.M.G.!" she squeals. Her voice is so high-pitched I think it might have damaged my eardrums. Now I remember why we didn't stay in touch after graduation. "Congratulations!"

Her ruckus attracts the attention of a few other women I recognize from attending these events over the years, and soon, two other women are gathered around my hand to get a closer look.

The universe must have decided it owes me one, because just then, I lock eyes with Helen Jacobs, a creative director I worked for almost ten years ago. She smiles and nods toward the empty barstool next to her.

"Excuse me," I say, pulling my hand back. "I'm going to grab a drink."

I make a beeline toward Helen and give my old boss a hug.

"Tell me what's new?" she says in lieu of hello, and I instantly remember why I liked her so much. You never had to wonder where you stood with Helen.

"Well . . ." I stall, not wanting to disappoint her. She was a mentor to me, and all I have to show for it is a weekly unemployment check. "I'm engaged," I tell her.

"Congrats." Helen takes a sip of her martini before adding, "And . . ." in a tone that makes it clear she's more interested in my professional accomplishments.

I smile, remembering one particular late-night conversation when we were working on a new business pitch for a brand of birth control. We talked about how society puts too much focus on marriage. As someone who was proudly married to her job, Helen didn't understand what the big fuss was about. I remember blushing as she told me she was having more and better sex than most of the married men in our office, including the ones who had a side piece.

I signal the bartender, buying a little more time to think of what "and" to tell her. I know being laid off is nothing to be ashamed of, especially in the advertising industry, but I don't want to tell her all the tired lines, and I know she doesn't want to hear them, either.

For a brief second, I consider telling her about everything going on. She would definitely give it to me straight—not that I think Maks or Margaux or Jeff are ever dishonest with me, but they see things from a place of love. And I could definitely use an objective, outside opinion.

After I order my vodka soda with a splash of cranberry, I turn back to Helen. "And . . . I recently found my biological father who I didn't know existed until FamilyTree.com told me so," I say with as little fanfare as if I was asking her to pass the sugar.

"Huh," Helen says. "So you didn't know who he was before?"

I shake my head and take a sip of my drink. "I didn't even know there was anyone to know about before. Until a few months ago, I would have told you my father was Mark Meyer." I realize my mistake as soon as the words are out of my mouth. "I mean, he's still my father in every other meaning of the word, just not biologically."

Helen nods slowly, and I get a sense of déjà vu. Except it's not an advertising campaign she's trying to wrap her head around; it's my life. "So, what happened? They emailed you—'Hello, meet your birth father!'?"

I smile. It's easier to talk about than I imagined it would be. "More or less."

Over two more drinks while people network around us, I tell Helen the whole story from the confusion of the first email to my mother's denial, Maks's Googling, my ambush bachelorette party, and, finally, the argument with my mother.

"Heavy," Helen says.

I laugh, because it is heavy, but the load feels lighter having shared it. "It's the weirdest feeling," I tell her. "Everything I thought I knew about who I was and where I came from is suddenly gone. It's like my life story has been wiped clean and now it's just a book of blank pages."

"That's where you're wrong," Helen says. "The only blank pages in your life story are the ones yet to be written."

I nod, taking in her perfect turn of phrase. Maybe it's not too late for me to write a new chapter. I've wasted enough time waiting for someone else to write it for me. After all, it's my story.

Chapter Forty-Five

Now

O NE, TWO, THREE, ONE, TWO, THREE," STEPHANIE, THE DANCE
teacher at May I Have This Dance, counts as Jeff and I awkwardly spin on the dance floor. The lessons were a wedding gift
from Maks and Margaux after I told them we weren't planning to
have a traditional "first dance."

They both vetoed our song, and we settled on Garth Brooks's
cover of Dylan's "To Make You Feel My Love." The song is sweet
and slow and easy to dance to—and seeing as I have two left feet,
the simpler the better.

"One, two, three," Stephanie says again, and Jeff spins me out.
This time, I manage to keep holding his hand. I smile, proud of myself.

"Good job," Stephanie says as I spin back toward Jeff's open
arms.

This is my favorite part of the dance, where we sway back and
forth, holding each other, before he dips me at the end. I tried to
protest that last move, but Stephanie convinced me it would be a
beautiful photo op.

"Let's take five, then we'll go again," Stephanie says.

Jeff gives me a kiss before heading to the water cooler, and I go to check my phone even though I know there won't be any missed calls. At least not one from the person I want to hear from.

I know I said I would call if I didn't hear from her by yesterday—but I'm scared I can't fix this. We've never had a great relationship, but I don't want to have *no* relationship with her. She's my mother, and unless I count Andy, she's the only parent I have left. I should have kept my big mouth shut.

"You okay?" Jeff asks, handing me a small paper cup of water.

"Just thinking about my mom."

Jeff nods. He's been good about listening and careful about not offering too much advice. As much as I would love for him to tell me what to do, I know this is something I need to work through myself.

"I keep coming back to something Helen said the other night," I tell him. "She said it might be easier if I try to think of my mom not as she is now but as the young girl she used to be."

"Betsy," Jeff says thoughtfully.

I nod, thinking of the nineteen-year-old girl in the drawing from Andy. The girl who was afraid and scared. I think about the choices she had and how by choosing my dad, she was choosing me. She loved me before she even knew me, so hopefully she can find a way to forgive me. If I can find a way to ask.

"I'm not mad at her anymore," I tell him. "But I think I had a right to be, don't you?"

"Of course," he says, smart enough not to disagree.

"Is it wrong that I want her to admit that?"

Jeff frowns for a moment, considering my words. "It's not wrong," he says. "But I don't know if it's worth drawing a line in the sand over. It's in the past, and if you ask me, the future matters more."

I nod, knowing he's right. "I just don't know how to start the conversation."

"By picking up the phone?" he suggests.

"I don't think this is a phone type of conversation," I tell him.

"FaceTime?"

I smile at the thought of my tech-unsavvy mother trying to figure out how to FaceTime. The last time we tried it, to show her the engagement ring after Jeff proposed, we spent the first half of the call staring at her ear as she held the phone up to her head.

"I think it needs to be in person," I tell him. "Think it can wait two weeks until the wedding?"

Jeff shakes his head, and I know he's right. But I'm still not sure what to do about it.

"Rested up, lovebirds?" Stephanie asks, walking back in the room. "Let's run through one more time and see if you've got it."

Jeff takes my hand and I smile, ready to dance with my groom. At least I know one thing at the wedding won't be an utter disaster.

AFTER OUR LUNCH-HOUR dance class, Jeff goes back to work and I go back to my office: the couch. With Maury Povich on in the background, I write Helen an email, thanking her for the conversation and the offer to send my portfolio on to a friend she thought might be hiring.

I hit send, feeling more accomplished than I have in weeks. Once the wedding is over, I really need to focus on what's next. And if I can't find a job at a traditional agency, then maybe I need to open myself up to new possibilities. Going client side, or maybe even starting my own thing. If Margaux can do it, maybe I can, too.

Instead of going back to check the NPE Facebook group again, I open another blank email.

The cursor blinks, as if daring me to say something.

Hi, Mom.

I stop typing, and the cursor continues to blink, taunting me. If I send her an email asking her to talk, she could say no. Or she could say nothing at all. But this is too important, for both of us. And like my dad used to say, a big apology needs a big gesture.

AN HOUR LATER, I'm standing outside Maks's office building, waiting for him to come down.

He smiles when he sees me. "What's the fire drill?" he asks.

"I'm going on a little road trip and could use some company," I tell him.

"You don't have a car," he reminds me.

I nod to the rental car parked on the street. "Want to go see me grovel and beg my mother for forgiveness?"

Maks pretends to clear out his ears. "Sorry, bad connection," he says. "Can you repeat yourself?"

"Are you coming or not?" I ask. When he doesn't make a move, I put my hands on his forearms and look into his brown eyes. "I might need a push."

His face softens, and he smiles. "I'll always be your pusher," he says. "Just give me four minutes."

Chapter Forty-Six

Then

Betsy swore their kitchen had been bigger when she and Mark moved in. Then again, she had been a lot smaller seven months ago.

Her back had been aching on and off all day, and the last thing she wanted was to be on her feet, but it was Mark's birthday—and she was attempting to cook his favorite dinner: chicken parmesan with spaghetti and homemade chocolate cake.

She looked at the clock on the wall—it was ten after six. Mark would be home from his last class any minute. Betsy had wanted to have everything ready and on the table, but the noodles were still boiling, and the cheese on the chicken hadn't melted yet. A perfect homemaker, she was not. But she hoped the effort counted for something.

Mark's real birthday gift was a book of poetry by one of his favorite poets. *First Blues: Rags, Ballads & Harmonium Songs*, by Allen Ginsberg. She hoped he would like it.

Betsy stopped stirring the noodles to put her hands on the small of her back and stretch. She wondered if pregnancy was always this hard, or if like Eve, she was paying the price for her sins. Betsy cringed as she felt her stomach tighten with a cramp.

"Not yet, baby," she said out loud. This was Mark's day; she couldn't ruin it by going into labor before she'd even finished making dinner. Betsy winced at another cramp, the pressure building. She glanced at the door, willing Mark to get home fast.

Betsy made her way over to the oven, where the cheese still hadn't started to brown. She sighed and rubbed her belly, hoping their son or daughter would stay put just a little longer. He or she wasn't quite done cooking yet, either.

The water in the pot was close to boiling over, so she lowered the heat. Betsy was starting to sweat now. So much for looking beautiful for her husband.

She checked the clock again—only two minutes had passed.

"Owww," she moaned as another cramp washed over her. She leaned against the counter, trying to breathe through the pain. Betsy had to take the noodles off the stove or they'd be ruined.

She took a deep breath and stood back up just as the front door opened and Mark walked in, holding a bouquet of fresh flowers.

Betsy couldn't believe he had gotten her a gift on his birthday. She forced herself to smile through the pain and made a mental note to do the same for him when her birthday came around again.

"Hey, handsome," she said, trying to sound upbeat. "Happy—"

A gush of liquid between her legs stopped her. She looked down at the floor and the puddle she was standing in. She looked to the pot of water, still on the stove, then back down to the floor before locking eyes with Mark.

He glanced down at the wet linoleum floor, then up to Betsy's face. His eyes widened in shock.

"I'm so sorry," she said through the tears she couldn't stop from falling.

FIVE HOURS LATER, Betsy was exhausted from breathing her way through increasingly intense contractions. The nurse had been in and out several times, checking Betsy's slow but steady progress. Betsy's world had narrowed into this small space: a hospital bed, a scratchy gown, the waves of building pressure, and Mark. He hadn't left her side.

Of all the days, she couldn't believe the baby would be born on his birthday. As much as she wanted her pain to subside, she hoped the baby would hang tight for another hour, until after midnight. Betsy didn't want either of them to have to share a birthday.

She wanted to give their son or daughter a childhood where their birthdays were celebrated like they were the most important person in the world on their special day. And after the fuss she'd made over her own birthday, Betsy hated herself for taking the day away from Mark. He deserved to have his own special day.

"I'm so sorry," Betsy said again, hiccupping through the tears after she finished another contraction. "I ruined dinner and your birthday."

"Sweetheart," Mark said, perching on the bed beside her. He wiped a tear away from her cheek before leaning over to kiss her forehead. "You haven't ruined anything."

His gentle sweetness made Betsy cry even harder. If he only knew how much she'd ruined.

Another contraction hit, less than a minute after the last one, and she groaned in pain. Mark rubbed her lower back in slow, steady circles while she moaned.

Finally, the doctor walked in, looked down at his clipboard, and then over to Betsy. The nurse followed after him, snapping on her gloves and moving briskly around the room.

"It's a beautiful night to have a baby," the doctor said. "Go ahead and lay back, Mrs. Meyer."

Betsy shook her head. "I'm not ready," she pleaded as she carefully lay down on the bed. "Can we wait until tomorrow?"

The doctor took a seat at her feet, moving the sheet up around her knees. "I'm afraid not," the doctor said. "Looks like somebody can't wait to join this party."

Another contraction hit, this one worse than before, and Betsy gripped Mark's hand in hers, squeezing through the pain.

"Go ahead and push," the doctor said.

"Breathe," Mark coached in a low, calming voice. "Breathe. You're doing great."

"Push, honey," the nurse said, taking her other hand.

Betsy closed her eyes and pushed. She pushed for Mark, for their child, and for their family. It seemed to go on for hours, until just when she thought she might split completely in half, she heard the most beautiful sound. A baby crying. Her baby.

"It's a girl," the doctor said. Her eyes found Mark, who looked blurry through her tears. He was holding their daughter, tears of his own streaming down his face. She'd never seen him cry before.

"I'm sorry," she said again. "I left your present at home."

Mark laughed, and Betsy cried even harder. She was failing him at every turn.

"Bets," he said, bringing the tiny bundle with flaming-red hair over to the bed. "Look at her. She's the best birthday gift I've ever gotten."

Betsy nodded, looking down at the human life she and Andy had created. She wished more than anything that the baby was Mark's, but Betsy sent her daughter a silent promise that she would never tell, so her daughter would always know the love of the most amazing father.

"Thank you for making me a dad," Mark whispered in her ear.

Betsy was crying too hard to answer. Luckily, Mark assumed they were happy tears.

Chapter Forty-Seven

Now

FIVE HOURS, THREE PIT STOPS, AND TWO BAGS OF PUFFCORN later, we pull into St. Louis. I already consider the trip somewhat of a success, because just south of Bloomington-Normal, I gave Maks the push he needed to finally end things with John for good. I think it's really going to stick this time. He downloaded the apps again and already has two dates lined up for when we get back to town.

My confidence fades the closer we get to my mom's neighborhood. It's almost eight o'clock, so even if she had dinner plans, she's probably home by now. Unless her plans were with Joel. I cringe at the thought of walking in on them in some state of undress.

"I think we should call first," I tell Maks.

"No way, José," he says. "Trust me, the element of surprise will work in your favor."

I sigh. He's been treating this like some critical mission in a spy movie. "I'm not planning an attack. It's just a conversation," I remind him.

"With your *mother*," he says before starting to hum the *Jaws* theme.

My stomach flutters. He's right. This is my mother we're talking about. And me. I close my eyes and try to calm my nerves.

"We're here," Maks says, pulling into the driveway.

The lights downstairs are on, and her car is the only one in the driveway. I take a deep breath before opening the car door. Maks stays put.

"Aren't you coming?" I ask.

He shakes his head. "Be strong, butterfly. You don't need me." He balls his hand in a fist and pumps his arm in what I assume is supposed to be an attempt to show his support.

"Wish me luck," I tell him.

"Luck," he says, before turning up the radio on the nineties gangster rap he's newly rediscovered.

My pulse quickens as I approach the front door. I take a deep, steadying breath. I can't believe I'm about to do this.

I can hear the TV on inside, the volume up so loud I wonder if she'll hear the door. Maybe I should wait until whatever she's watching is over.

Maks beeps the horn, and I turn to shoot him a dirty look.

I take a deep breath and knock.

"PAIGE? IS EVERYTHING okay?" There's panic in Mom's voice, and I add another thing to the list I have to apologize for. A knock on the door is how she found out about Dad, and I'm sure her heart leapt in her chest at the sound tonight.

"Everything's fine, I just—can I come in?"

"Of course." She steps back and lets me inside. Her lipstick looks freshly applied, and I wonder if she always wears makeup with her yoga pants, or if she put it on when she heard me knock. "I didn't know you were going to be in town."

"It wasn't planned," I tell her. "I was hoping we could talk?"

Mom looks at me like I'm a puzzle she's trying to solve. "Let me just turn off the TV."

I follow her into the living room as she turns off *How to Get Away with Murder*. I didn't know she watched that show—it's one of the shows Jeff and I watch together, but we're a few episodes behind.

"Do you want something to drink?" Mom asks. "Coffee or soda? Something stronger?"

"Nothing stronger," I tell her. "I'm still recovering from last weekend."

The wrong thing to say, I realize, when she purses her lips. She's still recovering from last weekend, too.

"That's actually why I'm here," I tell her. "I wanted to say I'm sorry."

"I got your note," Mom says, sitting down on the couch. The tone of her voice makes it clear she doesn't want to talk about it, and for a moment, I think maybe it would be better that way.

I should have just sent her an email or let her bury this the way we've buried every other issue between us. A lot of people don't have relationships with their mothers, and they're fine.

But then I remember how not fine I've been. As much as this is about her, it's also about me. I need this, I need her, and I think she needs me, too.

"I didn't hear back from you," I say, sitting down beside her.

She laughs, but it's not a happy sound. "What was I supposed to say, Paige?"

I shrug. This is already going all wrong. I look up at her, looking at me, and I'm twelve years old again, just wanting her to love me.

"I used to be jealous of the twins," I tell her.

"Why on earth?" Mom asks.

"Because they had you for a mom."

"So did you, Paige. You're not making any sense."

"I'm trying." I look down at my hands, folded in my lap, then back up at her. I'm not trying to hurt her feelings any more than I already have. I just want her to know where I'm coming from.

"They got a different you," I try to explain. "One that was ready to be a mom, one that wanted kids."

Mom inhales sharply, and I know I've hit a nerve.

"But this isn't about them," I say, pivoting. "It's about me." I pause to try to collect my thoughts, afraid to say another wrong thing. But I came here to be honest, and I know that's what I have to be. I take a deep breath before I say, "I used to think you resented me for being born."

"That's just silly," she says, dismissing me. It's obvious she wants to end this conversation before it's even begun, to retreat back into what's easier and more comfortable, avoiding conflict the way she's always done. The way we've always done. But I've come too far and waited too long to turn back now.

"It might be silly, but it's how I felt. I know you had to grow up too fast because of me, and I ruined your college years. You didn't want to get pregnant—not the way or how you did."

Mom flinches. "That's not—"

"Let me finish," I tell her. "I get it now. I mean, I wish it were different. But I can't imagine how hard it must have been. Every time you looked at me, you saw a reminder of everything you . . . of what happened. It explains so much, and I just . . ."

Mom's eyes are red and watering, and once again, I wish I'd started this conversation differently. I'm struggling to find the right words to say next when she surprises me and starts to talk.

"That's not what I see when I look at you," she says. "When I look at you, I see my beautiful daughter who has somehow managed to grow up to be a strong, wonderful woman in spite of me."

It's so unexpected I nearly laugh. "What do you mean?" I ask.

"It was too late when I realized what I'd done."

Now it's my turn to inhale quickly, wondering if she really just admitted that it had been too late for her to end her pregnancy.

"No," she says, clearly reading the shock on my face. "It wasn't that. It's just, your father loved you so much. I didn't want to take an ounce of that away from him."

"That's not how love works," I tell her, exasperated. "I had more than enough to give you both."

"I know that now," she admits. "But I was so young. I didn't know how to be a mother, but your father . . . somehow he knew exactly what to say and do. You two had such a special bond right from the start, I honestly thought I was doing you a favor," she says, then shakes her head. "I would have ruined you."

She curls her legs beneath her, and I see a flash of the broken girl Andy described.

"The more you grew, the more I knew I didn't have to worry about you," she says. "You were clever and smart and funny and so talented. But by then, there was already a wall between us. And I tried . . ."

I nod, looking at my past through a softer filter. The mother-daughter fashion shows, the manicures, even shopping for my prom dress. She was trying, all those times, in the only way she knew how. She's trying right now, too.

"I wasn't exactly open to it," I admit.

"No," she agrees. "But it wasn't your fault. Even as a little girl, you were so grown-up, I didn't think you needed me. But I always loved you. I love you, and I never regretted having you—not for one second. I'm sorry you ever felt that way," she says. "I'm just so sorry."

"I'm sorry, too," I tell her. My tears are falling freely now, and we're both sitting on our ends of the couch, crying.

My mom's arms are wrapped around herself, as if she's trying to hold her broken pieces together. I know exactly how she feels—and I also know that if we stay like this, both of us hurting in our own separate spaces, nothing will ever change between us. For the first time, I realize that she's just as scared of *me* rejecting *her*.

And in that moment, I see her for who she is now, who she was then, and who, I hope, she can be to me in the future. She's Betsy and Elizabeth at the same time; on some level, she's still that frightened pregnant college student, hiding a secret from the world. She's also a woman grieving the loss of her husband while trying to move forward. And she needs me as much as I need her.

I scoot to her end of the couch and lean in for a hug. For a moment, she stiffens, and I'm terrified she's going to pull away. But then she leans forward and wraps her arms around me, and I relax. She feels so small in my arms, her delicate shoulders shaking with sobs.

A chill runs down my spine, then a sense of calmness comes over me. I don't know if it's my dad's presence, but I hope it is.

Once our tears have dried, I pull back. There's one more thing I need to apologize for. "I know you loved Dad," I tell her. "I'm sorry I ever implied otherwise."

Mom smiles, and there's a faraway look in her eyes, and I wonder where she is in her memory. "I did love him, more and more each day."

I nod because I understand. I feel the same way about Jeff.

"Love means different things at different points in your life," she

359

says. "When I was younger, I thought I wanted passion like Sissy was always chasing. But sex isn't love. It can still be fun and exciting with someone you don't love—but it doesn't hold a candle to being with someone you do. When you're so deeply surrounded by love, it's like you're bathing in it, breathing it in."

I nod again, knowing what she means.

"Your dad loved me more than I deserved to be loved," she says, giving me a rueful smile. "You know, there's nothing more attractive than a kind, good man who values your opinion and what you have to say. Who encourages you to go after your dreams even if you think it's too late and reminds you why you're worth loving even on the days you feel like you're not. I tried every day to make him happy."

She looks like she's about to burst into tears again, so I reach out and squeeze her hand. "You made him so happy, Mom." I gaze across the room at the framed picture of my parents on the day they renewed their vows for their tenth anniversary. The love between them was so apparent, anyone who saw them could see. "I wish I'd met Jeff sooner, so he could have met Dad."

Mom nods and brushes a tear from her eye. "They would have loved each other," she says. "But for the record, I think your timeline has been just fine. It's a gift to have had time to really get to know yourself before you tie your future together with someone else."

We're both quiet for a moment, but it's a comfortable quiet now. Like we both appreciate the other's presence and don't have to fill the silence with chatter. As we sit together, I think back to what she said about love in different stages of her life. Her life isn't over.

"Can I ask you something?" I ask.

She nods, looking a little nervous.

"What kind of love are you looking for now? Is it Joel?"

Mom smiles but thinks for a moment before she answers. "At this point in my life, I just want someone who's good company, who treats me well and makes me laugh. Joel is really funny. And he's a good dancer."

"I'm happy for you," I tell her. "As long as he makes you happy."

"He does," Mom says. From the look on her face, I can tell it's true. Her eyes are shining, and she seems to be glowing—although I'm not sure if it's from love or her skin-care routine.

I sit back and realize there's one more thing I have to come clean about.

"And, Mom?"

"Mmm-hmm," she says, a soft smile on her face.

I take a deep breath and let the words tumble out of my mouth, "I'm sorry, but I don't like the anti-aging cream you got me. I know I said I did, but the smell—I just, I'm sorry, but I don't like it."

The smile on Mom's face fades, and I scold myself for not leaving well enough alone, but then she starts to laugh. It's the kind of deep, musical laugh that my dad used to get out of her. And soon, I'm laughing, too. Until we're interrupted by another knock at the door.

"Are you expecting anyone else?" I ask.

Mom shakes her head, and we both get up to see who's at the door.

"Ma'am," the neighborhood watch officer says when Mom opens the door. "This man was loitering outside your house."

"Maks," Mom says, reaching out to hug my best friend. "He's okay, thank you."

The officer nods and gives Maks a warning look before turning to go.

"I'm sorry," Maks says. "But I've got to go to the bathroom!"

He runs off toward the downstairs bathroom, and Mom and I both laugh. We've got a long way to go, but for the first time in a long time, maybe ever, I know we'll be okay.

Chapter Forty-Eight

Now

I LOOK IN THE MIRROR ONE LAST TIME, AND I CAN'T HELP BUT smile. Thanks to the magic of makeup and a talented hair tamer, I like what I see. I look like myself, just a more beautiful version. I don't look like an old bride, I realize, just a happy one.

"Ready?" Mom asks, walking up behind me.

My eyes meet hers in the mirror, and I smile. My biggest regret isn't what happened or how I came to be. It's that I wasted so many years believing that my mom's distance was her way of punishing me for being born, when she was really punishing herself. Now that the truth is out there, hopefully we can both forgive each other and ourselves.

I reach behind me and take her hand in mine. I give it a squeeze because I don't think I can say anything without crying, and I don't trust that this mascara really is waterproof.

"Ready," I tell her.

She drops my hand to gather the skirt of my dress so I can turn around without tripping over myself.

The wedding is small for St. Louis standards, just about sixty people. I decided not to have a bridal party, and I'd planned to walk myself down the aisle in respect to my dad. But this morning I woke up knowing there was someone else who deserved the honor.

When I asked Mom to do it, there was nothing fake about the smile she gave me. Her eyes flooded with tears, and she hugged me so tightly it felt like we were both making up for lost decades.

Now, we're standing outside the closed door to the Great Hall, our arms linked. I take a deep breath as the door opens.

My eyes immediately find Jeff's. He's standing at the front of the room, smiling the bright smile that anchors me. I nod toward Andy and Patrick, respectfully sitting in the last row on my side. Mom invited Andy over to her house yesterday afternoon before the rehearsal dinner so they could have a moment in private.

She wouldn't tell me what they said to each other—except that she apologized for not telling him when she found out she was pregnant, and he thanked her for keeping his secret. I don't know if we'll ever have big family dinners or holidays together, but I'm grateful there are no hard feelings.

Maks is grinning at me from the second row, where he's sitting between Margaux and Frank, a guy he swiped right on and has been out with every night for the last week and a half. Margaux brought Paul, an attorney she used to despise when they worked together. He'd asked her out once she'd stopped being his competition. She's already started her interior design classes, and I got Jeff to agree that she could practice on our apartment. It's the least I could do after all she's done for me.

The twins are sitting in the front row, with Joel Levy on one side, Sissy on the other. Annabelle is looking down, probably at her phone, but Frannie's eyes are brimming with tears, and she's giving me the smile she shares with Dad. I can't wait for her to move to

Chicago in a few weeks when she starts her new job at the nonprofit organization that teaches people in low-income neighborhoods about financial health.

I look back to Aunt Sissy. There are tears in her eyes, too, and I'm reminded how much like a second mom she is to me. I laugh at the realization that I have two moms and two dads.

Next to Sissy, there are two empty seats—one that Mom will take, and the other one will stay empty in honor and remembrance of my dad. And standing front and center is the only man I would go through all of this for. He looks nervous and handsome, and I can't wait to spend forever with him. He is all the kinds of love rolled into one.

The ceremony is short and sweet, just the way I wanted it. Not a lot of hoopla, just a lot of love. After the vows are exchanged, Jeff and I are whisked off to a room for a private moment together while the guests have cocktails and passed hors d'oeuvres.

"Thank god that's over," I tease, leaning in for a kiss as soon as the door behind us is closed.

Jeff laughs and kisses me back. "The party is just starting," he says.

I don't know if he's talking about the reception or the rest of our lives, but either way, I have to agree.

A few minutes later, there's a knock on the door and Mom comes in. "Sorry to interrupt," she says. "But they're all set to announce you whenever you're ready."

Jeff gives me one more kiss, then takes my hand in his. "We're ready, Mom," he says, and I watch as my mom's heart melts. She brings her hand to her chest, and her eyes sparkle with the hint of happy tears.

She lets herself back into the room to let the DJ know we're ready.

"Party people," I hear the DJ say. "Will everyone gather around the dance floor?"

Through the closed doors, I hear the happy chatter of people moving around. I take a deep breath and squeeze Jeff's hand. Being the center of attention isn't so bad when it's shared with him.

"Ladies and gentlemen, please join me in welcoming the brand-new couple, Mr. and Mrs. Jeff Parker!"

Jeff looks at me and frowns a quick apology that the DJ got our announcement wrong, but the doors fly open, and a spotlight is on us as we walk into the room, where everyone is clapping and cheering.

When we get to the center of the dance floor, Garth Brooks starts crooning through the speakers. I wrap my arms around Jeff's neck and try to remember the moves we rehearsed just last night.

"I forgot to tell you something," I tell him, as we sway back and forth.

"Oh, yeah?" he says. "Another family secret?"

"No more secrets," I promise him.

We're almost at the part of the song where we do our first big move. He must be able to tell I'm nervous, because he gives me an encouraging smile before spinning me out. The crowd cheers, and I stand there, smiling like I just won the world's biggest and best prize before he pulls me back in.

"I'm changing my name," I tell him, when I'm back in his arms.

"To Abrams?" he asks, and I love how there isn't any judgment in his voice.

"No, to Parker."

I study him, watching the thoughts flutter across his face. He said he didn't care, but I know there's a part of him that wants his wife to take his last name. Just like there's a part of me, albeit a small part, that wanted the whole white dress and big party.

"But your initials," he says, before spinning me out for the second spin of our dance.

"I'm not in elementary school anymore," I tell him, once I'm back in his arms.

"Paige Parker," he says, pulling me close. "I like the sound of that."

I like the sound of it, too.

He gives me a kiss before dropping me down in the dip I'd been so nervous about. But cameras flash, and I know this will be a moment I'll be grateful to have frozen in time.

I had a realization on the drive back from St. Louis after my talk with my mom. I'd been spending so much time worrying about whether I was a Meyer or an Abrams when they're both important parts of my past. But Jeff is my future. Besides, I am who I am, and a last name won't change that.

Chapter Forty-Nine

Then

BETSY LOOKED UP FROM THE COUCH WHERE SHE WAS NURSING Paige. Mark watched them with so much love in his eyes that it made Betsy want to do whatever he asked of her. But she wasn't ready for this.

"Why don't you go without us?" she said, trying again. "We'll go next time."

"Please," Mark begged. "Everyone is dying to see you, to meet Paigey."

She frowned, looking down at their daughter. Paige was almost three months old. Her hair was still just as bright red as it had been the day she was born, and she'd started smiling real smiles that weren't just gas.

Betsy had been nervous to take Paige anywhere near campus for fear of running into Andy. But she knew it was a pretty safe bet that he wouldn't be at Hillel tonight. She'd managed to keep subtle tabs on him through Sissy, who was always willing to catch her up on the latest gossip. Betsy was careful not to ask too many direct questions without asking about other people, first.

From the sound of it, Andy had kept his promise and had stopped taking girls from their sorority out on false dates. It seemed he had thrown himself into studying and the football team. Betsy hoped he was happy.

She was happy, or at least she was getting there. Which is why she didn't want to go to the Hillel event tonight. She preferred to stay in their little bubble, with just the three of them.

Betsy didn't want a reminder of all the things she'd lost. To see the girl she used be—the girl who didn't know a thing about chapped nipples, who could sleep through the night, who had no idea how it felt to feel so inadequate at something you were born to do.

"Please?" Mark asked again. "We can just go for a little while. We'll leave as soon as you want."

Betsy sighed, knowing she couldn't deny him. Not this, not anything.

So forty minutes later, after one false start and a blowout diaper change, they walked into Hillel as a family of three.

Deborah was the first one to greet them, cooing over the baby and telling Mark how beautiful she was. Betsy tried not to get anxious as people reached for her daughter, everyone wanting a chance to hold her. Betsy watched over them like a hawk, quick to correct the way they were holding Paige, making sure they supported her neck, that she wouldn't slip out of their hands.

When it was time to light the Shabbat candles, Mark handed Paige back to Betsy, who sighed in relief. She stood off to the side, feeling like an outsider, peering into the life that used to be hers.

Paige was starting to get fussy, but Mark was having so much fun showing off his girls that she hated the idea of making them leave. But then the front door opened, and Paige started to cry.

ANDY HAD HEARD through the grapevine that Betsy Kaplan, Betsy Meyer now, had had a baby. He hadn't seen her since the day he ran past City Hall, but he still kept an eye out for her at the library.

But the last place he'd expected to see her was at the Hillel event.

Andy stopped in his tracks, wondering if it was too late for him to turn and leave. He could pretend that he'd forgotten something, that he had some commitment for class or the football team. But Betsy's eyes locked with his from across the room, and he knew he couldn't walk away.

His smile was a question, asking if it was okay to come closer. Betsy smiled back, and Andy walked toward them. He was a few steps away when Betsy's daughter started to cry.

Betsy looked as if she was about to start crying, too. She looked panic-stricken as she rocked the baby back and forth, which only made the little girl cry harder.

Mark was by her side in an instant, and as soon as the baby was in his arms, her crying slowed to a whimper. Betsy looked embarrassed, and for the second time that night, Andy had a feeling he should turn and walk away. But Mark had already spotted him.

"Andy Abrams," Mark said. "It's been a while—come meet my best girl."

Andy sent a silent apology toward Betsy as he walked up to the new, happy family.

Mark was cradling the little girl in the crook of his arm, and Andy felt goose bumps as he saw her red curly hair.

"She's beautiful," Andy said. He tried to make eye contact with Betsy, but her eyes were trained on the ground. He sensed that she was trying to disappear, and Andy wished he could tell her he knew how she felt.

"I'm a little biased," Mark said. "But I have to agree."

Mark brought his free hand up and tickled his daughter's neck. The baby cooed, opening her eyes to reveal the most shocking blue. Andy startled at the sight of them. He stepped back to what felt like a safe distance.

His body was there, but his mind kept going back to that night, just over a year ago. He memorized the little girl's face, then looked over to Betsy. He kept his eyes on her until she reluctantly met his gaze.

So many unspoken words passed between them, it felt like time stood still. Andy had the sense that he was on the edge of one life, looking into the one he could have chosen.

"Mazel tov," Andy finally said. "I'm so happy for you both."

And he was happy for them. He was happy for Betsy, and he hoped she really was happy. He wanted the best for her, a life full of love and a house full of children. The kind of life a man like Mark could give her.

The baby started to cry again, and Mark and Betsy bent their heads around their daughter. Andy turned to walk away, stopping right before he reached the door. He looked back toward Betsy, who was holding their daughter tight. She looked terrified, and Andy wished he could tell her that she had nothing to be afraid of. Betsy was keeping his secret, and he would keep hers. Both of them.

Acknowledgments

First, I have to thank my friend Mia Phifer for inspiring this book and for sharing a little piece of her story with me. I'm grateful for your friendship and your willingness to answer a thousand different questions. Also for your killer brunch parties.

I owe so much to my incredible agent, Joanna MacKenzie. Not only is she the world's best agent—but this story wouldn't be what it is without her suggestion to take it apart and put it back together again. I can't wait until the world is safe enough for us to get back to our lunches!

To my editor, Tessa Woodward, I'm sorry for more tears! Thank you for believing in me and this book, and for pushing me to go deeper to make it even stronger. And for putting up with all my attempts to get an A+!

There aren't enough words to thank Bradeigh Godfrey—my critique partner, one of my very best friends, and now, my side-project cowriter. You make everything I write better, and I'm so grateful for you. (This paragraph could probably be better, since it's the only one in the whole book I didn't have you read!)

My family have been my biggest fans from day one. This novel is dedicated to my parents—Kathy Hammer and Dr. Randy Hammer—

who made me who I am and love me anyway. And I owe a lot to my sister, Elizabeth Murray, who didn't complain when I borrowed a few little pieces of her life for this book. I should note that she is not the inspiration for the Elizabeth in this book!

I'm grateful for my trusted group of beta readers, who have helped craft this story along the way: Lainey Cameron, Sharon Peterson, Kathleen West, and Nancy Johnson—who stopped me from making more than one mistake!

I've never been a big researcher, but I'm grateful to have friends who shared their expertise with me. Thanks to my cousin Grace Lewin for giving me the ins and outs of a courthouse wedding, Bradeigh Godfrey for the ugly and beautiful truth about pregnancy and childbirth, Mike Wegener for the refresher on the geography of the KU campus, Julie Clark for the advice on writing dual timelines, Elena Mikalson and Natalia Iwanyckyj for their insights on Ukraine, Pierrette Hazkial for letting me borrow some of her colorful language, Sheila Athens and Kyle Ann Robertson for their help with heartthrobs of the seventies, and Rabbi Amy Feder for answering Jewish questions I probably should have known the answers to!

And I have to give a shout-out to my Sigma Delta Tau sisters in the Beta Chi chapter, and to AEPi for throwing some memorable frat parties during my years at KU.

A special thanks to Adrienne Gentry and Vasyl Markus for letting me borrow pieces of themselves (including their beverages of choice) to help this story come to life.

My writing circle has grown so much over this past year. I'll always be grateful to my fellow 2020 debuts. I can't imagine getting through this crazy year without you all. A special shout-out to

Natalie Jenner, Christi Clancy, Julie Carrick Dalton, Lainey Cameron, Heather Chavez, and Suzanne Park. (I hope we make our livestream cake reveals a release-day tradition!)

I was so lucky when I got paired with Amy Mason Doan to be my mentor through the debut group. Thank you for answering all of my questions, making me feel not quite so crazy and becoming a good friend along the way.

I'm fortunate to have many talented friends who have been patient with giving me advice and support every step of this journey. Special thanks to Kristin Harmel, Camille Pagàn, Barbara Claypole White, Heather Webb, Kathleen Barber, Orly Konig, Laura Drake, Kristin Rockaway, Renee Rosen, Jamie Beck, Barbara O'Neal, Liz Fenton, Rebecca Makkai, Emily Henry, Rochelle Weinstein, Lisa Barr, and Erin Bartels.

I will always be grateful to the Women's Fiction Writers Association (WFWA) for introducing me to "my people"; to the Fictionistas who keep me sane, the Every Damn Day Writers who keep me motivated, and my Slice of Fiction ladies (Mary Chase, Amy Melnicsak, Kasia Manolas, and Nancy Johnson) for giving me an excuse to have pizza every once in a while!

I promised myself the acknowledgments would be shorter this time around, but I have so many amazing writer friends I have to thank, including Lyn Liao Butler, Christine Adler, Mary Hawley, Leah DeCesare, Peggy Finck, Kerry Ann King, Kathryn Craft, Robin Taylor, Denny Bryce, Michele Montgomery, Barbara Conrey, Kelly Duran, Megan Collins, and Therese Walsh. Also Donald Maass and my group from the 2017 WFWA workshop.

Thank you to Jennie Nash for inventing the Inside Outline, and for making me realize I had written a mother-daughter story without realizing it for the second time. And to Grant Faulkner for start-ing National Novel Writing Month (NaNoWriMo). My Novembers will never be the same, and I'm grateful!

Thanks to Rich Plum for your friendship and your generous do-nation to Rock By The Sea to have your name in the book. I hope you like the scene you landed in!

Thank you to Kristin Zuccarini, Kevin Grady, Jennifer Ludwig, and Colleen McTaggert for your friendship and your killer design eyes. And to my FCB family and CB team for the support and for being a big part of the reason I want to keep my day job! Also, thank you to Megan Colleen McGlynn for starting Girlsday and letting me fictionalize one of their happy hours.

To John Corry and the former Same Bar Saturday crew at Four Farthings, and to Tom Piazza for hosting the party where I had the conversation that sparked the idea for this book.

I'll always be grateful for my friend the talented photographer Will Byington for making me look better than real life, and to An-gela Carlson for the fine-tuning. To the Puffcorn Mafia, My Girls, Meg McKeen, Krissie Callahan, #LibbyLove, DJ Johnson, Michelle Dash, Shana Freedman, Marija McPherson, Robbie Manning, Christina Williams, Jenna Leopold, Teddy Brown, and Emalie Wei-land, thank you for your friendship and support. And thank you to Nate Godfrey for not throwing your wife's phone out the window!

Thank you to my extended family, all of the Hammers, Berg-ers, Lewins, Kirbys, Murrays, Blocks, Nancy Multin, and Carlene Jarrett. And I can't forget the Rock Boat and the Rock By The Sea family.

For all the behind-the-scenes work, thank you to the entire team at HarperCollins, including Elle Keck, Christina Joell, Kaitie Leary,

Jeanie Lee, Diahann Sturge, Allison Draper, Pamela Barricklow, Mark O'Brien, Robin Barletta, Jennifer Hart, and Kelly Rudolph. And to Kristin Nelson, Brian Nelson, Tallahj Curry, Samantha Cronin, Maria Heater, Angie Hodapp of the Nelson Literary Agency, and Alice Lawson at Gersh. And thanks to Ann-Marie Nieves of Get Red PR and M.J. Rose of AuthorBuzz.

There are a few people I owe delayed thanks to for *You and Me and Us* (you'd be surprised how early we have to turn in these acknowledgments!). Thank you to Jason Ryan for recording my audio extras, Nalana Lillie for the candles, and to everyone who was supposed to be in conversation with me at one of my events that never came to be: Emily Belden, Erin Bartels, Lori Rader Day, Bob Bergen, and Colleen Oakley. Maybe one day we'll get to have a do-over.

Thank you to Stephen Kellogg for turning lemons into lemonade and making my pandemic-launch something I'll never forget. I'm grateful for your friendship and inspired by your music. Can't wait to bring some of our ideas to life!

As writers, we write the words, but it's the booksellers, book reviewers, and bookstagrammers who help put them in the hands of readers. Thank you to Rebecca and Kimberly George, Javier Ramirez and Mary Mollman, Mary Webber O'Malley, Pamela Klinger-Horn, Maxwell Gregory, Ashley Hasty, Ashley Spivey, Andrea Katz of Great Thoughts Great Readers, Kristy Barrett of A Novel Bee, Susan Peterson of Sue's Reading Neighborhood, Annie McDonnell of the Write Review, Pamela Skjolsvik of the Quarantine Book Club, the Book Club Girls, the Girly Book Club, Friends and Fiction, A Mighty Blaze, the Book Sharks, Reader's Coffeehouse, Tall Poppy Writers, the Bookish Ladies Club, and so many more.

ACKNOWLEDGMENTS

Thank you to all of the book clubs who have read my books and invited me virtually into your homes for such interesting conversations. I'm so grateful.

And last, but certainly not least, thank YOU for reading this book and helping to make a lifelong dream come true. I'd love to hear from you at www.alisonhammer.com, on Facebook at www.facebook.com/ThisHammer, and @ThisHammer on Twitter and Instagram.

About the author

About the book

Insights,
Interviews
& More . . .

Meet Alison Hammer

Will Byington

ALISON HAMMER is the author of *You and Me and Us* and the founder of the Every Damn Day Writers Facebook group. A graduate of the University of Florida and the Creative Circus in Atlanta, she now lives in Chicago, where she works as a VP creative director at an advertising agency.

Behind the Book

It was late March 2017. A bunch of friends and I were meeting at Wrightwood Tap for one last hurrah before the neighborhood bar our friend owned closed the next day. The narrow room was already crowded by the time I got there, and I spotted my friend Mia sitting at the bar.

I said hello, and she said: "You'll never believe what I just found out through Ancestry.com."

Mia works in politics and is active in the Democratic community, so I said the first thing that came to mind. I asked if she'd found out that she was related to Trump.

"Worse," she said.

After I threw out a few other names from history she wouldn't like to be related to (Hitler and Mussolini, to name a few), she gave up on my ability to guess. That's when she told me she had recently gotten an email from Ancestry.com telling her she had a new parent-child connection with a man who was not her beloved late father.

She was right. I never would have guessed that.

After she told me more about her discovery, I said what any writer would've said after hearing such a ▶

goose bumps–worthy tale. I said, "That would make an incredible book."

At that point, I had recently finished writing the second draft of what would become my debut novel, *You and Me and Us.* I was still a year away from signing with my amazing agent, Joanna, but I was already on the lookout for an idea for my next book.

A few weeks after that night at the bar, I was still thinking about what Mia had told me. So when she reached out to say she wouldn't mind if I wanted to write about her crazy DNA story, I wrote back right away.

I was definitely intrigued, but I didn't want to write *her* story. I wanted to write a fictional story inspired by what had happened to Mia, and what, I was starting to realize, had likely happened to many other people, with the rise in popularity of these vanity DNA tests.

There were a few reasons I didn't want to write her specific story. Mainly, I didn't want to feel creatively limited or bound to her reality. When writing a story, you have to live inside your characters' heads to access their thoughts and feelings. I couldn't do that fully if I was trying to write about a real person. Real *people*, since her parents were obviously involved, too.

I did decide to give Paige, my main character, red hair like Mia, and also her drink of choice (vodka soda with just a splash of cranberry!). But other than that, Paige Meyer is her own, albeit fictional, person, and the specifics of her story and the way it all unfolded came entirely from my imagination.

Early that August, Mia and I met for lunch at Dublin's, one of her go-to spots, and also the location of the first chapter in the book. Over lunch (scallops for me, salad for her) she told me her story. How she felt when she got the email from Ancestry.com, what her initial response was, how she first reached out to her mom, and then two of her best friends—Vasyl and Adrienne, who helped her make sense of the news.

Mia also shared a few articles she'd found in her personal research, as well as the transcript from her chat conversation with the online customer service at Ancestry.com. Most of that exchange made it into the book—but I had to make a few tweaks because early readers flagged some of the back-and-forth as unbelievable. They do say that truth is stranger than fiction!

Over the next month, the story started to take shape. I decided to give Paige two friends to ground her during her journey, and to help remind her who she really is. Like Paige, her friends Maks and Margaux are fictional—but they each share a bit in common with their real-life inspirations.

I used the French spelling of ▶

Margaux's name as a nod to Adrienne, who found out through a DNA test that only half of her family history was accurate. The European part of her DNA she always thought was French had turned out to be Irish. Another thing the two women have in common is their impeccable style!

Vasyl and Maks are both from Ukraine—but Vasyl doesn't share Maks's challenges with the English language. That part is pure fiction. But they both can deliver one hell of a punch line, and they both drink "the cheapest whiskey with the most expensive ginger ale."

I used September and October to do a little more work on the characters—rounding out their backstories and personality traits and doing a rough outline of how I thought the story would unfold. Then I was officially ready for my second attempt at National Novel Writing Month (NaNoWriMo), an international program where writers around the world are challenged to write fifty thousand words in the month of November.

At the stroke of midnight on Halloween night, as soon as it became November, I started writing the first draft of the book, which I was calling "Blank Paige" at the time. (Like Paige and her dad, I have a love of puns!)

When I first wrote the story, it was

told in three parts. Part one took place in 2018, when Paige first made the DNA discovery. Part two took place back in 1974, at the University of Kansas, where Paige's mom, dad, and DNA Dad all went to school. Part three picked up in the present day, after we found out exactly what happened that night in 1974, and showed Paige trying to make sense of it all.

The book was good. But it wasn't great until my agent gave me the most amazing editorial suggestion. In the second part of the book, the reader goes into it knowing these two characters Betsy and Andy will wind up having sex that leads to Paige's conception. That gave the part a driving energy as readers turn the pages to find out exactly how and when that happened.

In my original draft, once the reader found out the real story, they still had about one hundred pages left to read, but the "mystery" had already been solved. So my agent suggested that I take the story apart and put it back together again. Instead of three parts, she thought I should try to weave the past and present timelines together.

After I got over the anxiety of how much work that would be, I knew she was right. So I cleaned off my kitchen counter and printed out a fifty-page chapter-by-chapter outline. I had the ▶

Behind the Book *(continued)*

present-day chapters in a blue font and the 1974 chapters in a red font so they were easy to tell apart.

I went all arts-and-crafts on the project, cutting the outline and taping pieces of the chapters together. After that, I physically laid the structure out on my kitchen counter and used Post-it notes as placeholders for the new scenes I would have to write (about four or five total). It was incredible the way the past and present stories flowed together. It was like it was meant to be that way.

There was one more thing I needed to do before the book was complete. I thought it was only right to take a DNA test of my own. But I wasn't going to do it alone—I got my family to join me under the guise of a holiday gift.

In December of 2019, when my family was together for the holidays, I handed an identically wrapped box to all the adults in my family—my mom, my dad, his girlfriend, my sister, and my brother-in-law. I made them open the gifts at the same time, and they laughed when they saw the Ancestry.com tests. But the joke was on me, because my dad got up and handed his own identically wrapped boxes to myself, my sister, and my brother-in-law. Apparently, he had the same idea, only he'd gifted us 23andMe kits.

From what I know about my

family history, I have roots in Germany, Russia, and, I believe, Czechoslovakia. I'd been hoping to find some specifics, but the results were pretty broad and unsurprising. It turns out I'm 99.5% Ashkenazi Jewish and 0.3% Eastern European. And in case you're wondering, all of my family members who took the test showed up on my family tree. No unexpected connections. At least not yet.

One last thing I'd like to call out is that the NPE (Not Parent Expected) Facebook group is a real community. It's a very private network that only allows in people who have a Not Parent Expected. I am not a member of the group, and all the posts mentioned in this book are fictional, based on a few articles I've read and some of the stories I've heard about how these DNA surprises unfold.

So that's the story behind the story of *Little Pieces of Me*. Thanks so much for spending a little piece of your time with Paige, Betsy, and Andy. ❧

Reading Group Guide

1. Do you think Andy suspected Paige was his child? If so, do you think he took the DNA test in hopes of connecting with her?

2. Paige is dealing with a crisis of identity. She lost her job, is about to get married, and then finds out about her Not Parent Expected. How much do your job, your family, or your social status play into your identity and how you see yourself?

3. Have you taken a DNA test? If you have, why did you decide to do so? If you haven't, would you consider it? Why or why not? If the DNA test revealed surprising information, would it change the way you see yourself or your family?

4. Do you think Betsy made the best choice for herself and her daughter by leading Mark to believe the baby was his? Do you think Mark ever suspected?

5. Paige tells her mom that she forgives her, and Elizabeth gets upset and says she doesn't need forgiveness for something that happened before Paige was born. What do you think

about that? Did Elizabeth owe Paige an apology for anything?

6. Paige's group of friends all struggle with feeling different at some point in their lives. It's one of the things they have in common. Have you ever felt different? How did you deal with those feelings? Do you have any groups of friends where you're the same kind of different?

7. In college, William is not very accepting of Andy's desire to stay closeted, even though William himself had a traumatic experience coming out. What do you think of their relationship? In what ways was it good, and in what ways was it destructive?

8. Do you think Maks made the right decision to trick Paige into going to Naples? How do you think he should have handled the situation, knowing what is best for his friend even if that friend doesn't see it?

9. Paige feels a lot of anxiety over her perceived judgment from both society and her younger sister about being an "old" bride. Do you think the wedding industry ▸

caters to young brides? Do you agree with Elizabeth that love at any age deserves to be celebrated?

10. Paige and Elizabeth have a conversation about different kinds of love throughout one's life. What kind of love do you think Elizabeth and Mark had? What kind of love do Paige and Jeff have? Has the kind of love you look for changed over time?

11. What do you think Paige and Andy's relationship will look like in the next five years? Do you think Andy and Elizabeth will have any relationship at all? How about Paige and Frannie? ❧

Discover great authors, exclusive offers, and more at hc.com.